# SILK AND STEEL

## A SELECTION OF THE DOUBLEDAY BOOK CLUB

## THE REVIEWERS RAVE OVER KAT MARTIN

"Kat Martin is pure entertainment from page one!"
—Jill Marie Landis

"Kat Martin shimmers like a bright diamond in the genre."
—*Romantic Times*

"Kat Martin keeps on getting better and better . . . A premier historical writer."
—*Affaire de Coeur*

"Kat Martin dishes up sizzling passion and true love, then she serves it with savoir faire."
—*Los Angeles Daily News*

## NIGHT SECRETS

"Lots of energy and adventure . . . The writing is crisp and clear, and the characters are larger than life."
—*Booklist*

More . . .

# WICKED PROMISE

"Conflict dogs the steps of the protagonists while tension keeps the reader alert. Humor is like icing on a cake in this delightful tale."
—*Rendezvous*

"This is a fast-paced and passionate story; as always, Ms. Martin is wonderful."
—*Bell, Book and Candle*

"A mistress of the genre, Kat Martin delivers what readers desire: an exciting, sensual, engrossing romance whose characters use the power of their love to give them strength."
—*Romantic Times* (4½ Stars, Top Pick)

# DANGEROUS PASSIONS

"Ms. Martin has an excitement and edge to all the books that bring the readers back time after time."
—*Bell, Book and Candle*

"War, lust, deception, and seduction make this thrilling historical come alive as this intense romance unfolds. Graphic war passages, sensuous romantic encounters, and the quest to find an unknown traitor make this historical masterpiece unforgettable. Kat Martin has once again given us an inspiring tale of love, hope, and promise."
—*Rendezvous*

"Kat Martin weaves a tale as compelling as any she has written. This novel is un-put-downable—a non-stop read filled with excitement, tempestuous passion, betrayal, mystery and everything romance readers have come to expect from a top-notch writer."
—*Romantic Times* (4½ Stars)

"The irresistible but scarred lead protagonists add the needed romantic element that turn a fabulous novel into a tremendous reading experience that will captivate readers."
—*Affaire de Coeur* (Five Stars)

"You'll enjoy every fast-paced minute!"
—*Interludes*

"Steamy, sensual, magnificent, and exciting describe the scintillating new novel by Kat Martin as she takes fans on a perilous journey through the tempestuous Napoleonic war. Ms. Martin weaves history into her story, creating a tapestry rich and elegant with romance hot enough to singe the fingers, curl the toes, and scorch the pages as we turn them ever fast. Destined to shoot to the top of the charts, DANGEROUS PASSIONS leaves the reader breathless, exhilarated, clamoring for more. A keeper!"
—*Romancing the Web*

## NOTHING BUT VELVET

"Kat Martin draws the reader into Regency England and the lives of wealth and privilege, with the assurance of a master . . . A writer of renown who thrills us."
—*Under the Covers Book Reviews*

"NOTHING BUT VELVET is nothing but brilliant. The lead characters are super, and the villain as vile as they come. The story line is fast-paced and extremely interesting."
—*Affaire de Coeur*

"What more could a romance reader want? . . . [NOTHING BUT VELVET] is a boisterous carriage ride in which Martin shows herself to have a firm grasp on the reins."
—*Publishers Weekly*

# Silk AND STEEL

St. Martin's Paperbacks

SILK AND STEEL

Copyright © 2000 by Kat Martin.

All rights reserved.

For information address St. Martin's Press, 175 Fifth Avenue, New York, NY 10010.

ISBN: 0-312-97281-4
EAN: 978-0-312-97281-3

Printed in the United States of America

St. Martin's Paperbacks edition / January 2000

St. Martin's Paperbacks are published by St. Martin's Press, 175 Fifth Avenue, New York, NY 10010.

10  9  8  7  6  5

*To my great friend, Meryl Sawyer,*
*and her beloved late husband, Jeffrey,*
*who will long be missed by all.*

# ONE

Lady Kathryn Grayson slipped silently into the shadows behind the door of the old stone stable. She shivered, her tattered, dirty night rail little protection against the chill, the straw on the cold dirt floor scratchy beneath the soles of her bare feet. At the front of the stable, she could see a skinny, freckle-faced groom and the gleaming black of an expensive traveling carriage.

Creeping closer to the door, she saw that the conveyance was ready to depart and that it bore the gilded crest of a nobleman—the head of a wolf above a silver sword. Two footmen stood in conversation with the driver a little off to the left and as she listened to their conversation, her heart began to pound. The carriage wasn't traveling to London, but preparing for a return to the country. Dear God, it was headed away from the city! If she could find a place to hide in it, she would be safe!

Her excitement increased, her breath coming faster, a frosty mist in the cold morning air. She had to get away and the sooner the better. The carriage was the perfect solution.

She watched a moment more, surveying the sleek, finely polished lines of the expensive coach, feeling a wild

surge of hope. The luggage boot at the rear would work—
if there was room for her inside. She prayed there was,
took a deep, steadying breath to calm the tremors running
through her, and prepared to move quickly, before the
footmen returned to their places aboard. When she heard
the men laughing, saw that their attention was focused on
a pair of barking dogs, she sprinted for the back of the
carriage, her bare feet flying over the muddy earth, her
dark hair swirling around her, a mane of tangles that
brushed against her shoulders as she raced along.

Jerking up the leather cover, she climbed inside, settled
herself between the trunks and satchels, tried to calm her
furiously beating heart, and said a fervent prayer that no
more luggage would be added before the coach departed.

Seconds passed. Her pulse rang in her ears. Though
the morning was chill, sweat dampened the hair at her
temples and trickled down her sides. She heard the men
approaching, taking their places on top of the carriage.
She felt it dip and sway with their weight, then the four
matched blacks strained against their traces and the carriage rolled off toward the front of the inn.

It paused only briefly, long enough for its single pas-
senger to climb aboard and settle himself against the
leather squabs. Then the driver whipped up the team and
they were off.

Hidden safely in the luggage boot, Kathryn breathed a
sigh of relief and allowed her weary body to slump against
the black laquered wood. She was tired. So terribly, incredibly tired. The night had been exhausting. Running,
then walking for miles in nothing but her dirty nightgown,
her legs aching, her feet cut and bleeding, terrifed all the
while that they would find her. When she stumbled upon
a road and the ivy-covered inn, she'd said a prayer of
thanks and carefully made her way to the stable at the
rear.

Several hours later, asleep in a pile of straw, she'd
awakened to the jangle of harness and the luffing of horses
as they were led into their traces. Kathryn had known in

an instant that this was her chance to get safely away.

Now, as the cool fall day began to warm, heating the space in the back of the carriage, her tired muscles relaxed and she began to doze. She slept off and on, awakened once when the carriage paused at a roadside tavern late in the afternoon and its occupant departed, probably for a bite to eat. Kathryn ignored the rumble in her stomach that motion brought and relaxed once more as the coach resumed its journey, too tired to even notice when the wheels jarred into the ruts in the road.

The hours dragged past. Her legs were cramped in the tight confines of the luggage boot. Her back and shoulders ached, and a dull pain nagged at the back of her neck. As the coach rolled along, she was almost grateful she hadn't had anything to eat or drink, since there was no possible way she could stop to relieve herself.

The rhythm of the carriage heightened her need for sleep. Her head slumped forward onto her chest, her slumber deepened, and Kathryn started to dream.

She was back at St. Bartholomew's Hospital, huddled on the cold stone floor of her dingy, airless cell. Fear surrounded her like a heavy morning mist, making her throat feel tight, and she eased farther into the corner, pressing her back against the rough gray walls, wishing she could disappear inside them. Along the row of cells, she could hear the other inmates and her hands crept up, covering her ears to block the screams, pretending she couldn't hear them.

Her heart beat raggedly, pounding into the silence she created inside her head. Dear God, she was living in hell itself, or at least man's version of it. What demon had fashioned such a place? How much longer could she endure it? The sound of footfalls traveled toward her, the rattle of chains as the guards approached, leading some poor unfortunate back to his cell.

Or perhaps they were coming for her.

Kathryn sank down, curling into herself, wishing she could disappear. She had eluded them for a time, been silent and docile enough they had left her alone. But sooner or later they would come for her as they had the others.

The footsteps grew louder. Her heart beat with fear. *Sweet God, don't let it be me. Someone else. Anyone else. Not me! Not me!* She saw them then, one tall and heavy through the shoulders, with thick lips and dirty blond hair queued back from his face with a thin piece of leather. The other was short and fleshy, his stomach protruding over coarse brown breeches stained with grease.

Kathryn fought back a sob as they paused at the door to her cell, a pair of heavy iron shackles draped over the fat man's arm.

Through the bars in the door, he flashed her a lecherous grin. "Evenin' missy. Time for us to take a little stroll."

"Nooo!" She began to back away, desperate now, her eyes darting around for any means of escape. She knew what they wanted, what they'd done to some of the other women. She'd escaped them until now, though she wasn't quite sure why. "Leave me alone! Get away from me! I'm warning you—go away and leave me be!"

The taller man merely grinned, but the fat man laughed out loud, a harsh, cruel, bitter sound that sent chills down Kathryn's spine—and jerked her from her dream.

Her heart was pounding, her nightgown damp with perspiration and clinging to her body. She tilted her head back against the wall of the luggage boot and reminded herself the dream wasn't real—not anymore. By some miracle of fate—or perhaps divine intervention—she had tricked the two vicious guards, escaped the end they had in store for her, and managed to flee St. Bart's.

Kathryn forced herself not to think of it, to bury it deep inside and dwell instead on keeping her hard-won freedom. She was free of the hospital, free of the madhouse she had been locked up in for nearly a year.

For the moment it was all she wanted, all she could think of. The future loomed ahead, but there would be time to plan, to decide what to do. If only she could keep from getting caught.

She slept again. She had no idea how many hours had passed when she was awakened with a fierce jerk on her arm that tumbled her forward out of the carriage. She would have landed in the mud if a second footman hadn't caught her other arm, hauling her upright with a rough jerk that snapped her head back.

"Let me go!" Kathryn struggled against him, trying to break his solid hold. "Get your hands off me!"

"It's a bleedin' stowaway!" one of the men called out, wrapping an arm around her waist and forcing her back against his chest. "More than likely, the chit's a thief." At the word, Kathryn kicked him hard in the shins and he jerked backward, knocking his silver wig askew. He swore and cuffed the back of her head. "Bloody beggar— do that again and ye'll be sorry."

Kathryn straightened. "Hit me again and I promise you, sir, it is you who will be sorry."

"All right, that's enough." The deep voice cut through the melee and both men instantly went still. For the first time Kathryn noticed the tall, imposing man who stood in the shadows, the owner of the carriage, she presumed. He was dressed in tight black breeches, a long black tail-coat and matching waistcoat with a fine silver thread. The frill on his snowy cambric shirt showed through the front, and a bit of white lace hung from each sleeve. His skin was dark, his hair even darker and slightly wavy, queued back with a broad black ribbon tied in a spreading bow.

"Let the girl go, Cedric. She seems quite able to talk. Give her a chance to speak."

They did so with some regret, releasing her arms and taking a single step backward.

"What's your name?" the tall man asked. "And what the devil are you doing in the back of my carriage?"

Kathryn squared her shoulders, trying not to think what a miserable picture she made in her filthy, dirt-stained nightgown, her hair a dark mass of tangles around her face. She summoned the lie she had concocted for just such a moment, the words tumbling past her lips with surprising ease.

"My name is Kathryn Gray and I tell you this, sir, I am not a beggar—nor am I a thief. I'm a gently reared lady who has encountered an unfortunate bit of trouble. If you are indeed the gentleman you appear, I pray that you will help me."

His black brows drew together over eyes that were equally black. In the last rays of late afternoon sunlight, they seemed to glint with silver. He surveyed her from top to bottom, taking in every inch of her seedy appearance, his gaze so intense her arms unconsciously came up to cross over her breasts.

"Come into the house. We can speak in my study."

She was surprised at his acquiescence. She was filthy from the top of her greasy, unwashed hair to the soles of her cold bare feet. God knew she must carry the foul stench of the madhouse in every pore. Steeling herself, ignoring the disbelieving looks of the footmen, she followed him into the house, which was actually a huge stone castle that had been added onto over the years. She stopped just inside the entry.

"I appreciate your courtesy, my lord, but there is a favor I would beg."

"You have yet to explain yourself and already you ask a boon? Whoever you are, you are not one to mince words. What is it you wish?"

"A bath, my lord. I can hardly discuss my circumstances, filthy as I am and indecently dressed. If you would allow me to bathe and borrow a change of clothing, I am certain we would both be more comfortable."

He studied her for long moments, weighing her words, contrasting her educated speech against her ragged appearance. Kathryn studied him in return, noting the well-defined angles of his face, his broad-shouldered, narrow-hipped build. He was a handsome man, she saw, but there was a hardness about him, an appearance of iron-hard will that warned her to beware.

"All right, Miss Gray, you shall have your bath." He turned to the long-nosed butler who stood just a few feet away. "Summon Mrs. Pendergass, Reeves. Have her see to the lady's needs then return her downstairs."

He turned back to Kathryn. "I shall await your presence in my study." His dark eyes sharpened. "And I warn you, Miss Gray, should your tale be anything but the truth, you will find yourself tossed out like so much rubbish. Do I make myself clear?"

A slight chill slid through her. "Yes, my lord. Perfectly clear." He nodded and turned to leave. "My lord?"

An exasperated sigh whispered out. "Yes, Miss Gray?"

"I'm afraid I don't know your name."

His brow hiked up. He made an extravagant bow. "Lucien Raphael Montaine, fifth Marquess of Litchfield, at your service." A mocking half-smile curved his lips. "Welcome to Castle Running."

He turned and walked away and this time she did not stop him. The housekeeper, Mrs. Pendergass, appeared a few moments later, and she was ushered to an elegant bedchamber upstairs. Ignoring the buxom woman's disapproving glare, she made her way behind the screen and relieved herself with a sigh.

Feeling better, she walked over to the window to await her bath. From there she could see down into the courtyard. The castle was magnificent, centuries old, with crenellated towers and a goodly portion of the outer wall still intact around what must have once been the bailey.

The house itself was immaculately well cared for, the bedchamber she occupied done in royal-blue and ivory accented with elegant oriental pieces. She couldn't fault the marquess's taste.

The housekeeper's voice broke into her thoughts. "Your bath has arrived. I don't know who you are or how you managed to foist yourself off on his lordship, but I would advise you not to try to take advantage. His charity stems from kindness not weakness. You would do well to remember that."

She would remember, all right. One look in those hard dark eyes and she knew he was far from weak.

"I shouldn't tarry, if I were you," the woman said. "His lordship would not be pleased." *And you do not wish to see him angry,* were the words she left unspoken.

Kathryn silently heeded the warning, stripping away her soiled night rail, grateful it was one of her own embroidered gowns and not one the hospital issued with the neck trimmed in a wide band of red. Crossing naked to the bath with only a trace of embarrassment, she climbed into the steaming copper tub, and sank down with quiet bliss, letting the heat soak into her aching muscles, the stench and dirt melt away beneath the scent of roses. She smiled as she settled against the metal rim, relishing the simple joy that was nothing at all like the monthly scrubbings she had endured at St. Bart's.

Mrs. Pendergass left as she washed her hair with the fragrant rose-scented soap that had been brought for her use, rinsed, then settled back once more. In a moment she would dress in whatever borrowed clothing the housekeeper managed to scavenge and face the black-haired lord. Before she went down she would rehearse the lie that she had prepared. For now she would allow herself the pure pleasure of simply sitting there in the warm sudsy water, a pleasure she'd not had for nearly a year.

Seated behind the wide mahogany desk in his study, Lucien Montaine, Marquess of Litchfield, leaned back in his tufted leather chair. He steepled his fingers, his mind on the woman upstairs, in truth, little more than a girl, certainly no more than twenty. Dirty and unkempt as she was, there was something about her . . . something he found intriguing. Perhaps it was the way she carried herself—more like royalty than the beggar she appeared.

She was taller than the average woman, thinner than she should have been, with dark chestnut hair, and firm little upthrusting breasts her ragged nightgown did little to hide. Her speech was certainly that of a lady. He wondered who the devil she was.

A knock at the door distracted him. At his command, the butler, Preston Reeves, ushered the girl into his study. Lucien found himself coming to his feet, barely able to believe the woman who stood in front of him was the same bedraggled creature who'd been hiding in the back of his carriage.

Even dressed in the simple white blouse and brown cotton skirt of a servant, there was no doubt she was a lady. The set of her shoulders, the look in her cool green eyes, said more than words ever could.

And she was lovely, he saw, her dark brows softly winged, her features fine, her nose straight, her lips full and perfectly curved. What he hadn't seen beneath the dirt on her face was more than apparent now, skin the color of honey mixed with cream, soft spots of rose tinting her cheeks.

"Perhaps you were right, Miss Gray. Your appearance is certainly improved. Why don't you sit down and tell me what this is about?"

She did as he commanded, seating herself in the chair across from him, her back ramrod straight, her hands folded neatly in front of her. He noticed they looked rough and slightly reddened, in contrast to the soft femininity of the rest of her. He wondered at the implication but let it pass, giving her his full attention.

"As I told you, my name is Kathryn Gray. I live in a village near Ripon, not far from York. My father is the vicar of the local parish church. He was away visiting friends when I was abducted."

"Abducted?" Lucien leaned forward in his chair. "You are saying someone broke into your home and carted you away?"

She nodded. "Exactly so, my lord. That is the reason I was dressed in my nightclothes. Who they were, where they came from, or why they chose me I couldn't say. I do know they had nefarious plans for me."

"Indeed. And just what plans were those?"

The girl cleared her throat but continued to face him squarely. "I overheard one of them say they were taking me to a . . . a house of ill repute. Of course, I didn't know at first what the man meant . . . being the daughter of a vicar and all. But after a while I began to understand what they were talking about. My father had preached sermons against such places, so I was able to discern their intentions."

"I see." Something about her story gave him pause, but he was fascinated at the cool control with which she told it, and under it there was an unmistakable hint of desperation. Considering her circumstances, assuming she was telling the truth, it was amazing she could hide it as well as she did. "Go on, Miss Gray."

"The men intended to sell me. I suppose that is the reason they left my . . . my person alone. Apparently there is a market for such things."

His mouth curved faintly. "So I've heard." And she would certainly have brought a fetching price. For an instant the annoying thought arose that he wouldn't have minded being a patron at such a house. He would indeed have enjoyed a night in the arms of the intriguing Miss Gray.

"Fortunately, I escaped," she continued in that cool, controlled way that made him wonder what emotion it was that seethed just below the her surface calm. Her breeding was evident in every movement, every gesture. If she hadn't told him otherwise, he would have been certain she was a member of the nobility.

"I ran as far and as fast as I could," she was saying. "I was hiding in the stable when—"

"How?" Lucien broke in. "How did you escape?"

"How?" she squeaked, for the first time unnerved.

"That is what I asked. How did you escape the men who abducted you? You are a lady and obviously no match for them. How did you manage to get away?"

Her hands trembled for a moment where she clutched them in her lap. She took a deep breath and straightened, once more in control. "We'd been traveling for days, staying in one foul place after another. The night before we reached London, we stopped at an inn. One of the men—a fat man with foul breath—dragged me into a room behind the kitchen. He and his friend—a tall, thick-shouldered man with dirty blond hair—must have decided that they would . . . that they would . . ."

She moistened her lips, her control slipping a bit. "The fat man took me into this room while the tall man waited outside. He started swearing, unable to unfasten the buttons on his breeches. While he was distracted, I hit him over the head with a chamber pot and escaped out of the window."

Lucien leaned back in his chair. "Very clever."

She nodded. "I was desperate. I had to escape. I walked through the night and finally ran across the stable in back of the inn. I was exhausted. I hid in the straw and for a while I fell asleep. When I woke up, I saw your carriage and . . . well, you know the rest."

"Yes, I suppose I do." Lucien stood up from his chair and rounded the desk, stopping right in front of her. "I'm going to presume, Miss Gray, that you are telling me the truth. You are, aren't you?" He looked at her hard and could have sworn he saw a slight hesitation.

Then she stood up as well. "I'm telling you the truth, my lord. And I am asking you, as the gentlemen you obviously are, to help me."

Lucien pondered that. He had decided to help her the moment she had walked through the door of his study, perhaps even before that. "All right, Miss Gray. In the morning I'll arrange for a carriage to take you home to your father. I'll have one of the housemaids accompany you and—"

He felt her hand on his arm. "Please, my lord. My father is not at home and I . . . I would be afraid to return while he is away. Perhaps you could send word to him, and in the meantime, I could wait here for him to come and get me. I realize it is asking a lot but—"

"Is there no one else you can go to for help?"

She shook her head. "Not really. My father will be back in a few more days. If you would send word, he would be happy to come for me."

Lucien watched her closely. He wasn't really sure how much of her story he believed. There was something incongruous about the woman in the carriage, the one in his study, and the one she had just described. No, he wasn't convinced she was telling the truth, though parts, at least, were certainly delivered convincingly. Still, as a gentleman, he was obliged to help a lady in distress—and there was no doubt this one was. And the mystery she posed continued to intrigue him.

"Staying here isn't a problem. My aunt will be home in the morning. She can serve as chaperone. In the meanwhile, I'll send word to Ripon to your father." He gave her a mocking half-smile. "Will that suffice, Miss Gray?"

"Yes, my lord, it will more than suffice. I shall be forever in your debt."

"Once my aunt arrives, she can find you more appropriate clothing. You and she are about the same size. In the meanwhile, riding in the carriage for as long as you did could hardly have been comfortable. You may occupy the room you used to bathe. We will speak again on the morrow."

She smiled with obvious relief. "Thank you, my lord." Turning, she started for the door.

"How long has it been since you've eaten?"

She whirled to face him and her posture suddenly drooped. For the first time he realized how much will it had taken to maintain her iron control. "I'm afraid it is difficult to remember."

Lucien swore softly. "I'll have a tray sent up to your room."

She nodded. "Thank you."

"Get some rest, Miss Gray. And do not worry. You are safe at Castle Running."

She gave him a wobbly smile and he thought he might have caught the glint of tears before she turned to walk away. Lucien took a deep, steadying breath and closed the door to his study. What had he taken on when he'd agreed to let her stay? He wasn't sure and yet he didn't regret it. That one quick glimpse beneath her careful control had told him how badly she needed his help.

The days ahead would be interesting.

He wondered what his betrothed would say when she discovered the presence of his latest houseguest?

# TWO

Kathryn slept better than she had in as long as she could remember. Last night she had eaten till she nearly burst at the seams, then climbed between clean white sheets that smelled of lavender and starch, and rested her head against a soft feather pillow.

Her bedchamber at Milford Park, the home she had lived in until she been committed to St. Bart's, had been even more elegant. Her clothes had been fashioned of the finest silks and laces, the food she ate rich and expensive. Her father was the Earl of Milford, and as his daughter, she had taken such luxuries for granted. After she entered the filthy, brutal world of St. Bart's, she realized just how lucky she had been.

Kathryn glanced down at the borrowed gown of moss-green cambric printed with tiny yellow flowers she wore and felt the sudden sting of moisture in her eyes. It was such a lovely dress and, except for a bit of extra fullness in the bust, it fit her almost perfectly. A year ago, she would hardly have noticed but now . . . now she saw life in a completely different way. Seating herself on a petit-point stool in front of a gilded ivory mirror, she brushed her long dark hair and thanked the lucky turn of fate that had brought her to Castle Running.

And the tale that had convinced the tall, dark marquess to take her in. The story of being sold into prostitution was more fact than fiction, a tale she'd been told by one of the women at St. Bart's. Unfortunately, unlike the story Kathryn had told, that young woman had not escaped her abductors. Instead she'd gone a little insane at the cruelty she'd suffered in the brothel where they'd taken her, and wound up in the madhouse.

Kathryn shivered to think of it—or the part of the story that had been true. She'd escaped the guards just as she had explained: the fat guard had dragged her into a room off the kitchen, intending to rape her while the tall guard waited his turn outside. As the first man was struggling to get his breeches undone, she'd hit him over the head with a pot and climbed out through a small kitchen window into the darkness of the night.

She forced the ugly memory to the back of her mind. As the marquess had said, she was safe at Castle Running and she would stay as long as providence—and his lordship—would allow. At least a week, she imagined. It would take a minimum of three or four days' travel by mail coach each way before Litchfield's messenger could reach Ripon, discover there was no vicar named Gray at the local parish church—or anywhere else thereabouts—and return to the castle with the news.

By then she would be gone.

For the present, Kathryn intended to enjoy the comfort and safety of Castle Running. She needed time to recuperate from the terrible months she had spent at St. Bart's, and even more importantly, time to make plans for the future. She wasn't certain what she was going to do, but somehow she would find a way to make a life for herself.

Unfortunately, with nowhere to go and no money to get there, she wasn't looking forward to leaving. But facing the Marquess of Litchfield when he discovered her entire tale was false was something she dreaded far worse.

Kathryn picked up a pin and sank it into the tidy bun she had fashioned at the back of her head, preparing herself to face his lordship in the breakfast room where he had summoned her to meet his aunt. She noticed her hand was shaking. Each person she met posed a threat to her safety, each was an enemy who could see her returned to the madhouse. Kathryn shuddered to think of it.

She didn't know the marquess's aunt, didn't know what kind of woman she was, or if she would believe Kathryn's made-up tale. If she didn't . . . dear God. If she convinced the marquess to call the authorities. . . .

Kathryn forced the thought away. She would play her part as well as she could, pray the lady would be as sympathetic as the marquess was, and Kathryn would indeed be allowed to stay.

Taking a deep, shaky breath, she smoothed the fabric of her borrowed gown, appreciating the luxurious feel as she never had before, and headed downstairs.

Lucien Montaine was waiting, dressed for riding in tight brown breeches and a full-sleeved white lawn shirt. A jacket of fine brown wool hung over the back of his chair. He rose as she entered, smiled a greeting and inclined his head toward the attractive blond woman sitting beside him.

"I should like you to meet my father's sister," he said. "Winifred Montaine Dewitt, Viscountess Beckford, may I present to you Miss Kathryn Gray."

Kathryn dropped into a curtsy. Her palms were sweating and her chest felt tight. "Lady Beckford. It is a pleasure to meet you."

Lady Beckford smiled. She was a woman in her early forties, with blond hair faintly graying at the temples, and deep-set, clear blue eyes. They seemed to hold a world of compassion, as if she wished she could somehow make up for whatever Kathryn had endured. A look of sympathy passed over her face that did something to Kathryn's insides, and for a moment she felt dizzy. Her mother's pretty face appeared in the eye of her mind and Kathryn thought for a horrifying second that she might simply unravel, hurl herself at the poor woman's feet and blurt out the truth.

Last night she had been strong. She'd had no choice if she meant to survive. But this woman with the tenderness in her eyes made her think of home and family, made her wish there was someone she could turn to, someone who would help her.

It took sheer force of will to pull herself together, to merely return the smile.

"Please join us, Miss Gray," Lady Beckford said, studying her with those wise, discerning eyes. "My nephew has told me what happened. My poor dear child, I can only imagine what you must have suffered."

No, Kathryn thought, you couldn't begin to imagine. Not even in your cruelest nightmares. "I am only grateful I happened upon Lord Litchfield and that he was kind enough to help me." The marquess seated her on his opposite side and she could feel those arresting dark eyes on her.

"But of course he would help. Lucien is a gentleman. He might seem a bit daunting at first, but once you get to know him you'll discover he is really quite harmless."

The marquess arched a brow. "Harmless? I would hardly call that a flattering description, Aunt Winnie."

Nor was it correct, Kathryn was sure. The tall, black-haired man at the head of the table with the hard jaw and steely black eyes was anything but harmless. Inwardly, she shuddered to think what would happen when he discovered that she had duped him.

I'll be gone, she told herself firmly. I'll be miles away by then.

"Do eat something, my dear. You're pale and a little too thin. You need sustenance after what you've been through."

Kathryn smiled, liking the woman more each moment, but still uncertain she could trust her. "It looks delicious." She accepted the plate a footman filled and handed her, a heartier meal than was usually served this early, and attacked the food as if she might never get another bite, forgetting completely where she was. She glanced up to see the marquess watching her with eyes that held a look of speculation, while Lady Beckford's gaze was filled with pity.

She set her napkin aside, her appetite suddenly gone. "I'm sorry. I just . . . I . . . They didn't give me very much to eat." That was the truth. Watery gruel and a hard crust of bread, an occasional slice of maggoty meat.

"It's all right," the marquess said with a surprising amount of gentleness. "My aunt is right. You need to regain your strength."

She glanced down at the eggs remaining on her plate, the succulent slice of roast partridge, and her mouth watered. She took another forkful, then another, careful to eat more slowly this time, more like the lady she had once been. Still, she finished every bite on her plate.

"More?" the marquess asked.

Kathryn shook her head. "Thank you, I've had quite more than my fill."

"Good," said Lady Beckford. "Then if you are through, we shall go for a stroll in the gardens and you can tell me all about yourself."

Kathryn's insides churned and she thought for a moment she might lose the delicious food that she had just eaten. Sweet God, walking with the woman, sharing a conversation about herself was the last thing she wanted. She would have to lie again and she didn't want to do that. She swallowed past the nervousness tightening her throat. Perhaps it would be all right. Perhaps if she simply stayed as close to the truth as she dared. . . . That seemed to work last night.

Though her heart was pounding with trepidation, she forced herself to smile. "That would be lovely."

"The castle has beautiful gardens. Perhaps Lord Litchfield will join us."

The marquess smiled indulgently, rose and assisted

each of them to their feet. "I'm sorry, ladies, not this time. I'm afraid I have some work to attend," His gaze swung to Kathryn, seemed to linger on her mouth. "Enjoy your stroll, Miss Gray."

Kathryn unconsciously wet her lips, her heart fluttering oddly. "Thank you, my lord. I'm sure I will."

By the time they returned to the house several hours later, she was far less tense, actually able to smile with a certain amount of sincerity. Lady Beckford had talked to her as if they were longtime friends, insisting Kathryn call her Aunt Winnie as her nephew did. She had spoken about the husband she had lost just two years past, and her eyes had filled with tears at the mention of his name.

Kathryn had cried as well. She had tried not to say too much, had been careful to speak in generalities, but questions about her family had resulted in talk of her mother and sister, dead these past ten years, which had led to unspoken thoughts of her guardian, her vicious uncle Douglas, and her hellish year at St. Bart's. Her tears had fallen unchecked, and Lady Beckford had held her, certain she was crying about the trials she had faced with her abductors.

It didn't really matter. Kathryn took comfort in the slender woman's concern, and by the time they returned to the house, the two were becoming friends.

Days slipped past. She saw the marquess at luncheon and usually at supper, but spent most of her time with Aunt Winnie or simply by herself. As Lady Beckford had said, the gardens were lovely, and she spent time there whenever she could.

The castle library was extensive and she found herself drawn as she had always been to the comforting world of books. Kathryn loved to read: poetry, novels, and especially such philosophers as Socrates, Plato, Aristotle, Descartes. One day she came upon a section of the library that held medical tomes, books on medicine, healing, and herbs, and from that day forward she spent every extra hour poring over the volumes.

On her fourth day at the castle, the marquess discovered her there. Spotting his tall frame standing in the doorway, she snapped the book she was reading quickly closed, hid it beneath her skirt, and picked up a different volume.

When Litchfield read the title of the one she held, his fine black brows arched up. "Descartes's philosophy on the existence of man? It's rare a woman holds an interest in such matters."

She simply shrugged her shoulders. "I have always been interested in philosophy. Plato says, 'The life which is unexamined is not worth living.' "

He smiled. " 'There is only one good—knowledge, and only one evil—ignorance.' "

"Socrates," she correctly guessed, returning the smile. "He also said, 'I know nothing except the fact of my ignorance.' "

The marquess laughed at that. He had a pleasant laugh, she thought, not rusty, but deep and melodic. A well-oiled laugh, as if he used it whenever he wished.

"What is that other book you are reading?"

A sliver of tension ran through her. "What . . . what other book?"

"The one you are hiding beneath your skirt. You may as well confess, Miss Gray. I realize there are a few books here some might consider inappropriate for a young lady, but I don't believe there is anything so far beyond the pale I would be shocked if I found you reading it."

There was nothing for it but to hand him the book. She did so with a good deal of reluctance.

"William Harvey, *On the Motion of the Heart and Blood in Animals*?" He looked amazed.

"You've a very nice collection of books on medicine and herbal healing. I realize Mr. Harvey's book is a bit outdated, but I thought he might have some insight into . . ." Her words trailed off as his brow arched up even more.

"You thought he might have some insight into what,

Miss Gray? Why on earth would you be interested in reading a book like this? It is hardly the vogue."

She felt the heat seeping into her cheeks. His distaste was apparent in the set of his shoulders, the cool look in his eyes. Reading so graphic a text was simply not done by a woman. "My sister and mother died of a fever when I was ten," she explained, telling him the truth and hoping he might understand. "I was distraught, of course. I felt so completely useless. None of the doctors were able to help them. No one could. A few years later, I began to study herbs and their uses in healing. My interest in medicine stems from that."

"I see." But she wondered if he saw anything beyond the fact it was a highly unsuitable subject for a lady to pursue. Merely the mention of one's body parts was frowned upon. For an unmarried young woman to be studying diagrams of anatomy and reading articles discussing arteries and vessels and the pumping of blood was definitely suspect, as she had been certain it would be.

He handed her back the book. "Well, I suppose there is no accounting for taste. My library is at your disposal for as long as you remain, Miss Gray."

"Thank you, my lord."

He left her then and she didn't see him again until supper. Since Lady Beckford was feeling a bit under the weather, they dined alone. Fortunately, by the time she arrived in the drawing room and the marquess escorted her into the dining room, his good humor had returned and he smiled at her with a hint of indulgence.

"I hope you enjoyed your books."

"Yes. I have always loved to read."

"You are quite unique, I believe, Miss Gray. One rarely meets a woman whose interests range from Descartes to anatomy." He seated her at the long, ornately carved table lit by silver candelabra.

Kathryn took a sip of the rich red wine the footman had poured. "Aside from philosophy, what interests you, my lord?"

The crystal goblet he held in one dark hand slowed midway to his lips. His glance strayed down to the swell of her breasts, lingered on the flesh rising slightly above the neckline. Her breath caught and her stomach did an odd little twist.

Then he realized what he was doing and returned his attention to her face. "Any number of things interest me, Miss Gray. I enjoy managing my estates. I find it challenging to make improvements in the land and watch the way the crops respond to them. I like horse racing. I like to hunt. I took up the sport of boxing some time back."

"A man of diverse tastes."

"Yes, I should like to think so."

"You seem to be a very busy man."

"Very busy, indeed."

"Too busy for a wife and family? Your aunt tells me you are not yet married."

He swallowed the bite of roast quail he had been eating. "Did she not also tell you that situation is soon change?"

Kathryn sat up a little straighter in her chair. "No, actually she must have forgotten."

"The fact is, Miss Gray, I am betrothed to Lady Allison Hartman. We are to wed less than two months hence."

Kathryn smiled, but the task seemed surprisingly hard. "Congratulations, my lord."

"Thank you. Lady Allison and I have been acquainted for the past five years. Recently, I decided it was time to enter the marriage mart and get on with the job of producing an heir. Lady Allison was amenable to the notion."

*Amenable.* It was hardly a word she would use to describe what one might feel about wedding the intriguing, darkly handsome Marquess of Litchfield. She wondered if the lady's feelings for him were as bland as his seemed to be for her.

It was only the following day that she got the chance to find out.

A coach and four arrived early in the afternoon. At the

sound of a commotion outside, Kathryn's heart started pumping. Dear God, had they somehow found her? Her first impulse was to hoist her borrowed skirts and race for the door. Instead, she ignored her leaping pulse and remained where she sat on the peach brocade sofa.

For the past half hour, she'd been sitting in the drawing room with Lady Beckford, enjoying a cup of tea and listening to stories of the marquess's youth, misadventures he had shared with his best friend, Jason Sinclair, the Duke of Carlyle.

Now Lady Beckford's words faded away, buried beneath the fear coursing through Kathryn's veins and the sound of voices in the hall.

Winnie glanced toward the door. "That must be Lady Allison and her mother, the Baroness St. James. They visit the castle quite often, since the baron's estate is only a few miles away."

The tension drained from Kathryn's body, leaving her almost dizzy with relief. She didn't recognize the names, and there was no way that they would know her. "I didn't realize you were expecting visitors."

Winnie sighed and shook her head. "I suppose I should have mentioned it, but I guess I was hoping they would not come. It always puts me out of sorts, all that tittering about the wedding—what sort of decorations they should choose for the feast tables, what color gown Lady Allison should wear. Gossip about the guests—who should be invited and who should be ignored. It's all a pack of nonsense, but poor Lucien indulges them. In truth he would far rather be off riding about his estate."

"Lady Allison is his betrothed. I am sure he enjoys spending time with her."

Winnie gave her an "if you knew her you wouldn't think so" sort of look. She sighed and shook her head. "I'm sorry. I know I should be more discreet but the girl is nothing but ribbons and fluff. My nephew will rue the day he binds himself to her and I have told him so on more than one occasion."

Kathryn mulled that over, taking a sip of her tea. "Perhaps he is in love with her."

Winnie rolled her eyes and blew upward through a curl of silver-blond hair above her forehead. "My nephew doesn't know the meaning of the word. He has never been in love, and considering the way he was raised, I doubt it is a state he ever wishes to experience. If you haven't noticed, Lord Litchfield prefers an orderly existence. He is a man of iron control and he is determined to keep it that way. Love has a way of making a man lose his head. That is what happened to his father—with disastrous results—and my nephew has never forgotten it. By marrying Lady Allison he can fulfill his duties as heir without taking any sort of risk."

Kathryn made no reply to this, but she found the notion rather sad. For herself, she had always dreamed of falling in love. She had hoped one day to marry a man who loved her as she loved him. She knew it would probably never happen now, not when mere survival required her total attention.

"Oh, dear, they are headed this way," Lady Beckford said, and Kathryn steeled herself. She hadn't thought the marquess would want it known she was there but apparently he had no such reservations. Or perhaps he did, since when the women walked in, Lord Litchfield did not accompany them.

"Lady Beckford—how good it is to see you!" Gowned in a confection of pink silk and white lace over wide panniers that lifted the skirt up above her stockinged ankles, the porcelain-faced blond girl looked like a doll made of sugar candy. She was shorter than Kathryn, rounder and softer in all the right places. With her pale skin and pink cheeks, she was the image of female perfection.

Kathryn felt an unwanted twinge of jealousy. With her own taller height and too thin frame, she felt gangly and awkward in comparison. The girl was undeniably a beauty. No wonder the marquess had chosen to wed her.

The butler called for tea, and introductions were made all round, Kathryn introduced simply as Miss Gray, a friend of Lady Beckford's from York.

Even at that, the baroness eyed her with some suspicion. She was even shorter than Allison, or perhaps it was the width of her bulky frame that made her appear that way. "Then you are not here to visit his lordship?" she said in a voice that sounded a bit too probing.

Kathryn forced a smile. "Actually, Lord Litchfield and I are barely acquainted. He has been busy a good deal of the time. In truth, I have rarely seen him."

For the first time, Lady St. James smiled. She accepted the teacup Winnie had handed her and set it down on the table. "Where is he now? He was expecting our call. I assumed he would be here when we arrived."

"My apologies, ladies." Litchfield strode through the doorway, as dark and imposing as ever. "The meeting with my steward ran longer than I had planned." He bowed over the baroness's plump hand. "I hope you both will forgive me."

Lady Allison beamed up at him. "Of course, my lord. A man of your position has any number of responsibilities. Mama and I quite understand."

Litchfield gave her one of his indulgent smiles. For an instant his eyes lifted over her head and fixed on Kathryn. His gaze was dark and unreadable, but it lingered an instant longer than it should have and something hot tugged at her insides. Then his attention returned to the vision in pink.

"Your note said there was a matter of importance you wished to discuss. Perhaps you would prefer to be private. If that is the case—"

"Oh, no, my lord." Lady Allison set her gold-rimmed teacup down on the table. "It is simply the matter of Lord Tinkerdon. What he has done is hardly a secret, so there is no need for discretion."

"Tinkerdon? What has Tinkerdon to do with me?"

The baroness leaned forward, her plump figure straining against the tight-fitting bodice of her blue silk gown. An air of authority exuded from her stout, rigidly postured frame. "Surely you've heard the news. Tinkerdon has lost his fortune in some grand scheme to extract silver from lead in which he was swindled. His creditors have all come forward, demanding he pay his bills, but apparently the man is penniless. He is certain to be banned from Almack's. No one will want to have anything to do with him."

"And?"

"And we have invited him to the wedding!" Lady Allison cried as if the man were a convicted killer instead of simply broke.

"The invitations have already been sent," the baroness put in. "Lady Allison was hoping that you, as a man of discretion, would contact Lord Tinkerdon and quietly suggest he be too busy to attend the affair."

Litchfield frowned. "Whether or not Lord Tinkerdon attends the wedding is hardly a matter of importance. The man has lost his fortune, but he is still a member of the aristocracy. You've invited half of London. His presence or absence will scarcely be noted."

Sitting next to him on the sofa, Lady Allison caught his arm. "Please, my lord. Where would we seat him at the wedding feast? Someone might be offended and there could be an incident. Something might happen to spoil the affair and we certainly wouldn't want that."

For a moment, Kathryn thought he would concede to Lady Allison's ridiculous plea, and began reevaluating her opinion of him. Instead, he patted the girl's white-gloved hand.

"I'm sorry, my dear. You are young yet. In time you will learn that how much money one has is not always the most important consideration. You may approach your father if you wish, but I imagine he'll feel just as I do. In the meantime, I suggest you busy yourself with more important matters than poor old Tinkerdon's lack of funds— which is exactly what I intend to do."

Rising to his feet, he flicked Kathryn a last quick glance and started for the door. "I hope you ladies will excuse me."

He didn't await their reply, simply strode across the room on those long legs of his and slid open the drawing room doors. Sunlight gleamed on the glossy black hair tied at the nape of his neck. Without looking back, he disappeared into the hallway. Hearing his retreating footfalls, Kathryn felt a growing respect for him, and a strong suspicion that Lady Beckford's assessment of his upcoming marriage was extremely astute.

Lucien couldn't sleep. He kept dreaming of the ragged waif who had hidden in the back of his carriage. Over and over, he saw her, filthy and unkempt yet facing him with the dignity of a queen.

Then the dream would shift and he would see her as she was now, her lovely face clean and shining, her eyes a deep, mossy green, her mouth full and tempting. She was gowned in silk and sitting in a sumptuous drawing room as if she belonged there. Only the book she was reading, a thick tome on physical anatomy, on arteries, vessels, and blood, seemed incongruent with the picture.

Lucien jerked awake, his mind still spinning, disturbed by the conflicting images, wondering why they didn't fit together. He lay back on the pillow with a sigh, still seeing her face in his head. What pieces of her story were missing? How much had she left unsaid? His instincts told him she was telling only part of the truth. He wondered how much was a lie.

Whatever the answer, he intended to find out. He had dispatched his messenger a day earlier than he had told her. He would know the answers and soon.

The wind kicked up outside, rattling the windows, the chill of mid-October just beginning to settle in. A thin moon hung in a pitch-dark sky masked by a thin layer of clouds. Sleeping naked as he usually did, Lucien swung his legs to the side of the bed and drew on his black silk dressing gown. If he couldn't sleep, he might as well get something to read.

Lighting the branch of candles on the dresser, he made his way downstairs, pausing at the thin blade of yellow streaming out from beneath the library door. Aunt Winnie wasn't much of a reader. Only one other person would be in there at this hour of the night.

Lucien eased open the door, his eyes searching the dimly lit interior, finding the slim figure in his aunt's satin wrapper curled up in the window seat, her long legs tucked up beneath her. Open and resting on the seat beside her, lit by a single beeswax candle, sat a worn, leather-bound volume with gold-edged pages.

"Couldn't sleep, Miss Gray?"

She gasped at the sound of his voice, jerked her head up from her study, so engrossed she hadn't heard him walk in. Her hair was unbound, streaming down around her shoulders past her waist. It was thick and shiny, as dark as the shadows flickering on the walls, but for the first time, he noticed it was highlighted with lustrous red.

"I had a nightmare," she said. "I decided I would rather read than suffer it again."

He walked toward her, taking in the firm points of her breasts outlined by the robe, the sash that marked the circle of her tiny waist. "Have you had this dream before?"

She bit her lip and shook her head. "It was real before," she said so softly he almost didn't hear.

"You are speaking of your abduction."

She nodded a little too quickly and glanced away. "Of course." But the words somehow didn't ring true.

Lucien stopped beside her, studying her face, close enough that the satin of her wrapper brushed the black silk of his dressing gown. The sight was oddly erotic and his body began to harden. Inwardly, he cursed and took a step away.

"What are you reading this time, Miss Gray?" He watched the shifting of her features, watched her expression close up. She wanted to hide the book. He could see it in her eyes. He reached out and closed it so that he could read the title, careful to mark her place with his index finger.

*"The English Midwife Enlarged."* Reading the smaller letters below, he continued. "Containing Directions to Midwives. Herein is Laid Down What is Most Requisite for the Safe Practicing of her Art." He frowned, lifting his gaze to her face. A dozen thoughts rolled through his head, but a disturbing one remained at the forefront.

"You said the men who abducted you did not . . . that they left your person alone. If it happened otherwise, it is certainly not your fault. If you are worried that you may be with child, do not be afraid to tell me, Miss Gray."

Even in the dim light of the candle, he could see her cheeks infuse with pink. "They did not . . . nothing of that sort occurred." She straightened a little in the window seat, lifted her chin. "I am merely interested in the subject, is all. As I told you, I have been interested in the healing arts since I was a child. I found your books and I wanted to read them. You said that it was all right."

He stared at her for long, silent moments, wondering if this were the truth or another lie. "So I did. Read them as you like, Miss Gray. I won't stop you. Nor will I caution you to be discreet. You seem to know how such study by a woman would be frowned upon."

She straightened even more, squaring her shoulders. "I know, but I don't agree. I believe a person, male or female, should be allowed to study whatever interests him. But I shall heed your advice and continue to behave accordingly."

Lucien nodded. His attention had begun to stray from the words she was speaking, to the slim, bare foot that had edged its way from beneath her satin robe. It was pale and high-arched, her ankle slender and shapely. The arousal he had suppressed began to rise up once more beneath his robe. Lucien turned away, busied himself among the texts along the bookshelf, found the volume he had come to retrieve, and strode to the door.

"Perhaps those books are the source of your bad dreams, Miss Gray."

She smiled faintly. "I suppose in a way they are. But they are also my salvation."

Lucien made no reply. She was an odd little creature. Too intelligent to be fashionable, yet strangely enticing. It bothered him that in the few days she had been at Castle Running, he had begun to feel an increasing desire for her. He was betrothed to another; he had to remember that.

He only wished Allison Hartman could stir him as easily as Kathryn Gray did with merely a glimpse of her ankle.

# THREE

Dear God, how she hated to leave. Kathryn's fingers ran over the deep blue silk counterpane, down along the heavy velvet bedhangings that surrounded the big four-poster bed where she had been sleeping.

She would miss the soft life of privilege she had once taken for granted and never would again. She would miss Lady Beckford's friendship, even her often unnerving conversations with the handsome owner of the castle. But she would survive without them. As long as she had her freedom, she could survive most anything.

Kathryn pulled the snowy embroidered case off a fluffy down pillow. She would use it to carry the food she had been hiding away for the last three days. She would have to take one of the gowns Lady Beckford had loaned her, along with a pair of kid slippers and one of her borrowed night rails, but there was no help for it.

She wished she had money to pay for the clothes, or at least a few coins to help with her journey, but she refused to take anything more from the only people who had been kind to her in nearly a year. She would find work along the road, she vowed, enough to make her way.

She had decided to head for Cornwall, rural country

where she could find a job of some sort, earn enough to make a life for herself, and simply disappear. She would leave later tonight, as soon as she was sure the others were asleep. Earlier she had pled a headache and taken supper from a tray sent to her room. She'd needed time to gather her courage, time to accept what must be done and prepare herself to do it.

With a heavy heart, she walked to the cream and gilt armoire across the elegant bedchamber to change into the simplest of her borrowed gowns, a heavy dark green woolen trimmed with ecru lace, but a knock at the door interrupted her.

The long-nosed butler, Reeves, stood in the opening. "Lord Litchfield requests your presence in his study."

A shiver of unease rippled through her. "It's getting rather late. Are you certain he wants—"

"He wishes to see you. That is all he said."

She nodded, shoving down her fears. "Tell him I'll be down in a moment."

The butler didn't move. "He said that I am to wait."

Dread moved through her. There was something implacable in the tall butler's stance, something that warned her of Litchfield's mood. Sweet God, his messenger wasn't due back for at least another day. Perhaps it was something else, something simple, like making plans for an outing on the morrow. She hoped so. Prayed it was so with all her heart.

She descended the stairs with no little trepidation, her heart pattering hard, her palms beginning to sweat. When she walked into the study, the marquess stood at the window, his back turned toward her, his long legs braced slightly apart. She couldn't miss the rigid set of his shoulders, though she prayed that she was wrong.

He waited until the butler shut the door, the sound like the closing of a coffin lid behind her, then he turned, his dark eyes glittering with unmistakable anger as they came to rest on her face.

"Who are you?" There was such soft menace in his

voice Kathryn unconsciously took a step backward. She wanted to run. She wanted to be somewhere—anywhere—but there in his study. She wet her lips but couldn't seem to make them move.

"You let me send my messenger on a wild-goose chase halfway across the country. You lied to me. You accepted my aunt's kindness, and took advantage of my generosity. Now I want to know exactly who you are and why you are here."

She did run then, bolted toward the door, jerked it open and fled like a deer down the hall. Litchfield caught her before she reached the entry, gripping her waist, spinning her around and slamming her hard up against his chest.

"You're not going anywhere," he said in those soft, dark tones that were far more terrifying than if he had shouted. "Not until you tell me the truth." She could feel the ridges of muscle beneath his white ruffled shirt, feel the hardness of his thighs pressing against her, and her body began to tremble. Tears burned the backs of her eyes, but she blinked them away.

She tilted her head, stared into the hard lines of his face. "I'm sorry I lied to you. I was leaving tonight. By morning, I would have been gone. Dear God, I never wanted to lie—especially to someone who helped me. I didn't want to deceive you. I had no other choice!"

His mouth curved up in a ruthless half-smile. "You've a choice now," he said. He released his hold, but kept a tight grip on her arm, dragging her back down the hall toward his study. "You can tell me the truth, or I can turn you over to the authorities. That is your choice, Miss Gray."

She struggled for a moment, tried to wrench free, but his hold was implacable. He didn't release her until she was back inside the room and the door firmly closed. He cranked the key, locking them both inside, then he turned to face her.

"All right, Miss Gray, what is your choice? The truth? Or the authorities?" He folded his arms across his wide

chest, which made him look even taller and more imposing than he did before. "Rest assured, Miss Gray, I am
not bluffing. And I shall know in an instant should you
spin another false tale."

Kathryn stared at those hard, determined features and
a wave of defeat washed over her. "Oh, God." She sank
down on the brown leather sofa in front of where he
stood, and against her will, her eyes filled with tears.
"Can't you just let me go? In time I can earn enough
money to repay you for the food I've eaten. I don't have
any clothes, but surely you could find something old
that—"

"Listen to me," the marquess said more gently. "Whatever you have done, I cannot believe it is as bad as all of
this. If you have stolen something, if you have hurt someone—just tell me and I will find a way to help."

She only shook her head.

"I have to know, Kathryn. Tell me what it is you have
done."

Kathryn shot to her feet, her hands clenching into shaking fists. "I've done nothing! Nothing—do you hear!"

"Then why are you running away?"

She bit down on her trembling lip. Dear God, she
wanted to tell him, wanted with all her heart to trust him
with the truth.

His hands gripped her shoulders and he shook her.
"Tell me, dammit!"

She raised her eyes to his face, her heart like a lead
weight in her chest. "All right. I'll tell you the truth—on
one condition."

He frowned. "I am not in the mood for accepting con-
ditions."

Kathryn said nothing, simply held her ground.

"All right, what is it?"

"After . . ." She wet her trembling lips. "After you hear
my story—if you decide you don't want to help me—
you'll let me go."

"You expect me to let you just walk out of here, with no money and no place to go?"

"Yes."

His jaw tightened. She could see he didn't like the notion, but finally he nodded. "All right, then, you have my word."

Kathryn sucked in a shuddering breath and forced courage she didn't feel into her spine. "I'm not Kathryn Gray. I am Lady Kathryn Grayson. The Earl of Milford was my father."

The marquess's brows drew nearly together. "Milford was your father?"

"You knew him?"

"I knew of him. He was well thought of among his peers."

She smiled with a touch of sadness. "He was a good man, a wonderful father. He was also extremely wealthy. When he died five years ago, he left an enormous estate. Unfortunately, I was his only heir."

"Unfortunately?"

A lump began to form in her throat. "I'm afraid so."

He coaxed her to sit back down on the sofa and took a chair across from her. "Go on, Lady Kathryn. Tell me your story."

She smoothed her skirts, gazed down at the hands she clutched in her lap. When she started to speak, her voice came out stark and rusty. "By the time my father died, my mother was already dead, which meant my inheritance required a trustee. That duty fell into the hands of my guardian, my mother's brother, Douglas Roth, the Earl of Dunstan."

He leaned a bit forward. "Dunstan. Yes, I know him fairly well."

No one knows him, Kathryn thought. Not the man he really is. She simply nodded. Hearing his name brought his image to mind and she had to force it away.

"At first I allowed him unlimited control of my money. It never even occurred to me to question what he might be doing with it, how he might be spending it. We were in residence at Milford Park and even I knew the upkeep on such a place would be outrageously expensive. As I grew older, I began to grow suspicious. I discovered he was squandering my father's enormous fortune, and that if I didn't do something to stop him, the money would all be gone."

"I always believed he had plenty of money of his own," Litchfield said.

"That's what everyone thinks. In truth, the money he is spending is mine, and when I began to speak out against him, to demand an accounting of my funds, he had me sent away."

"How long ago did this happen?"

"Ten months ago."

His eyes moved over her face. "Where did he send you?"

The word stuck in her throat. She worked to force it out. "St. Bartholomew's Hospital."

His dark eyes widened; his expression became incredulous. "Dunstan had you committed to St. Bart's?"

Kathryn glanced away, afraid of what she would see in his face. "Yes."

"Forgodsake, on what grounds?"

She blinked and fresh tears rolled down her cheeks. "He told them that I was insane. He said he was doing it for my own good, that he wasn't capable of dealing with a madwoman." It was all she dared to tell him. Sweet God, she prayed he'd never discover the last bit of evidence that had finally sealed her fate.

The marquess came up from his chair, moved toward her, reached down and took her hand. She realized it was shaking.

"You are unique, Kathryn, but to say that you are insane . . ." He squeezed her hand, shook his head. His eyes looked dark and forbidding. "I cannot imagine a man doing such a thing to a woman in his care."

"Please, Lord Litchfield, I beg you to help me. I'm not

insane. I never was. Uncle Douglas has friends in high places and money enough at his disposal to pay whatever it might take to see his ends served. If he finds me, he'll force me to go back to that place and . . . and." She swallowed past the lump in her throat. "And this time I couldn't survive it."

She started crying in earnest then, deep wracking sobs that shook her whole frame. She felt the sofa dip beneath the marquess's substantial weight as he sat down beside her and eased her into his arms.

"It's all right, love, don't cry. You're safe here. I'm not going to let anyone hurt you." She felt his hands stroking over her hair, fine hands, long-fingered and graceful. She could feel the solid strength of his arms and chest and the comforting warmth of his body. Minutes ticked past. He didn't try to quiet her. He simply held her, let her sob out her tears, and in time her crying ceased.

Kathryn dragged in a shaky breath and drew back a little to look at him. "I have nowhere else to turn. Will you help me?"

The marquess's face looked grim. "I know Douglas Roth. I never imagined him capable of something like this, but he is certainly not a man I would trust. I'll hire men to look into the matter, see what I can discover. In the meanwhile, you can stay here."

"I'll pay you back. If you can find a way to protect me from my uncle, I can repay whatever it costs. It won't be for some time yet, not for another few years. But once I'm four and twenty, Milford Park and my father's fortune will finally belong to me and I'll be able to pay back the debt."

He smiled faintly. "The money isn't important. What matters is keeping you safe. You will stay here at Castle Running until this matter is resolved."

She brushed at the wetness on her cheeks. "Thank you. Thank you so much. You'll never know how much your kindness means."

Litchfield simply nodded. But the look in those hard

dark eyes had slowly turned to stone. She was grateful that look was reserved for Douglas Roth and no longer directed at her.

Lucien sat in a comfortable leather chair in the corner of his study. Across from him, his best friend, Jason Sinclair, Duke of Carlyle, stretched his long legs out in front of him. A small fire blazed in the hearth, warming the room against the building October chill.

"So that is how the girl wound up here," Lucien finished, leaning back in his chair.

" 'Tis hard to believe even Dunstan would do such a thing," Jason said. "It makes my skin crawl just to think of it." He was a big man, slightly taller than Lucien and more muscular, thicker through the chest and shoulders. His hair was a wavy dark brown, shoulder length, tied back with a thin black ribbon. They'd been friends since they were boys, their family estates not far apart. Lucien could always count on Jason. He wasn't afraid to trust him with his secrets, nor even with his life if it ever came to that.

"If you could have seen the poor girl that first day, you might have an inkling of what she must have suffered. The poor child—"

"Child?" Jason interrupted. "I thought you said the girl was twenty."

"Yes, well, I suppose she isn't exactly a child, though I prefer to think of her that way. It makes things . . . simpler."

"Which I take to mean you're attracted to her."

Lucien sighed. "She's lovely in the extreme."

"Need I remind you the girl you are to marry is only nineteen?"

"Allison is different. I don't—"

"What? Lust after her as you do Lady Kathryn?" Jason grinned. "You want to bed her, but she's an innocent, so you're forced to ignore the attraction."

"I'm not certain she is still as innocent as she was ten

months ago. God only knows what they did to her in that place. But the fact remains she's a lady and well out of my reach. Aside from that, I'm betrothed to Allison and very soon shall be wed."

"That hasn't kept you away from the pretty widow in the village."

Lucien made a gruff sound in his throat. "A man has needs, and I am not yet married. And of late, I have given up seeing even her."

"You mean since Lady Kathryn has arrived."

He didn't deny it, though he didn't like to hear it put quite that way. In truth, he hadn't been interested in the widow Carter since Kathryn Grayson's appearance at Castle Running. Unsettled by the notion, he returned to the problem at hand.

"I can't help feeling sorry for her. I visited Bedlam once. It was a scene from the very depths of hell."

"I know. There are actually tours of the city that take you there. God, can you imagine people paying good money to witness that kind of suffering?"

"No. Nor can I imagine the fear this girl must live with every day, worrying if she's going to be sent back there."

"What do you plan to do?"

"Whatever it takes. First we need to gather as much information as we can."

"Perhaps Velvet can help." Jason's wife, a short, auburn-haired ball of fire who was the love of his best friend's life. It was Jason's headlong tumble for Velvet Moran, bringing him near to disaster, that made Lucien even more certain he never wanted to fall in love.

"Velvet has a friend," Jason continued. "Actually, the man is an old friend of her grandfather's—head of the London College of Physicians. Perhaps he can find a way to obtain Kathryn's records from St. Bart's."

"Is she certain she can trust him? If word leaks out of Kathryn's whereabouts before we are ready, we'll have no way to keep them from hauling her back."

"Velvet has known Dr. Nolan since she was a child. He has long been a trusted family friend."

"All right, we'll start there. In the meantime, I've instructed my solicitor to discover what avenue we might take to have Kathryn's guardianship changed."

"Good idea. Where is the lady in question? I'd like to meet her."

Lucien nodded. "I imagined you would. She's in the drawing room with Aunt Winnie. We're to join them for tea, but I think I can arrange for something a bit stronger."

Jason grinned. "What are we waiting for?"

They made their way down the hall to the Green Drawing Room, a favorite of his aunt's, and found both of the women deep in conversation. By now Winnie knew the truth of Kathryn's situation and had taken up a stance even more protective than Lucien's.

The ladies looked up at their approach. Jason paused for a moment in the doorway, his bright blue eyes surveying Kathryn Grayson from head to foot, seeing the same rare beauty that Lucien had seen. Even dressed as she was in a borrowed rose silk gown cut a little too full in the bodice, a concession to his aunt's more ample bosom, Lucien could see the small, elegant swells that had a different, more exquisite, even more enticing appeal. It was obvious Jason noticed as well.

Lucien frowned, not liking the notion. Striding toward the women, he paused in front of Kathryn, whose look had turned wary as Jason walked in. Lucien gave her a reassuring smile and some of the tension went out of her shoulders. For safety in regard to eavesdropping servants, Kathryn was introduced as Kathryn Gray. It was a ruse they would continue until she was no longer in danger.

"Miss Gray," Jason said, bowing with great formality over her slim, gloved hand. "Lucien speaks highly of you. Since he rarely goes on in such glowing terms, I hope we shall become great friends."

Kathryn smiled. "Lady Beckford has shared a number

of stories about you and his lordship when you were boys. I feel as if I already know you. I look forward to meeting your wife."

"As I am equally eager to meet you," said a bright voice from the doorway. Velvet Sinclair bowled into the drawing room with all the energy of a whirlwind. "It's a pleasure . . . Miss Gray? Wasn't it?"

"Yes . . ."

"My wife, the Duchess of Carlyle," Jason said, completing the introduction.

Velvet looked her over with a different sort of eye, sizing her up then staring hard at Lucien, who found himself glancing away. Whatever she saw in his face made her smile. "Yes, Miss Gray, a rare pleasure, indeed. Lucien is a dear and loyal friend. I'm sure we shall become good friends as well."

Kathryn smiled broadly. "I should like that above all things."

It occurred to Lucien how treasured such a friendship would be to a woman who had spent nearly a year away from home and family, even if that family was Douglas Roth.

"I thought you had gone to the village?" Jason captured his wife's hand. In an unselfconscious gesture, he brought it to his lips.

Velvet smiled up at him. "I returned home shortly after Lucien's note arrived, but you had already left for the castle. Since it has been some time since we've all been together, I thought that I would join you."

*And after reading my note mentioning "a matter of greatest urgency," your curiosity wouldn't let you stay away.* Lucien inwardly smiled. Even after the birth of their two children, Alexander Jason and little Mary Jane, Velvet was the same high-spirited young woman she had always been. She wasn't the sort of woman he would want, but she and Jason were perfectly suited. Thank God, she had married the one man who could handle her.

"Why don't we close the door?" Aunt Winnie said,

breaking into the easy camaraderie. "Lucien brought us all together for a purpose. I realize Kathryn has only just met Jason and Velvet, but she has asked for our help and now she must trust us to give it in the best way we know how."

Grateful to his aunt for getting to the point in the least painful manner, Lucien firmly closed the door.

"As my aunt has so eloquently put it, we are here for a purpose." His glance fixed on Velvet. "Since the subject is undoubtedly painful for Miss Gray, I shall summarize briefly for you, Duchess, then we shall put all of our heads together to discover the best way to help our lady in distress."

Kathryn looked up at him with such gratitude and hope shining in her eyes, something tightened in Lucien's chest. He told himself any man worth his salt would be willing to help her. It had nothing to do with the surge of desire he felt whenever he looked at her. It wasn't because he wanted to bed her, though more and more it was true.

It was simply that Kathryn needed him so badly. She had no one else to turn to, no one to count on but him. She needed him as no woman in his memory ever had, and he wasn't about to let anyone hurt her. Not Douglas Roth or anyone else.

Returning from a brief sojourn to Castle Running with her maid the following day, Lady Allison Hartman untied the fastenings on her satin-lined cloak and tossed it to the butler. As she stormed into the drawing room where her mother sat penning a letter, her cheeks still burned from the anger coursing through her. Her fingers bit into the cream silk reticule she clutched in one hand.

She waited till the butler discreetly closed the drawing room doors and her mother glanced up from the foolscap on her small, portable writing desk. One look in her daughter's troubled blue eyes, and she set her plumed pen back in the inkwell.

"What is it, dearest? What has so upset you?"

"Oh, Mother, you were right. Something *is* going on. The marquess was outside with that . . . that *woman* when I arrived. They were discussing philosophy. *Philosophy!* What woman talks to a man about such a thing? It simply is not done."

Allison closed her eyes and she could still see the willowy, dark-haired woman, Kathryn Gray, walking beside Lucien out in the garden. He listened to some jest she made and his chest rumbled with mirth.

" 'Were Democritus still on Earth he would laugh,' " Lucien said.

"Democritus . . ." said the woman, as if every female in England should recognize the name. "The laughing philosopher. You are quoting Horace."

Lucien smiled at her with obvious admiration . . . and something more. A look Allison was certain she had never seen on his face when he looked at her.

"Oh, Mama! What should I do?"

"There, there, dear heart. I'm sure whatever you saw was harmless. Lord Litchfield is a man of honor. He has asked you to marry. I do not believe his intentions have changed."

"You are the one who has always said a woman must guard against the treacheries of men."

The baroness straightened her large bulk, making the small rosewood chair creak beneath her weight. "I am not saying we shouldn't be wary. Lord Litchfield is a handsome, wealthy man. He would be quite a catch for some little untitled nobody from the country. Until the two of you are well and truly wed, it is safer to guard against such a threat."

Lady St. James rose ponderously to her feet. "I have friends in York. I shall write to them, see what they know of Litchfield's Miss Gray."

Allison smiled. She could always count on her mother. "Thank you, Mama." She bent and bussed her mother's plump cheek, then wrinkled her nose at the taste of rice powder on her lips. "Now, I believe I shall go up and

change for tea. I've yet to wear my new yellow gown—
the one with the striped silk underskirt. I think it will look
quite fetching."

"I'm sure it will, my dear."

As Allison left the salon, her thoughts returned to the
woman at Castle Running. Now that her mother was in
charge, they would learn all about Kathryn Gray. They
would discover the woman's family and friends, her past,
perhaps even her plans for the future. In time, every secret
would be exposed. Allison smiled. Her mother would
know how to deal with a woman who had obvious designs
on her future husband. She had nothing more to worry
about. Nothing at all.

She hurried to her room, her thoughts on the new silk
gown she would wear, and whether or not she should also
have purchased a new pair of yellow kid slippers.

# FOUR

Kathryn stared down at the lovely emerald silk gown Winnie had brought to her room and insisted she wear.

"I couldn't possibly accept another of your beautiful dresses," Kathryn argued, admiring the exquisite cut of the fabric, the deep, shimmering hue of green.

Aunt Winnie just laughed. "Nonsense. Most of the gowns I've given you have grown too snug for me—I am sorry to say. They look splendid on you, however—now that we've had the bustline taken in."

"I still feel guilty. Perhaps one day—"

"Don't be silly. I told you, they are far too snug. I already had this one altered, and I'm having some new gowns made for me. I am merely glad to see these old things go to some use."

*Old things.* Dressed and standing in front of the cheval glass, Kathryn smoothed the green silk bodice that came to a sharp vee in front. The sleeves, tight halfway down, cascaded in rows of frothy white lace from elbow to wrist, and the skirt floated out around her, draped over wide panniers. Her small breasts thrust above the square-cut neckline, forming pale, delicate mounds.

The marquess was entertaining guests tonight, the

Duke and Duchess of Carlyle. As Kathryn made her way downstairs to join them, she straightened the pleats below the vee of her skirt, a little nervous, she discovered. She tried to tell herself it was the presence of the duke and duchess, but she knew that wasn't the truth.

It was the handsome marquess with the silvery glint in his eyes, a spark that seemed to burn whatever it touched. Whenever she was with him, she found herself gazing at his lips, wondering if they were as hard as they looked; somehow she didn't think so. She wondered what it might be like if he kissed her, then felt ashamed of the thought. He belonged to Lady Allison. In less than two months, he would be wed.

Still, she couldn't stop thinking about him, couldn't stop hearing his deep, silken laughter, couldn't stop seeing the dark, smoldering look that came over him whenever he glanced her way. It made the breath catch in her chest and the inside of her mouth feel dry, just as it did now, simply at the thought of seeing him tonight.

Kathryn paused at the foot of the stairs, took a last glance in the ornate gilded mirror, checked the cluster of powdered curls at the side her neck and the black heart-shaped patch at the corner of her mouth. She had never been so formally dressed in the marquess's presence and she couldn't deny the flutter in her stomach or the hope that he would approve.

Taking a final deep breath, she walked into the drawing room where her newfound friends stood conversing as they waited to go in to supper. Lucien was the first to notice her. For an instant, the silver light in his eyes seemed to glow.

"Miss Gray," he said, walking toward her, bowing gracefully over her hand. "We were beginning to wonder if you had found company more to your liking."

"I'm sorry. I didn't mean to be late. I didn't realize how much time had slipped away."

"You are scarcely late. Besides, wasn't it Pepys who said, 'Better now than never'?"

She smiled. "Yes, though he is often misquoted. I believe that is in his diary."

A corner of his mouth curved up while his gaze drifted down to the tops of her breasts. "You look ravishing . . . Miss Gray."

A little thrill shot through her, though she tried her best to ignore it. "Better, I hope, than the first time we met."

He laughed in that deep, appealing way of his. " 'Tis the greatest of accomplishments, the ability to laugh at oneself."

Kathryn frowned. "I'm sorry, I can't seem to recall who said that."

The marquess grinned, making the angular planes of his face appear softer, less forbidding. "That is because I am the man who said it. You are quite an amazing woman, Miss Gray."

She could feel herself blushing at the compliment. She couldn't remember the last time flattery had been able to make her blush. Unable to come up with a suitable reply, she was grateful to Aunt Winnie for stepping into the breach.

"If my nephew is determined to monopolize Miss Gray's attention, I suggest we go on in to supper."

"Good idea," Jason said. "I'm starving."

They adjourned to a sumptuous meal of roast swan and oysters, sweetbreads of veal, potatoes in shells, and a delicious orange and apple pudding. Kathryn found herself seated next to Litchfield, which was odd because they should have been seated by rank. The duchess must have been guilty of the change, for when the marquess realized what had occurred, his dark gaze swung in her direction. It held a look of amusement tempered with a hint of warning.

For a moment, Kathryn found her cheeks heating up once more because in truth she liked sitting beside him.

"Perhaps Her Grace was right in seating us together," the marquess said easily. "I've been meaning to speak to you. I heard from my solicitor today. He's been making discreet inquiries about your guardianship. One of the Crown judges is a friend of his. He thinks the man would be amenable to the idea of removing you from Lord Dunstan's control."

Hope shimmered through her. "You are saying he might be able to arrange for a different guardian?"

"Yes."

"I should like nothing better, of course. Unfortunately, I can't imagine anyone who might accept the position."

Jason grinned as he leaned across the table. "How about the Duke and Duchess of Carlyle?"

Kathryn could have shouted out loud. Instead she felt the unexpected bite of tears. "That would be wonderful. I don't know how to thank you."

"There's no need for thanks just yet," Jason said. "One judge's opinion is far from enough to make that sort of change, should Dunstan oppose it."

"Which most likely he will," Lucien said darkly.

"With your father's will to support his position, it won't be an easy matter to accomplish," the duchess said. "But in time I'm certain Lord Litchfield will succeed."

"Until then," said Winnie, "you are safe here with Lucien and me. We've enjoyed your company immensely—haven't we, my lord?"

His eyes held hers for an instant. "That we have," he said a bit gruffly. "We certainly have, indeed."

Across the table the duchess glanced at her husband, who was frowning, but the duchess simply smiled.

After dinner, the ladies retired to the drawing room while the men remained in the dining room to smoke their pipes or take snuff and enjoy a glass of brandy.

Kathryn spent the better part of an hour talking to Lady Beckford and the duchess, who insisted she dispense with formality and call her Velvet and carefully avoided painful questions about Kathryn's months in St. Bart's. Instead they spoke of children and marriage, Kathryn admitting those sorts of thoughts hadn't occurred to her since the day she'd been locked away.

"Well, you are free of that awful place now," Velvet said with feeling. "And Lucien shall see the matter resolved once and for all. He is very good at that sort of thing."

An image came to mind of the marquess as she had seen him that morning, riding with flawless grace across the fields, his sleek black horse almost a part of him. "The marquess is very good at a lot of things, I should think."

Velvet cast her a speculative glance. "You like him, don't you?"

A flush rose into her cheeks. "Lord Litchfield has been very kind to me."

Velvet smiled. "He is a kind man, yes. He is also handsome, intelligent, and incredibly male."

The flush was spreading down across her breasts. She had thought those things more than once. She glanced over at Lady Beckford who, like the duchess, seemed oddly interested in her reply. "Yes . . . I suppose he is."

Velvet glanced at Winnie, whose blond brows climbed a bit higher on her forehead.

"Lucien is a good man," Velvet said. "One of the very best. He can also be stubborn, brooding, and bad-tempered. He and my husband are both men used to having their way. They are constantly giving orders and they expect to be obeyed." She laughed. "Of course that has changed a good deal in the years since Jason married me."

Velvet plucked a piece of lint from her gold satin skirt, considering her next words. "Lucien, even more than Jason, expects his life to be orderly and exactly as he has planned. When things don't go just that way . . . well, he can become extremely difficult."

Kathryn frowned, trying to make sense of the conversation. "Are you giving me some sort of warning, Your Grace?"

"I suppose I am merely saying that Lucien's . . . friend-ship . . . might come at a certain price, but whatever that price is, if you care for him enough, it would be worth it."

Kathryn stared at both of the women, trying to discern the cryptic words but completely unable to do so. She felt a rush of relief when the butler appeared to announce that the gentlemen would be joining them for tea and cakes.

A few minutes later, her relief slid away as the marquess strode into the drawing room. From the moment he arrived and all through the balance of the evening, she could feel his gaze on her. Always he forced it away, as if he were surprised that it had strayed toward her again.

She was grateful when the evening finally came to an end. She thought that perhaps Lord Litchfield was equally thankful.

Lucien paced his study the following afternoon. Long angry strides carried him from one end of the thick Oriental carpet to the other and back again, wearing a path in the colorful patterns in the wool. The fire in the hearth had burned low, just a few flickering flames that burned orange and red and popped occasionally against the grate. Outside the window, a stiff wind whipped branches against the panes, and cold air seeped over the sill, but Lucien didn't feel the chill. He was too damned bloody angry.

He barely heard the knock at the door, just crossed the room and jerked it open.

Reeves's head snapped up at the dark look on his face. "You sent for me, my lord?"

"Fetch the girl," he commanded. "Bring her here at once."

"Yes, sir. Right away, sir. I shall return in all haste, your lordship."

"See that you do and the girl had better be with you."

"Yes . . . yes of course, my lord."

Only a few minutes passed before another knock sounded and the door swung open again, though it seemed like an hour to Lucien. Reeves ushered Kathryn Grayson into the room and backed away, hurriedly closing the door.

He gave her an evil half-smile. "Well, *Miss Gray,* how good of you to join me." He approached where she stood, his look so hard he could see the color drain from her cheeks.

"You're angry. What . . . what have I done?"

"It is not what you have done, *my lady,* it is what you have not done."

"I don't understand. I told you the truth. I told you who I am. I told you where I've been and how I got there."

"Who you are and where you have been, yes. Not exactly how you got there."

She began to wring the hands she had unconsciously clasped together in front of her. "What . . . what do you mean?"

"I mean you very conveniently left out the part where you attempted to poison your cousin, Lord Dunstan's daughter. That is what I mean. You also neglected to mention that the reason your uncle had you committed was that he found you in the process of cutting up a dead body!"

Her eyes looked like two green saucers. Her hand crept up to the base of her throat and her mouth opened up but she didn't say a word.

"What's the matter, Lady Kathryn? Has your tongue suddenly stopped working? Or are you simply attempting to concoct another falsehood? If that is the case, it is far too late for that. A doctor friend was good enough to procure your medical records. They are sitting over there on my desk. Those things happened—did they not, Lady Kathryn? That is the truth of why you were sent to St. Bart's."

A little sound escaped her throat, a sound of pain that made his chest feel suddenly tight. Pity had no place in this conversation and he ruthlessly forced the feeling away. Dammit, he'd had such faith in her. He felt furious and betrayed that this woman he had come to admire had lied to him again—or even worse—that she might in fact, actually be insane.

Kathryn tilted her head back and looked up at him. "I don't care what is in those papers," she said at last, "it wasn't that way. Whatever it says—it wasn't that way!"

"Are you telling me you did not try to poison Lady Muriel?"

"No, of course not! Muriel was sick with an ague. I gave her a potion to help cure it, but the medicine affected her adversely and she became violently sick to her stomach. No one had ever reacted that way—not in all the times I had used the same herbs. I wasn't trying to kill her—I was trying to help her! Lady Muriel knew it and so did her father."

"Then might I also assume the body you were cutting up was not someone you were more successful at killing?"

Tears filled her eyes, yet angry sparks seemed to shoot out from the centers. "It was a course of study, nothing more. There was a doctor in our village—Dr. Cunningham. Since I had been interested in medicine for quite some years—"

"Since the deaths of your mother and sister."

"That's right. Since that was so, Dr. Cunningham and I became good friends. We shared a common interest. I had been studying herbal cures. The doctor showed me more. He taught me anatomy, showed me how the human body works, ways to treat different maladies. In exchange, I helped him with his patients whenever I was able to slip out of the house."

Lucien mulled that over. He didn't like what she was saying, but at least it had the ring of truth. "And what of this body you were found with? You are saying this was part of your course of study?"

She stared down at the toe of her low-heeled slipper, then looked back into his face. "Dr. Cunningham was actually the one involved in dissecting the . . . the subject.

He knew some men who provided him with . . . with a means to further his studies."

"Grave robbers, you mean. Resurrection men. Or were they out-and-out murderers, paid a tidy sum by your surgeon friend to provide him with a means to continue his studies? There have been any number of such cases."

"I don't . . . I don't know where he got it. But Dr. Cunningham is a man of honor. However he came into possession of the . . . cadaver . . . it was by honest means. I was interested to learn more of how the body functioned so the doctor let me watch." Her eyes slid closed for a moment, trying to hide the terror she was feeling, her fear of what he might do. Her hands were shaking, he saw. She looked as pale as parchment and for a moment he felt guilty.

Lucien steeled himself and forced the guilt away. He was tired of her lies and half-truths. If he was going to help her, he had to know the whole of it, no matter how damning it was.

"You are telling me that you—a young woman of the tender age of what? Twenty? That you were caught in the process of dissecting a human corpse?"

Her face went even paler. She swayed on her feet and he reached out a hand to steady her. Kathryn straightened away from him, forcing a stiffness into her spine. "I only wanted—"

"Let me guess—to further your education."

She shrugged her shoulders but her eyes were full of misery, and he couldn't miss the fear. "Some women are interested in painting or embroidery. I happen to be interested in learning ways to heal. What is so terrible about that?"

"If you were simply involved in a course of study, why did this Dr. Cunningham not come to your defense?"

"He tried to. My uncle threatened him. Douglas Roth made his life so difficult he finally left town. I haven't seen or heard from him since."

"Assuming that is the truth, what else have you neglected to tell me?"

Her head snapped up; her lashes were spiked with tears. "Nothing! I swear to you—there is nothing else for you to learn. I would have told you . . . the rest, but I was afraid of what you might think. I know the way you feel about my studies. I was afraid you wouldn't help me, and I desperately needed your help." Her eyes locked on his face, big green tear-filled eyes full of pain and desperation. "I still do."

Something in that look pulled hard at his insides. Kathryn Grayson was, without doubt, the most unusual female that he had ever encountered, but he believed her. And he knew without doubt that she wasn't insane. Different, determined, too smart for her own good, but certainly she wasn't mad.

"And what of Lady Muriel? What does she think of all this?"

"She's never liked me. I'm four years older and she has always resented me. For some reason she is jealous, but I haven't the slightest notion why."

*Perhaps because you are beautiful and intelligent and dedicated to your beliefs, no matter where they might lead.* It was odd. Though he highly disapproved of a gently bred lady involving herself in such an inappropriate subject, in a strange way he found himself admiring her even more than he had before.

"Is there anything else you wish to add?" he asked, making her squirm beneath the intensity of his gaze.

Kathryn shook her head. "No, my lord," she said softly. "I would, however, remind you that should you decide you no longer wish to help me, you have agreed to let me leave. I would hold you to your word."

A picture arose in his mind of Kathryn as he had first seen her, filthy and ragged, hungry and exhausted. He couldn't bear to think of her suffering that way again. Lucien cleared his throat, which felt oddly tight and made it difficult for him to speak.

"You will stay here, as we decided. With these additional marks against you, Dunstan will have a much stronger case, but sooner or later, we shall discover a way to get round him."

"You . . . you are still going to help me?"

"Aye, Lady Kathryn, that I am."

Her spine seemed to go even straighter. "Do you believe that I am insane? I have to know the truth."

"It doesn't matter what I think. What's important—"

"It matters to me, my lord."

Lucien shook his head. "No, Kathryn. I don't believe you are insane."

Something close to relief washed over her features. She nodded, brushed the dampness from her cheeks. Lucien found himself staring at her mouth and his breathing began to quicken. He noticed the way a strand of her long chestnut hair, loose from its tidy bun, floated down to tickle the soft mounds of flesh above the neckline of her dress. Inside his tight black breeches, his body began to grow hard and Lucien inwardly cursed.

"That is all, Miss Gray," he said matter-of-factly, though he was far from feeling matter-of-fact.

"Thank you, my lord."

He didn't answer. As he watched her leave, he kept thinking of her pretty pink lips and her small, exquisite breasts, and rueing the day that she had climbed aboard his carriage.

Kathryn sat curled up in the window seat, her favorite place in the library. She was poring over a volume by a man named Jean di Vigo entitled *Of Wounds in General*. Many of the books in the library were over a century old but medical treatment had changed very little in the past hundred years and each held something of interest that might come in useful.

Her mind shifted from the book in her lap to the marquess and their conversation that afternoon. Though Litchfield had stood by her once more and she was in-

credibly grateful, his disapproval was more than apparent.
Perhaps his lordship was right. She would never be a physician, no matter how long or hard she studied, and in
truth, she didn't really want to be. All she wanted, all she
had ever wanted, was to study the fascinating field that
had captured her interest as a girl and be able to give aid
when it was needed.

Kathryn scanned the pages of the book, which said that
firearms caused poisonous wounds because of the powder
and that one must cauterize the injury with scalding hot
oil of elder mixed with a little theriaca. A later volume
she had read by a man named Pare had advised against
such measures, suggesting instead the wound be dressed
with a mixture of egg yolks, oil of roses, and turpentine,
a far less painful procedure. She wished Dr. Cunningham
were here to advise her which was the better course.

Then again, hopefully a gunshot wound wasn't something she was soon to encounter.

Kathryn read on, the ticking of the clock on the mantel
beginning to fade as the hour grew late and she grew
sleepy. She must have dozed, for somewhere between di
Vigo's medical writings and her thoughts on Pare, she
found herself dreaming.

She was back in her airless cell at St. Bart's and a child
was there with her, little Michael Bartholomew, a scrawny
towheaded seven-year-old orphan who'd been named after
two of the saints. Saint Michael, whom one of the women
had seen in a vision the night he was born. She was certain the child was an angel fallen to earth—and he surely
looked like one with his golden hair and deep green eyes,
though as he got older he rarely behaved that way. Bartholomew, his surname, was simply the saint after which
the hospital he had been born in was named.

Kathryn ruffled his dirty blond hair, felt his small hand
reach out and clasp hers. His mother had died a few days
after his birth, leaving him to the care of a woman named
Cleo, an inmate of the madhouse who still had milk from
the child she had lost. In her squalid London flat, her babe

had suffocated during the night, its tiny face buried in the corn-husk mattress on the floor. Cleo had gone completely mad, tearing off her clothes, pulling out her hair, running about the London streets stark naked, winding up at St. Bart's.

She had mothered little Michael the first four years of his life, then Cleo had withdrawn completely, refusing even to speak to the boy she thought of as her son, leaving Michael to be raised by the inmate population. Why he had been drawn to Kathryn, she didn't know. She simply felt lucky that he had.

"Did you hear that?" Michael asked, staring up at her. "I think the guards is comin'."

Kathryn felt a chill whisper through her. "What . . . what day is it?"

"It's bleedin' Friday," Michael grumped. "They's comin' to give us a bath."

"Oh, God." She hated the last Friday of the month, though it was the only way she could keep track of the time. From one horrible Friday to the next a month away. This was the last Friday of September. She had marked the date on the wall. The keys rattled in the lock and the heavy oak door swung open. Michael was the only one allowed to freely roam in and out of the corridors and cells and he darted out now, hoping to escape the fate that she could not.

"Get ye arse out here, ducky," a bulky matron commanded. "Ye know well enough what day 'tis."

How could she so love to be clean and so hate the process by which she got that way? It was crystal clear when the matron stripped her and the other women naked and forced them to walk beside two burly guards down the chilly corridor to the room where the women were scrubbed.

"Get your filthy hands off me!" she shouted to one of the men whose big hand "accidentally" squeezed her breast when she didn't take her nightgown off fast enough.

" 'Ere now. I was only tryin' ta help ye. Ye best keep a civil tongue in yer head, gel, if ye know what's good fer ye."

She clamped down on her jaw to keep from spewing out the vile oath building inside her. Instead she walked down the hall in line with the rest of the women to the row of tubs where a matron would scrub her skin and hair until her flesh was raw and red and burning. They would touch her as if she were nothing more than a slab of meat, and as much as she tried not to care, humiliation scorched through her.

"No . . ." she said, starting to shake her head. "I'm a person. I can wash myself. I won't let you do this to me again."

Kathryn cried out at the harsh slap that stung her cheek.

"You'll do what I say and if ye give me any more a yer lip, you'll be scrubbin' the floor on yer hands and knees when yer finished in here."

"No . . ." Kathryn whispered as the dream continued, beginning to toss and turn on the window seat. "You can't do this . . . I won't let you . . ."

Lucien watched from the doorway for only an instant. Then he crossed the library and sat down on the window seat beside her. He knew she was dreaming and it was obvious her nightmare was not pleasant.

He shook her gently. "Kathryn, wake up. You're having a nightmare."

"No!" she cried out the moment he touched her. "Take your filthy hands off me!" She came up swinging, but he gently caught her wrists and pulled her firmly against him.

"It's all right. You're just dreaming. It's Lucien. I'm not going to hurt you."

Her eyes popped open. She blinked and slowly sagged against him. "Lucien . . ." It was the first time she had ever said his name, which sounded breathy and slightly throaty on her lips. She was breathing hard, her forehead covered with a sheen of perspiration. He could feel her slight frame trembling.

"Want to tell me about it?"

She sighed, but she didn't pull away, just rested her head on his shoulder as if it somehow gave her strength. He hoped that it did. He hoped that in some small way he could help to erase her painful past.

"There was a child there . . . a little blond boy named Michael. He was my friend."

"Was Michael in the dream?"

She nodded. He could feel the movement of her head against his chest. Wisps of burnished dark hair floated up against his cheek.

"Michael was there when the guards came. It was the end of the month. Time for . . . time for the women to bathe. I hated being dirty, but I hated what they made us do even worse."

Lucien said nothing. His heart was beating, hammering away inside him. He didn't want to hear this, but he didn't stop her. Some perverse part of him had to know the hell that she had endured.

"They stripped us naked in front of the men. They treated us as if we were cattle. If we argued with them, they beat us." She swallowed hard. He could feel the movement against his shoulder. "Some of the women sold themselves for better treatment," she said. "Most of them weren't coherent enough to know where they were or care what was being done to them."

She looked up at him with eyes that were dark and haunted. "I can't go back there, Lucien. Not ever. I would rather be dead."

His chest squeezed, pressing down on his lungs. He held her tighter, stroked her hair, wished there was something he could do to make her forget. Kathryn slid her arms around his neck and leaned her head into his shoulder.

"You won't have to go back," he said. "I promise you, Kathryn."

She made no comment, just dragged in a shaky breath of air. When she realized how intimately they were entwined, she eased away, a slight flush coloring her cheeks.

"I'm sorry. I didn't mean to burden you with my past."

"It wasn't a burden."

Her eyes locked on his face. Something moved between them. Kathryn stood up from the window seat and took a step away. He knew what she was feeling, the hot, sweet thickness that had risen in the air around them, the awareness that suddenly pulsed like a living thing between them. Feelings that had nothing to do with comfort and everything to do with desire.

Inwardly he cursed. That he wanted her made no difference. He had obligations, commitments. His life was laid out exactly as he had planned, his future as unchangeable as if it were drawn in indelible ink.

There was no place in it for Kathryn Grayson. And even if there could be, he wouldn't want it. She wasn't the sort of woman he wished to marry. He wanted a sweet, docile, manageable female like Allison Hartman.

"It's getting late," Kathryn said, the words little more than a whisper. "I had better be going upstairs."

"Yes . . . I believe I shall retire myself." But he wondered if he'd be able to fall asleep. Or if he would lie in the darkness, imagining the feel of Kathryn Grayson's firm little nipples as they had pressed into his chest, the soft look in her eyes when she had said his name.

# FIVE

Winifred Montaine DeWitt looked down from the window of her bedchamber. In the garden below, Lucien strolled the gravel paths with Lady Kathryn Grayson. Winnie knew he was attracted to the girl and she understood the attraction. They were both intelligent, strong-willed people. People who knew what they wanted and weren't afraid to go after it.

Kathryn was determined to pursue her medical studies, no matter that society forbade such an unsuitable course. Her childhood, the loss of her sister and mother, had spawned a fascination she could not ignore. She had already suffered greatly for the path she had chosen, but Winnie believed even her ordeal in the madhouse would not be enough to snuff out her need for learning.

Lucien's own desires were equally strong. He wanted to protect the Litchfield title, to increase the productivity and value of his lands and estates, and build a future for his sons. He had made plans to do just that, and no matter what problems might arise, that is exactly what he would do.

That Kathryn didn't fit the image of wife he had created in his mind only made it easier for him to hold his course. He disapproved of her interest in what he saw as unfit subjects for a lady. Winnie thought that perhaps, deep down inside, he still harbored an ill will toward his mother. Charlotte Stanton Montaine was also a brilliant young woman who refused to follow the dictates of society.

Her uniqueness had sparked Lucien's father's interest from the moment he first met her, and he had fallen wildly, insanely in love with her. But unlike Kathryn Grayson, Charlotte was selfish and spoiled. As a child she had wanted be an actress—an outrageous notion, considering she was the daughter of an earl. But Charlotte craved attention the way a thirsty man craved water, and she would do anything to get it. In the end, she had run off with an Italian count, abandoning her twelve-year-old son and leaving behind a besotted husband who became addicted to opium and died far too young.

Winnie believed that when Lucien looked at Kathryn, he saw the strong sort of woman his mother had been, felt the same pull of attraction his father had felt for such a woman, remembered the terrible consequences and unconsciously rebelled.

It was a pity, Winnie thought, recalling the love she had found with Richard. Though her husband wasn't the passionate sort of man her nephew was, though he never looked at her with those hot, burning glances Lucien directed at Kathryn Grayson, they had been happy together. Winnie missed the closeness, the sharing that she would never have with another man.

She stepped back from the heavy velvet draperies with a sigh. In her own way she had come to love her husband. As a girl, she had once even fallen in love.

When she looked at Lucien, she thought of Allison Hartman and wondered if her nephew would ever learn the meaning of the word.

Lucien dismounted from his black Arabian stallion and handed the reins to the stable lad who rushed up beside him.

"I'll take 'im, milord."

Lucien patted the animal's sleek neck, still damp with sweat from his afternoon run. "He's had a long day, Timmy. See he's well cooled out and be sure to give him an extra portion of grain."

"Aye, milord."

The horse nickered softly as Lucien walked out of the barn, both of them grateful to be returned from a day of calling on tenants and surveying the fields. They were harvesting the last of the corn stubble to fatten the geese and the rest of the poultry. Pigs were being slaughtered for market, the bristles bringing a good price for brushes, their lard also a valuable commodity.

Lucien strode off toward the house, hungry for a good hot meal and a restful evening. Perhaps he would play a game of chess with Kathryn. He had discovered she was good at the game, and yesterday she had actually won.

He found himself smiling at the thought. He wouldn't have believed the day would come when a woman could beat him at chess. He glanced toward the door and his smile slid away. Reeves was racing toward him, his coat-tails flapping, his face flushed beet-red.

"My lord—come quickly! There are men in the house and they—" He stopped to wheeze in a breath, his powdered wig slipping sideways as Lucien gripped his arm.

"What is it, man? What's happened?"

"The constable. He and his men—they've come for Miss Gray. I tried to—"

Lucien didn't wait to hear the rest. Already he was running, shoving through the heavy oak door, his heart pounding as loud as his boots, anger making his fists clench. By the time he reached the entry, the house was in chaos. Kathryn was surrounded by a group of five men, Aunt Winnie standing beside her, gripping Kathryn's arm, refusing to let them take her away. One of the constable's men was prying on Winnie's fingers, trying to break her hold.

"What the devil is going on here?" Lucien's voice rang

like a cannon shot above the melee. He stopped just paces from the heavyset man who appeared to be in charge. "You are trespassing in my home," he continued in his most severe tone. "You are assaulting one of my guests. Release Miss Gray at once." He had yet to look at Kathryn and he didn't intend to. He knew the terror he would see on her face and what it would do to him when he did. He couldn't afford that moment of weakness. He needed his wits about him.

"I'm sorry for the inconvenience, your lordship. I'm Constable Perkins," said the heavyset man with the hard gray eyes and heavily powdered hair. "The man to my right is Henry Blakemore, the dean of admissions for St. Bartholomew's Hospital." He was slimmer, his nose long and thin, his hair slicked back in a face that was gaunt and a little bit sallow. "This woman is Lady Kathryn Grayson. We have been looking for her for some time. After a considerable effort, we discovered she was here. We've come to see her returned to the hospital."

Kathryn made a little whimpering sound but Lucien still didn't look at her.

"This woman's name is Kathryn Gray. She is a guest of my aunt's. Since there has obviously been some mistake, I strongly suggest that you leave."

"I'm sorry, your lordship, we can't do that. Dr. Blakemore has known her ladyship for more than ten months. He has identified her as the woman you know as Kathryn Gray."

He did look at her then, saw her sway toward Aunt Winnie, who still clung to her arm. Two watchmen still held her prisoner between them while another stood a few feet away. Her face was ashen, her eyes huge and glassy, like a moss-covered stone at the bottom of a stream.

"I tell you there is some mistake. I demand that you leave this instant." The men did not move, nor did they release their hold on Kathryn's arms. Lucien wanted to rip their hands away, to tear her free from their grasp and spirit her to safety. Instead he clamped down on his formidable temper and maintained his careful control.

"I warn you, gentlemen. Continue in this endeavor and you will not like the consequences."

"I'm afraid you don't understand, my lord. This woman is a danger to you and your family. She nearly killed the Earl of Dunstan's daughter. For your sake as well as her own, she must be returned to St. Bart's."

"Noooo!" Kathryn's voice, high-pitched and keening, rang across the foyer. She struggled against the watchmen's hold and unconsciously his hands balled into fists. "I didn't try to kill her," Kathryn cried. "She got sick, is all. It was an accident—I swear it."

"Take her away," Constable Perkins told his men.

"No!" Lucien stepped in front of the door. "You aren't taking her anywhere. She is a guest in this house and she is not leaving."

The constable's face turned hard. "There are five of us, Lord Litchfield. We will subdue you if we must. This woman is a danger to society. We have orders to bring her back. That is what we intend to do."

"Lucien?" Aunt Winnie's worried face looked up at him for a solution. Short of battling a constable, a doctor, and three seasoned watchmen, he could think of none. And even if he called in his servants, the men would simply return. Better to deal with the matter and have it settled once and for all. He turned his attention to Kathryn, whose head hung forward in defeat.

"I won't let them keep you," he told her. "I'll go to London straightaway. I'll have you out of there in a day or two."

Kathryn stared down at the floor as if he hadn't spoken, her eyes more glazed than before.

Lucien gripped her shoulders. "Listen to me, dammit. I won't let them hurt you. I'll come for you. As soon as I can arrange it, I'll have you out of there."

She looked up at him, but he didn't think she really saw him. "I can't survive that place again," she whispered. "I would rather be dead than go back there." Her eyes locked with his and her meaning was more than clear. "Do you hear me? I would rather be dead!"

Fear unlike any he had known tightened like a band around his chest. He knew what she was saying and he believed her. She would die in that place, if it had to be by her own hand.

Perkins made a motion toward the door, ordering his men to lead her away. As they started in that direction, Lucien stepped in front them, blocking her way. He reached up and caught her chin, cradled her face between his palms, and gave her a fierce, hard kiss on the mouth.

"Listen to me, Kathryn. I'll get you out of there—I give you my word. Don't do anything until I come for you—do you understand?"

Kathryn ran her tongue over her lips, tasting him there, looking at him for the first time as if she really saw him.

"Just find a way to survive," Lucien told her. "I'll get you out—I promise you I'll find a way."

Kathryn gazed into his face and finally she nodded. Then she turned away. He could hear his aunt crying in the background, and the sound ate at the last shreds of his control.

He turned a hard warning gaze on Blakemore. "I'll hold you personally responsible for this woman's treatment. If anything should happen to her—anything at all—I'll come for you. And a brigade of watchmen won't be able to save you from my wrath."

The doctor turned as gray as his powdered hair, but he nodded. "I'll see she receives the best possible care, your lordship."

Which meant nothing at all in a place like St. Bart's. Lucien felt sick to his stomach. As he watched her climb into the carriage, he wanted to bury his fist in Blakemore's self-righteous face. He turned to Reeves, who stood in the shadows of the hall, looking nearly as distraught as his aunt.

"Have my carriage brought round. I leave tonight for London."

"Yes, my lord."

Aunt Winnie stepped forward, catching his arm. "I'm going with you. Kathryn may need me and I mean to be there if she does."

Lucien didn't argue. The look in Winnie's eyes and the tears on her cheeks warned him it would do no good.

Dressed in a worn white cotton gown with a bloodred band around the neck, Kathryn walked down the hall toward her cell. Ignoring the fetid odor of unwashed bodies, urine, and feces, she held her head high, fighting against the crushing weight of defeat that had settled in her breast. She wouldn't cry, she vowed—not now, not ever again. She wouldn't give them the satisfaction.

"Get a move on, wench!" The bulky matron shoved her down the hall. "I ain't got all day to be nursemaidin' the likes o' ye back where ye belong."

Kathryn ignored her and simply kept walking.

"What's the matter, *yer ladyship*? No servants ta cart ye about in yer bleedin' sedan chair? No footman ta serve yer bloody meals on a silver tray?"

Another shove and Kathryn stumbled. She caught herself, straightened her shoulders, and walked on. They had almost reached her cell when she heard the sound of small racing footsteps and the loud cry of her name.

"Kathryn! Kathryn, ye came back!" It was the one sound in this foul, dismal world she was happy to hear.

She turned outside the door to her cell and felt his small weight rush into her arms. Tears threatened again, and this time she almost gave in to them, but these were tears of joy at the feel of Michael's warm little body held tightly in her arms. Sweet God, she hadn't realized just how much she had missed him.

The matron stepped back, scowling but allowing them a moment. Not even Miss Wiggins was immune to Michael. Kathryn hugged him hard, then stepped back to survey his thin frame from top to bottom. "My goodness, Michael—look how much you've grown!"

He beamed up at her, a lock of his blond hair sticking straight up on the top of his head. "Do ye really think so?" They had cut his hair again, cropped it short around his head so that it wouldn't tangle.

She nodded and smiled. "I think you've sprouted at least two inches."

Michael laughed at that, knowing it was a lie but wishing it were true. "When I get big," he said, tossing a look at the matron, "I'm gettin' outta here—and they won't be able ta stop me."

"Ye'll be gettin' a cuff on the head," the matron said, "ye don't get away from here and go on about yer business." But there was no anger in her voice. That she saved for Kathryn. Miss Wiggins shoved her into the cell and the door slammed closed with an eerie clank, locking her inside.

She came up to the window and looked down through the bars. The matron was walking away, her heavy girth making her brown linen skirt sway back and forth around her thick ankles, but Michael remained in the hallway, staring up at her from below the bars.

"I thought ye'd gotten away," he said. "I thought ye was gonna be free."

She blinked against the sting behind her eyes. "So did I, Michael." She forced herself to smile. "I almost made it. I wish you could have come with me." It was surprising how much she meant it. Perhaps if the marquess managed to free her, he would also free the boy.

Kathryn felt a tightness building inside her. She was back where she had started, her life stretching hopelessly in front of her. But she had made a friend in the world outside, perhaps more than one. Litchfield had given his word to help her. He had promised to get her out of St. Bart's. She wanted to believe it would happen. Dear God, she wanted to believe it so badly. But hope was a dangerous, even lethal emotion in a place like St. Bart's. Better to resign yourself, to close yourself off against the terrors in the world that surrounded you.

And yet deep inside hope remained, burning as it hadn't since she'd been locked away. The marquess was the strongest, most honorable man she had ever met. If anyone could help her, it was he.

She remembered the way they had parted, the fierce, unexpected kiss that had reached her as nothing else could have. Kathryn ran her tongue over her lips and thought that if she closed her eyes, she could still taste him. She could still hear his words, his promise to free her, and the conviction in his voice when he had said it.

His promise and the memory of his kiss would keep her alive, at least for a while. Until the pain and humiliation were simply too great to bear. Then she would decide what she must do.

Lucien sat across from his solicitor, Nathaniel Whitley, in Nat's office on Threadneedle Street. It was six o'clock in the morning. It was raining outside, a thick mist enveloping the city, a cold that seeped into the bones.

Sitting behind his desk, Nat looked sleepy-eyed, his clothes wrinkled as if he had slept in them, which Lucien guessed he might have, considering the pressure he'd been under.

Five days ago, Lucien had arrived at Nat's West End town house at an equally outrageous hour, rousing him from slumber and demanding Nat start to work immediately to find a way to free Lady Kathryn Grayson from imprisonment in St. Bartholomew's Hospital.

So far, in five long, grueling days, his efforts had come to naught.

"I wish I had something positive to tell you, my lord." Nat was an attractive man in his late forties, average in height and build, his dark brown hair shot with silver beneath his gray bagwig. A pair of gold-rimmed spectacles perched on a straight, well-formed nose. "The fact is, Dunstan is dead set against Lady Kathryn's release—even into the custody of someone as respected as you and your aunt. As soon as he was informed of your efforts, he began his own campaign to thwart them. He's a powerful man, Lucien. Where you have always shied away from politics and social intrigue, Dunstan thrives on them. He has friends in the highest places, and money to line the pockets of any man who might oppose him."

"Lady Kathryn's money," Lucien said blackly, running a hand over his hair, smoothing it back toward the wide black bow at the nape of his neck.

"Perhaps. We haven't been able to discover the source of the earl's funds. I've got a man working on it, though it won't really matter whose money it is, as long as he has legal control."

A faint tremor ran through him. He leaned back in his chair. He hadn't been eating lately. Every time he thought of Kathryn locked up in that place, of her suffering God only knew what, his appetite fled completely. He hadn't been able to sleep. Every time he closed his eyes, he imagined them stripping her naked, imagined the guards leering at her small pert breasts. He remembered her keening cry for help and the sound sliced right through him, dragging him to wakefulness even if he managed to fall asleep.

He shifted on the hard leather chair. "How did they discover where she was?"

"Servants' gossip. There were a number of them there the night she arrived at the castle. From what you have said, it was a rather memorable occurrence."

Lucien merely nodded, having come to the same conclusion. He had foolishly believed word wouldn't reach Dunstan until he had matters firmly in hand. "What's our next move?" he asked, praying there was one.

"I'm not sure. The more information we have the better chance we'll turn up something that will help us. I've been trying to locate this Dr. Cunningham her ladyship mentioned, but so far we've had no luck."

Lucien flexed a muscle in his jaw. "It's been nearly a week. I've got to see her, convince her to be patient. She needs to know we haven't given up, that we still mean to help her."

Nat shook his head. "They won't let you in. Dunstan's adamant about that. She's not allowed any visitors—she's too dangerous—that's what Dunstan and Dr. Blakemore say."

He ground his teeth. "Blakemore. That little weasel will be lucky if I don't kill him. As for Dunstan—I haven't yet devised a punishment that is nearly cruel enough for him."

Nat removed his glasses, folded them, and set them on top of the papers spread before him. "Take it easy, Lucien. You and your aunt are the girl's only hope. You've got to keep your head. Dunstan is cagey. Anything you do wrong he'll use against you."

Lucien sighed, feeling exhausted clear to the bone. "I thought this would be easy. I thought I'd have her out of there long before this. I don't know how much longer she'll be able to hold on."

Nat stood up from his chair and leaned forward, bracing his hands on the desk. "You're doing everything in your power. No one can ask more than that."

But it wasn't enough. Not nearly enough. Somehow he had to help her. Lucien wasn't sure just how it had happened that Kathryn Grayson had come to mean so much to him. Whatever it was, he considered her a friend and he wasn't a man to let his friends down in time of need.

"Thank you, Nat, for all the work you've done."

"It's all right," his friend said gently. "I don't like injustice any more than you do, particularly when it involves an innocent young woman. And I don't like Douglas Roth."

Lucien almost smiled. Instead he simply nodded, turned and started for the door.

"Lord Litchfield?"

Lucien paused and looked over his shoulder.

"Try to get some sleep," Nat said. "And you might

also try eating something. You can't do the girl a lick of good if you fall ill."

Lucien dragged open the door and stepped out into the hallway. Nat was right. He had to take better care of himself. He told himself he would head for the top of St. James Street, visit White's, his club, and get something to eat. The thought had only begun to take root when a picture of Kathryn arose, hungry and dirty, her eyes full of fear and desperation. He shoved the image away and climbed into his carriage, but he didn't head for St. James's.

The thought of food suddenly made his stomach lurch.

Eight days passed. Eight endless, humiliating days with no word from Lucien. Perhaps the marquess had forgotten all about her. Perhaps he never intended to help. Perhaps he had spoken to her uncle, and Douglas Roth had convinced him she actually was insane.

Whatever the reason, the hope she had clung to had begun to slip away. Only little Michael had been able to keep her spirits up. His laughter, echoing in the dirty, dimly lit halls, gave her strength and the will to go on. She wondered at the despair that weighed her down like a heavy iron shirt. Why was it so much worse this time than it had been before?

Perhaps because she had been living again the sort of life she'd enjoyed before her father died, waking up each day among friends in a house of comfort and warmth. Or perhaps it was simply that her failed escape had forced her to see the truth. Even if she got away, no matter where she went, no matter how far she ran, somehow her uncle would find her. He couldn't risk losing control. He needed her money and he would do anything in his power to keep it.

She heard men's footsteps coming down the hall. She wasn't frightened of the guards, as she had been before. The marquess had accomplished one thing the day of their parting—he had terrified Dr. Blakemore with his threats.

Upon her return to St. Bart's, the man had given strict instructions that none of the guards were to touch her. She was no longer afraid one of them might force himself on her, which was not to say she didn't feel the back of a hand should she dare to speak her mind, or the sharp lash of a matron's tongue.

Or far worse, she discovered, the day she protested one of the men's ill treatment of little Michael. She was working in the laundry, bent over a huge iron pot filled with scalding water, stirring a long wooden stick through a bubbling vat of lye soap to clean the hundred dirty nightgowns even filthier than the one she wore.

She heard Michael's high voice even before she saw him. "Bugger off, ye bleedin' sod!" he called out, and Kathryn winced at the words. Poor little Michael knew every curse word in the English language. He had developed a thick Cockney accent learned from the guards. She could only imagine what his life would be like if he ever escaped to the real world outside the hospital walls.

Through the open door, she saw him round the corner and race toward her. A big beefy guard named Otis rounded the corner right behind him, thundering along and shouting equally offensive curses.

"Ye little prick! I'll be tannin' yer arse with me belt once I get me hands on ye!"

Michael's feet kept moving but his face went pale. He'd received more beatings than she could count, most for the slightest misdemeanors. She'd always thought this man, Otis, actually looked for an excuse. He seemed to get a thrill out of hurting someone smaller than he was. And there was an odd look in his eyes whenever he glanced at Michael.

As if he wanted something from the boy and was only biding his time until he got it. Kathryn had heard of men who preferred other men over women. She wasn't exactly sure how it worked between them, but she wondered if Otis might be one of those men and if it were possible for him to be thinking those sorts of thoughts about a little boy.

Michael raced up beside her, breathing hard, his small hand clutching her nightgown as he ducked around behind her.

Otis roared up a few seconds later, his thick chest rising and falling with each breath. "Bloody little thief stole me purse!"

Michael poked his blond head out from behind her. "Did not, ye lyin' sod!"

Otis made a grab for him, but Michael jerked away, careful to keep Kathryn between him and Otis.

"Michael says he didn't take it." Kathryn straightened, blocking Otis even more. "Isn't there a chance you misplaced it?"

Otis's hard gaze swung to her. "The little whelp's comin' with me. I'll teach him to steal from Otis Cheek." Otis tried to step around her, but Kathryn blocked his way.

"I'm sure he didn't do it. Perhaps if you looked again—" His hand snaked out, slapped her hard across the face.

"You stay outta this—ya hear?" He stared down at the top of Michael's head and something hot and sordid flashed in his eyes. "The boy's comin' with me."

"Nooo!" Michael shrieked, and she thought that he too must have seen something in Otis's gaze. The boy was truly frightened and her own fear for him began to pound in her ears.

She tucked him farther behind her. "You aren't taking him anywhere. I'm not going to let you."

The evilest grin she had ever seen split across Otis's face. "You ain't gonna let me? You and who else is gonna stop me?"

"I am!" Michael shouted, kicking Otis hard in the shin. Otis howled and made a violent grab for him, catching his thin arm and jerking Michael clear off the floor.

"Let him go!" Raising the stick she had been using to

stir the boiling pot of laundry, Kathryn crashed it down on Otis's head with all her strength. He roared like an injured lion and whirled in her direction, giving Michael the chance to jerk free. Otis cursed and slapped her. Michael shrieked an equally dirty word and leapt on the huge man's back, pounding away with his small bony fists.

Arms and legs were everywhere. Shouts and curses rose above the sound of running feet as three husky matrons burst through the door of the laundry. Seeing Kathryn still wielding her stick, they began to shout orders and race madly about. The next thing Kathryn knew, she was down on the rough stone floor, surrounded by matrons and guards, a screaming Michael being dragged away by one of the women. At least he would be safe, she thought as she struggled against the heavy weight pinning her down. Rough hands pried open her mouth and someone poured something bitter onto her tongue.

She didn't remember much after that, only barely recalled being dragged back to her cell. She slumped down in the corner, feeling weightless and slightly dizzy. Her eyes felt heavy-lidded. Her surroundings appeared softly blurred. It was odd, she thought dimly. For the first time since her return to the madhouse, she felt good . . . almost . . . happy. As she sagged down on her filthy straw pallet, the walls of the cell seemed to recede and she was standing on the soft grassy lawn at Milford Park. The trouble and pain of St. Bart's slid away, leaving her with only a vague sense of numbness.

Kathryn leaned back against the wall, unaware of the cold stone at her back or the stiff straw pressing through her thin cotton night rail. Instead she closed her eyes and gave herself up to the pleasing numbness. She thought of Lucien and she smiled.

# SIX

Douglas Roth, Earl of Dunstan, sat behind the huge rosewood desk in his study. Outside the window, the lawns of Milford Park stretched like an elegant carpet, sloping down to a babbling steam that meandered beside the sprawling brick house. The leaves had fallen from most of the trees and a stiff November wind clipped along, rifling through the branches, but the manor still carried an air of magnificence unmarred by the weather, its handsome lines and sturdy façade a testament to the architect Robert Lyminge and a young Inigo Jones, who had designed it a hundred and fifty years earlier.

Douglas pulled his diamond studded snuffbox from the pocket of his waistcoat and took a pinch. He sneezed several times and turned away from the window, back to the papers strewn across his desk. Somewhere on nearly each one was the name of his niece, Kathryn Grayson.

He found himself grinding his teeth just to think of her. He had become her guardian five years ago—a stroke of good fortune for him that the late earl, her father, couldn't have begun to guess when he had bestowed the honor upon him. Since then she had been headstrong, willful, and impossible to manage. But her fortune was huge and well worth the effort, especially since his own meager estate had dwindled to near nonexistence.

Douglas began to shuffle through the papers, searching for the stack of bank drafts his accountant had sent for his signature, notes drawn to pay the tailor, the haberdasher, the shoemaker—a tidy sum, as Douglas refused to dress in anything but the very best. There was a draft made out for his new carriage and a rather large amount he had incurred while gaming at Madame Duprey's pleasure barge.

No one ever questioned his use of funds—no one but Kathryn. The others were well paid to look the other way, and after all, his niece still had an extravagant amount of money.

Douglas smiled as he picked up the letter he had received from Dr. Blakemore, the dean of admissions at St. Bart's. Upon her return, Kathryn had engaged in an encounter with one of the guards, displaying once again her unstable, violent nature. But, the letter said, Lord Dunstan need not be concerned. His niece had been subdued without harm to her person and been brought once more under control. Blakemore assured him there would be no more such incidents and that Lady Kathryn was being well cared for.

There wasn't the slightest hint in the letter for another "contribution" to the doctor in gratitude for his service. He knew Douglas would send it, now that the girl was once more well in hand. It went unsaid that she wouldn't be allowed to leave the hospital again.

That possibility was past, and any attempts by the Marquess of Litchfield to intercede on her behalf had already been quietly thwarted. All was in order, Douglas thought with satisfaction, his world returned to normal.

He paused at a light knock at the door, glanced up to see his daughter, Muriel, standing beside the butler, who had fetched her at his command and now eased slowly back into the hall.

"Good afternoon, my dear."

"You wished to see me, Father?" She fidgeted, straightened a bit from her usual slump. She was slightly taller than Kathryn, too tall for a woman, with bright red hair that stuck out in little frizzles all over her head, and freckles across her nose and cheeks that no amount of effort could disguise. She wasn't pretty like Kathryn. Muriel took after his late wife's mother, but she was his daughter, his own flesh and blood. And unlike Kathryn, she had learned to obey his commands.

"Actually, my dear, I merely wished to learn what you were doing at Mary Williams's house last week with that abominable Osgood boy."

Muriel's face turned red, partially hiding her freckles. "Truman is only a friend. He was there to visit Mary's brother."

"Good. I am glad to hear it. He is only a second son, after all. The lad is penniless and always will be. He is certainly not for you."

She met his gaze for only a moment, then she stared down at the floor. She was a big girl, not the sort in vogue, but even at sixteen she had the full ripe curves of a woman and he had no doubt she would prove useful in the marriage mart.

"You may go now." He reached up to adjust his white pigtail wig, then flicked a piece of lint from his gold velvet tailcoat. "Just remember, I have plans for you that do not include an untitled nothing like Truman Osgood."

Something flashed in her eyes, then it was gone. For an instant he imagined it was defiance. He shook his head at the ridiculous thought.

"I'll remember, Father," Muriel said meekly.

Turning away from him, she walked out the door, and Douglas returned to the papers on his desk. His life was back on course, his future once more secure. Even the interference of a man as powerful as Lucien Montaine didn't upset him. Douglas had matters well in hand.

•       •       •

Jason Sinclair stepped out of the mist into the entry of Lucien's town house in Grosvener Square. It had been raining for the past three days, making the trip from Carlyle Hall a muddy, difficult journey.

He untied his cloak from around his neck and swirled it toward the butler, slinging water on the polished marble floor. "Where is he, Reeves?"

"In his study, your lordship. He rarely comes out these days. Lady Beckford has been worried sick about him."

Jason nodded, his jaw tightening. He turned and strode down the hall, knocked briefly on the study door, then shoved it open without waiting for Lucien's permission. Even knowing how upset his friend must be, Jason wasn't prepared for the haggard, unkempt man who sat hunched over his ornate desk.

"Good God, man—you look like bloody hell." Jason strode toward him, didn't stop till he reached the desk, then leaned over it, bracing his big hands on the top. "When is the last time you've eaten? Not for a fortnight from the look of you. You probably aren't sleeping much, either. What are you trying to do—kill yourself?"

Lucien straightened, raked a hand through his thick black hair, which was unbound, as it rarely was, and hung down to his shoulders. It looked as dull as his eyes.

"What am I trying to do? Whatever it is, I am not succeeding. I haven't accomplished a bloody damned thing since I've been here."

"Christ, man. It isn't your fault she's in there. You didn't put her there—her uncle did."

"I gave her my word. I told her I'd get her out. It's been nearly two weeks. Can you imagine what could have happened to her in two bloody long weeks?" He sat wearily back in his chair. "By the way, what the devil are you doing here?"

"Looking for you. Aunt Winnie sent word of what happened at the castle. I thought you'd have this whole thing settled by now and be back home. When I didn't hear from you and you still hadn't returned, I figured you might need some help."

"I've hired the best help money can buy. It hasn't done a lick of good."

Jason sat down in the leather chair across from him, stretched his long legs out in front of him. "Dunstan probably has half the people you're trying to deal with in his pocket. We don't even know who all of them are, so we can't very well offer them more money."

"No, I don't suppose we can, more's the pity." Lucien ran his hands over his face, which was darkened by a day's growth of beard. In all the years Jason had known him, he had never seen his friend look so weary. "I tell you, Jason, I am at my wit's end."

"I realize this may sound a little strange, since you're betrothed to another woman, but what if you simply married her?"

Lucien shook his head. "Kathryn can't marry me or anyone else—at least not for another year. Until she is one and twenty, she would have to have her uncle's permission, and considering her husband would then control her fortune, Dunstan would scarcely be willing to give it."

Jason leaned back in his chair, steepling his fingers beneath his chin. "On the way here, I had time to do some thinking. I figured if you couldn't find a way to get Lady Kathryn out, there was probably little more that Velvet and I could do."

Lucien looked surprised. "Velvet is here as well?"

"She wanted to be, I can tell you. If the baby hadn't come down with the croupe, I wouldn't have been able to stop her."

A corner of Lucien's mouth curved up. "No, I don't suppose you could have."

"I got in late last night. I knew you were an early riser and I wanted to speak to you as soon as I could. I was glad Velvet couldn't come, since I wanted to talk to you alone."

Lucien cocked a sleek black brow. "Since when did

you begin keeping secrets from your wife?"

"Since I decided to suggest we do something highly illegal."

"Illegal? What on earth are you talking about?"

"I'm talking about breaking into St. Bart's and rescuing your lady."

Lucien made a rude sound in his throat. "She isn't my lady—and breaking into St. Bart's is completely absurd."

"Then you're content to leave Kathryn in there?"

"Actually, I was thinking of calling on Dunstan. I figured if I threatened him at the point of a gun—"

"Now *that* is absurd."

Lucien did smile then. "I know, but I'm getting more desperate every day."

"Desperate enough to ride with One-eyed Jack Kincaid? If I recall correctly, there's a hunting lodge hidden in the woods not far from Castle Running. It would be the perfect place to hide Lady Kathryn until we could find a way to remove her from Dunstan's control."

Lucien's black brows drew together. "You're serious."

"As an epidemic of the Black Plague."

A spark of interest moved over Lucien's sharp features. "Do you actually think we could do it?"

"It won't be as tough as you think. It isn't often someone wants to get *into* St. Bart's. They won't be expecting that sort of problem. All we have to do is figure out where Kathryn is and take her out of there."

"She's probably locked up. We'd have to have a key."

"We won't go in unprepared. It may take a few days to gather the information we need, but if Dunstan can find willing cohorts for a bit of coin, so can we. We'll have the whole thing well planned. We'll use horses to go in but have a carriage waiting at the outskirts of town." He grinned. "Trust me in this, my friend. I may play the part of gentleman once more, thanks to you and Velvet, but a man doesn't forget the things he's been forced to learn, and this is a subject I know a great deal about."

Something glinted in Lucien's dark eyes. "All right.

I'm willing if you are." With those simple words, his hollow, defeated expression seemed to fade, replaced by a look of fierce determination.

"I'd prefer we didn't inform my wife," Jason said. "I don't want her involved in this. We both know it might be dangerous."

Lucien simply nodded. "The lady will remain uninformed, as will my aunt. For their sakes as well as our own."

"All right, then, let's get started." Jason stole a last glance at his friend, who looked once more like the self-assured, strong-willed, imposing man he was. Whatever his friend's feelings were for Kathryn Grayson, he was a man who didn't break his word and clearly he meant to keep it this time.

Jason inwardly smiled, wondering where his friend's concern might lead, more certain than ever he was doing the right thing.

Kathryn turned her head away and some of the dark, bitter liquid dribbled off her chin and ran down her neck. "No . . . I don't . . . want it."

"Shut yer mouth and drink it like I told ye." The matron ruthlessly pinched her arm, then caught her jaw and squeezed until Kathryn finally opened her mouth. The bitter brew spilled over her tongue and down her throat, forcing her to swallow. She hated the foul-tasting stuff, but in truth, she liked the way it made her feel, so languid and warm, so comfortably unaware.

The matron wiped the wetness from Kathryn's face and neck. "All right, now, that's more like it. Ye're finally learnin' to mind yer manners." She chuckled, shaking her bulky girth. "With a wee bit o' help from a friend." She lifted the empty glass that had contained the dark powder mixed with water she gave to Kathryn every day. "Ye've a visitor wantin' ta see ye—little Michael's come ta call."

Kathryn worked to recall the name. Slowly the little blond boy's image formed in her mind. "Michael . . . ?"

For a moment, she'd thought it might be Lucien. For the past few days, she'd been seeing him in her dreams, reliving his kiss, tasting it on her lips. In the dream he came for her, appearing like a knight out of the shadows to carry her away from St. Bart's. In the dream he kissed her again and again, and oh, it felt so good.

But she was glad to see Michael. She had missed him these past few days . . . or perhaps it was weeks . . . she couldn't be sure. The minutes and hours all seemed to run together. Her mind was too fuzzy, too out of focus to know where one day ended and another began. And in truth she no longer cared.

"Kathryn?" Michael squatted down on the dirty straw pallet beside her. "Ye never come out and play no more. Are ye mad at me, Kathryn?"

"No . . . Michael . . . of course not." She didn't remind him she had never come out to play. She'd been busy scrubbing floors or washing laundry, busy darning the matrons' clothes or working in the kitchen. Still, they'd talked as she worked and Michael had played at one thing or another close by. "I'm just . . . a bit tired . . . is all. Miss Wiggins has been . . . letting me . . . rest."

Standing near the door, the heavyset matron cackled some sort of response. "Bang on the bars, Mikie, when ye decide ye want ta come out." She locked the cell door, though Kathryn had no thought of escape even if she hadn't.

Michael sat down beside her on the scratchy straw. "Do ye want to hear me sing?" he asked. "I learnt a new song. I'll sing it if ye want." Kathryn nodded. They had sung songs while she was working, she recalled, to block the screams of one of the inmates down the hall. She had taught him several verses of "Greensleeves" and in the past they had sung it together.

Michael started singing his new song, his voice high and wavery, his enthusiasm making up for any notes in the tune he sang off key.

> *There once was a maid from Sark*
> *Who walked with me in the park.*
> *I put me 'and on her knee,*
> *She put 'er 'and on me.*
> *We laid down on a grassy patch,*
> *She pushed me over onto me back.*
> *She laughed as I raised 'er skirt—*

"Michael—" Even in her hazy state, Kathryn recognized the bawdy lyrics were not the sort to be sung by a child. "Michael . . . you mustn't . . . sing songs like that. It isn't . . . proper."

"Why not?" He screwed his face to look up at her, his pale gold brows pulling nearly together. "Old Sammy Dingle taught it to me." One of the guards. " 'E used ta be a sailor."

She tried to clear her mind, concentrate on what he was saying, but her thoughts kept slipping away, returning to Lucien, remembering the taste of his kiss.

"Do ye want to play cards?" Michael asked, tugging on the sleeve of her nightgown.

"What?"

"I said do ye want to play cards?" He rammed a small hand inside his shirt and pulled out a dog-eared, dirt-stained deck of playing cards. "Sammy taught me ta play. He said I could use these to practice. I bet I can beat ye."

Kathryn didn't answer, she was too sleepy for cards, too tired to notice Michael tugging again on her night rail.

"Don't ye want ta play?"

"Not now, Michael."

"Ye never want to play no more. Ye ain't no fun no more." She thought she heard him pounding on the door, thought she heard it swing open, but her eyelids felt heavy and she couldn't lift them enough to see.

Instead she sagged down even further in the dirty straw and propped her head against the wall. Her gown was twisted up above her knees, but she hadn't the energy to pull it down. Her mouth felt dry. She wet her lips, which felt oddly numb, looked down to see her hands were shaking.

Her body felt light and oddly distant, but her dreams—ah, her dreams were so pleasant. Kathryn closed her eyes and gave herself up to the warm sensation of the marquess's kiss.

# SEVEN

Dressed in tight black breeches, high black boots, a black jacket that hid the white of his full-sleeved cambric shirt, Lucien strode beside Jason, also dressed in black, toward the stables at the rear of the town house.

The waning moon, no more than a sliver, hid its pale light behind a dense layer of clouds hanging over the city. In silence they mounted their horses, Jason's big gelding, Blackie, and Lucien's prize black stallion, Blade. Taking the back roads through the city, they wound their way through the darkest parts of London, heading toward a massive, stone-walled, four-story structure, St. Bartholomew's Hospital, which sat on a knoll at the outskirts of town.

Beyond the hospital, on the road that would lead them back to Surrey, a carriage awaited, ready to speed Lady Kathryn Grayson to the safety of Lucien's hunting lodge in the forests near Castle Running.

All they had to do was reach it.

Lucien's jaw tightened. What would they find when they arrived at St. Bart's? If Kathryn had been mistreated . . . if one of her so-called guards had put his filthy hands on her . . . Silently, he cursed. He had meant what he had said. If Blakemore had allowed her to be hurt in any way, he would face Lucien's wrath and the results would not be pleasant. He didn't ask himself why it mattered so much, or think, even for a moment, how Kathryn had managed to breach the distance he kept between himself and other people. Right now his only concern was getting her out of there.

Blade shied beneath him as a brown and white dog broke out of an alley, its tail tucked between its legs. It whimpered when a rotund tavern-keep stepped out of a door behind him, hefted a stone and pelted the dog on the rump.

"And stay away, ye good-fer-nothin' cur!" The man shook a meaty fist, turned and disappeared back inside the tavern, letting the door slam shut behind him.

Lucien urged his horse forward and Jason did the same, the animals churning up mud beneath their hooves as they made their way along the dirt street. There were no cobblestones in this part of town, just narrow, rutted lanes piled high with garbage. The smell of rotting offal hung heavy in the air and Blade's nostrils flared in protest. Beggars huddled in doorways, and drunken sailors staggered along, singing bawdy tunes.

They rode on and eventually the area began to change. Buildings became fewer, the streets not so littered. Grass grew along the edges of the road. On the knoll up ahead, a huge structure loomed out of the night. St. Bartholomew's Hospital.

It wasn't the first time Lucien had seen it. They had come in the daytime two days ago, to survey the layout and decide on a plan. The back door of the building seemed the best route in. Jason motioned him in that direction, and Lucien urged the stallion forward. There was only one guard at the gate. He lolled at his post, half-asleep. As Jason had said, there weren't many people interested in breaking *into* St. Bart's.

Jason dismounted, motioned for Lucien to do the same,

and they tied their horses beneath a tree out of sight in the shadows.

"Count to fifty," Jason instructed, his tall, cloaked figure rising like a specter in the darkness. "Then follow me in through the gate. It'll be safe by then."

Lucien nodded and Jason stole silently away. Beginning his silent count, Lucien untied a heavy woolen cloak from behind his saddle and draped it over one arm. The night was cold and Kathryn would need something to keep her warm until they reached the carriage. He finished his count and slipped farther into the shadows.

By the time he reached the gate, the guard was sitting beside it, his head slumped over his chest as if he were merely asleep. Lucien guessed his slumber would last well past the time they left St. Bart's. He passed silently through the gate and found Jason waiting just inside the door leading into the massive stone building.

"Our sources were right. The door isn't locked. Let's just hope the rest of our information is equally correct."

It had better be, Lucien thought. Every minute they were there increased the chances of their getting caught. He could only imagine the embarrassment a duke and a marquess would suffer if they should be arrested for breaking into a madhouse. Worse yet would be the knowledge that he had failed Kathryn again.

This time it might be a fatal breach of promise for Kathryn.

The heavy oak door opened soundlessly. He thanked whoever it was that kept the hinges so well oiled. He paused inside the hallway, glanced around to be certain it was safe. The smell assailed him like a blow to the stomach, the stench of unwashed bodies, the foul odor of feces. Lucien set his jaw against it and tried not to think of Kathryn living each day in a filthy place like this.

They headed down the hall, their boots ringing on the dense gray stone, but the noise was lost in the eerie sounds around them. Some of the cells were more open than others. Patients moaned and thrashed; some talked, though it was well past midnight and there was no one to listen. A woman sobbed quietly in the dim light of a single lantern. A man snored loudly, scratching himself in his sleep, then curling into a tight, jerky ball on a pile of dirty straw.

Kathryn's image arose and a tightness crept into his chest. She was here, forced to live in this hellish place not fit for the lowliest beast. The smell of urine and vomit grew stronger as they moved deeper into the building, and the bile rose in Lucien's throat. Anger began a slow burn that licked like flame through his blood. Kathryn didn't deserve this. He wasn't sure anyone did.

What kind of a man would put an innocent young woman in a wretched, filthy, stinking place like St. Bart's?

"Dunstan." He nearly spat the word. He didn't realize he had said it out loud until he noticed the bitter taste in his mouth. "I swear I'll kill the bastard."

Jason's eyes swung in his direction; clearly he was thinking the very same thing. "You can deal with Dunstan later. For now, your lady is more important."

Lucien started to correct him, but decided it could wait. They had reached the staircase leading up to the second-floor block of cells and a guard was posted at the bottom.

"Leave this one to me," Lucien said, slipping silently away. Jason made no move to stop him. The hard glint of fury in his eyes was enough to warn him not to. Dealing with the guard, Jason knew, would provide some measure of release.

Lucien approached him on silent feet. He was a tall, bone-thin man with mouse-brown hair and a scar on his cheek. Lucien tapped him on the shoulder, and when the guard turned, Lucien's fist shot out, clipping him solidly on the chin. He crumpled like a puppet whose strings had been cut, and Lucien caught him before he hit the ground.

"Let's hide him under the staircase," Jason suggested from behind him.

Already heading in that direction, Lucien dragged the man into the darkness below the stairs. They climbed quickly to the second floor and started along the row of cells. Kathryn's was on the right halfway down, they had learned from one of the matrons, who had gladly given up the information to a man in Lucien's employ—along with a key—for a hefty pouch of coins.

He paused at the door, his heart thudding uncomfortably, worry making the sweat bead on his brow. A glance inside told him someone was in there, but it was too dark to see who it might be.

"Kathryn?" He called her name softly into the shadows, but whoever was there didn't answer. Perhaps she was soundly asleep. "Hand me the key." Jason complied and Lucien shoved it into the heavy iron lock. Down the hall he could hear the rattle of chains and the moan of the man who wore them.

He clenched his jaw and opened the lock. Iron clanked and the door creaked as it swung open. Lucien stepped into the darkness while Jason kept watch outside.

"Kathryn, it's Lucien." Still no answer. He moved toward the slight figure huddled in the dirty straw, saw that it was a woman, saw that it was Kathryn, and his heart squeezed hard. The moon slipped out from behind a cloud, and for a moment he could see her, the dirty white nightgown with the wide red band, the long dark brown hair that hung in tangles around her face. The nightgown was ruched up to her thighs and her legs were bare. When he touched her, her skin felt as cold as ice. Lucien swore softly.

"Kathryn, can you hear me?" He shook her gently and her eyelids slowly opened.

"Lucien . . . ?" She dragged herself upright with what seemed a gargantuan effort, swayed, and he steadied her against him. "Is it . . . really . . . you?"

God, he felt like the lowliest villain. "I would have come sooner. I should have. I thought I could find another way." A legal way, he thought. But seeing her like this, legal didn't seem to matter anymore.

"Will you . . . take me . . . home?"

His eyes slid closed, blocking out a needle of pain.

"Yes . . ." he said softly. "That's exactly what I mean to do." Taking the cloak from his arm, he shook it open and spread it around her, tying it loosely, then wrapping her up in the soft warm folds. She leaned against him and he saw how weak she was, recalled her speech, and noted for the first time the odd slur of her words.

Another shot of anger speared through him. Blakemore. He would deal with the good doctor, too. Lucien bent and lifted her gently into his arms. "Just hang on to my neck. I'll do the rest."

He thought that perhaps she nodded. He felt her slim arms encircle his neck, the brush of her hair as she rested her head against his shoulder. Her feet were bare and icy cold. He wanted to warm them between his palms. He wanted to strip away her soiled night rail and look for bruises, make certain that no one had hurt her.

"Is she all right?" Jason asked with a frown, the moment Lucien stepped out of the cell.

"I'm not sure." A muscle tightened in his jaw. "Let's get out of here."

Jason nodded and led the way downstairs. Another guard was silently dispensed with, and in minutes they were out the back door and heading for the horses. Jason held Kathryn while Lucien mounted Blade, then he lifted her up to Lucien, who settled her sideways on the saddle in front of him. He wrapped his cloak around her, making sure to cover her feet.

Jason mounted his big black gelding, which tossed its massive head, eager to be on its way. "Let's get the hell out of here." He urged the horse toward the road and Lucien fell in behind him.

In minutes they were galloping along the lane, Kathryn tucked safely against his chest, one of his arms wrapped tightly around her. He could feel her steady breathing and the slow beat of her heart. She never spoke, only occasionally opened her eyes, and never really seemed to see him. Something was wrong, he knew, his worry increasing with every passing mile. What the devil had they done to her? God's blood, he would make them pay—every last one of them!

They kept the pace steady and fast and eventually reached their destination. An unmarked carriage and four black horses sat behind the Marsh Goose Inn, exactly where Lucien had instructed. He swung down from Blade and lifted Kathryn down, cradling her gently in his arms. The coachman waited beside the carriage. He jerked open the door before they reached it and Lucien climbed the iron stairs, ducked his head, and carried her inside. Settling himself on the carriage seat, he rested Kathryn in his lap, tucked the woolen cloak around her, and pulled a lap robe over her legs. The moment Jason climbed aboard, he rapped on the top of the carriage. The driver slapped the reins, and the horses leaned into their traces.

It was hours yet to the lodge. They had decided Jason would accompany them that far in case any sort of trouble arose along the way. From there he would return to Velvet and Carlyle Hall. Once Kathryn was settled, Lucien had planned to return to the castle. He would send a serving woman to stay with her until Aunt Winnie arrived from London, where she'd been determined to stay until Kathryn was released.

In time he would send for her, tell her that the lady was safe, but not yet. He wanted to be certain she was truly all right and he wanted time to consider what course he should next take.

In the meantime, he simply sat there, holding his slight burden, worrying about her, wishing he knew what was wrong. Sitting across from him, Jason assessed her with his piercing blue eyes, his thoughts apparently running along the very same lines.

"What's the matter with her?"

Lucien unconsciously tightened his hold. "I don't know. They must have given her some sort of sleeping potion." He looked down at her, saw her eyes were only half open. "Kathryn, it's Lucien, can you hear me?"

A soft smile tipped her lips up at the corners. "Lucien

... I dreamt you would come." She shifted on his lap, leaned over and pressed a soft kiss on his cheek. Surprise, and a fine sliver of heat ran through him. "I prayed . . . you would come."

"How are you feeling?"

"Lovely . . ." she said with a throaty sort of drawl. "Now that you are . . . here." She relaxed once more, snuggled into his shoulder, and her eyes drifted closed.

"What the devil have they done to her?"

"Opium," Jason said, his jaw tight. "I've seen it before."

"Opium? Good God—what will it do to her?"

"Depends on how long she's been on it. The stuff's incredibly addictive. As long as she keeps taking it, she'll stay just like she is."

"Like a trained puppy, you mean. Someone they can control."

"Exactly so."

"What happens now that she won't be getting it any longer?"

"In time she'll return to normal."

Lucien frowned. "How long a time, and what happens between now and then?"

"Once the stuff wears off, she'll get sick. Her body will crave the drug and until it's completely gone from her system, she'll be pretty bad off."

Lucien tried to clamp down on his anger, but it seemed to swallow him whole. "Damn the bloody bastards to hell."

"They wanted her malleable, easy to handle. They might have kept her that way for years."

"Thank God we didn't wait any longer."

"Thank God we got away with it."

Lucien glanced toward the window, but the heavy red velvet curtains were drawn, keeping the flickering light of the carriage lantern well hidden inside. "I was planning to leave her alone at the lodge once we got there. I thought

I'd send a lady's maid over in the morning to see to her needs."

"I'm afraid it isn't going to be that easy."

Lucien stared down at the top of her dark head. Even unwashed and tangled, her hair glinted faintly red in the light of the candle. She must have felt him watching her for she tilted her head back and her eyes slowly opened. Kathryn looked up at him and smiled. "Will you . . . kiss me? I liked it . . . when you kissed me . . . before."

Lucien groaned, and Jason chuckled, a rumble in his broad chest. "I thought she was just a friend."

"It wasn't like that. They were taking her away. I couldn't seem to reach her. I—oh, dammit, never mind. You wouldn't understand."

"Lucien . . . ?" she whispered, the sound of his name soft and low and oddly enticing.

"What is it?" he snapped, still disgruntled, sorry the moment the words left his mouth.

Kathryn didn't seem to notice the gruffness. "In my dreams . . . you kissed me . . . over and over. Will you . . . do it . . . now?"

For a moment he didn't answer, for even in her dirty nightgown, with smudges on her face and her hair in tangles, he wanted to. He could feel her small breasts pressing into his chest, feel the roundness of her bottom against his groin, and inside his breeches he went hard.

"This is insane," he grumbled.

Jason just laughed. "Looks like you're going to have an interesting night ahead . . . at least what little is left of it."

"Don't be absurd. The girl doesn't know what she's saying."

"I'm sure she doesn't. But opium has a way of getting to the truth."

Lucien ignored him. Kathryn needed his help, nothing more. He had failed her once but he wouldn't do so again.

They rode in silence for most of the journey, Kathryn opening her eyes now and then, several times repeating her soft request for a kiss. By the time they reached his hunting lodge deep in the Wealden forest, his nerves were on edge.

Jason just kept grinning in that way that made Lucien want to hit him.

Fortunately, the lodge had been cleaned and prepared as Lucien had instructed. Though the night was nearly ended, candles burned in the windows and a fire roared in the hearth. Bennie Taylor, a tall, thin boy who had worked for him for years, was waiting by the door as he carried Kathryn inside. With his angular face and thick sandy hair, he was growing into a handsome boy.

"Everything's ready, milord, just like ye said." The son of a tenant, Bennie was seventeen now, one of his best grooms and most trusted employees.

"Thank you, lad. That'll be all for now." The boy slipped quietly out the door and Lucien carried Kathryn toward the fire. Remembering their first encounter and the lady's penchant for cleanliness, he had instructed Bennie to have a bath ready and waiting. A steaming tub of water sat in front of the blazing hearth. More kettles hung over it, and a bar of rose-scented soap rested on the floor next to the tub beside a stack of clean white linen towels.

"Looks like you're all set," Jason said with a quick survey of the room.

"A bath . . ." Kathryn said with a wistful sigh as Lucien set her on her feet. "How wonderful." She swayed toward the tub and might have fallen in if he hadn't caught her around the waist and pulled her back against his chest.

"Take it easy. You don't want to go in headfirst."

She smiled up at him through heavy-lidded eyes and thick black lashes, and pulled the tie at the neck of her gown. It slid slowly off one shoulder. "I feel so dirty. I can't wait . . . to be . . . clean." She leaned toward the tub, but her knees seemed to sag. Lucien tightened his hold and hauled her back to her feet.

Jason chucked and Lucien swung a hard glance in his direction. "What the devil am I going to do?"

Jason just grinned. "I told you the night would be interesting." He jerked open the door and stepped outside, then closed it firmly behind him. Lucien could hear him chuckling as he swung up on the back of the fresh horse that was waiting for him in the stable. The thunder of hooves sounded and Jason was gone. The two of them were left alone.

Kathryn stared with longing at the tub, then looked back into his face. "I seem to be . . . having a bit of . . . trouble."

"So I see," Lucien said dryly, trying not to notice the ever-widening expanse of skin at the neck of her nightgown. The opening was so large any moment the damned thing would slip down to her waist.

"Do you think you could . . . help me?"

Lucien ground his jaw, knowing he had no choice, trying to discipline the part of him that was swelling with anticipation at the thought of seeing her naked. God's blood, he had always considered himself a gentlemen. He couldn't remember a time when his attraction for a woman had affected his careful control.

Kathryn swayed toward the tub. Lucien steadied her, but the nightgown slipped out of his grasp and pooled in a heap at her feet.

"Damn and blast!" She was lithe and supple, all smooth skin and gentle curves. She was tall for a woman, yet she fit neatly beneath his chin. She slid her arms around his neck to steady herself and his hands settled at her waist. It was impossibly small, her hips flaring gently. He closed his eyes for an instant, sucked in a steadying breath, and lifted her into the tub.

The water made her smile. She sank down into the warmth with a soft purr of pleasure and tiny bubbles lapped at her breasts. They were cone-shaped, he saw, heavier at the bottom, the nipples a dusky rose, small and tight and incredibly erotic.

Lucien steeled himself. He wasn't a man to take advantage, and Kathryn was hardly in the right state of mind to encourage his advances. Besides, he was betrothed to another woman, nearly a married man. In truth, he couldn't imagine how he had let himself get so involved with her, wasn't even certain exactly why he was going to all of this trouble. Except that Kathryn had somehow become a friend and friends didn't abandon each other when they were in trouble.

Assuming a businesslike persona, he soaped a cloth and washed her neck and shoulders. Kathryn washed her face, sloshed some of the water around in her mouth, spit it up in the air, and it landed on the floor. She gave him a saucy grin and Lucien rolled his eyes.

"We had better do your hair."

Kathryn nodded and he helped her slip below the surface of the water. He washed the heavy mass with the rose-scented soap and helped her rinse it out.

Kathryn smiled up at him. "That feels . . . so good."

God, did it. Her hair was like dark, wet silk, her skin as smooth as the petals of a flower. By the time he was finished and had lifted her out of the tub, he was hard and aching. He was furious at himself for his unseemly lack of control and angry at the fate that had put him in this position.

He steadied her with one hand while he dried her with the other, surveying her body for any signs of injury she might have suffered. He saw no marks, only the roundness of her bottom and her long, shapely legs, the graceful line of her torso from neck to hip. She was lovely in the extreme, sweetly curved and incredibly feminine. He fought to ignore the throbbing in his groin, and it occurred to him it was he who was suffering, and mightily.

"I feel so much . . . better."

Lucien cleared his throat. "I'm sure you do." A clean white night rail sat next to the tub. He pulled it over her head with brisk, efficient motions, then breathed a sigh of relief once she was decently covered again.

She smiled up at him. "Now will you . . . kiss me?"

*God's teeth!* "Listen to me, Kathryn. You don't understand what you are saying. You don't want me to kiss you. It was simply something you dreamed. In the morning you'll be able to see things more clearly. In the meantime, I'm going to carry you upstairs so that you can get some sleep."

"What . . . what about my hair?"

"Your hair? What about it?"

"We have to get out the . . . tangles."

She was right, of course. He gave up an inward groan. He would have to brush it out, run his hands through the heavy damp strands, watch the way it glistened in the firelight as it dried. Lucien shook his head, disgusted at his train of thought. He set Kathryn down on the camelback sofa, propped her against the arm, and set to work on her hair. It took a goodly amount of time, yet oddly he failed to notice, engrossed as he was in the job he'd undertaken. Once the tangles were gone and he began to brush it dry, Kathryn made little sighing sounds of pleasure, and he found himself smiling, oddly pleased by the sound. His fingers combed through the softly curling heavy strands and desire flared inside him. He tamped it down and hurriedly plaited the dark lengths into a single long braid.

Dammit to hell, he wasn't interested in Kathryn Grayson, at least not beyond bedding her a time or two. His life was laid out exactly as he wanted it, as he had been planning for years. Even if it weren't, she was the last woman he would consider taking to wife. She was headstrong and stubborn, too smart for her own good, and far too bloody independent for a woman. He couldn't help thinking of his father, thinking of the terrible mistake he had made in marrying that sort of woman.

He wanted a docile wife, a pleasant, manageable little dove like Allison Hartman. Allison would obey his wishes, raise his children as he saw fit, and allow him the freedom to live his life as he wanted. If that meant having a mistress—if it meant having a dozen—he would do so if he chose. He couldn't imagine Kathryn Grayson meekly accepting any of those things.

They reached the top of the stairs, and she turned her head to look up at him. "Lucien?"

"Yes, love?" He carried her into the bedchamber and set her down gently on the edge of the bed.

"Will you . . . kiss me . . . now?"

He went instantly hard again, pressing painfully against the front of his breeches. Kathryn was smiling up at him, her eyes a deep forest-green, her body soft and supple where it leaned into his. What would it hurt? he thought. One little kiss. What could it possibly hurt?

He bent his head and gently covered her mouth with his. Her lips were full and incredibly soft, fitting perfectly with his own. He drew her full bottom lip between his teeth, kissed the corner of her mouth and it parted slightly, allowing his tongue to slide in. He hadn't meant for that to happen, but now that it had, he could taste her feminine sweetness mingled with the faint copper flavor of his own desire.

Kathryn slid her arms around his neck and kissed him back, and a wave of heat washed over him. Lucien deepened the kiss, slanting his mouth over hers, first one way and then the other, cupping her face between his hands and kissing her more deeply still. A tiny mew of pleasure bubbled up from her throat as his hands found her breasts and he cupped one, the fabric lightly abrading her nipples where he rubbed it with his thumb. Heat sank low in his belly. Need licked fiercely through his blood.

Lucien jerked away as if he had been burned, swearing a savage oath. "Damn and blast, woman! What the devil are you doing to me?"

Kathryn's dark brows pulled faintly together, as if she were pondering the question. She touched her moist, kiss-swollen lips and looked up at him. "I thought you . . . wanted to kiss me."

"Of course I wanted to kiss you, dammit! That is only the beginning of what I'd like to do." He jerked the blankets up over her, tucked them beneath her chin. "Now go to sleep before I lose the last of my sanity and do something both of us will regret in the morning."

Turning away, he strode to the door and yanked it open, but he couldn't resist a last glance over his shoulder. Kathryn's eyes were closed and he thought that already she was sleeping.

"Good night . . . Lucien," she whispered, her eyes still closed. The tiniest smile curved her lips.

Lucien blew out a breath and smoothed back his hair, which had come loose from the ribbon at the nape of his neck. He closed the door with a heavy sigh, and set out to find the lost strip of velvet, determined to put both his person and his mind back into some sort of order.

His jaw clenched on his way down the stairs. He didn't like the lust he felt for Kathryn Grayson. He didn't like the protective instincts she stirred in him. He felt out of control in a way he couldn't remember, and he didn't like that most of all.

"Damnation." What the devil was he doing mixed up in the woman's affairs? How had he gotten so involved with her? He had troubles of his own, a marriage to arrange, lands and estates to manage, an aunt who depended upon him. Kathryn had no right to interfere in his life as she had.

And yet he knew he would continue to help her. She was alone and afraid and she had no one else to turn to. He thought of her lying upstairs in his bed and tried to block the image of her sweetly feminine body, of her eyes on his mouth as she had asked him to kiss her.

That he wanted her, he couldn't deny. He only hoped she would awaken on the morrow once more in her right mind and he would no longer have to suffer such an agony of temptation. If she continued her innocent enticement, he wasn't certain how much longer his frayed grip on control would last.

# EIGHT

Kathryn awoke with a start. She blinked several times, oddly out of focus, and glanced at her surroundings, finding herself in an upstairs bedchamber with a sloping wooden ceiling and a wide-planked wooden floor.

Ruffled muslin curtains hung at the windows and an oak bureau sat against one wall, a blue willow porcelain bowl and pitcher resting atop it. She ran a hand over the colorful blue quilt on the bed, then looked down at her night rail and saw that the sleeve was not frayed as she remembered. It was spotlessly clean, and no red band marked the neckline as if it were stained with blood.

Wherever she was, it wasn't St. Bart's, and a feeling of relief overrode her uncertainty.

Kathryn frowned, trying to put the pieces together, snatches of memory rising here and there. Her head ached abominably and her mind felt muzzy and out of focus. Her tongue seemed to stick to the inside of her mouth and her stomach felt queasy.

She concentrated harder, recalled riding somewhere in a carriage, thought back further, remembered being lifted into a man's strong arms. Lucien! The memory arose with a jolt of awareness and an odd little tingle that filtered into her heart.

Lucien had come for her. He had brought her here to safety in this place. Surely he was somewhere near.

Ignoring the pounding in her head, Kathryn swung her feet to the edge of the bed, but a wave of dizziness assaulted her. She sat there a moment, fighting down the spinning in her head, her limbs weak and oddly shaking. With a surge of effort, she forced herself up on her feet and made her way behind the screen in the corner to relieve herself, holding on to the wall for support.

When she finished, she poured water into the basin on the dresser and completed her ablutions as best she could. Her hair was clean and it had been braided. She wondered who had helped her bathe.

She lifted the latch and stepped into the opening, stared down into the single, cozy room below. Lucien stood in front of a big stone hearth, his dark head bent over a heavy iron kettle, stirring something in the pot.

She must have made some sound for he looked up just then and saw her. "Kathryn!" He was on his feet and racing up the stairs, his arm coming around her waist to steady her there in the doorway.

"You shouldn't be out of bed. You're too weak."

Her eyes found his face, saw the concern there. "You came for me. You took me away from that horrible place."

His gaze met hers, assessing her in some way. "Do you remember what happened?"

"Not much, only an image here and there."

Some of the tension seemed to drain from his shoulders. He smiled, softening the hard lines of his face. "I had to come. I'd left you there too long already." He lifted her hand, pressed a light kiss on the palm, and a warm little shiver slid up her arm. " 'My ever-esteemed duty pricks on me.' "

Kathryn frowned, trying to drag the author of the quote into her head, but her thoughts were simply too fuzzy. "I know it, but I can't seem to get it clear in my mind."

Lucien gave her hand a gentle squeeze. "Shakespeare. In time you will once more recall."

"In time? What has happened to me, Lucien? What did they do?" A wave of dizziness rocked her and she bit down on her lip. Lucien's hand shot out to steady her. "They gave me something. I remember now. At first I didn't want to take it, but after a while I didn't care. In a strange way, I even began to like it."

He slid an arm beneath her knees and lifted her up, carried her back to the bed. "It was a drug. In time the effects will wear off."

"What sort of drug?"

"Opium. Do you know it?"

Her brows came together in a frown. "It is sometimes used to alleviate pain. I should have suspected something like that. I should have guessed what it was. I would have fought them harder."

"You weren't thinking clearly. And you couldn't have stopped them even if you had tried." He set her down on the feather mattress, helped her slide beneath the covers, then tucked them beneath her chin.

"Where are we?"

"My hunting lodge. It's impossible to find unless you know where to look. You'll be safe here until we can see you safe from Dunstan."

The drum inside her head pounded harder against her skull and her stomach rolled again. "I know what opium does in small doses. I don't know what happens to someone who has been given as much as I have."

Lucien sat down in the chair beside the bed. "Jason says your body will crave the drug." He looked down at her hands, saw how badly they were shaking. "I believe it does so already."

"You are saying it will make me ill? How bad will it be?"

He shrugged wide shoulders. "We'll have to wait and see. I know little about such things."

"Oh, dear Lord—I've been such a burden already."

"You are no burden. And soon you will be as strong as you were before."

She only shook her head, which continued to pound like a battering ram.

"Perhaps you will be lucky," Lucien said with a look of encouragement that gave her a thread of hope. She was healthy. Perhaps her body would shake off the drug without much of a problem.

But she wasn't lucky, and by morning of the following day she was in agony. Her body was drenched in perspiration and her heart beat frantically. Her breath came in shallow little pants. She was alternately hot and then cold, her muscles aching and twitching, her body so restless she thrashed on the mattress and couldn't stay still.

Lucien had come to her room several times, but each time she had sent him away, embarrassed that he should see her this way. A few minutes later, he would return on one pretext or another, his face dark with concern, and what she thought might be a deep-rooted sort of rage.

Again his knock came at the door and he shoved it open without her permission, correct in assuming it would not come.

"I have a cup of broth for you. Bennie brought it over along with some bread and meat. I'm afraid I can't cook a lick." He glanced down at the cup she made no move to reach for. "Perhaps you can take just a bit."

Kathryn shook her head, her stomach rolling at the thought, but the marquess paid no heed, just sat down on the edge of the bed and pressed the cup against her lips. Kathryn turned her head away, the steam from the broth making her nose start to run. She sniffed, then swiped at it with the sleeve of her night rail, her face heating up with embarrassment.

Lucien paid no heed, just retrieved a handkerchief from the top bureau drawer, handed it over, and waited while Kathryn blew her nose. "Please go away."

"You are in no shape to be left alone."

A fresh round of chills began, shaking her body so hard

she could barely speak. "I'll be f-fine as soon as the drug wears off. You s-said so yourself."

"I'm certain you will."

"Then p-please, just leave me alone."

Lucien turned away, his hands balling into fists. "Damn the lot of them. Damn them to bloody hell." He strode to the door and yanked it open, slammed it loudly behind him.

Kathryn curled up on the bed, drawing her legs up beneath her. Her body spasmodically twitched and jerked, and the chills returned with a vengeance. This time not even the stack of covers the marquess had piled on top of her was enough to keep her warm. Her teeth were chattering so loudly she was certain the noise must have summoned him up the stairs.

The door opened and the marquess walked in. His bold black brows drew nearly together at the sight of her shivering on the bed.

"You're freezing. Dammit, I knew I should have stayed with you."

"I've b-blankets enough to outfit a s-small regiment of soldiers. Nothing seems to h-help."

He pondered that. Then he was striding toward her, sitting down on the edge of the bed and tugging off his black knee-high boots.

"W-what are you d-doing?"

"Getting you warm, but you'll have to move over so that I can get in."

She started to protest. It was hardly seemly to allow a man into her bed, especially one as handsome as the Marquess of Litchfield. But another round of chills rattled through her, and he simply gave her no choice, urging her firmly toward the opposite side of the bed, lifting up the covers and settling his long length beside her. Even through his linen shirt and snug black breeches, she could feel his heat and the hardness of his body. Litchfield pulled her into the curve of his arm, surrounding her with his warmth and his tall, lean form, tugging the blankets up over them both.

She had never been this close to a man before, never been pressed so fully against one. She was certain few men were as beautifully built, as cleanly muscled. She could feel the hard ridges across his ribs and the flat indentation of his stomach. Long sinewy thighs pressed against her, and the muscles in his arms and shoulders bunched whenever he moved. Even as sick as she was, the feeling stirred an odd little thrill of pleasure and she found herself wondering how all that sleek muscle would look unhampered by clothes.

It was an unwanted thought and she forced it away, concentrated instead on the warmth seeping into her body. In minutes, the shaking began to ease. She was tired, she realized, exhausted clear to the bone. Her eyelids felt thick and swollen, drooping lower and lower until finally she fell asleep.

As she slept, she dreamed. Images appeared. She was riding in the marquess's carriage, sitting on his lap as the vehicle rumbled along. She saw herself asking him to kiss her, not once but again and again. The dream shifted and he was removing her clothes, lifting her into a steaming tub of water, soaping a cloth and running it over her body. She dreamed he carried her upstairs and settled her on the bed. In the dream, he finally kissed her, ravishing her mouth, gently cupping a breast.

A spiral of heat slid through her, settled low in her stomach. Kathryn awoke with a start, her mind still churning with disjointed images. Lucien was no longer beside her, nor anywhere in the room. She dragged in a steadying breath, still weary and slightly out of balance, but for the most part, the aftereffects of the drug appeared to be gone. She roused herself from the bed, her limbs feeling heavy, her eyelids gritty.

She pulled on the heavy silk wrapper she found at the foot of the bed, washed her face, unbraided and brushed her hair, but the jumble of images in her mind remained.

*It was only a dream,* she told herself. *Put it out of your mind.* But something wouldn't let her, and suddenly she knew why. It wasn't a dream, she recalled with sudden clarity. It was a memory!

A sweet, warm memory.

A hotly embarrassing memory.

Dear, sweet God!

She heard him coming up the stairs a few minutes later, and her body went rigid with tension. The awful notion occurred to her—she had asked him to kiss her and he had complied. Dear Lord, what else had they done?

Litchfield knocked on the door, but he didn't walk in. Instead he waited patiently for her invitation. She swallowed back her worry and opened the door, her cheeks going warm at the sight of him.

He was dressed in tight-fitting breeches and a full-sleeved white shirt, ruffled at the wrist and down the front. His dark hair was left unpowdered as it usually was and queued back with a wide black bow.

His eyes ran over her face, noting the flush in her cheeks, the hair she had brushed and tied back with a length of yellow ribbon she had found on the dresser.

"How are you feeling?"

Kathryn glanced away, thinking of his kiss, unable to face him. It was early morning outside the window, the forest streaked with sunlight slanting down through the needles on the evergreen trees. "How am I feeling?" She worked to make the words come out light. "As if I've been run over by a loaded freight wagon. Other than that I am fine." She forced herself to look at him, saw his mouth curve up at one corner.

"You are better, I think. How about something to eat?"

Her stomach rumbled just then. Apparently she *was* feeling better. "All right. As long as it's nothing too heavy."

"Some porridge and a cup of hot chocolate? Bennie's mother is a very good cook."

She nodded, but her eyes slid away from his. Litchfield

left the room, returning a few minutes later with a tray, which he set on the table beside the bed. Steam curled up from the bowl of porridge and the chocolate looked rich and dark.

"Come. Sit down in the chair and eat." He reached a hand in her direction but Kathryn drew away.

Lucien frowned. "What is it? What's wrong?"

She stared into his handsome face, thinking of his kiss, embarrassed yet determined to know what else her memory might have buried. "You kissed me, didn't you? The night you brought me here from St. Bart's."

Color crept beneath the dark skin over his high cheekbones. "So, finally you remember."

"I remember asking you to kiss me, so I suppose it was my fault, not yours."

His lips drew into a harsh line of self-reproach. "Don't be ridiculous. It was scarcely your fault. You were drugged, certainly not in your right state of mind. I am to blame and I apologize. I didn't mean to take advantage. Somehow it just happened."

Kathryn worried her bottom lip, afraid to ask more. "I didn't . . . We didn't do anything else, did we?"

"Good God, no! You don't think that I—"

"No! That isn't what I meant. I just thought . . . I wasn't sure what I might have encouraged you to do."

Lucien glanced away. "I won't deny I feel an attraction to you, Kathryn. But surely you know I wouldn't do anything to hurt you."

She sighed and sat down on the chair beside the bed, feeling better now, certain the marquess really was the gentleman she had believed. Recalling his usual iron control, she felt a trickle of satisfaction she had been able to tempt him. "I'm sorry. I'm afraid I'm still not thinking very clearly."

He seemed satisfied with that, his smile slipping back into place. "I had your things brought here, clothes you wore while you were at the castle."

"Thank you."

"Now that you're feeling better, I'll be returning home. I'll send someone to cook for you and act as your lady's maid, someone you can trust. No one will find you here. You'll be safe until we can figure a way to remove you from your uncle's control."

She was free of St. Bart's and, at least for now, she was safe—thanks to the Marquess of Litchfield. So why was she disappointed? Because Lucien was leaving. Good heavens, she wanted him to stay! *I won't deny I feel an attraction to you, Kathryn.* And in truth she felt no small amount of attraction to him.

Perhaps she *was* a little crazy. The man was not for her—he was betrothed to someone else. And even if he weren't they were hardly suited. Lucien disapproved of everything she believed in, everything she worked for.

"I'm grateful, my lord, for all that you've done. I'll never be able to repay your kindness."

Litchfield smiled. "Seeing you safe is payment enough. You might want to thank the Duke of Carlyle, however, once this is over and done. It was his plan and his aid that helped to get you out of that place—at no small risk to himself."

"And no small risk to you, my lord," she said softly, knowing it was true, realizing for the first time how great the danger must have been. "You could have been arrested or perhaps even killed."

Litchfield smiled in that disconcerting way of his. "Well, I wasn't and you are safe." He glanced toward the tray of food on the bedside table. "And very nearly recovered. Which means, you had better eat your breakfast before it gets cold."

Kathryn merely nodded, picked up the spoon, and began to stir through the porridge.

"If there is nothing more you need, I shall leave you. Bennie is here. He'll be working outside. Should you require anything at all just let him know. I'll send a servant as soon as it can safely be arranged."

She poured chocolate from the pot on the tray into a

simple china cup. "When will I see you again?" she asked from beneath her lashes. She glanced up. "I mean . . . it's quite remote and I shall no doubt be lonely. Perhaps you might visit me from time to time."

"My aunt will certainly be along as soon as she returns from London. And I shall make it a point to stop by every couple of days."

Relief poured through her. It was amazing how strong it was. She took a sip of chocolate, grateful for the distraction. "How long do you think it will take to settle matters with my uncle?"

Lucien sighed. "I'm afraid it could take quite a while. I'm sorry, but that is simply the way it is."

She only nodded. Whatever happened, she was free and this time she meant to stay that way. But the danger her two protectors had faced reminded her of the danger she still faced every day. If her uncle found her as he had before—

Kathryn shivered to think of it.

She couldn't afford to wait for fate to turn in her direction. She had tried that avenue before. This time, Kathryn meant to drag fate, kicking and screaming, along whatever path it took to keep her safe.

Allison Hartman was frantic. First her betrothed had raced off to London as if a fire had been set beneath him, following after Kathryn Gray—no, not Kathryn Gray. Lady Kathryn Grayson—not a commoner, but an aristocrat. Allison nearly swooned to think of the deceit the woman had perpetrated upon them. Lord protect us—Kathryn Grayson was a mental patient escaped from the madhouse at St. Bart's!

Now Lord Litchfield was returned and so immersed in some secret business he hardly spared her a glance. It was frustrating. It was frightening. Allison was certain she was losing him, and that awful woman was the cause.

Allison had heard the story. Her mother's lady's maid, Gladys Honeywell, was a friend of one of the servants who worked at Castle Running. To garner the baroness's favor—and a few extra shillings in her pay—Gladys had been relaying the gossip she overheard at the castle ever since Allison's betrothal, and recently she had uncovered quite a juicy morsel.

"You won't believe it, milady," Gladys had said, her eyes as big and round as the porcelain saucer beneath the baroness's teacup. " 'Twas scandalous, it was, the house overrun with constables, his lordship shoutin', commandin' them to leave. They told him the girl was dangerous—that's what they said. Said she tried to murder her cousin, the Earl of Dunstan's daughter. Then they carted her off to St. Bart's, dragged her right back to the madhouse, and her ravin' like a lunatic all the way."

That had been more than three weeks ago. Lucien had left the same night for London and only just returned. Since then Allison had seen him just once, and aside from a few words assuring her Lady Kathryn wasn't the madwoman she had heard, he refused to discuss the subject at all.

And now there was more bad news.

"I can't believe it, Mama, surely there is some mistake." Allison paced the room where the baroness sat at a small French writing desk, sorting through engraved wedding invitations that had already been addressed and were ready to be posted.

"I am certain it is true," her mother said. "Gladys said two men came yesterday to the castle. They told the marquess that brigands had broken into St. Bart's and abducted Lady Kathryn. They said they were worried about her safety in the care of such men and asked if he knew anything that might be of assistance, or if he had any idea where they might have gone."

"How would the marquess know something like that? And who in the world would abduct a madwoman?"

"I'm sure I wouldn't know. But I am truly disappointed. I heartily disapprove of his lordship's involvement, however slight, in such a scandalous affair. Your father and I had a lengthy discussion on the subject just this morning."

Allison paused in front of the big gilt mirror over the fireplace to check her appearance. "And?" She straightened the whalebone panniers beneath her peach silk skirts, which fell to just the right length to expose a glimpse of her stockings.

"And your father has agreed to look into the matter—discreetly of course. If the marquess had something to do with Lady Kathryn's disappearance—"

Allison's sharp intake of breath stopped her mother mid-sentence. "You aren't suggesting . . . ? Surely you and Papa don't believe the marquess was behind Lady Kathryn's abduction? Why on earth would he do such a thing?"

"I am not saying he was responsible. But he was certainly opposed to her being locked away."

"You're wrong, Mother. Lucien wouldn't involve himself in something like that." But in truth she wasn't so sure. How much did she really know about the Marquess of Litchfield? Other than the fact he was handsome, rich, and titled, that he was the most sought-after bachelor in London and marrying him made her the envy of every woman in society, she knew almost nothing of her betrothed.

"Whatever the case," her mother said, "we will soon discover the truth. Your father has employed a Bow Street runner to ferret out the facts of the matter. The baron will do whatever is necessary to protect you and your future husband's good name."

Allison relaxed a little at that. She knew her parents wanted this marriage. Her father admired the marquess and wanted her to have the luxuries such a wealthy, titled aristocrat could provide. Her mother wanted the prestige she would gain with her daughter married to such a man.

Whatever the reasons, her parents would take care of the problem as they always did. Allison could return to the ladies' book of fashion that she had been reading, confident everything would be all right.

Winifred Montaine Dewitt stepped down from the plain black unmarked carriage that pulled up in front of Lucien's hunting lodge. She had taken only two steps when the door of the lodge burst open and Kathryn Grayson rushed out.

Winnie simply opened her arms and, without a moment's hesitation, Kathryn stepped into her embrace.

"I'm so glad to see you," the girl said with such a fierce hug Winnie felt the sting of tears. "Lucien . . . I mean, the marquess said you would come, but I wasn't really sure."

"Don't be silly. Of course I would come." Arm in arm, they started back to the house. "I would have been here sooner. In truth, I'm still mad as fire at my nephew for not telling me he intended to spirit you away."

Kathryn smiled. She looked healthy, her cheeks blooming with color, no longer wan and pale from the effects of the drug, as Lucien had described. "I'll never forget what the marquess has done for me."

*Nor will my nephew easily be able to forget you,* Winnie thought, seeing in her mind's eye Lucien's determined efforts to help her and the constant worry he tried to hide. He had always been a caring man, especially loyal to those he called friends, but Winnie had never seen him quite like this.

Back inside the cozy lodge, Kathryn motioned her toward the camelback sofa in front of the hearth.

"The marquess has been in constant contact with his solicitor since his return to the castle," Winnie told her. "Nathaniel Whitley is a very competent man."

"Do you know him?"

Winnie felt an unexpected warmth rise into her cheeks. "I knew him when I was younger. I hadn't seen him in years. Last week, he came to the castle to discuss the matter of your guardianship." And he was still as handsome as ever. More so, perhaps, with the gangliness of youth long gone and the touch of silver in his hair. There was none of the boyish shyness so much a part of him when he was younger. Nathaniel Whitley was a man, strong and competent, and undeniably attractive.

Perhaps it was the way he had looked at her that had made her take notice. As if she were still a desirable, attractive woman. It bothered her to think that she had responded to that look, since Nat was a married man.

"Make yourself comfortable, Aunt Winnie, and I'll fix us some tea." Kathryn bent to fill a teapot from the kettle of boiling water that hung from a hook above the fire. "In the meantime, you can tell me what progress the men are making."

Winnie sighed. "Not much, I'm afraid. Every legal avenue seems to be blocked, or is, as soon as they discover it. Your uncle is an extremely powerful man."

A shudder passed over Kathryn's willowy frame though the room was cozy and warm. She threw a handful of loose tea into the china pot and replaced the lid, allowing the leaves to steep.

"The earl has my money at his command, and there is a good deal of it. Does Lord Litchfield have any idea what we might do?"

Winnie leaned forward, accepting the steaming cup of tea Kathryn had poured for her. "He's frustrated, I can tell you. But he isn't about to give up."

Kathryn sighed and sank down on the sofa beside her, steadying the teacup in her lap. "I feel so useless. I can't simply stand by and do nothing, and I can't stay here forever. Sooner or later, my uncle will discover where I am. Once he does . . ." Kathryn didn't finish. Instead her gaze slid off to the low-burning flames of the fire.

Winnie's heart went out to her. She couldn't begin to imagine the terrible things Kathryn had suffered in a place like St. Bart's. But Lucien had told her some of what he had seen, and it was more than enough. Winnie set her cup on the table in front of the sofa, reached out and clasped Kathryn's hand.

"You mustn't lose heart, my dear. The marquess will find a way to help you. He won't give up until he does."

Kathryn tried to smile, but her face looked suddenly pale. "You don't know what it was like in there. I won't go back—not ever. I'll do whatever it takes—anything I have to—in order to protect myself."

Winnie squeezed her hand. "Lucien will find a way," she said firmly. But as much as she wanted to believe it, she couldn't really be sure.

# NINE

Kathryn inspected her small cottage domain, making certain everything was in proper order for the visitor soon to arrive. That morning Bennie Taylor had brought word that Lucien would be joining her for supper. It would be the first time she had seen him since the day he had left for his home.

Kathryn leaned over and lifted the heavy iron lid on the kettle hanging over the fire. The servant the marquess had sent to help her, a girl named Fanny Pendergass who was the housekeeper's daughter, had prepared a simple meal of mutton stew, fruit, cheese, and fresh baked bread for the occasion. Fanny was staying with Bennie's family in a cottage in the woods not far away and would return to the lodge on the morrow.

Though it was highly improper to entertain the marquess alone, Kathryn had given the girl leave to retire for the evening early. There were matters she wished to discuss and she wanted to do so in private. Besides it really didn't matter. Her reputation had been destroyed the day she'd been committed to St. Bart's. What little might have remained slipped away with her soiled nightclothes the evening Lucien had helped her to bathe.

As it always did, Kathryn's face heated up at the thought. And deep inside something soft unfurled, making her stomach feel fluttery and warm. She tried to tell herself it was simply the anticipation of a visitor after so much confinement, but she knew it wasn't the truth. Though Aunt Winnie had come to call, and the Duchess of Carlyle had paid her a very enjoyable, unexpected visit, she had missed the marquess's presence more than she cared to admit.

It was Litchfield she was eager to see, and as much as she tried to fight it, she couldn't contain her excitement that he was soon to appear. Wanting to look her best, Kathryn chose a simple gown of soft yellow wool that draped over a quilted petticoat. She pinned her braid into a wreath above her head and pinched her cheeks to give them color, pining for the days when she'd owned a pot of rouge.

Kathryn shoved a strand of dark hair into place as she checked the stew to make sure it wouldn't burn and waited impatiently for the marquess to appear.

Lucien left the castle late in the afternoon for the two-hour ride to the lodge. He hadn't seen Kathryn Grayson in nearly a week, not since his return to Castle Running. His aunt had paid a call, and Velvet Sinclair had gone to see her as soon as Jason had confessed to freeing the girl from St. Bart's.

According to the duke, his fiery-tempered wife had been furious—not at the role Jason had played in aiding Kathryn's escape, but simply that he had seen fit to act without her assistance.

Lucien smiled. Jason was lucky to have found such a lady, a woman who fit his volatile disposition so perfectly. Lucien's own tastes, however, ran in a different direction. He didn't want a headstrong, willful wife. A woman like Velvet was simply too much trouble. He wanted a mild-tempered, obedient sort of woman.

And less than one month hence, he would have one.

The wedding was set, the invitations posted. In the beginning, Allison had tried to convince him to wait until after the first of the year, till spring and the Season began. He had politely but firmly refused. He wanted to get on with the marriage and the business of siring an heir, and once his decision had been made as to whom he would choose for the role of wife, he was ready to proceed with all haste.

In truth, his physical needs had also played a part in his decision. He was used to taking his pleasure as often as he wished, but now, with his wedding so close at hand, he refused to embarrass his betrothed and her family by risking gossip of his amorous affairs.

Lately, after the days he had spent at the lodge, he was more impatient than ever for the wedding to take place. His confinement with Kathryn had left him badly in need of a woman, his blood running hotter than it had in as long as he could remember. Thank God he would be married and the problem remedied in less than three weeks.

An image of his young wife-to-be appeared in Lucien's mind and he smiled. Allison was a sweet little thing, rather like a bite of sugar candy. He had never been passionately attracted to the girl, certainly he had never felt the hot lust he felt for Kathryn Grayson, but she was young and pretty, and bedding her would certainly not be a burden.

Allison was even-tempered and well schooled in the art of being a wife. Her reputation was flawless, her family background impeccable. Allison would get on well in society and make a very appropriate marchioness. She would bear him the sons he needed to insure his family's lineage, and he could go on with his life as if nothing much had changed.

Lucien straightened in the saddle as a gust of wind rose up through the trees, rustling dead leaves along the path. Blade snorted and tossed his head, flinging his glistening black mane. Lucien leaned over, ran a gloved hand along the animal's neck.

"Easy, boy, we're almost there." Almost to the place deep in the forest that he had been avoiding since his return to the castle. Guilt had forced his decision to come back, the promise he had made to see her.

It was caution that had kept him away.

Every time he thought of Kathryn Grayson, he saw her slender, graceful body as she had stood naked beside the bathing tub. He imagined her small pointed breasts, the feel of her soft skin beneath his hands as he had lifted her into the steaming water, her tiny waist, and long shapely legs. He remembered the way she responded to his kiss, the pliant fullness of her lips, her little sigh of pleasure, the intriguing weight of her breast in his palm, the stiffness of her nipple.

Every time he thought of Kathryn, he remembered those things and he went rock-hard.

Just as he did now.

Damnation! Lucien swore several silent oaths, adjusting himself inside his tight black breeches, trying to ignore the ache, trying to get comfortable with his groin so heavy and full. That he wanted her went without saying. Which was why he had stayed away as long as he possibly could.

This morning, the promise he had made to her nagged at him until he was forced to act. He prayed the little maid he had sent to the house would be there to act as chaperone and remind him to keep his wits about him.

He arrived at dusk, the windows of the lodge glowing with the soft light of candles. He had always loved the old log house, an unpretentious structure in a lovely secluded glen where the trappings of his position could be forgotten, at least for a while. As he stepped down from his horse, he saw Kathryn's silhouette outlined in the window. She greeted him at the door with a smile that beckoned him in.

"Good evening, my lord."

His eyes ran over her from top to bottom, taking in the rose in her cheeks, the healthy color of her skin. Bothersome memories arose and his body stirred, but Lucien battered them down. "It's good to see you, Kathryn. I'm glad to find you looking so well."

The rose in her cheeks went deeper. "I'm feeling quite fit, thanks to you."

He ducked his head beneath the door frame and walked in, inhaled the aroma of fresh bread and simmering meat. "Whatever you have on the fire certainly smells delicious. I didn't realize how hungry I was until now."

"Mutton stew and fresh baked bread. Simple fare by your standards, my lord, but by mine, it's a meal fit for a king."

He frowned at the reminder of what her life had been at St. Bart's. "I wish you could stay at the castle, but for now I'm afraid this will have to do."

She smiled. "I am hardly complaining. As I said, even this simple existence seems a luxury to me."

Lucien glanced toward the table and chairs positioned near the fire. "I see you have the chessboard set up. I had hoped we might play a game."

"I feared you might not be able to stay that late."

He shouldn't, he knew. Not when he found her so bloody attractive. Even now, his palms itched with the memory of cupping those small, soft breasts and he began to grow hard. He wondered where the serving maid was and found himself hoping, against all common sense, that the girl had left for the night.

"It isn't wise for me to stay," he said. " 'Tis hardly seemly to be here with you at all, but I suppose the point is moot at this juncture, and in truth I have missed our games."

Kathryn grinned. " 'Of joys departed, not to return, how painful the memory.' "

Lucien laughed. "Robert Blair. So your taste runs to more modern works as well as the ancient Greeks."

"I admit I'll read most anything. And I am cursed with a memory for such things."

"I should think such a memory would come in handy

with the medical texts you are interested in." As he wouldn't have at home, he shrugged out of his riding coat and tossed it over a chair, leaving him in boots, shirt, and breeches. "You don't mind, I hope. Somehow it is difficult to be formal here."

Kathryn smiled. "I don't mind in the least. And you are right. My memory has served me well in my studies."

He didn't pursue that topic and Kathryn seemed grateful. It wasn't a subject that sat easily between them. Instead, while he seated himself in a wing-back chair, Kathryn made her way to the fire and began to serve up the meal.

"Tell me what is happening with my uncle," she said over her shoulder. "Have you been able to make any progress where he is concerned?"

At the thought of Dunstan, Lucien bit back a foul curse. "The man is an outrage. There are no limits he will not go to where you are concerned. I've had constables at my door asking questions about your disappearance, and my solicitor has been warned by the magistrates to cancel our petition for a change of guardianship. They say they will oppose whatever we present to the courts. I must tell you, Kathryn, I am hard-pressed to know where to go from here."

In the light of the fire, he could see the frown that formed on her forehead. The ladle of stew paused at the edge of the heavy iron pot. "Perhaps I should leave the country. In the Colonies, I could make a new life. I wouldn't have to worry about my uncle and the power he holds over me."

Lucien rose from his chair and crossed the room to where she stood. He hated to bring her more bad news. He didn't want her to worry, but it was better that she knew the truth. "I'm not certain you could get there even if you tried. Your uncle has men scouring the country. Every port has been alerted. They'll be watching for a woman of your description who might be trying to book passage. Even bribery might not be enough to ensure your safe escape."

The color bled from her cheeks. "He has gone to those lengths to find me?" Her fingers went lax and the ladle dropped back into the stew pot. Lucien took the handle from her shaking hands and set the pot down on the table.

"I shouldn't have told you. I thought you would want to know."

Kathryn straightened, dragged in a shaky breath of air. "I'm glad you did. I have to know the truth if I'm going to protect myself." Unconsciously she twisted the apron she'd tied over her pretty yellow dress. "I don't understand it. Why won't he just let me go? Surely if I left the country—"

"He has to keep you under his control. As long as you're free, there is always the risk the truth will come out and he'll lose access to your fortune—to say nothing of the scandal. Dunstan has political aspirations. He can't afford to take that kind of risk." He didn't add that her age was also a factor. Once she reached her majority at the age of four and twenty, should she prove to be sound of mind, her inheritance would pass out of Dunstan's hands and into her own.

"I have to do something. Sooner or later he'll find me. I can't just sit here and let that happen."

Lucien reached out and gently caught her shoulders, felt the tremors that ran through her body. "You mustn't lose faith. I have half a dozen of the best legal experts in England working on this. I've hired men to investigate Dunstan. They'll ferret out every detail of his past and whatever misdeeds he is up to at present. Sooner or later, one of them is bound to come up with something that will help us."

Kathryn only shook her head. "I can't take that risk. I have to do something—I have to find a way to protect myself." She turned away, but not before he caught the shimmer of tears.

Lucien caught her chin, turning her head and forcing

her to look at him. Her eyes were closed but drops of moisture leaked from beneath her thick dark lashes. The concern he was feeling swelled, blossomed into a fierce urge to protect her.

"Trust me to help you," he said. "If something doesn't break soon, I'll find a way to get you out of the country."

She nodded but her throat constricted and the wetness spilled onto her cheeks. Lucien eased her into his arms and she rested her head against his shoulder, her slim fingers pressing into the front of his shirt. He could feel her heartbeat, feel her warmth and womanly curves, smell the rose soap she had used to wash her hair. Desire arched up, swift and hot, making his body go hard.

He wanted to slide the soft yellow gown off her shoulders, to see her naked as he had before. He wanted to pull the pins from her hair, to run his fingers through it, to bury his face in the shiny dark strands and inhale the faint rose scent of her.

Instead he drew away, used the pad of his thumb to wipe the tears from her cheeks. Unconsciously, his gaze drifted down to her mouth. Such a soft mouth, full and perfectly curved. He imagined the ruby hue deepening beneath the pressure of his kiss and couldn't seem to tear his gaze away. Kathryn must have noticed for her small pink tongue flicked out to moisten the corners, and Lucien groaned, the last of his control leaching away as if it had never existed. He had to taste those soft lips—God's breath, he would die if he didn't.

Leaning toward her, he bent his head and kissed her even as he pulled her into his arms. It was a gentle kiss, a tender exploration. Then those warm, full lips parted under his, and he was lost. Desire crashed in on him in storm-force waves. His stomach muscles clenched and his body went rock-hard.

He kissed her fiercely, savagely, his tongue sliding in to taste her more deeply, his mouth moving over hers, first one way and then the other. Kathryn made a soft sound in her throat and her arms slid up around his neck.

He could feel her trembling, feel the soft crush of her breasts, and a fresh burst of heat surged into his loins.

He cupped her bottom, silently groaned at the firm, intriguing roundness, pulled her more tightly against his arousal, and deepened the kiss, unable to get enough, lost to the world around him.

God only knew where the next few moments might have led if it hadn't been for the slight knock at the door. Lucien jerked away as if he had been burned, and Kathryn swayed against him, her big green eyes heavy-lidded, her mouth damp and rosy from his kiss. He reached out to steady her, cursing himself for what he'd let happen, fighting to bring himself under control.

"Stay here. I'll see who it is."

Kathryn said nothing. Her attention swung to the door, and the glow of desire faded from her face, replaced by a look of fear. Striding to the window, Lucien glanced outside, saw that it was only Bennie Taylor, and silently thanked the gods of fate for their timely intervention.

He lifted the latch and opened the door. "What is it, Bennie? What's happened?"

The lad nervously twisted the brown felt hat he had wadded up in one hand. "Your aunt sent me to fetch ye." The boy glanced past him to where Kathryn stood at rigid attention. "Some of the constable's men come lookin' for ye. She told 'em you was away on business, but she was afraid they might come back and she thought ye might want to be there if they did."

Lucien nodded. "That I do." He turned back to Kathryn, his body still pulsing with unspent heat, grateful for the chance to escape. "Since your maid has apparently abandoned you, I'll have Bennie spend the night in the stables. I don't want you here alone."

Kathryn stiffly nodded. Though she held her head high, hot color burned in her cheeks. She knew, just as he did, what had happened between them should not have occurred. Lucien inwardly cursed. He realized he should apologize, but he had done that before and it hadn't stopped him from repeating the offense.

Damnation. Where this woman was concerned, perhaps *he* was the one who was mad.

"There is no need for worry," he said. "I'll send word if there is a problem." He forced himself to smile. "I'm sorry I missed out on the stew."

Kathryn said nothing. Just stood there looking fragile and uncertain, and he cursed himself all over again. He would stay away from lodge, he told himself.

He would have to for both of their sakes.

In the meantime, he would deal with the constable's men.

Kathryn spent a torturous night filled with exhausting dreams of the past and terror of what might lie in the future. She awakened at every sound, certain the constable's men had found her, wishing she had some way to protect herself if they did. When she wasn't afraid, she was thinking of Lucien, torn between bitter self-rebuke for what she had done and regret that their encounter had ended so soon. Memories of the marquess's hot, soul-burning kisses clashed with her fears and left her feeling tense and drained, more exhausted than when she had gone to sleep.

It wasn't until late the following afternoon that a note arrived from Lucien. The constable had merely wanted to ask a few more questions, he said. They had no idea where she was, though they continued to search.

"You are safe, Kathryn," the note had ended. "There is no need to fear."

But there was every reason to be afraid and Kathryn knew it. She was more desperate than ever to find a way to protect herself, and after the marquess's last, passionate visit, Kathryn had come up with a plan.

At first she had thought that she would just tell him, beg him to help, and he would agree. But the more she thought about it, the more she knew he would never consent to such a scheme. It was too risky. Too reckless. Too completely insane.

It was also totally and unequivocally selfish. She couldn't possibly expect the Marquess of Litchfield to cancel his wedding and marry someone else—even if the union would only last a year. And this would be no simple marriage, for unless her uncle was coerced by a higher authority, he would never simply give his permission.

Kathryn paced the floor of the lodge, trying to convince herself to forget it. Lucien would never agree and doing it without his consent would be unthinkable. That she would even consider betraying the one man she could trust, a man who had risked himself for her and continued to do so every day in an effort to protect her, made the notion even more despicable.

Her conscience warned her to discard the notion, to simply stay in hiding and pray Lucien would find a way to help her, or that she would not be found.

She had almost convinced herself when Bennie Taylor raced up and madly slammed his fists on the door.

"I seen 'em, milady! I seen 'em down in the village!"

Kathryn hurriedly pulled it open. "For heaven's sake, Bennie, what are you talking about?"

"The constable's men, milady. I'm seen 'em down in Gorsham askin' questions about ye."

"Oh, dear God."

"They was pressin' real hard for information. No one there knows where ye are, of course, but I thought ye'd want to know."

Kathryn swallowed hard. Of course she wanted to know. Her legs started shaking beneath her skirt.

Bennie tugged on the brim of his brown felt hat. "I'll keep a sharp eye, milady, don't ye worry. If I see any sign of 'em headin' this way, I'll come get ye. You can hide somewheres in the forest till I can fetch his lordship."

Kathryn wet her lips, which felt as dry as bone. "Thank you, Bennie. You did just right." The lad nodded and raced off into the woods as Kathryn closed the door. She closed her eyes and leaned against it, her whole body shaking. She was already frightened. Now she was terrified. If she closed her eyes, she could almost hear the guards' debauched laughter as they stripped away her clothes. Any minute the authorities could arrive at the lodge. They would drag her back to that horrible place and there was nothing at all she could do.

Tears burned her eyes, but Kathryn forced them away. She wouldn't sit idly by and let them destroy her. This time she would protect herself. The plan she had only half concocted rose into her mind with blazing force, and in that moment, she knew what she had to do.

She was in more danger than she had ever been and time was running out. Before she could change her mind, she crossed to the sideboard and pulled open the bottom drawer. Taking out pen and ink and several sheets of foolscap, she sat down at the heavy plank table off to one side of the great room and began penning the letter she had mentally composed that morning. Her hand shook, scattering drops of ink across the page.

She took several calming breaths and started over, taking care to make the strokes of her quill bold and broad, different from her usual more delicate script. She was writing to a man who had once been a friend of her father's, Bishop Edwin Tallman.

Though the bishop had believed her uncle's story when she was sent away and sadly refused to intercede on her behalf, he was a man of principle, a highly respected figure in the church. He held one of the twenty-four senior bishop seats in the House of Lords and was influential with all the members of the peerage.

Aside from being notoriously uncompromising in his beliefs, the bishop was one of the few men with enough power to impose his will on the Earl of Dunstan. Kathryn finished the missive, slipped the quill pen back in the inkwell, and read over the letter.

*I write to you, Bishop Tallman, as I have learned
you were a longtime friend of the late Earl of Milford.
If you wish to help Lady Kathryn Grayson, bring her
uncle, Lord Dunstan, to the hamlet of Gorsham on the
night of November 20. There, in the Wealdon Forest,
a secluded hunting lodge lies south, half a mile off the
road leading into the village. You will find her there
at exactly ten o'clock with the man responsible for her
abduction. In memory of the friendship you once
shared with her father, do not let Dunstan go after her
alone.*

Kathryn swallowed down the fear that overrode her
guilt. If her plan succeeded, Bishop Tallman would travel
to Gorsham with the earl and his men. They would arrive
at the lodge around ten to find Lord Litchfield in a compromising circumstance with Lady Kathryn Grayson.

With the marquess's recent efforts to free her from St.
Bart's, his insistence that she was not in the least insane,
and the fact that she was an innocent, the bishop would
insist—she hoped—that Lucien marry her.

And should her uncle refuse to allow the match, he
would be as ruined in the eyes of society as the Marquess
of Litchfield.

Kathryn folded the note and sealed it with a drop of
melted wax. She would ask Bennie Taylor to pay one of
the boys in the village to see it delivered.

She looked down at the letter and a shiver of dread
passed through her. She was risking all, taking the gravest
of chances. If she failed, she would be returned to St.
Bart's—or someplace worse, if there were such a thing.

But if she succeeded, she would be free.

She thought again of the terms of her guardianship that
had set her on this course, a clause that freed her from
her uncle's control in the event that she should marry. To
escape the earl, she would have done so years ago, but
her inheritance would then have gone to her husband, and
her uncle would never have given his permission.

If her plan succeeded, he would have no choice.

It was a brilliant scheme—assuming it actually worked.

Lucien was the fly in the pastry. She didn't want to hurt him. He was a good man—the most loyal friend she had ever had. She didn't want to involve him in her life any more deeply than he was already, but the constable's men were practically knocking at her door, and every day brought her uncle closer to finding her. Once he did and she was returned to the madhouse, her life would be over.

Her conscience warred with her feelings for Lucien, feelings, she confessed, that went far deeper than friendship, but she rationalized her role in the destruction of his carefully orchestrated life. He wasn't in love with Allison Hartman—at least she didn't think so. His fiery kiss of the night before was hardly that of a man in love with another women.

And even if he were, in less than a year, Kathryn would be one and twenty, the legal age to marry without her uncle's consent. Lucien could obtain an annulment, leaving both of them free to marry whomever they wished. With the lure of her inheritance, Kathryn could surely find a man more suitable for her to wed.

Still, it was a complex plan and a dozen things could go wrong. She prayed that they would not.

An image of Lucien in one of his tirades arose in the back of her mind and a trickle of fear slipped down her spine. He would be angry, furious in fact. But once the deed was done, surely she could find a way to convince him to forgive her. Certainly he would do so when he realized that in time he could return to the life he had planned.

In the meanwhile, all she had to do was think of a way to lure the marquess to the lodge on the night of November 20. Once he was there, she could find a way to seduce him—or at least lead him far enough along that path to appear convincing.

An odd little shiver ran over her skin, making it feel

tingly and tight. Kathryn told herself it was fear of what lay ahead and not anticipation.

Standing behind the desk in his study, Douglas Roth, Earl of Dunstan, reread the note the bishop had handed him one last time.

*I write to you, Bishop Tallman, as I have learned you were a longtime friend of the late Earl of Milford. If you wish to help Lady Kathryn Grayson, bring her uncle, Lord Dunstan, to the hamlet of Gorsham on the night of November 20. There, in the Wealdon Forest, a secluded hunting lodge lies south, half a mile off the road leading into the village. You will find her there at exactly ten o'clock with the man responsible for her abduction. In the memory of the friendship you once shared with her father, do not let Dunstan go after her alone.*

He studied the bold, slightly uneven script, wondering who could have composed it, though he really didn't care. At long last, his relentless search had paid off. In a matter of days, his long-lost, infuriating niece would be returned. Once he had her, he would deal with her in a manner that would end his problems once and for all, and his interests would again be secure.

"What do you think, my lord?" Bishop Tallman, silver-haired and stately, arose from his chair on the opposite side of the desk and braced his palms on the top, the bones in his elegant hands protruding beneath his thin, heavily veined skin.

Douglas smiled. "I believe you have done a very great service in bringing this letter to me. As you can imagine, I've been extremely concerned for Kathryn's safety."

"Then you wish to accompany me as the note suggests."

"Accompany you? There is certainly no need for you

to trouble yourself any further. I shall leave within the hour, take a handful of men, and—"

"I shall go, and we shall comply with the message exactly. It is our best hope of finding Lady Kathryn. Lord Milton was a very dear friend. I have suffered any number of sleepless nights worrying about your decision to place his daughter in a place like St. Bart's. I realize you had your reasons, and considering the circumstances, I did not dispute them. But I owe it to my old friend to do my best for his daughter. I will do as the note requests."

Dunstan clamped hard on his jaw. He didn't need the old man's interference, but perhaps he was right in following the note's instructions. Arriving too soon might frighten his quarry away.

Inwardly he sighed. It would be so much easier if he could simply kill her.

Unfortunately, if he did, her inheritance would pass to a string of cousins, daughters of the late earl's younger brother. No, he had to find the girl and lock her away. As long as she was simply mad and not dead, her money was his to control.

Douglas shoved back his chair and rose to his feet, rounded the desk to join the bishop. Perhaps this time, instead of shipping her off to St. Bart's, he should simply lock her up in one of the towers at Milford Park. Earlier he hadn't wanted the inconvenience, but considering the problems she had caused, perhaps it was the better solution. With Kathryn close at hand, he could make certain she didn't escape—and see that she stayed healthy.

At least for a while . . . long enough to siphon off the balance of her inheritance without getting caught.

He smiled at the tall, silver-haired man standing in front of him. "All right, Bishop, we shall do as you wish. You may spend the night here and we shall leave on the morrow. We should reach the village early the following evening and be ready to approach the lodge exactly at ten o'clock. Hopefully, whoever sent the note has given us the correct information."

Bishop Tallman nodded, apparently satisfied with his decision. "Very good, my lord. Now if you will excuse me, I believe I should like to retire."

"Of course," Douglas said. "I'll have my housekeeper prepare a room, and my daughter will see you upstairs as soon as it is ready."

He watched the old man walk away, his back ramrod straight. The bishop was a man of dignity and honor. He had believed Dunstan's story and been horrified to think the daughter of his dearest friend was involved in something he saw as very close to witchcraft.

Douglas inwardly laughed to think what the old man's conscience would say if he knew the girl had suffered because of his prejudice, his inability to see things beyond the scope of his beloved church. He'd been blinded by Kathryn's unseemly, highly improper interest in the study of medicine.

And fool enough to let that blindness convince him of a well-concocted lie.

# TEN

So far, as nearly as she could guess, Kathryn's plan was proceeding on schedule. Requesting an urgent meeting with Lucien on the night of the twentieth, she had received a note that relayed his agreement to come. He would arrive for supper at eight, as she requested. They could discuss, his reply had said, whatever it was she believed was so important.

That he didn't wish to come was apparent in the tone of the letter. Only grudgingly had he agreed. He was worried about a recurrence of what had happened before, she knew, as well he should be. Kathryn intended to make certain that very thing transpired.

But how exactly to go about it?

And just how far in her seduction was she actually willing to go?

*As far as you have to,* said the voice inside her head.

It was an unnerving thought, yet she would do what she must. Hopefully, her uncle would arrive long before such a thing could actually occur.

The night of the twentieth arrived like a dark wind from the north, chilling her with an icy sense of dread. Kathryn paced the floor of the lodge, her gown of pale mauve silk swirling about her ankles. Her little maid, Fanny, had altered the gown at Kathryn's request, lowering the square-cut neckline to expose more of her breasts. She wore no panniers, only her heavy quilted petticoat and the stiff whalebone corset that thrust her bosom into what she hoped were tempting swells above the low-cut bodice. She'd left her hair loose down her back, and clipped it back on the sides with pretty little tortoiseshell combs.

Kathryn checked the clock ticking on the wall, its long brass pendulum wagging endlessly back and forth. Eight-fifteen. Lucien should have been there by now. He was rarely late. The marquess was a man of exacting discipline who prided himself on a life of order and precision. She studied the clock, watched the minutes tick past, felt the perspiration begin to trickle between her breasts. Something must have happened. Dear God, what on earth could be keeping him?

Kathryn tugged at the cuticle on her thumbnail, so nervous she felt sick. Surely he would come. He had said so and he never broke his word. She tried to calm herself, told herself how crucial it was that nothing seem out of order when he arrived, but her hands had begun to tremble. Her stomach was a bundle of nerves and she was torn between fleeing the lodge while she could still get away, or praying Lucien would come before it was too late.

Ten minutes later, he arrived and Kathryn nearly sobbed with relief when she saw him ride into the glen, leading Blade across the yard toward the stable. By the time he had reached the lodge, she was almost under control. Pasting on a smile and taking a deep, steadying breath, she pulled open the door at his knock.

"My horse picked up a stone," he said simply. "He was limping badly. I had to walk the last mile."

"I was afraid something had happened. Please come in. You must be extremely tired."

He stepped inside, but she saw that he was frowning and a faint tension showed in the straightness of his spine.

"I know you're busy," she said. "I'm grateful you could come."

"You said it was important. From the tone of your message, I couldn't very well refuse." He glanced around, searching for her maid, and a slight flush rose in Kathryn's cheeks. "Where is Fanny?"

She moistened her lips, which felt stiff and brittle. "I gave her the evening off. I—I needed to speak to you in private. I thought it best if we were alone."

His dark brows pulled even farther together and his jaw looked tight.

She tried to smile, but it came out wobbly. "I realize you would probably rather not have come, but I truly needed to see you." She moved toward the table, where a pitcher of ale sat beside a heavy pewter tankard. "You must be thirsty after such a difficult journey. There is brandy or sherry. Bennie's mother sent over a pitcher of ale."

He let out a long breath of air, relaxing a little or perhaps simply accepting that he was there and could not politely leave. "A tankard of ale would do wonders."

Kathryn filled the pewter mug and poured herself a glass of sherry. She took a hefty sip, hoping it would help her to relax. "Supper is ready. We can talk after we eat." She turned toward the fire, to the venison pasties warming on the hearth, but Lucien caught her wrist, bringing her to a halt and forcing her to face him.

"I want to know what's going on. Why did you send for me? What was so important you practically insisted that I come? What is it you want to discuss?"

Her insides clenched. Oh, dear God! What could she possibly say that he would believe? How could she have ever thought to fool him? Her stomach was quivering. She was making a muck of things and time was running out. She was going to fail, and if she did, her uncle would arrive and her life would be over.

Unexpected tears welled in her eyes. She tried to blink them back, but they spilled over onto her cheeks. She tried to calm herself, but her body started to tremble and she couldn't make it stop.

"I know you didn't want to come. I know it was a terrible imposition, but I—I—"

He tipped her chin up, looked into her teary eyes. "Tell me what is wrong," he said more gently than before.

Kathryn shook her head. "I'm just so frightened. I tell myself it will all work out, but as hard as I try, I can't make myself believe it. He's going to come, I know he is. He's going to find me and take me away. I feel like running but I have noplace to go. I feel trapped and confused and you . . . you are the only one I can turn to." Her voice broke on this last, and something flickered in his eyes.

"Kathryn . . ." A single word and she was in his arms. He was holding her and she was clinging to his neck, pressing her body against his long, lean frame. None of the words she had said were what she had planned. She had simply blurted out the truth.

"I'm sorry, Lucien. I know I've been nothing but trouble." She felt the soft press of his lips on the top of her head. In her heart, she felt the agony of involving him in her plan.

"This isn't your fault. None of this should have happened to you."

She tilted her head back, looked into those piercing dark eyes, caught the glint of silver around the rim of his pupils. There was heat there, she saw, a hunger she had seen in his gaze before.

"Would you kiss me, Lucien?" she asked softly. "I know it's wrong, but I don't care. I need you, Lucien. I need you so—"

He made a low sound in his throat. His hold tightened almost painfully and he silenced her with his mouth, taking her lips in a fierce kiss that stole her breath along with her words. His hands dug into her hair and he held her immobile for the plunder of his tongue, tasting her deeply, making her knees go weak. His kiss was rough, hot, hun-

gry. It was wild, savage, and in some strange way, unbearably tender. The room swirled around her. The walls
seemed to fade. She swayed and would have fallen if he
hadn't been holding her up.

The kiss went deeper, hotter. Lucien's hand found her
breast and he tested the weight of it through the lustrous
silk fabric, his thumb massaging her nipple. It tightened
and swelled, and a soft ache arose there, pulsing with each
beat of her heart. Her insides trembled and heat surged
into her belly. It sank into her limbs, seeped into her core,
left her damp and aching.

"Lucien . . ." she whispered, kissing him just as
fiercely, amazed at the need that rose inside her, needing
him as she had never imagined. Kathryn laced her fingers
in his shiny black hair, freeing it from the ribbon at the
nape of his neck, and he groaned. She sucked in a breath
as his long dark fingers slid inside the bodice of her gown
to curve over a breast and his mouth traveled down the
side of her neck. Hot, moist kisses burned her skin. Graceful hands stroked and teased until she thought she would
surely swoon.

He worked the buttons at the back of her gown, pop-
ping them open one by one, then he slid it off her shoulders, exposing her corset and chemise. He kissed his way
across her shoulders then moved lower, easing the chemise down over her arms, pulling the lacings on her corset. He loosened it enough to shove it down, then took
the weight of her breast into his mouth.

Kathryn's legs started shaking. The earth seemed to
open and swallow her up. A soft sob escaped, the pleasure
more intense than anything she could have imagined. Little tongues of heat seemed to lick at her insides, following
the path of his kisses. Kathryn's head fell back, giving
him freer access to first one breast then the other as he
laved them, tasted them, circled the stiff peaks, then returned to suckle the fullness.

Dear God, she was on fire for him. Her body throbbed
all over and a soft ache shimmered in the place between

her legs. She had meant to seduce him, but she never would have guessed that in doing so she would also be seducing herself. Vaguely, she wondered how much time had passed, but Lucien kissed her again and the thought slid away, buried beneath the skillful fire of his mouth and hands.

She barely noticed when her gown fell into a useless heap on the floor. The petticoat was stripped away, the corset dispensed with. Her chemise bunched around her hips. She scarcely noticed when he lifted her into his arms and carried her over to the sofa, realized only dimly that he had stripped away his shirt.

Kissing her again, he came up over her, her bare breasts pressing into smooth, hard bands of muscle. Such a magnificent chest. Sinfully dark and hard as the stone floor beneath them. She traced the rigid sinews with her fingers and then with her tongue. She tested the springy black chest hair and touched a flat copper nipple, amazed to feel it contract, to hear a tight hiss of breath escape from his throat.

He kissed her again, and her whole body trembled. Her nipples ached, and she was damp and hot at her feminine core. In the far reaches of her mind, the thought occurred that it was past the time she should stop him. It wasn't part of her plan to let her seduction go so far. She had to end this dangerous game before it was too late, but she couldn't find the will.

He eased her legs apart and settled himself between them. He was unbuttoning his breeches, raising the thin chemise that still covered her from waist to thigh, when the door to the hunting lodge burst open and her uncle walked in, followed by three of his men, and the tall, dignified, silver-haired Bishop Tallman.

For an instant, Lucien went dead still.

"Forgodsake, what the devil—" Dunstan didn't need to finish. It was more than obvious exactly what was going on.

Lucien swore an oath even as he jerked Kathryn's chemise back up over her breasts, grabbed his coat and tossed it over her nearly naked body. Clenching his jaw, he turned away to refasten the buttons at the front of his breeches and grab up his shirt.

"Wait outside," her uncle ordered his men, who stood gawking for an instant, then silently slipped away, closing the door behind them. "So it was you after all," her uncle said to Lucien with a curl of his lips. "I didn't think you had that kind of nerve."

"What is the meaning of this?" the bishop demanded. "You're Litchfield, are you not? I believe we've met once before."

Lucien nodded stiffly. "I'm Litchfield." He dragged his full-sleeved shirt on over his head, but didn't bother to tie the string that closed the opening at his throat. "Bishop Tallman, if I'm not mistaken. How is it you are both here, trespassing on my property?"

The bishop made no reply, simply pulled the note Kathryn had written from a pocket inside his robe. Lucien scanned it and handed it back to him, his expression even more grim.

"I received this three days ago," Edwin Tallman told him. "As you can see it wasn't signed, but it was, apparently, quite accurate." He cast a glance at Kathryn, who huddled beneath the woolen coat, her face a flaming shade of red. She had known this would be hard, but it was worse than she could ever have imagined.

His gaze returned to Litchfield and did not waiver. "You realize this is Lady Kathryn Grayson, daughter of the late Earl of Milford."

Lucien ground down on his jaw. "I do."

"Well, then, you must also realize exactly what this means. You have seduced an innocent young woman, the daughter of an old and noble family. There is no course open to you but marriage."

Dunstan's head jerked up at the words, his eyes going wide in astonishment. "Marriage? Now wait just a minute—"

"As I said, the girl is an innocent," Bishop Tallman said to Lucien as if the earl hadn't spoken. "You, however, are reputed to be quite a libertine. You have ruined the girl. Now you are honor bound to marry her."

Lucien's hard black gaze swung to Kathryn, and in a single moment of clarity, he knew exactly what she had done. He realized that she had been the author of the note, that she had arranged for all of this to happen. He knew that he was well and truly trapped and that she was the cause, and though he understood why she had done it, he was furious to have been so viciously maneuvered.

A muscle tightened in his jaw. Anger made his face take on a dark reddish cast. He might have made some reply but her uncle broke in just then.

"You can't possibly ask the man to marry the girl. The poor child is quite mad."

The bishop pinned the marquess with an unrelenting glare. "Is that what you believe, my lord? That Lady Kathryn is insane? There were rumors that you were trying to arrange for her ladyship's release from St. Bartholomew's Hospital, that you were convinced she was not at all mad but completely and totally sane. Is that not so, my lord?"

Kathryn held her breath. If he said the right words, he might yet escape his fate. Was he so angry he would abandon her to whatever fate her uncle had in store for her? She bit down on her trembling lip, praying that he would not.

Lucien's eyes remained locked on her face. "Lady Kathryn is not insane." *Far from it,* those dark eyes said. *A conniving, deceitful little harlot, willing to use her body to gain whatever it is she wants, but she is certainly not insane.* Kathryn felt that icy glare like a knife sliding into her heart.

The bishop moved farther into the room, his robes floating out around him. "If you truly believe she is sound of mind, it is your duty to marry her."

"The girl is dangerous," Dunstan argued. "She tried to poison my daughter. She tried to—"

"I did not!" Kathryn came up on her knees on the sofa, clutching Lucien's coat around her. "I was trying to help her and you know it!"

"Are you afraid of the girl, my lord?" the bishop asked calmly.

A muscle tightened in Lucien's jaw. "No. I don't believe she would purposely do harm to anyone." But his fierce expression said she had certainly dealt a deadly blow to him.

"Then I will send word to the archbishop on the morrow. It is not all that far to Canterbury. The two of you should be able to marry in a couple of days."

"This is absurd!" Dunstan strode forward, his tricorn hat gripped tightly under one arm. "The chit is not in her right mind. I tell you she's—"

The bishop's warning glance cut him off. "You are her guardian. Her father gave her into your care because he trusted you. It is your duty to do what is in Lady Kathryn's best interest. Do you truly believe that marriage to the Marquess of Litchfield would be worse for her than sending her back to St. Bart's?"

Her uncle cleared his throat. His face was red and his eyes darted around like those of a cornered animal. "Well, no, of course not, but—"

"Then the matter is settled. The marriage will take place as soon as a special license can be obtained." Dunstan said nothing more, but the look of fury on his face said that murder would have been far more to his liking.

"In the meantime—with Lord Litchfield's permission— Lady Kathryn and I will accompany his lordship home, where we will remain until the ceremony has been performed. I intend do the honors myself. I owe it to Lady Kathryn's father."

Her uncle's jaw clamped so hard his teeth made a grinding noise. With a stiff nod of his head, he turned and stalked out of the room. She could hear him shouting to his men, then there was the creak of saddle leather and the jangle of bridles and bits. The rumble of horses' hooves followed, fading into the distance as he and his men rode away.

"My carriage is parked down the lane. If you will join me, Lord Litchfield, we will give her ladyship a moment to make ready."

Lucien merely nodded. It was difficult to know exactly what he was thinking for his mask of control had been skillfully set back into place. But Kathryn could easily guess. If anger could be bottled and hidden away, the marquess would no doubt have stored a cellar full. Thinking of his friendship, of the fiery, passionate kisses they had shared before her uncle's arrival, a painful ache rose inside her.

He would marry her, but she was no longer sure he would ever forgive her. She had betrayed him in the cruelest, most vicious manner, and it was obvious how bitter he was.

*You only did what you had to,* said the voice inside her head. But her heart clutched at the guilt she felt, and the thought occurred, as it should have before, that the Marquess of Litchfield wasn't a man who would easily forgive.


Jason Sinclair sat on the sofa in the Red Salon of Castle Running, his wife perched nervously beside him. They had arrived just minutes before and been immediately ushered into the elegant salon by a grim-faced Reeves, Lucien's long-nosed, exceedingly proper butler.

Velvet reached over and captured his hand. "I'm worried, Jason. Something must be terribly wrong."

Jason made no reply, distracted by the sound of the ornate walnut doors sliding open. He came to his feet as his best friend walked in and the butler closed the doors behind him. From the set of Lucien's jaw and the hard look on his face, it was obvious his wife was not wrong.

"We came as soon as we received your message." Jason strode toward him. "You said it was urgent. Obviously something has happened. I hope this has nothing to do with Lady Kathryn."

A corner of Lucien's mouth tipped up in a tight smile that was merely a curl of his lips. "You're right, my friend. Something has happened. And it has everything to do with Lady Kathryn Grayson."

Velvet surged to her feet. "Good heavens—they didn't discover she was hiding at the lodge?"

His features seemed to harden. "Not exactly." He moved to the sideboard and began to pour himself a drink, every movement stiff and punctuated with what Jason suddenly realized was anger. He was dressed more formally than usual, especially for so early in the afternoon. His navy blue velvet coat, white cravat, and tight navy satin breeches fit perfectly. The froth of lace hanging below his cuffs looked stark against the darkness of his long-fingered hands. His queued-back hair was powdered, as Lucien rarely wore it.

"Would either of you care for a drink? Some brandy or sherry, perhaps?"

Jason shook his head and so did Velvet. "Just tell us what this is about."

That sardonic semblance of a smile reappeared. "I'm sorry for imposing upon you on such short notice, but I've invited you here for a special occasion. You're both to be guests at a wedding."

"A wedding?" Velvet repeated. "Whose wedding?"

Lucien's mouth went thin. He tossed back the brandy as if it were water. "Mine."

Jason arched a brow in surprise. "From the tone of your voice, I take it you aren't exactly pleased. I thought you wanted to get married."

"I did. Unfortunately, the bride-to-be is not of my choosing. I'm to marry Kathryn Grayson at exactly two o'clock. That is in precisely"—he glanced at the clock—"forty-five minutes."

Velvet's voice carried a higher pitch than normal. "Oh, my." Her hand moved down to the waist of her burgundy velvet traveling gown as if something fluttered in her stomach. "I believe I shall take that glass of sherry."

"I'll get it," Jason said. "I think I need one, too." He moved to the sideboard, lifted the stopper off a crystal decanter, and poured them both a glass.

Lucien began to pace. "I still can't quite believe it. That conniving, deceiving little baggage trapped me as neatly as you please. She played the sharper as if she were born to it, seduced me into marriage as if I were a callow boy, and there isn't a damnable thing I can do about it."

He went on to tell them what had happened at the lodge, omitting a goodly bit of detail, Jason imagined, but saying simply that he and Lady Kathryn were discovered in a compromising situation. The lady's reputation was ruined, and the bishop had insisted they wed.

"She planned the entire bloody affair. After everything I've done to help her, it's damnably hard to believe."

Velvet crossed to his side, rested a small gloved hand on his forearm. "She was frightened, Lucien. She was desperately afraid she would have to go back to that terrible place. She did the only thing she could think of to protect herself."

"I would have protected her. I would have seen to her safety, if she had simply trusted me. Instead the little fool has ruined both of our lives."

"Maybe it won't be so bad," Jason put in. "I didn't want to marry Velvet—at least I didn't think so at the time. Now I'm damned glad I did. It was the best thing that's ever happened to me."

"This isn't the same and you know it. Kathryn and I are not suited to each other in the least. And even if I wanted to marry the chit—which I don't—I want nothing to do with the sort of female who would use her body as a weapon to get what she wants." He walked to the sideboard to refill his snifter of brandy, and Jason thought he had rarely seen his friend so near the edge of his control.

"You aren't a man who is easily duped. Surely there is some way out, if that is truly your wish."

Lucien ground down on his jaw. "She's a clever little wench. She had it planned right down to the instant. She is lucky her bloody uncle arrived on time, or I would have quite properly dispensed with her maidenhead. I don't believe she would be feeling so smug if I had taken her as well and thoroughly as I intended."

Jason watched him closely, assessing the bitterness that blazed in those fierce, dark eyes. "You could always send her back," he said softly. "If you told them she was truly insane, there is no way they could force you to wed her."

"Jason!" Velvet gasped. "What are you saying?"

"I'm telling him the truth. He could send her away and be done with it. One word is all it would take." Jason studied his friend's features, certain of his response.

Lucien drained the contents of his snifter, his fingers tight around the bowl of the glass, anger making the movement jerky. A tic appeared in his cheek. Still, he shook his head. "I can't do that. No one deserves that sort of punishment. I'm damned if I'll make this a legitimate marriage, but I refuse to let Dunstan hurt her any more than he has already."

Velvet sagged in relief. "Have you spoken to her? What does Kathryn have to say?"

"We've spoken only briefly, as the bishop allowed us to do. In a year, Kathryn will be one and twenty, able to marry without her uncle's consent. According to her, an annulment at that time would give us both the chance to marry as we wish. Unfortunately, Lady Allison is hardly likely to wait, considering the embarrassment she and her family will suffer—thanks to Kathryn's deceitful machinations."

Velvet tilted her head back to look up at him, Lucien so much taller she looked like a pixie standing at his feet. "If Allison loves you, she'll wait. She'll forgive your momentary indiscretion and she'll wait for you to marry her."

Lucien eyed her darkly. "If Jason had been found in a passionate embrace with a half-naked woman, would you have forgiven him?"

Velvet glanced away. "It would have been hard. My pride would not have wanted me to do so, but I might have, if I had believed it was me he truly loved and not her."

Lucien scoffed. "Well, I am not in love with Allison Hartman and she is not in love with me. I was, however, looking forward to a long and comfortable life with her as my wife—a life that has now been ruthlessly stolen from me. Kathryn Grayson is responsible for that misdeed and I shall never forgive her for it."

The hard look on his face confirmed his words. The path Kathryn Grayson had chosen would not be an easy one. Jason thought that perhaps the girl had made a mistake in choosing to match wits with the Marquess of Litchfield. Lucien was the best friend a man could have— and the very worst enemy.

"It's nearly two," Jason said, finishing the last of his drink. "Knowing you as I do, I'm sure you don't want to be late for your own wedding."

Lucien's mouth curled ruthlessly. "On the contrary," he said. "I see no reason to rush, and I am in need of another brandy. If that means I shall be late, then the lady will simply have to wait."

Jason inwardly groaned, feeling even more anxious for Kathryn Grayson. If he knew his friend, the next year would be hell on earth for the woman who had betrayed him.

# ELEVEN

Candles burned in the small ivy-covered stone chapel behind the castle, lighting the centuries-old stained-glass window above the altar at the far end of the room. Kathryn listened to the wind howling outside the walls and an icy shiver ran through her. A loose shutter banged incessantly against the window and a leafless branch scratched at the mullioned panes, grating on her nerves.

Dressed in an elegant cream silk gown trimmed at the neck and sleeves with heavy gold lace, Kathryn stood next to Aunt Winnie, awaiting the arrival of her groom, her stomach in such turmoil she feared she would be sick.

She nervously adjusted her wide panniers, which felt as if they were fashioned of stone instead of whalebone and had a stranglehold on her waist. Sweet God, where was he? The marquess should have been there ten minutes ago, but there was still no sign of him. She tried not to glance at the heavy oak door, but her eyes strayed in that direction time and again.

Aunt Winnie patted her hand. "He'll be here, my dear. You mustn't worry."

Kathryn tried to smile, but her face felt brittle and her lips barely moved. The minutes crawled past. She began to wonder if he had changed his mind about the wedding and would not come. If he didn't, she would be left to the mercy of her uncle, who sat in one of the polished walnut pews staring at her with icy eyes and a look of such malice her stomach churned and bile rose into her throat.

Only Lord Dunstan, Bishop Tallman, Aunt Winnie, and the Duke and Duchess of Carlyle were in attendance. The marquess had made no pretense of being happy about the marriage, not even for the benefit of the servants. It was not a joyous occasion and he meant for one and all to know it.

Kathryn's fingers bit into the gold-trimmed lace handkerchief she gripped in one damp hand. Of all the weddings she had ever dreamed up, never could she have envisioned a day as miserable as this.

Assuming Litchfield actually went through with it.

A second wave of nausea rolled through her. Please let him come, she silently prayed. Please let him stand by me just this one last time.

It would be the last, she knew. She had betrayed him and now she knew he would never forgive her.

The bishop cleared his throat. "Your bridegroom seems to have been detained," he said with a thunderous glare toward the door. "I wonder where . . ."

But he didn't have to wonder anymore. Lucien strode in behind the duke and duchess, whose worried expressions mirrored her own, though theirs held a trace of pity. Her gaze swung to the man who followed them up the aisle, the man who would be her husband. Tall and graceful and breathtakingly handsome—cold and hard-eyed, and more angry than she had ever seen him. Lucien strode toward where she stood near the bishop and Aunt Winnie at the front of the chuch.

"Ah, there you are, *beloved.*" Sarcasm dripped from every word and his eyes held an edge of steel. He made a slight, mocking bow. "I hope I haven't kept you waiting.

I had important matters to attend." As if his wedding were not among them.

Kathryn turned away at the words he had purposely said to hurt her and blinked to hold back tears. She deserved this—every bit of it. But God, it made her heart ache unbearably.

"If you are ready, Bishop Tallman," Lucien said, taking her shaking hand and resting it on the sleeve of his navy blue velvet coat. "I believe you have a wedding to perform."

The bishop nodded, his white hair glistening in the light of the dozens of candles that lined both sides of the chapel. "Quite so," he said, and they followed him to a spot in front of the altar.

It was fashioned of ornately carved wood, draped with a length of aging ivory silk, and a massive Bible sat open atop it. The bishop began to read, but Kathryn barely heard him. She could feel Litchfield's powerful presence beside her, feel the heat of his anger as if it were a tangible thing.

The torturous moments wore on, but she couldn't seem to focus on what was being said. Her heart was pounding so hard it threatened to tear through her chest. Her mouth felt so dry she could barely repeat the bishop's words. Lucien said them with a lethal calm that matched the killing look on his face. Fury flashed in his dark eyes like a deadly bolt of lightning every time he glanced in her direction.

At last the brief, emotionless ceremony came to an end, but instead of a bridegroom's kiss, Litchfield gave her a stiff bow of acknowledgment that said he was well and truly wed, and turned to take his leave. The high-pitched gasp of horror that came from the open door stopped him cold.

Kathryn swayed at the sight of Allison Hartman, Lady St. James, and Allison's father, the baron, blocking the entrance to the chapel. Dunstan turned to stare. Carlyle started and the duchess made a soft little gasp of horror.

With a shaking hand, Kathryn gripped the altar to steady herself.

At the opposite end of the room, the baron's thunderous voice overrode the stunned silence of the guests. "Good God, Litchfield—what is this outrage? What the devil is going on?" A portly man with a barrel chest and heavy, white-stockinged calves, his immaculate forest-green velvet tailcoat flapping as he moved, St. James strode like a maddened bull up the aisle, stopping in front of Lucien, who stood half a head taller, his broad shoulders rigid. The baron craned his thick neck to look him in the face.

"Tell me my eyes deceive me. Tell me I did not just witness your marriage."

"I sent you a note," Lucien said. "I asked for a meeting with you and your family at your home on the morrow at two. Did you not receive my message?"

"I received it. When I showed it to my wife, she begged me not to wait. Martha was afraid something untoward was going on. She feared you were somehow still involved with that madwoman from St. Bart's." He cast a hard glance toward the altar. "If the woman you just wed is Lady Kathryn Grayson, obviously my wife was correct."

Clutching her mother's hand, Allison made a fluttery little sound in her throat. "Lucien? My lord? You did not truly marry her?" She stared at Litchfield with big blue teary eyes, moisture streaming down her cheeks. Gowned in a dark blue silk traveling dress, she looked pale and shaken, and Kathryn's guilt rose up again.

Lucien moved past the baron down the aisle and stopped in front of Allison, his whole body tense. He made a slight bow and took her trembling gloved hand.

"Lady Allison. I have done you a grave disservice. It was never my intention to hurt you in any way, but that, it seems, is what has occurred. It is not enough to say that I am sorry. I do not ask for your pardon, merely that in time you may somehow come to forgive me."

"Forgive you?" She pulled her hand from his, pressed a fine lace handkerchief beneath her nose, and very daintily sniffed. "You have ruined my life, sir. You have made me a laughingstock in front of all of London. I shall never, ever forgive you!" Whirling away, she lifted her wide blue silk skirts and raced from the chapel, the heels of her matching blue slippers clicking against the stone floor.

Her mother, her face an angry mottled red, glared up at Litchfield. "You and that . . . that harlot. I knew something like this would happen. If that little slut hadn't come along—"

"Madam," Lucien quietly warned, "I realize this has been upsetting, but I remind you, you are speaking of my wife."

Her cheeks puffed in and out, heaving in rhythm to her bosom. "You, sir, are no gentleman!" Turning, she pounded after her daughter, letting the heavy door slam behind her. The rest of the guests in the chapel sat in fascinated silence, staring at the scene as if a great Shakespearean tragedy were being played out before their very eyes.

The baron's hard gaze bored into Litchfield. "I should call you out for this."

Lucien's face looked suddenly haggard. "That is certainly your right. I shall, of course, pay for any expenses you have incurred in regard to the wedding and allow you to explain what has happened in any way that you and your daughter see fit." Some of the stiffness left his posture and fatigue seemed to settle over his broad shoulders. "I'm sorry, Edward. I truly am. I have always valued your friendship. It pains me greatly to know that I have lost it."

For a moment the older man just stood there, his jaw squarely clamped. Then he released a weary sigh and made a curt nod of his head. With his thick neck slumped slightly forward, he walked past Litchfield out of the chapel.

The marquess cast a last glance at Kathryn. She could

read the turbulence in his eyes, the humiliation. Regret
knifed sharply through her. Dear God, she hadn't meant
for any of this to happen. She had only been trying to
protect herself. She had thought that it would all work
out, that in a year he could marry whomever he wished.
Now she saw that the plans he had made had been destroyed forever. She wondered if the price had been worth
it.

She didn't realize she was crying until she felt Aunt
Winnie's arm around her shoulder. "Give him time, my
dear. In time it will all work out."

But Kathryn didn't think so. Not anymore. And as she
watched the tall, handsome man she had married walk out
the door, she realized with sudden, painful clarity she had
lost more than just a friend. She didn't know exactly how
Allison Hartman felt about the Marquess of Litchfield, but
in that final moment when she had looked into her husband's angry face, Kathryn had discovered with dawning
horror that she was totally and irrevocably in love with
him.


Sprawled on a tufted leather sofa in his study, the rain
beating down with unrelenting force, Lucien lifted his
glass of brandy and drained the contents, then refilled the
glass, knocked it back, and filled it again.

He was blindly, stupidly drunk as he hadn't been in
years and he didn't give a bloody damn. His debacle of
a wedding was over. At long last, he was a married man.

He scoffed at the notion. He was married, all right,
outfoxed by a slip of a girl who had tricked him with her
tempting little body. Kathryn Grayson was a deceitful little harlot—nothing at all like Allison Hartman—and now
she was his wife. He thought of the scene with Allison in
the church, grimaced, and took another long drink. He felt
guilty for hurting her, though what she mostly suffered
was disappointment and embarrassment. She didn't love
him. He wasn't certain she was the type of woman who

was capable of that sort of emotion. It was one of the things he'd liked best about her.

He wasn't worried about her future. With the face of an angel and a ripening figure to match, together with the sizable dowry her father had provided, it wouldn't be long before she was betrothed again, wed, and out of the marriage mart for good.

The thought set his teeth on edge and made him angry all over again. Angry at the woman upstairs. Angry at himself for having been such a fool.

Kathryn was responsible. She was the one who had caused all of this. He consoled himself with the reminder she was his wife in name only. A year from now he would be free of her. He would find another girl like Allison, a sweet, well-bred young woman who would make a good mother for the children she would bear him.

Lucien set his drink down on the table in front of the sofa, his temper still raging. Reaching across the polished marble top, he picked up a small mother-of-pearl inlaid snuffbox, lifted the lid, and took a pinch of snuff. The white lace on his cuff brushed against his jaw as he drew in the robust, slightly sweet tobacco.

He rarely overindulged in anything. He intended to do so tonight—his wedding night—and to hell with Kathryn Grayson.

His mind formed a memory of her that evening at the lodge, of her feigned passion and heated responses, of the innocent kisses that had seemed so real he had tumbled in their thrall down the road to disaster.

Instead of sitting there feeling sorry for himself, what he should be doing was striding up the stairs to take what Kathryn Grayson had so convincingly offered. What she had bartered for the safety of his name. Lucien snapped the lid closed on the snuffbox a little too hard and tossed the box back down on the table. Strands of disheveled black hair moved against his cheek. He jerked the ribbon from the nape of his neck and tossed it away, letting the hair fall unhindered around his face.

Taking another sip of his drink, he leaned back against the deep leather sofa, thinking of Kathryn's sweet little body, remembering the softness of her lips, and wishing he could make her pay.

Kathryn stood mutely in the center of the same royal-blue bedchamber she had stayed in at the castle before. She wasn't ensconced in the marchioness's suite as she should have been, considering she was Litchfield's new bride. But then, she hadn't expected she would be.

The wedding was over and she was married. Well, almost married. The vows had not been consummated and never would be. She would never be Lucien's wife and, in truth, it was just as well. She might be in love with him, but he would never return that love. He wanted a sweet, docile wife like Allison Hartman. Kathryn was hardly that. He disapproved of her studies, couldn't understand her determination to learn more about illness and healing, yet it was something that consumed her, something she would never be able to give up.

Kathryn crossed the room and sat down in the window seat, listening to the sound of the icy rain that tapped against the panes. Every time she closed her eyes, she could see the awful scene in the chapel, see the tears in Allison Hartman's eyes and the anger on Lucien's face.

"The worst is past," the duchess had said as Kathryn and Aunt Winnie had led her out of the chapel. "It's a shame it happened as it did, but it's over now and done. From now on, things can only get better."

Kathryn shook her head. "He hates me. I ruined his plans to marry Lady Allison and shamed him in front of his friends. Lucien will never forgive me."

"You did what you thought you had to. Perhaps in time—"

"I was wrong. No matter what might have happened to me, I shouldn't have done it—not to him. Not after all he's done to help me."

Velvet laid a hand on Kathryn's shoulder. "Lucien

wasn't in love with Allison Hartman. He told me that himself. And I don't believe she was in love with him. Give him some time, Kathryn. He cares for you; he has from the start. Perhaps in time he'll be able to put all of this behind him."

Kathryn felt a fresh stab of pain. It had occurred so many times since the wedding it was almost a constant throbbing. "I betrayed him. I didn't want to, but I did. I only wish there was a way I could make it up to him."

Aunt Winnie marched into the bedchamber just then, ending her reflections and bringing Kathryn to her feet. Still gowned in mauve silk, her silver-blond hair glinting in the firelight, Winnie bustled across the room with a smile and a sense of command Kathryn welcomed. At least she could still count on Aunt Winnie.

"Come now, dearest," she said. "Time to get you out of those clothes. After all, this *is* your wedding night."

Kathryn felt a sharp jolt up under her ribs. Unexpected tears welled and spilled over onto her cheeks. She tried to brush them away, but Winnie saw them.

"There, there, child. You mustn't cry—not tonight. If all goes well, by the morrow, at least a portion of my nephew's anger will have faded."

Kathryn's head came up. "What are you talking about?"

"I'm talking about the marriage bed. There is no better place to soothe a man's ire." She smiled. "You will see."

Kathryn stared off toward the window. "There isn't going to be a wedding night. This is a marriage of convenience. A year from now, our wedding will be annulled and the marquess will marry someone else."

Winnie waved her words away. "Nonsense, my dear. You are his wife and exactly the right woman for him. Besides, you are in love with him. You couldn't possibly wish for him to wed someone else."

Kathryn swayed on suddenly unsteady limbs. She reached out and caught hold of the bedpost. "I'm not . . . not in love with him and he is certainly not in love with me. He loathes the very sight of me. He will hardly be coming to my bed."

Aunt Winnie frowned. "That is the trouble with my nephew." She turned Kathryn around and started on the buttons at the back of her cream silk gown. "One never really knows what he is thinking."

But it was only a matter of minutes until Kathryn found out. A knock came at the door and a footman appeared carrying a silver salver, a note folded and perched on the top, addressed in a man's bold hand.

"What does it say?" Winnie asked, peering over her shoulder.

Kathryn nervously opened the note and read her husband's words. "Prepare yourself. Tonight I intend to claim what you so eagerly offered at the lodge." It was signed simply "Litchfield."

Kathryn's stomach knotted. "Dear God," she whispered, hardly aware she had spoken. The marquess was furious that he had been duped into marriage. Now he meant to claim his husbandly rights whether she was willing or not.

She stared up at Winnie DeWitt. "He . . . he means to have a wedding night, just as you said." Kathryn sank down on the padded velvet bench at the foot of the bed, her legs suddenly too weak to hold her.

Aunt Winnie simply smiled. "Well, there you have it, then. There will be no annulment and in time everything is going to work out."

But it wouldn't work out. Not after what had happened in the chapel. Not when it was obvious how much the marquess despised her. Not when he only wanted to punish her for duping him into marriage.

But Kathryn didn't say the words. What happened between them was no one else's concern. And whatever punishment Lucien intended to mete out, she well and truly deserved. She would submit to him, if that was what he wanted. She owed him at least that and more.

Swallowing back her fears, Kathryn let Aunt Winnie

help her into a filmy pale blue silk night rail that appeared from among the woman's apparently limitless wardrobe, then sat down on the tapestry stool in front of the gilded mirror while Winnie removed the pins from her hair.

"Is there anything you would like to ask, my dear?" Winnie took the silver-backed hairbrush and stroked it through Kathryn's dark hair, spreading it out around her shoulders.

Kathryn's hand was shaking. She rested it against her thigh to still the movement. "I'm sure I'll be fine."

Winnie bent and kissed Kathryn's cheek. "My nephew can be a hard man at times and he is not one who easily forgives. Try not to judge him too harshly for whatever might happen tonight."

Kathryn suppressed a shiver. Sometime tonight, Lucien would come. He meant to take what he wanted and there would be no tenderness in his touch this time, no kisses so hot they made her weak and light-headed. He would use her body as he pleased, take his pleasure and leave, and if she tried to stop him, the consequences would only be worse.

Kathryn fought back her growing despair, so mired in misery she didn't hear the sound of Aunt Winnie's departure, only the soft thud of the door as it closed, leaving her alone to await her fate.

Hours passed. The tension grew until Kathryn found herself jumping at every sound. A mouse in the walls, the creak of the rafters, the scraping of the branches against the panes. Still he did not come.

She paced for a while, until fatigue set in and her legs began to feel shaky. She lay down on top of the covers, but didn't dare fall asleep. Instead, she lay like a stone, listening for Litchfield's footfalls, her stomach tied in knots.

Another hour passed. Exhaustion pulled at every muscle and bone. If he hadn't arrived by now, surely he wasn't going to come. Her eyelids had begun to drift closed when the door flew wide and Lucien walked in.

Kathryn's eyes snapped open and her heart began to thunder. In the light of the single candle still burning beside the bed, she could see that his coat and cravat were gone, his white lawn shirt open nearly to the waist, exposing a hard chest and a mat of curly black hair. His hair was slightly mussed and hung in loose waves to his shoulders.

He closed the door solidly behind him and the sound rang like a death knell.

"I hope I didn't keep you waiting, *beloved*." The way he said the word, without the least sincerity, made her inwardly cringe. Lucien walked toward her and it was obvious from his dishevel that he had been drinking. Still, he didn't look all that drunk. When he paused at the foot of the bed, a little skitter of fear tripped along her spine. His eyes ran over her body, taking in the sheer blue silk gown and unconsciously Kathryn's hands came up to cover her breasts.

A fine black brow arched up. "The blushing bride? Surely you have not turned shy all of a sudden. As I recall, the last time we were together you weren't shy at all." He rounded the end of the bed and paused beside her. Kathryn shrank away from the hard look in his eyes. "Ah, but that night you were pretending."

Kathryn frowned, confused by the words.

He ran a finger along her jaw. "Perhaps you can do so tonight. Perhaps it will make things easier."

She drew her legs up beneath her, curling into herself protectively and wishing she could find the strength to run. She didn't like this Lucien. She didn't know him and she was afraid. "What . . . what are you talking about?"

He flashed a smile that really wasn't, his teeth gleaming white in the light of the candle. "I'm talking about enjoying the body I have purchased with my future. Remove your clothes, Kathryn, so that I may see what my devil's bargain has wrought."

A shiver of dread ran through her. Who was this man she had once called friend? This man who had kissed her with such fierce tenderness? Shaking her head, she inched away until her back pressed into the carved wooden headboard. Her eyes found his in the flickering light. They looked cold and unrelenting. Kathryn's nails dug into the palms of her hands.

"I realize you are angry," she said. "You have every right to be. I was wrong in what I did. I was so afraid my uncle would find me I was willing to do anything to save myself. It was selfish, I know. I thought that in time it would all work out. I was wrong and I'm sorry. If I had it to do again, I would not do what I did."

"What you did?" His eyes turned even harder. "But you didn't do anything, my dear. You merely pretended to. That is the reason I am here. This time, I mean to take what you pretended to offer." He reached for her, grabbed hold of her gown, twisted it in a fist, and ripped it viciously down the front.

Kathryn shrieked and tried to scoot farther back, but there was no place to go. Trying in vain to cover herself, she huddled nearly naked against the headboard, staring up at him, unable to believe this cold, unfeeling man was the same man who had kissed her so passionately that night at the lodge.

"I mean to have you, Kathryn. You may as well resign yourself."

She wildly shook her head, her whole body trembling. Fear ate at her. She had meant to submit, but now she found that she could not. The anger seething from Lucien's hard body brought the sting of tears.

"Not like this," she whispered. "Please, Lucien, not like this."

Something shifted in his features. He paused in the act of unbuttoning his fly. Kathryn glanced down, saw that he was hard and straining against the tight dark blue fabric, and heat burned into her cheeks.

"You are the one who made this bargain," he said, his eyes scorching into hers. "You pretended to feel passion before. You can do so again."

Surprise jolted through her, dispelling some of her fear. "Pretended? You think I was pretending that . . . that night at the lodge?"

He paused on another button and glanced up. "You are saying that you were not?"

She swallowed past the dryness in her throat. Her chest felt tight and an ache throbbed near her heart. "I sent the letter to Bishop Tallman. I meant for it to appear as though you had compromised my virtue, but what happened between us that night, I was not . . . It was not . . . I was not pretending." She blinked and glanced away, no longer willing to face him. "When you kissed me," she whispered, "when you touched me . . . it was magic."

Some painful emotion flickered in his eyes. They closed for a moment and he seemed to draw inward, collecting himself. When he looked at her again, some of the harshness had seeped from his features. "You were not pretending," he repeated as if he needed to be certain of her words.

"It was different between us that night," Kathryn told him, her mind recalling the scene all too clearly. "You wanted me then. Now you only want to punish me."

For long seconds, he just stood there. When he spoke again, his voice sounded thick and gruff. "Never doubt that I want you, Kathryn. I have since the moment you first stepped into my study. But perhaps it is better this way." Turning, he crossed the room and pulled open the door. "Wife or not, I discover I am not in the mood for an unwilling woman. Besides, an annulment would be impossible should I manage to get you with child."

Kathryn stared at his retreating figure as he stepped out into the hall and closed the door behind him. Looking down at the tattered remnants of her blue silk gown, her body still trembling with hurt and fear, it occurred to her that Litchfield had achieved his purpose after all.

He had punished her, just as he had intended. He had made her suffer, yet he had left her innocence intact. The vows remained unconsummated. In a year, the marriage would be annulled.

For the first time since her uncle's arrival at the lodge, Kathryn rolled over on the bed, buried her face in the pillow, and began to weep.

# TWELVE

Lucien rose late the following morning, his head throbbing like an anvil against the side of his skull. His mouth tasted foul and his tongue felt swollen, and as dry as an aging sheet of foolscap. When he walked into the sunny little parlor at the rear of the house where breakfast was usually served, the light slashed into his eyes and he winced. Blinded for a moment, he nearly collided with Kathryn, who was just then walking in.

She gasped as he caught her shoulders to keep her from falling and her face went a little bit pale. "My lord, I—I didn't think to see you. You are usually such an early riser." Faint purple smudges darkened the skin beneath her eyes, which looked red-rimmed and swollen.

Guilt trickled through him, and something else he couldn't quite name. She looked fragile in a way he had never seen her, and thinking of last night, he could hardly believe what he had very nearly done.

He cleared his throat, suddenly uncomfortable. "Yes, well, it wasn't the best of nights. I'm afraid I didn't get much sleep."

"Neither did I," she said softly with a glance away. "Perhaps tonight will be better."

Regret made his chest feel tight. He was angry, yes, but he had never really meant to hurt her. Lucien reached out and caught her chin, turned it with his hand. He studied her face with its dark, finely arched brows and innocently sensuous lips, the troubled green eyes that stared up at him with uncertainty.

"Yes," he said softly, "I'm sure tonight will be better." He thought that she might smile at his words of reassurance, but she did not, and a vision of the Kathryn he had seen that first day crept into his mind. Kathryn in her filthy, tattered night rail, facing him with all the courage and composure of a lady of her station. Kathryn beseeching him for a bath.

St. Bart's had not been able to break her. Last night, he very nearly had.

"The footman is waiting to serve our plates," he said, fighting an urge to comfort her, yet wanting in some way to allay her fears. "Why don't we sit down and have something to eat?" She nodded, but she still looked uneasy. Lucien cursed himself. He had never been cruel to a woman, and even the volume of liquor he had consumed was no excuse for the way he'd behaved.

It was this damnable hunger he still felt for her. Even now, just watching her skirts sway around her hips as she crossed the room made his body begin to harden. Last night when he had seen her in the sheer blue nightgown lying in the big four-poster bed, he'd very nearly lost control. It wasn't like him. He regretted his brutal treatment, but at least he had an answer to the question that had haunted him.

*When you kissed me . . . when you touched me . . . it was magic.* Her words filtered through like a sweet, soothing balm. Kathryn's passion had not been a trick. Her response to him had been as real as his own. She might have played at seduction, but she was no harlot, and she had wanted him just as he had wanted her. The knowledge eased his mind, made him feel less a fool, even though a marriage between them could never work.

They sat down to a pot of hot chocolate and a platter of sugary cakes, which was about as much as Lucien's stomach could stand at the moment. "What are your plans for the day?" he asked, hoping to assuage a little of his guilt, though he'd be damned if he would apologize.

She glanced up, surprised he wished to converse. "I'm not . . . not exactly sure. I shall read for a while. Her Grace the duchess ran across a text she though I might enjoy. *On the Causes of Disease* by a man named Morgagni. She found it in the library at Carlyle Hall and was kind enough to lend it to me."

He couldn't help the frown that settled between his brows. Why she wanted to dabble in such a vulgar pastime he couldn't imagine. If she were his wife in truth, he would certainly put a stop to it.

"What about you, my lord?"

His eyes swung to hers. He was heading into London to visit his mistress, though he could hardly tell her that. He had suffered his lust for Kathryn long enough. He meant to take his ease with a warm, willing female, and the sooner the better. "I've business to attend in London. I won't be back till the end of the week."

If she was sorry he was leaving it didn't show, and for some strange reason the notion annoyed him. "I'm certain you'll be able to entertain yourself while I'm away—unless of course you wish to go with me," he added just to be perverse, knowing after what happened last night she was certain to refuse.

"I—I'm sure I would just be in the way," she said, with a quick glance out the window.

He took a sip of his chocolate, felt his stomach roll, and set the cup back down in its saucer. "Perhaps you're right. At any rate, I shall see you upon my return."

She said nothing more, and a few moments later, he excused himself and left her, making his way out of the breakfast parlor and heading upstairs to instruct his valet to pack a valise for his trip. He could nap in the carriage, sleep off the pounding in his head, and once he got to

Anna's, he could take his pleasure. Anna Quintain was as skillful a lover as she was beautiful, and he intended to ride her hard and often, till he drove all thoughts of Kathryn away.

He was certain it would work. It always had. The easiest way to get over his lust for a woman was to replace that woman with another.

It was exactly what Lucien meant to do.

Standing at an arrow slit that now served as a window in the Great Hall, Kathryn's favorite room in the castle, she watched the marquess climb aboard the Litchfield carriage. Her heart beat dully. As he rapped on the top with his silver-headed walking stick, instructing the coachman to make way, she felt a painful yearning in her breast.

It was unseemly for a bridegroom to abandon his wife the day after the wedding, but Lucien didn't care. There were no pretenses where this marriage was concerned. Considering it would be over in less than a year, it was probably better that there weren't.

Still, even after his treatment of her last night, she felt sad and lonely without him. She was no longer afraid of him. As angry as he was, the marquess hadn't hurt her. And this morning she had seen the regret in his eyes.

She tried to tell herself it was better he was gone, that perhaps she wouldn't feel that painful ache in her heart every time she saw him. Perhaps she wouldn't remember how incredibly virile he had looked when he had come into her bedchamber with his black hair mussed and his shirt undone, how, just for an instant before she'd seen the hard look on his face, she had wanted him to make love to her.

Kathryn walked over to the huge stone hearth, big enough to hold five grown men. She remembered the pride in Lucien's voice when he had spoken of the castle, telling her how Edward III had gifted it to his ancestors for valor in service to the king.

She wondered what he was doing in London and part

of her regretted that she had not gone with him. She missed him already, and if she had gone to London, she could have visited little Michael. Just the notion of returning to St. Bart's made her stomach roll with nausea, but she would have done it for Michael.

A dozen times since her escape from the madhouse, she had thought of the towheaded child. In the days that had followed, with her own life at risk, there was nothing she could do to help him. Now that she was free, her determination had begun to grow.

Though Michael had survived at St. Bart's the seven years since his birth, she couldn't stand to think of him living in that terrible place as he grew up. She wished she could go to Lucien for help, but after the trouble she had caused, she could hardly ask him now.

More and more she struggled with the problem of how she could help the child and prayed that until she did, he would be all right.

She thought of Michael and tried not to think of Lucien, tried not to wonder if the desire she had seen in his eyes last night would be satisfied by some other woman.

Sitting on a lavender satin chair in the corner of the frilly purple and white bedchamber of the town house he had let for Anna Quintain, Lucien took a sip of his brandy and propped a booted foot on the lavender satin ottoman in front of him.

For an instant, Anna frowned, then her smile fell back into place. "Make yourself comfortable, my lord. It won't take a moment for me to finish changing."

His eyes took in her voluptuous curves, the long, pale blond hair she had freed from its pins and allowed to stream down to her waist. "Take your time," he said, swirling the liquor in the bottom of his snifter. "I'm content just to watch the show."

Anna laughed at that, a throaty, seductive sound that slipped over a man like warm, clear honey. He had heard

it before, of course. Until now, he had never noticed how
false it rang.

He watched her movements as she propped a shapely
leg on the bench at the foot of the bed to remove her silk
stockings. The rest of her garments were mostly gone, her
hat and gloves, her plum silk gown and whalebone panniers. Only her corset and chemise, stockings and garters
remained.

Once those were gone, he would feast his eyes on the
her rose-tipped breasts and the thatch of pale hair at the
juncture of her legs. He was already aroused. As he
watched her bare more and more of her smooth, unblem-
ished skin, he could feel his shaft hardening uncomfortably inside his clothes.

His body had needs and Anna Quintain could fulfill
them. It was his mind that was having a problem.

Lucien watched her remove her lacy satin garters, strip
away her stockings one by one and toss them over a chair.
He waited as she crossed to where he sat and turned
around so he could unlace the corset that thrust up her
plump white breasts. He did so with less anticipation than
he had imagined, then waited as she slowly stripped away
her embroidered chemise.

She was naked and he was hard. His body wanted to
take her, to satisfy its lust as it hadn't been able to do for
weeks.

His mind thought of Kathryn and rebelled at the
thought.

Lucien swore a silent oath, hating Kathryn Grayson in
that moment, wishing he had never laid eyes on her.
When he had married her, it never occurred to him he
would feel guilty for bedding another woman.

It never occurred to him he wouldn't really want to.

Anna smiled in that teasing way of hers, moving the
small black patch on her cheek. "Come, my lord. Let me
help you undress." Anna reached for his hand, urging him
up from the chair.

He rose in the hope she could stir his interest as well

as his body, but the moment she slid her arms around his neck and kissed him, pressing her pendulous bosom against his chest, he knew that hope was lost. Her breath tasted faintly of mutton and wine, and her heavy perfume engulfed him. He cupped a breast but it felt too full, too weighty, and he thought of another, smaller, more delicate, perfectly formed to fit his hand.

Her tongue slid into his mouth with practiced skill, and he thought of Kathryn's tentative, innocently seductive kisses that night at the lodge. *When you kissed me ... when you touched me ... it was magic.* When Anna reached down to cup his fly and began to massage him, he swore another silent oath and pulled away.

"My lord?"

"I'm sorry, sweeting. This isn't going to work. Not tonight." Or any night in the future, he inwardly added. Whatever pleasure he'd once found with Anna Quintain was apparently gone.

"I apologize, my lord, if I have done something to displease you. If you'll just give me a moment—" She reached down to stroke him again, but he turned away, his groin still hard and throbbing.

"It's nothing you've done, Anna. At present, I simply have too much on my mind." Anna looked genuinely upset. It was the first real emotion she had shown since his arrival at the town house. Turning away from her, he reached for his waistcoat, drew a pouch of coins from the pocket, and set them on the dresser. "Buy yourself something pretty to wear for the next time I am here."

It was a small lie, since he wouldn't be returning, but it would save them both embarrassment. In the morning, he would send word to his solicitor, have Nathaniel settle a reasonable sum on her and end the arrangement.

He was surprised to feel a trickle of relief.

He told himself it wasn't because of Kathryn. Anna Quintain simply didn't interest him as she had before. He would visit Madame Charmaine's Pleasure Barge and find a woman who did.

Lucien set his jaw as he stepped out onto the porch of the town house. He was lying to himself and he knew it. The woman he wanted was living under his very roof, sleeping down the hall from the master's suite at Castle Running. The trouble was, once he bedded her, he would be stuck with her.

Lucien clenched his teeth so hard a pain shot into his jaw. Kathryn Grayson was the last person he wanted for a wife, the very sort of woman he had sworn never to marry. For a few nights of pleasure, he would face a lifetime of hell with a willful little baggage so outrageous in her pursuits she had wound up in a madhouse.

A woman, forgodsake, who had cut up a human body to discover the way it worked! What sort of a woman would attempt such an abomination? What sort brewed potions and read books on disease and gunshot wounds? Whatever sort it was, it wasn't the sort he wanted.

What he wanted was a sweet, docile wife like Allison Hartman, a pretty bit of fluff who would obey his commands and bear him half a dozen children. In less than a year he would be free to find another such woman. All he had to do was stay away from Kathryn, and in a short time his life could be put back in order. His plans to marry and produce an heir could go forward exactly as he had intended.

He would do it, he vowed. How hard could it be to resist one slender woman?

From her upstairs bedchamber window, Winifred Montaine DeWitt watched her nephew lead his tall black stallion to the front of the stable and hand the reins to a groom. After a brief sojourn to London, he had returned to the castle more restless and withdrawn than he was before. He had been riding every day, inspecting his properties, visiting his tenants, spending his evenings at the Quill and Sword Tavern in the village.

Winnie knew the reason, of course. Lucien was a normal, virile man, married to a young and beautiful woman. He wanted to make love to her.

The problem was he refused.

Winnie let the heavy green velvet curtain fall back into place, turned and crossed the room. She was determined to speak to him, to try and talk some sense into his stubborn head. Out the door and down the hall. She had almost reached the bottom of the stairs leading into the entry when the front door opened and Nathaniel Whitley walked in.

Winnie paused on the stairs to watch his graceful movements as he removed his tricorn hat, handed it to the butler, and swept off his heavy woolen cloak.

When he glanced up, he saw her and smiled. "Lady Beckford. It's a pleasure to see you again."

"You're looking well, Nathaniel." And impossibly handsome, she thought, with the silver sparkling in his coffee-brown hair and a look of appreciation in his eyes. They were the same summer-blue she remembered, though now tiny laugh lines crinkled at the corners. He had been such a serious youth. She wondered if the man he'd become had learned to laugh at the oddities of life.

"I'm here to see your nephew. I've started the procedure to secure Lady Litchfield's inheritance. I believe the marquess is expecting me."

"I saw him ride in. I'll have Reeves tell him you are here. In the meantime, why don't you wait for him in his study?"

Nathaniel made a faint bow of his head and she led him down the hall. Once they were inside the dark, wood-paneled room that smelled faintly of candle smoke and aging leather, she moved to the bell pull and rang for tea.

"Lucien should be here any moment. Make yourself comfortable until he arrives." She started for the door, but Nat's voice stopped her.

"I don't suppose you would be willing to keep me company until he gets here?"

A flush rose into her cheeks. She shouldn't. Nat Whitley was far too attractive. "All right," she heard herself say, and inwardly she winced. Nat waited while she took a place on the sofa, then sat down across from her in a deep leather chair.

"How long has it been, Winnie? By my calculations nearly twenty years." Almost twenty-one, she thought. She would never forget the last time she had seen him. The day her father had denied Nat's suit and decreed she marry Richard DeWitt, a wealthy viscount more suitable to her station as the daughter of a marquess.

"It seems forever, doesn't it? In those days we were so young."

"You're still young, Winnie. You look more like a girl than the woman you have become." Winnie glanced away, trying not to be flattered by his words, fighting not to look nervous. All the while he watched her, his eyes so blue and intense. It did odd things to her insides, made her want to run from the room.

Made her want to stay right where she was.

He had a way of looking at her that made her remember the past, the days when she had been a foolish young girl who'd believed she was in love with him. Twenty years later, those bright blue eyes still created all manner of havoc, made her feel that same sweet stirring in her blood that she had felt as a girl.

The tea arrived, but Lucien didn't. Winnie poured and handed Nat a cup, then poured one for herself.

"I've been thinking about you," Nat said softly. "I've thought of little else since I saw you the last time I was here."

Something tightened in her stomach. Her teacup clattered as she set it down in the saucer. "As you said, we haven't seen each other in a good many years. I suppose it's only natural you would be curious about me."

Nat frowned. He uncrossed his legs and set his cup and saucer down on the table. She couldn't help noticing the fine muscles in his calves beneath his white silk stockings, the breadth of his shoulders in his tailored brown wool coat.

"That isn't what I meant," he said.

The heat returned to her cheeks. The conversation was growing highly improper. "What do you mean, then, Nat?" She hoped she had misunderstood. In their younger days, they'd thought they were in love, but that was years ago. Since then he had met and married Emma Hanson. They had at least three grown children, probably even grandchildren.

"I mean that I would very much like to see you. I realize what I'm asking has caught you off guard. I'm sure there would be problems in doing so, but—"

Winnie came to her feet, her face hot with indignation. "You overstep yourself, Mr. Whitley. I realize there was a time we meant a good deal to each other, but that was long ago." *Before you were someone else's husband.* "If you think I am interested in any sort of relation with a . . . with *you,* you are very sorely mistaken."

Nat clamped his jaw. He made a curt inclination of his head. "Then I beg your pardon, my lady. I am sorry if I have offended you." But he didn't look sorry at all. Instead, he looked angry.

Winnie ignored the way those accusing blue eyes made her feel. "Good afternoon, Mr. Whitley. If you will excuse me, there are matters that need my attention." Stepping out into the hall, she closed the door behind her, feeling as if a heavy weight had settled itself on her chest. Nat had always been a man of the highest morals. At least she remembered him that way.

Once she'd believed she was in love with him. Perhaps she still imagined he was the gallant hero she had thought him then—instead of the unconscionable rake that he had become.

Lucien stood at the rear of the stable, watching Kathryn and a groom ride out across the fields toward the woods. In the past two weeks, she had taken up riding late in the morning, heedless of the dampness or the frosty chill in the air. Last night a thin layer of powdery snow had fallen over the landscape, making the tracks of the horses' hooves clearly visible in the light coating of ice.

"Saddle Blade," Lucien said to Bennie Taylor, returned now to his job as a groom. "I've an errand to run in the village. I believe I shall take the shortcut through the forest."

"Yes, milord." The lanky boy headed off to do his master's bidding. Lucien watched Kathryn disappear into the woods, her dark red velvet riding habit flashing here and there between the trees. She was an excellent rider, he had discovered, and obviously enjoyed the out-of-doors. Why he decided to follow her he couldn't really say, only that he was curious where she might be going.

Since his return from London, he had been scrupulously avoiding her, which, he'd discovered, was no easy task. Kathryn had more energy than any two normal women. Wherever he went he stumbled upon her: in the breakfast parlor, though he arrived at an hour that was unfashionably early; in the library, where she holed up to read her damnable medical texts; in the conservatory, where she had planted a small patch of herbs; and now here in the stable.

Each time he saw her, he would notice something new about her, the way the dark centers of her eyes would expand the moment he appeared, the way the wind tossed wisps of her hair so appealingly around her face, the way her small breasts moved beneath the bodice of her gown. Each time he saw her, his desire for her grew, yet he was determined to ignore it.

Still, he was curious. She was his wife, at least for the present. What she did reflected on him and was, therefore, his business until they parted. There were a number of handsome young rogues in the village, and he had experienced firsthand her passionate nature. He'd be damned if he would allow her to trifle with one of them.

He followed the tracks into the woods and out into the

open field beyond. Instead of heading into the village as
he had been certain they would, the tracks angled off to
the west toward a small parcel of land that was occupied
by one of his tenants. When he topped the rise, he saw
her horse out in front of the whitewashed, thatched-roof
cottage, her groom holding the reins while she went inside.

Lucien watched from a cluster of trees on the knoll,
saw her come out of the house wearing a smile and clutching a cloth sack in her hand. She tied it behind her saddle
and the groom helped her remount the little sorrel mare.
She said something to the gangly young man who accompanied her, wheeled the horse, dug in her small booted
heels, and made a mad dash up the hill, the groom trying
frantically to catch up with her.

They were racing, he saw as she flashed by him with
a burst of speed, and he felt the pull of a smile. He could
hear her laughter echoing through the woods and it was
obvious how much she was enjoying herself. For an instant, he wished he could take up the challenge she had
posed to the groom and race after her. Instead he reined
the stallion back onto the trail and down to the house to
discover what Kathryn was about.

Sarah Whitelawn came to the door at his knock, a little
blond girl peeking around her skirts. Lucien made the
apropriate greeting, then asked after Kathryn.

"Her ladyship were bringin' me babe a potion," Sarah
Whitelawn replied. "Little Andy'd been sick with the
colic for nearly a week when I chanced upon your lady
on the path to the village. She were kind enough to offer
her help."

Lucien frowned. "If the child needed a remedy, there
is an apothecary in the village. Why did you not merely
go to him?"

"Oh, I did, milord. Didn't seem ta help and cost three
shillings, ta boot." She smiled, showing a hole where one
of her eye teeth was missing. "Her ladyship's potion done
the trick. Said it were made of angelica seeds, honey, and

water. She brought me a bit more today, just in case it were ta come back again."

Lucien said nothing to that. Thank God the damnable stuff had done a better job with the babe than the one she had concocted for Muriel Roth.

Lucien stepped back from the porch. "Thank you, Mrs. Whitelawn. Be sure to tell Terence if he needs any help repairing that broken plough shed, I'll be happy to send over my cooper."

The woman smiled. "I'll tell 'im, milord."

Lucien nodded in farewell and swung up into the saddle, heading back up the hill toward the castle. The sun was warm on his back across the fields, but it was shady and colder in the shadows of the trees in the forest. The stallion followed the winding path, heading deeper into the woods, then a flash of dark red on the ground up ahead caught his eye.

Worry splintered through him. He urged the horse into a gallop, racing over the uneven trail, saw Kathryn lying on the ground in a heap of red velvet, her jaunty little hat a few feet away. Her eyes were closed and there was no sign of the groom or Kathryn's little mare.

The beating of his heart jolted up another notch. He swung down from the stallion before the horse had come to a stop and raced to where she lay beside a fallen tree. Her cloak had been spread over her, but the ground was so cold she shivered. Her eyes came open at the sound of his rapid footfalls crunching on the thin layer of snow.

"Kathryn! Forgodsake, what happened?"

She gave him a valiant smile. "My fault. We were racing. There was a branch I didn't see. Knocked the wind out of me and scared poor Joey half to death. I sent him back to the castle for help."

He pulled off his kidskin gloves as he knelt beside her. "Dammit, you are smart enough to know better than to be racing in a place like this. It's too bloody dangerous."

Some of the pallor left her cheeks, which flushed a soft

shade of rose. "I know. We were just having so much fun."

Lucien felt a twinge of irritation. Fun riding with her groom instead of with him. He was her husband, yet he enjoyed none of the pleasures that went along with the dubious title. He tamped the feeling down. "Let's see if there is anything broken."

"I don't think there is, but I jarred my ribs a good bit. And I must have sprained my ankle."

Lucien gently made his way up each of her arms, looking for lacerations, checking for fractures, then he carefully probed her rib cage, eliciting a sharply sucked-in breath. "You may have cracked a rib. We had better wait for the wagon before we try to move you."

"Perhaps they are only bruised. They don't really hurt enough to be broken."

He nodded, hoping she was right, thinking there weren't many women who would know that much about ribs. Thinking how slender her body felt beneath his hands, and how hard it was to stop touching her before he reached those small, enticing, cone-shaped breasts. "Let's take a look at that ankle."

Reaching for the hem of her heavy velvet riding skirt, he raised it, her cloak, and several layers of petticoats up to her knees, trying to ignore the feminine display of lacy garters and white silk stockings.

"It's the left one," she said with none of the maidenly embarrassment he would have encountered with another woman. Unlacing her leather riding boot, he gently pulled it off and couldn't help noticing her pretty stockinged feet.

"It's badly swollen." He moved the ankle gently, testing it but trying not to hurt her. "I don't think it's broken."

The wagon rumbled around a corner in the distance, Aunt Winnie on the seat next to Bennie Taylor while young Joey Hampton, Kathryn's groom, rode in the back.

"Lucien!" Winnie leapt to her feet so quickly she almost fell out of the wagon. "Thank heavens you are here.

How is she? Is she all right?" The wagon creaked to a halt and he went to help her down.

"She's injured her ribs and sprained an ankle. We'll have Dr. Fredericks take a look at her as soon as we get home."

Kathryn tried to sit up, hissed as pain shot into her ribs, and lay back down. "I don't need a doctor. If you'll wrap my ankle in some snow and I stay off it, I'll be fine in a couple of days. We can bandage my ribs when I get home."

Lucien frowned. " 'Physician, heal thyself'? If that is what you are thinking, my lady, you may simply think again."

" 'God heals and the doctor takes the fee,' " she tossed back to him. "I tell you I shall be fine."

His lips twitched. He couldn't help it. She was a saucy little baggage. "You're my wife. As long as that fact remains, you are my responsibility—hence, you will do as I say."

Kathryn didn't argue, just set her mouth at a mulish angle and let him lift her up. Her arms slid around his neck and the moment they did, her eyes locked with his. Something passed between them, something hot and intense that had nothing at all to do with Kathryn's injury and everything to do with the last time he had carried her that way, over to the sofa in the lodge where he meant to, very slowly and quite thoroughly, ravish her beautiful body.

Kathryn quickly glanced away. Inside his breeches, he went hard. Lucien silently cursed. Setting his jaw against the throbbing in his groin, he carted her over to the wagon, gently laid her down on the pallet of blankets in the rear, and they set off for the house.

Lucien couldn't wait to get her there. With every passing day, his vow to ignore Kathryn Grayson was getting harder and harder to keep. With a last glance at the wagon, he grimly gripped the reins and swung up on the back of his horse.

# THIRTEEN

Jason Sinclair reined up in front of the huge stone castle just three miles west of Carlyle Hall. Swinging down from the saddle, he handed the reins of his big black gelding to the tall, thin footman who rushed down from the porch.

"Evenin', Your Grace," the young man said, careful to stay back from Blackie's dancing hooves.

"Don't worry, lad, he'll settle down in a minute. Had a good run across the fields, but it never seems to be enough. Take good care of him, will you?"

"Aye, sir." As the footman led the horse off toward the stables at the rear of the house, Jason climbed the wide stone stairs leading into the entry, eager for his evening of gaming with Lucien.

As often as they could manage, the two men met to play chess, sometimes at Carlyle Hall, tonight at Castle Running. Busy with some important papers he'd had to finish, Jason had sent word that he wouldn't be able to join the marquess for supper as he usually did, but was still planning to arrive for chess. Though the air was chill, the sky remained clear, lit by a big silver moon and a bright scattering of stars, making the shortcut he took through the fields easy to traverse.

He'd thought about postponing the game, since he would have to be late, but Velvet had been worried about Lucien and concerned for his bride, and she was determined Jason should discover how things were progressing between the pair.

With a brief nod at the butler, Jason continued past him down the hall to Lucien's study. The door was open, the marquess seated behind his desk, sipping a glass of brandy.

It was obviously not his first.

"For a man who is usually a moderate drinker, you are certainly becoming a sot." Jason grinned. "Then again, perhaps I should pour you another—you'll have a deuce of a time beating me at chess."

Lucien grumbled something beneath his breath, set the half-full snifter back down on his desk. "This is only my second glass. I am hardly foxed, and tonight I intend to trounce you quite soundly."

Jason glanced toward the chessboard, the beautiful carved ivory and ebony pieces waiting on a mother-of-pearl-inlaid black chessboard on a table before the fire.

"All right, then, let's get to it . . . though first I believe I shall join you in that drink." He moved to the sideboard while Lucien settled himself in a comfortable leather chair on one side of the board.

"How is Velvet?" Litchfield asked.

"Busy with holiday preparations. The children love Christmastide, and it is certainly my wife's favorite time of year. Her grandfather has been regaling us with tales of family holidays past. It's amazing the way the earl can remember what happened twenty years ago, but not what happened at supper the night before."

Lucien nodded. He had always liked the aging Earl of Haversham, Velvet's grandfather, even if he was growing more and more forgetful. "My aunt has been muttering about my lack of holiday spirit. Now that my wedding to Allison is a thing of the past, Aunt Winnie grows eager to entertain. I suppose I shall have to give in to her nagging and allow her to plan a few festivities."

"Sounds like a good idea."

Lucien took a sip of his drink. "Lately, she's been a bit out of sorts. I imagine it is simply the holidays and perhaps missing her late husband. It is her first Christmas here at the castle. Perhaps it would help if we did some decorating, gave the place a bit of cheer."

Jason smiled. "I'm sure it would, and your wife might enjoy it as well."

Lucien's long-fingered hand paused in the act of lifting the ebony pawn he was about to move, the white lace on his cuff draping gracefully over the piece he held several inches above the board. "Kathryn is my wife in name only. What she would or wouldn't enjoy is of no concern to me."

Jason wisely ignored that. "How is she?"

He shrugged as if he didn't really care, but a slight tension crept into his shoulders. "She took a bad spill riding last week. Sprained her ankle and bruised her ribs. Thankfully, she is very nearly recovered." The edge of a smile touched his lips. "She is a feisty little baggage. Quite an accomplished rider. Took the spill racing her groom through the woods. Witless thing to do, and you may be certain I told her so. Still, she was quite a sight with her red skirts flying and that young groom racing along in her dust."

Jason smiled and took a sip of his drink. "From what I've seen, the lady has any number of interesting qualities."

"I suppose that's true."

"But still, you are determined to end the marriage."

Lucien moved another of his pawns out two spaces. "We are not at all well suited."

Jason countered the move with an up-and-over jump of his ivory horse. "You want her," he said casually. "I can see it in your eyes whenever you look at her."

Lucien's gaze found Jason's across the chessboard. It suddenly looked hard as steel. "The woman duped me.

She made a fool out of me in front of half of England. Do you actually believe I can simply forget that?"

"She was desperate. Perhaps in her situation, you would have done the same."

Lucien made no comment, but his fingers tightened around the bishop he slid out through the opening he had created on the board.

"You told me when I married Velvet and refused to consummate the marriage that I was a fool. You said if she belonged to you, she would be spending her nights in your bed. Well, now I am saying those words to you."

Lucien's mouth went thin. "The woman betrayed me, dammit. For all I know she *is* insane. Forgodsake, man, the woman escaped from a madhouse!"

A small gasp sounded at the door and both men turned in unison to see Kathryn standing in the opening clad in a blue quilted wrapper, her hair unbound and hanging down past her shoulders. Her hands were shaking, her face as pale as the white beeswax candle she carried.

"Kathryn!" Lucien stood up so quickly, the chessboard toppled over, scattering pieces across the parquet floor. He cursed roundly, but didn't stop walking, striding rapidly toward the door. By the time he reached it, Kathryn had fled, her footsteps ringing down the hall, her injured ankle giving the sound a slightly out-of-rhythm cadence.

"Kathryn!" Lucien quickened his pace, determined to catch her, his heavier footfalls pounding along behind her.

As the sounds began to fade, Jason sighed and came up from his chair. It was obvious the chess game was over. He frowned to recall the look of horror on Kathryn's pretty face and wondered at the upcoming encounter between the two. Walking out of the study, he made his way back to the entry where the tall, stoic Reeves handed him his hat and cloak.

Sounds drifted down from the upstairs hallway, but Reeves dutifully ignored them. The last thing Jason heard as he strode out to collect his horse was the sound of his friend's broad shoulder slamming against Kathryn's locked door.

Jason grinned and continued on toward the stable.

"Dammit, Kathryn, let me in!" Lucien swore a savage oath, but it didn't do the slightest bit of good. The door remained solidly closed and that made him even more determined. He slammed his shoulder against the heavy wood one last time, and the iron latch gave way, tore out of the frame on the opposite side, and he exploded into the room.

Kathryn gave a little gasp of surprise and took a step backward, her green eyes huge in the pale oval of her face. Ignoring the broken latch, which hung in useless pieces, he paused long enough to close the door, then continued toward his quarry, who stood facing him a few feet away, her chin up and her shoulders squared. In the flickering light of the candle, he could see there were tears on her cheeks.

His breath hissed out as something painful squeezed inside him. He thought of all Kathryn had suffered and hated himself in that moment for hurting her again.

"I'm sorry," he said softly, gently, moving toward her as if she were some small injured animal who might decide to bolt, which was exactly how she looked. "I didn't mean that, Kathryn. You know I didn't. I was angry. I have been since that night at the lodge. You tricked me and I resented you for it. But I didn't mean what I said. You are not the least insane."

Kathryn shook her head, brushed at the wetness on her cheeks. "But you aren't certain, are you? You don't . . . don't really know for sure." She looked fragile and vulnerable, and a band of regret squeezed around his chest.

"Of course I know, dammit. If I really believed you were crazy there is no one on this earth who could have forced me to marry you." But she didn't look convinced and again he regretted his thoughtless words.

Big green eyes fixed on his face. "If I could only do

it over . . ." She wiped at the wetness. "I'd never trap you the way I did. I was just so desperate . . . and I really believed it would all work out."

He moved slowly toward her and she didn't run, just let him pull her against him and enclose her in his arms. She turned her face into his shoulder, curled her slim fingers into the lapels of his coat, her slight body trembling with sobs.

"Hush," he whispered, stroking her hair. "What's done is over and past. Crying will do neither of us any good."

"I never meant to hurt you. You were the best friend I ever had."

But he wasn't simply a friend, he thought. He was her husband. And the feel of her slender woman's body, the scent of her soft perfume, reminded him how much he wanted her. Her hair felt like silk in his hands, and beneath her quilted wrapper her small breasts rubbed against the front of his white lawn shirt.

Lucien tilted her face up, used the pad of his thumb to brush away the last of her tears. "Come, love, please don't cry."

Her bottom lip trembled. Her lashes were spiky with moisture, her eyes softly luminous. Inside his breeches, he was hard and throbbing. Need pulsed in his blood, began to grow like a beast inside him. His thumb caressed her jaw, sliding back and forth, testing the smoothness of her skin. Her lips were full and slightly parted. He remembered how sweet they tasted that night at the lodge, how perfectly they molded with his own. He remembered the way she had melted against him, fitting her body to his like the missing piece of a puzzle.

He leaned toward her, bent his head and kissed her as he had wanted to do for so long. It was a gentle kiss, undemanding, and Kathryn's surprise lasted only an instant, then her eyes slowly closed, her arms crept around his neck, and her slender body pressed the length of his.

Lucien groaned. Heat unfurled in his belly. Desire sank into his bones. He told himself to end the kiss, that nothing but disaster could come of it, but his body wouldn't listen. Blood pounded in his ears and surged into his groin. Need rushed over him, hot and unbearably intense. Her small pointed breasts pillowed against his chest. He thought how sweetly erotic they felt, and his hold on rational thought eroded even further.

Lucien deepened the kiss and a soft sob of surrender escaped from Kathryn's throat. He ravaged her mouth, took her deeply with his tongue, and felt the silky glide of hers in response. Beneath her quilted wrapper, her nipples formed hard little buds and he wanted desperately to touch them. He pulled the sash on her robe, worked the buttons down the front one by one, and eased the robe off her shoulders, letting it fall to a heap on the floor. She wore a night rail beneath, a thin white barrier that reminded him of her innocence and inflamed his passions even more.

He wondered vaguely if she had been misused at St. Bart's, but her sweet return of his passion said that she wasn't afraid, and the thought slid away on a wave of heat.

He kissed the side of her neck, then returned to her mouth, tilting his head first one way and then the other, wanting more, unable to get enough. He felt as if he were drowning, barely able to breathe, yet he refused to surface for air. His thigh pressed between her legs. Kathryn made a soft little gasp at the feel of his hardness against her and her fingers dug into his shoulders.

Heat rolled through him. He kissed her again, almost savagely, and Kathryn returned the kiss. His hand cupped a breast through the cotton of her gown, but it wasn't enough. He pulled the string on her night rail and slid it off her shoulders, ripping it a little in his haste to be rid of it. He kissed his way down her neck to the tight, trembling bud of her nipple, laved the end, then sucked the fullness into his mouth.

His loins were on fire. He shoved the nightgown off

her hips to the floor, lifted her naked body into his arms, and strode over to the bed.

"The door . . ." she whispered, staring worriedly at the broken latch.

"No one would dare," he said, and it was the truth. He kissed her again, then paused to strip off his shirt. He didn't want to wait, wanted to simply unbutton his breeches, release himself, and bury himself inside her; to impale himself and satisfy his aching need. Instead, he sat down and tugged off his boots, unfastened and removed his breeches, then joined her on the bed. When he started to kiss her again, Kathryn pressed a hand to his chest to stop him.

"Are you certain, Lucien? Are you sure this is what you want? If we make love, the annulment . . . we won't be able to—"

He silenced her with a long and very thorough kiss, kissed the side of her neck, then her ear. "You're my wife," he said softly. "I want you and nothing else matters." Some vague part of him warned him it wasn't the truth, that what happened this night mattered a very great deal, but he was too far gone to care. Instead, he kissed her, stroked her small, exquisite breasts, slid his palm over the flat spot below her navel and eased a finger inside her.

Kathryn went tense, her long legs closing around his hand.

"Trust me. Let me make this good for us both."

His words seemed to reassure her. She relaxed a little, and he settled himself between her legs. Stroking her gently, then more deeply, he set up a rhythm that had her squirming on the mattress, her fingers biting into his shoulders.

"Lucien, please, I can't . . . I don't . . . don't think I can stand any more."

"Relax, love. Just take it easy." He was achingly hard, his heavy arousal throbbing. He shifted his position and his hardness pressed into the warm, slick flesh at the opening of her passage. "Trust me and let yourself go." Gently he eased himself inside, trying not to hurt her. She was wet and hot, and so tight he set his jaw against the excruciating pleasure that threatened to shatter his control. When he reached her maidenhead, his eyes closed briefly in relief. He held himself in check a few moments more, letting her adjust to him.

"Lucien?" Tentative and uncertain, yet her body moved restlessly beneath him.

A hot fierce kiss, and he drove himself home, impaling himself to the hilt. A single, sharp breath came from Kathryn, then she was returning his kiss, reaching up to touch him, stroking her hands over his ribs, testing the muscles and sinews as if she wanted to learn every inch of him.

"God, Kathryn . . ." Her innocently passionate response drove him nearly insane. He couldn't hold back any longer. He'd been celibate too long and he wanted her far too badly. Dragging his hardness out, he drove into her again. Out and then in, taking her deeply, pounding and pounding, feeling the heat boil up through his skin. His climax loomed near. He teetered on the brink, holding himself in check by sheer force of will, determined to give her pleasure.

When Kathryn arched upward, taking him deeper still, he exploded over the edge. A few more driving thrusts, and her body tightened around him. Kathryn arched beneath him, reaching her own release, her body straining upward like a bow.

Though pleasuring her was exactly his intention, surprise filtered through him. Kathryn had been a virgin, untried and completely naïve, yet her body had responded with the passion of a seasoned lover. As forthright as she was, perhaps he should have guessed she would enjoy the pleasures of the flesh. Still, it reminded him how different she was from the sort of woman he had wanted to marry.

As the hot sensations faded and his senses slowly returned, he couldn't help wondering what his wedding night might have been like with Allison Hartman.

•      •      •

In the late hours of the night, Kathryn lay awake in her big four-poster bed, staring up at the plaster molding on the ceiling. Her body ached in places it never had before and the soft throbbing between her legs reminded her that she was no longer a virgin.

Lucien had made love to her. He had given her pleasure unlike anything she could have imagined. He had been savage in his need of her and yet he had been gentle. Afterward she had fallen asleep in his arms.

She'd awakened a few hours later, disoriented at first, until she realized exactly where she was and that the man beside her was her husband, that he was also awake and watching her with those fierce black eyes, that his hard length pressed against her, wanting to be inside her again.

Kathryn had turned to welcome him, glad he had made her his wife, eager to experience the incredible passion she had known with him before. She was in love with him. She wanted to show him how much she cared, to make up for the trouble she had caused him.

Instead, he turned away, kissed the top of her head, and enfolded her in his arms.

"Go to sleep," he said softly. "You will be sore in the morning."

At the time she had told herself he was simply taking care not to hurt her. Now, staring at the empty place in the bed beside her, she remembered the faint tension in his jaw, the glint of something she couldn't quite read in those black, silver-flecked eyes.

Her husband was gone and worry coiled up beneath her ribs. For hours, Kathryn lay beneath the covers, wishing the dawn would come, wishing it wouldn't. Wishing she could see him, know what he was thinking. Wishing she wouldn't have to face him and remember the intimate things they had done.

Finally, the light of day slipped through the windows, and Kathryn, her muscles sore and aching, dragged her sluggish body out of bed. Choosing a simple burgundy wool gown, she sent for Fanny to help her do up the buttons, braided her hair and pinned it up, then made her way downstairs. Whatever problems had been created by their rash behavior last night she would have to face, and sooner was better than later.

Kathryn entered the breakfast parlor at the rear of the house, hoping Lucien would be there, but she found only Aunt Winnie. The slender blond woman was staring out the window, her expression quietly pensive, perhaps even melancholy, and Kathryn wondered what it was she was thinking.

She didn't have time to ask. Winnie spotted her and the moment slipped away.

"My dear, you look exhausted," she said with a worried frown. Then she smiled. "Ah, but I suppose that is to be expected. Appeasing the needs of a virile man like my nephew would tax any mortal woman."

Kathryn flushed to the tips of her toes. "How did . . . how did you know?" Good lord, did she look different somehow? Could Winnie guess the intimate things the marquess had done to her? The things she had done to him?

Winnie just laughed. "Good heavens, my dear, when a man breaks down a woman's bedchamber door, it only stands to reason he has more in mind than simple conversation."

Perhaps that was so, but thinking of the way he had left her, she had the terrible suspicion his goal had not been met. Surely, if she had pleased him, he would have wanted to make love to her again.

Kathryn sat down at the table across from Winnie, and the footman served her, filling a plate with an array of foodstuffs she would never be able to eat. Basted eggs, roast pheasant, a slice of Gloucester cheese, and a piece of fresh baked bread. Kathryn took a tentative bite, but the food tasted like paper in her mouth.

She pushed it around on her plate. "Do you know where the marquess has gone?" she asked in a manner she hoped sounded nonchalant.

Winnie's pale brows pulled into a frown. "Why, I assumed he was with you . . . at least until you came down here. Are you saying he did not spend the night?"

"No, he . . . No," she whispered, barely able to force out the word.

"Oh, dear." Winnie pasted on a too-bright smile that didn't fool Kathryn for a moment. "Well, he probably had important business, perhaps an early meeting with one of his tenants. You know how he is. Everything according to schedule."

But his "wedding night" was highly unscheduled and obviously Lucien was filled with regret. Kathryn tried to force down another bit of eggs but they tasted cold and greasy and stuck in her throat. She shoved back her nearly untouched plate and set her napkin back down on the table.

"I hope you don't mind, Aunt Winnie. I discover I'm not feeling very well. I'm sure it's nothing, perhaps a little too much . . . excitement."

Winnie smiled kindly. "Of course, my dear. Why don't you go back upstairs and rest? I'll have a bath sent up to your room. Afterward you can nap for a while. I'll have Fanny bring up something for you to eat a little later."

Kathryn simply nodded. Her heart beat dully and her chest felt tight. She was more miserable now than she had been before. It seemed every time she tried to make things right, instead she made them worse.

*Even if you're married to a man who doesn't want you, at least you are safe from Dunstan.*

The words rose out of nowhere, comforting words, for she recognized them as the truth. The notion cheered her a little. True, she was in love with a man who didn't love her, but she was young and she was free and her whole life stretched before her. She had her own future, her own dreams. She refused to spend time languishing over a man who didn't want her.

Though it took a burst of will, Kathryn stiffened her spine. She didn't need Lucien Montaine to make her happy. She had her studies, the challenge of her work, and she had already begun to help a few of the people in the village. Aside from that, there was little Michael to consider. One way or another, she intended to free him from St. Bart's.

Kathryn squared her shoulders. She'd been taking care of herself since her father died. Except as protection from her uncle, she didn't need a husband. She had never really wanted one. And if, after last night, she was not with child, they could still get that annulment.

If Lucien didn't want her, so be it. She was tired of begging his forgiveness, tired of trying to make up for the mistake she had made in forcing the marriage. From now on, she would stay away from Lucien Montaine. For all she cared, the man could go straight to Hades.

# FOURTEEN

Light snow flew, more an icy sleet, and it melted as soon
as it hit the ground. Still, a chill air whipped through the
trees and slithered beneath the mullioned windows of the
Quill and Sword Tavern.

Sitting at a scarred wooden table in the corner, Lucien
absently sipped a tankard of ale. The taproom was dark
and smoky, the stone walls thick, and the timbered ceiling
low. It smelled of sour ale and stale tobacco.

Still, it was his secret hideaway, a place he came when
he wanted to escape his duties at Castle Running, as he
was doing tonight. He glanced around the taproom, mildly
observing the occupants: a pair of red-uniformed soldiers,
home on leave and already well into a deep rum fuddle;
the smithy from the stable who was dealing a hand of
cards; the big-breasted tavern maid who always let him
know she was eager for a tumble if the notion should
arise—along with anything else.

He had never taken her up on the offer. As randy as
he was in the days since he had taken his little wife to
bed, for a moment, he actually considered it.

Lucien sighed into the smoky, dimly lit interior. How
the bloody hell had he gotten himself into such a fix?

Damn, but he was a fool. Though he wasn't in the mood for liquor, he sipped his drink, just to have something to do. Tipping his chair back against the wall, he stretched his legs out in front of him and thought how much his life had changed since he had met Kathryn Grayson.

His sigh was lost in the noise of the taproom. Why did everyone around him seem so cheerful, while he felt so morose? He sat for a while in silence, then glanced up as the door to the tavern swung open, letting in a cold draft of air. Lucien watched a familiar brawny figure duck his head through the opening and step inside the taproom.

By the light of the fire in the old stone hearth, Jason Sinclair surveyed the occupants in the tavern, grinned, and strode straight toward him. He dragged out a ladder-backed chair, flipped it around, and sat down astride it.

"I went by to see you," Jason said. "When no one seemed to know where you'd gone, I figured you might be here."

Lucien straightened, righting the chair he leaned back in, and set his nearly full tankard back down on the table. "Well, you've found me. This is the only place I could think to go where I could keep my sanity."

Jason arched a brow. "Trouble at home?"

"You might say that."

"Worse than the night I came to play chess? I heard you pounding away at Kathryn's door. I imagine you got in."

Lucien didn't reply and the fact he didn't was answer enough for Jason.

He smiled. "I wish I'd been a fly on the wall. I would have loved to have seen your wife's face when you came charging through the door like a raging bull."

Lucien grunted, remembering the scene all too well. "Suffice it to say, the lady is now my wife in truth. There won't be any annulment."

The tavern maid, Sadie Jenson, arrived just then, interrupting the conversation. "What can I get for ye, Yer Grace?" she said to Jason, who was also well-known in the tavern. She was pretty in an overblown way, her hair a flaxen blond, her hips wide, but round and tight and enticing when she moved.

Jason cocked his head toward Lucien. "Bring me a tankard of whatever it is my friend is drinking."

Sadie nodded. "Right, ye are, luv." She walked seductively back to the rough plank bar and Lucien's gaze followed. He noticed Jason's did not. Unlike himself, it was obvious his friend was well satisfied at home. The fact was more than a little disturbing.

"You said you were looking for me. Did you want something, or were you simply dropping by to see how I'd fared with my wife?"

"Actually, Velvet wanted me to come. She was hoping I could convince you and Kathryn—and your aunt, of course—to join us for a small house party on the eve before Christmas. I realize you might have plans, now that you have a family of your own, but—"

"A family? I'd hardly call it that."

The tavern maid appeared, set the pewter tankard of ale down on the table, smiled at Lucien, then faded quietly away.

"Well, you've a wife now, at least. That is a start."

"Physical attraction has never been part of the problem."

Jason frowned. "Then what the devil is?"

Lucien ran a hand over his hair, smoothing several loose black strands away from his face. "God help me, I don't know. Every time I look at her, I want her. She is nothing at all what I imagined a wife to be, but I want her just the same. The odd thing is, the more I lust for her, the more I stay away."

Jason mulled that over, took a long drink of his ale. He mopped the foam from his mouth with the back of one big hand and set the mug back down on the table. "You know what I think? I think she scares you. She is intelligent, well educated, and extremely passionate by nature. She makes you feel things you don't want to feel and it frightens you to death."

"That's ridiculous. She is barely a woman, little more than a girl."

"She's courageous and full of fire. She's strong-willed and determined, and she isn't afraid to meet you head-on. You never expected that in the woman you married. You wanted someone like Allison Hartman, a woman you could pat on the head and ignore. You can't do that with Kathryn."

"You're as mad as she is."

Jason grinned. "She's not mad and you know it. I'll grant your wife may be a bit eccentric, but there really isn't anything wrong with that."

Lucien arched a brow. "Eccentric? Yesterday she came to my study and asked if she could set up her laboratory in the little stone cottage down by the creek. Her laboratory, forgodsake. The woman is the Marchioness of Litchfield and she wants to be some sort of bloody healer."

Jason chuckled softly. "She is definitely not your shy, retiring miss."

"A woman belongs at home, caring for her husband and children, not out roaming the countryside, dispensing herbs—half of which have the opposite result she intends."

Jason sipped his ale. "Did you let her use the cottage?"

"No."

"She said her mother and sister died and no one could do a thing to save them. Obviously, their deaths hit her hard."

Lucien leaned back in his chair. "Kathryn has suffered more than enough grief in her life. She hardly needs more. That is exactly what will happen if she tries to help every bloody vagrant in England. Hopefully in time she'll come to her senses and end this ridiculous notion she is on some sort of mission."

Jason raised his tankard of ale toward Lucien. "I wish

you luck, my friend. You are definitely going to need it."

Lucien said nothing more. As far as he was concerned the subject of Kathryn Grayson Montaine was closed. Perhaps if she followed his dictates and from now on acquiesced to his wishes, they could begin to have some semblance of a normal marriage.

God, he hoped so. He wasn't sure how much longer he could stay away from his pretty wife's bed.


"Do ye see 'im?" Hollis Wills stood in the dark outside the mullioned windows of the Quill and Sword Tavern. He pulled up the collar of his ragged woolen jacket against the cold.

"Yeah, I see him. He's talkin' to that bloody big duke what is his friend."

"God's eyes, Murray—we can't take on that big blighter. We're likely to get ourselves kilt." A short, stocky, tree trunk of a man, Hollis flapped his arms around his body against the cold.

Murray Tibbons continued to watch through the window. "Don't look like we're gonna have to. The duke's leavin'. Looks like the bleedin' marquess is stayin' behind."

Hollis grinned, revealing the gap between his two front teeth. " 'E's a dead man, then."

Murray just grunted. He was taller than Hollis, a former freight-wagon driver, with thick arms, strong legs, and a streak of meanness that had a way of keeping his pockets full of coin. He made a sideways movement of his head. "Come on. We'll wait for him round back. Sooner or later, he'll have to come out that way to get his horse."

Hollis rubbed his hands together against the cold. He had poked his blunt fingers through holey mittens, but they did little to keep him warm. He followed Murray around to the rear of the tavern and they took up places in the shadows.

They didn't have to wait long. The sound of boots

crunching against the frozen earth alerted them to someone's presence.

"It's 'im!" Hollis whispered, the sound hissing past the
space between his teeth.

"Keep quiet," Murray warned. "Do you want him to
know we're here?" They waited until the marquess drew
closer, waited till he rounded the corner and walked into
the shadowy darkness, then Murray stepped out and neatly
brought a length of wood down on the man's dark head.

Litchfield was a tall man, lean and hard and strong. He
took the blow and staggered, shook his head and came up
swinging, his fist connecting like a hammer with Murray's
jaw. Murray swore foully as he tumbled backward, land-
ing arse over teakettle on the cold snowy ground. Hollis
charged in just then, the blade of his knife flashing in the
moonlight.

"Bloody hell!" The marquess dodged the blade far
more agilely than Murray would have guessed, stepping
back just in time, seeming to grow taller as he straightened to collect himself. Keeping his weight on the balls
of his feet, his long legs splayed for balance, Litchfield
pulled off the scarf he wore around his neck and wound
it around his arm as protection against the blade.

"Get 'im!" Hollis shouted, slashing wildly with the
knife. The marquess smoothly evaded the blade but Murray came at him from behind, shoving him into the sharp
edge of steel. Hollis's blade arched upward, across the
marquess's chest, cutting through his woolen coat and
white cambric shirt, slicing a thin line through hard-
muscled flesh.

Litchfield grunted in pain and spun away to grapple
with Murray, knocking them both to the ground, rolling
in the dirt, first one on top and then the other. He slammed
several hard blows into Murray's face, then rolled to his
feet and whirled to face Hollis, who slashed downward
with his knife just then, the arc of the blade slicing into
the marquess's arm. A sharp hiss of pain cut through the
night, then Litchfield's long leg lashed out, his high black

boot cracking against Hollis's wrist, the knife spinning away into the darkness.

Murray's head pounded and his lip was swollen. Blood leaked from his nose and mouth. Panting for breath, he looked around for Hollis, but the runty little coward had fled.

The marquess stepped back, gathering his strength for the next attack. "If you know what's good for you," he warned in a voice edged with steel, "you'll follow the tracks made by your friend."

Murray sneered. "Like bleedin' hell!" He wasn't about to run, to let some fancy aristocrat make a fool of him. Circling, his eyes on his quarry, he spotted the knife Hollis had lost, reached down and scooped it up, holding it up like a trophy. "I'm gonna cut yer pretty face all to pieces," he warned, "and I'm gonna enjoy it."

In the sliver of moon slanting down through the clouds, the lines of Litchfield's face looked carved in stone. Murray wet his lips. The hand that held the knife was slick with sweat. When he'd taken the job, he hadn't expected the man to be such a fearsome opponent. He'd thought the other half of the quid he'd get for killing the bastard was as good as in his pocket.

Now he wasn't so sure.

"You can still leave here alive," Litchfield said with soft menace, as if, should Murray stay, his death was already a fact. Murray shoved back the greasy hair that had fallen into his eyes and continued to circle his prey.

"You're bleedin' like a stuck hog," Murray said. "You ain't got the strength to fight me. I'll kill ye and be gone."

The edge of the marquess's mouth barely curved. "I don't think so."

Murray could feel the sweat running down his rib cage. He noticed the marquess was favoring his injured arm, saw the blood trickling down the sleeve of his dark blue riding coat. Still, there was something in the man's black eyes, something that said even the knife wouldn't be enough to stop him.

The sound of voices reached his ears. God's teeth—someone was coming! It was the incentive he needed to set his legs into motion. Whirling away, Murray made a break for the stable, rounding the corner to where his horse was tied, running as fast as he could, certain the marquess was right behind him. He didn't waste time, just vaulted up on the horse's back, jerked its ugly head around, and dug his heels into the beast's bony ribs.

He didn't look back, just kept on riding till he reached the safety of the trees. There he reined up, but only for a moment. Looking back at the outline of the tavern, he swore an angry oath that he had failed.

Then again, the money was not yet lost. It was still there for the taking. The next time he encountered the bloody noble bastard, he would simply be better prepared.

Kathryn leaned over the rail at the top of the sweeping stairs down to the entry. A commotion below had pulled her from the solitude of her bedchamber. Now she saw a big-breasted woman dressed in the full skirt, low-cut peasant blouse, and stomacher of a tavern maid step into the entry. Behind her, two men half carried a third between them, an arm draped over each man's shoulder.

Kathryn gasped in horror as she realized who the injured man was.

"Lucien! Oh, dear God!" Lifting her skirts up out of the way, her heart clattering against her ribs, she raced down the stairs, nearly tripping in her haste to get there, skidding to a halt in front of them. "What in God's name happened? How badly is he hurt? Can you get him upstairs?" She whirled toward the butler. "Reeves—you must send for the doctor right away."

"I have already done so, my lady."

Lucien groaned just then and his eyes slowly opened. One of them was swollen nearly shut and his lip was cut and bleeding.

"I'm all right," he said, his voice edged with pain. "Ran into a little trouble outside the tavern."

"Me and Marty, we found him unconscious out near the stable," said the buxom, pale-haired woman. " 'E's lost a good bit of blood, milady. Be best we got 'im into bed."

"Yes, yes, of course. Please follow me." They followed her up the stairs, Lucien trying to navigate the steps but mostly being dragged by the men up to the second floor. His coat dripped blood. The ruffle at his cuff was stained crimson, and Kathryn bit back a wave of fear.

The man named Marty, young and gangly with long, unruly blond hair, spoke up. "Knifed him, they did. Cut his arm and across his chest. Bleedin' sods." He flushed. "Beg pardon, milady."

Kathryn's heart constricted. She covered her worry with anger. "It's all right. That is exactly what they are." The young man flashed her a grateful smile as they carried Lucien down the hall and settled him beneath the dark blue canopy on his big four-poster bed. With shaking hands, Kathryn pulled open his torn and filthy riding jacket and white cambric shirt, ripping it the rest of the way down the front, then she steadied herself as she looked at the slash across his beautiful chest.

"How bad is it, milady?" the buxom maid asked, hovering at the foot of the bed.

"The chest wound is only a scratch." Gauging the amount of blood soaking his sleeve, she decided that the other wound was more worrisome. Kathryn untied the makeshift bandage that had been tied around Lucien's arm to slow the bleeding, then tore open the sleeve of his ruined coat enough to survey the deep gash in his flesh.

"His arm has been cut very badly. I'll have to sew it up."

The barmaid lifted a pale winged brow. "Are ye sure ye hadn't ought to wait for the doctor?"

"Dr. Fredericks is at least two hours away. This bleeding needs to be stopped and I am as capable at sewing a wound as he is."

The blond woman said nothing more, but she looked at Kathryn with a hint of respect.

"Oh, my lord!" With a horrified gasp, Aunt Winnie rushed into the bedchamber, her slim hands pressed over her mouth. "He isn't . . . he isn't . . . ?"

Lucien's one good eye cracked open. "I assure you, madam, I am not dead yet. Quite possibly I will be after my wife attempts to practice her stitchery upon my ravaged person."

"Don't say that," Kathryn warned, "and don't you dare fight me over this, Lucien. We need to stop the bleeding and I am quite capable of doing it."

He might have argued if he hadn't noticed the glitter of tears in her eyes. His mouth curved faintly. "If that worry I see is for me, then I suppose I shall have to acquiesce."

Embarrassed, she blinked at the wetness, wiped the last trace away with the back of her hand. "All right, then." She turned to the others. "Aunt Winnie, I shall need my satchel. You will find it in my bedchamber beneath the bed. I'll need hot water to cleanse the wound and some clean cloth strips to bandage it. And fetch a decanter of brandy."

She turned her attention to the others. "The rest of you will have to leave." She tried to smile, but it came out wobbly. "I am extremely grateful to all of you for seeing to my husband's care. I shall be happy to pay you for your trouble—"

"No, milady," the woman interrupted. " 'Is lordship's done plenty for those of us what live in the village. You just see he gets back on his feet."

She nodded. "I will . . . and thank you again."

They left her alone, and a few minutes later, Aunt Winnie returned with the satchel that contained her precious medicinal supplies. Rooting through the contents, she set out a jar containing woundwort to help stop the bleeding, then drew out a needle and thread for the stitches. She located a salve of hound's tongue, foxglove flowers, and white dead nettle to keep the wound from putrefying and also set that out.

A footman appeared just then, carrying a pan of steaming water while another arrived with a decanter of brandy and a tray laden with bandages.

"Perhaps, Aunt Winnie, you should hold him."

"Oh, dear."

Lucien's voice rolled up from the bed. "I won't move. I don't need my aunt's help or anyone else's." He gave his aunt an exhausted smile. "It would be best, Aunt Winnie, if you waited downstairs until Kathryn is finished."

Winnie looked so relieved, Kathryn didn't argue. She supposed not everyone was cut out for this sort of thing. "Go ahead," she said. "This shouldn't take long."

"Well, all right . . . if you're certain you don't need me . . ."

Kathryn simply nodded. As soon as the woman left the room, she reached for the brandy, poured some into a glass, and handed it to Lucien, who drank the contents in a single gulp and hissed in a breath. She refilled the glass and held it out, but her husband shook his head.

"I swear I have never drunk so much liquor as I have since I met you."

"It will help with the pain," Kathryn told him, ignoring the jibe, but he still refused.

"I'll be fine."

Hoping he was right, she arranged the supplies she needed on a cloth-covered tray beside the bed, then placed the pan of hot water beside it.

"First we have to get you out of those filthy clothes."

The first flicker of interest shone in those silver-black eyes. "If I didn't know it was going to hurt like the bloody devil, I should like nothing better than to have you help me undress."

Something warm moved through her, stirring a memory of the night that they had made love. His words were the first reference of a sexual nature he had made since they had lain together. Since Kathryn was certain she had been an utter disappointment in that regard, she decided to ignore it.

"Perhaps I should ring for your valet. Holcomb could help me lift you up."

"I'm not an invalid, Kathryn. I've suffered a minor cut on my arm. If you will be good enough to help me a little, I can get the damnable coat off myself."

She didn't argue, nor mention the wound was scarcely minor at all. It was enough he was letting her take care of him. Leaning over, she untied the cloth she had retied around his arm, then slipped a hand behind his back to lift him up while he struggled to undress. It took a little doing, but eventually she was able to help him peel away the bloody coat and shed his torn and dirty shirt. Naked to the waist, he lay back down on the bed, the cut in his arm bleeding again quite badly.

Kathryn clamped down on her bottom lip to steady herself. Being nervous wasn't usually a problem, but somehow this was different. The blood spilling onto the sheets belonged to Lucien and she couldn't stand the thought that he was in pain. Her heart was pounding and she had to fight to keep her hands from shaking. She reached for the cloth, dipped water from the bowl, and swabbed the wound clean, then picked up the needle and thread she had prepared and settled herself on the mattress beside him.

"As you said, this is bound to hurt."

"Just get it done."

She took a deep breath and focused her attention on the work she had to do. Though Lucien didn't flinch or move even a single muscle, each time she pushed the needle through flesh she felt the pain as if it were her own. "I'm nearly through."

"It's a damned good thing."

She felt the tug of a smile. "One more stitch and I'm finished." Drawing the thread snug, she tightened the knot and tied it off, then bit the thread in two. She cleansed the wound on his chest, smeared both cuts with the me-

dicinal salve, applied a bruised woundwort leaf to his arm
and bandaged him up.

When she had finished, she smiled down at him, her
heart full of worry and love. She had tried to fight it, but
seeing him tonight, she knew she loved him even more
than she had thought. Ill-suited though they were, she
loved him. She cursed herself for a fool, but there was
nothing she could do.

"You were incredibly brave," she said, smoothing back
a lock of his wavy black hair. "I'm proud of you." Now
that his injuries had been tended, she moved to the foot
of the bed to tug off his boots, unfasten and roll down his
stockings.

The breeches were another matter. Just the thought of
what lay beneath the cloth reminded her of making love,
of how she had felt when he had been inside her, and a
little ripple of heat trickled through her.

Kathryn wet her lips, which suddenly felt as dry as the
powder she had used in her healing ointment. "I believe
I shall leave the rest to Holcomb," she said, trying not to
think of him naked, to ignore the warmth sliding into her
belly.

"I'll ring for him in a minute," Lucien said when she
returned to the side of the bed. His good arm moved and
his hand came up to her cheek. "You look nearly as tired
as I feel. Why don't you lie down beside me for a while?"

It was odd how much she wanted to. "I shouldn't. We
need to get you undressed so that you can get some sleep.
In the morning you can tell me how all of this happened."
*And perhaps I shall work up the courage to ask you about
the blonde.*

"I'll sleep better if you stay . . . just for a while."

She smoothed back his hair. "All right," she said softly.
"I'll stay. Just for while." She lay down on the mattress
and settled herself beside him, and Lucien snuggled her
closer. She rested her head against his shoulder and felt
his arm close around her. She should go, ring for Holcomb, and see him put comfortably to bed. Instead, she

lay at his side, absorbing the warmth of his skin, the faint smell of tobacco and leather, watching the long muscles move over his ribs with each rise and fall of his chest.

She was in love with him. A single night of passion didn't change things. In less than a year, their marriage would be ended. It was the right thing to do, the right thing for both of them.

Kathryn's heart squeezed hard inside her. She only hoped when the time came, she would have the courage to let him go.

# FIFTEEN

Christmastide was nearly upon them. By the night of the Duke of Carlyle's party, Kathryn's worry for Lucien had faded. Though his eye was a yellowish-purple, a corner of his bottom lip scabbed over, and his arm in a sling, he was feeling nearly himself.

She had asked him what had happened at the tavern and he had explained that brigands had attacked him as he had left the building on his way out to the stable.

"I assume they were after my purse. Most of the people in the village know I am the Marquess of Litchfield. My attackers probably assumed that as a member of the nobility, I would be carrying a substantial sum of money."

Sitting beside his bed, Kathryn skillfully cleansed his wounds, then applied a fresh bandage to his arm. He wore no night rail and the sheet rode low on his hips. Curly black hair arrowed down from a broad, muscled chest and every time she looked at him, Kathryn felt overly warm.

"The woman who brought you home . . ." she said, careful to keep her eyes on her work. "She seemed to think a good deal of you."

"Did she?"

"You go to the tavern quite regularly. I suppose you know her fairly well."

One of his sleek black brows arched up. "How well do you mean?"

Her cheeks burned with color. "It isn't really my business. I just thought . . . I mean, she seemed so very concerned and . . . well, I just wondered . . ."

A corner of his mouth curved with amusement. "If you wish to know if I have bedded the lass, the answer is no."

Kathryn glanced away, even more embarrassed, and wishing the news didn't make her feel nearly giddy with relief. "As I said, it isn't really my business. We have an arrangement, after all, and—"

"An arrangement?" Silver glinted in the midnight eyes that locked on her face.

"Yes, well, that is something I've been meaning to talk to you about. I realize . . . after what happened between us the other night . . . you might think you are now obliged to remain locked into our marriage. The fact is, I am fairly certain I did not conceive. Therefore we can still go through with the annulment as we had planned."

Instead of looking happy, Lucien looked annoyed. "So that is still your wish?"

She supposed it was. It was the right thing to do. She had trapped him into marriage. He didn't love her. She had to set him free. "Of course." But the thought made a soft ache throb in her chest.

Lucien's face looked grim. "If that is what you want, then that is the way it shall be."

Kathryn simply nodded. Her throat felt too tight to speak. It was ridiculous to feel this way, and yet she couldn't help it. Neither of them spoke as she tied off the clean white bandage on his arm and left the room.

Over the next few days, Lucien's family physician, Dr. Fredericks, appeared several times to examine the patient and look over her work, but he seemed pleased with what she had done and urged her to continue. He suggested the marquess might be bled a time or two but Lucien flatly refused, and Kathryn was secretly glad. Jason and Velvet came to call as soon as gossip of the assault reached Carlyle Hall. They were relieved to see the marquess was recovering and would soon be back on his feet.

Improving though he was, aside from her care of his wounds, it wasn't until the morning before Christmas that her husband sought her out.

"You haven't forgotten our plans to spend the evening with Velvet and Jason?" Earlier, he had mentioned the invitation he'd received from the duke and duchess to join a gathering of friends for the lighting of the Yule log that would begin the holiday season.

"I didn't forget. I didn't think you'd be feeling well enough to go." *And after our last conversation, I had no idea what you might be thinking.*

"I feel fine. I may not look so pretty, but if you and Winnie can stand the sight of me, I would be more than pleased to attend." Lucien smiled and even the bruises on his face couldn't disguise the beauty of his strong, carved features. "We haven't had much holiday spirit around here so far. With the Sinclair children scampering about, perhaps a bit of good cheer will rub off on us."

Kathryn smiled back at him, her heart beating a little faster. "I'd like that very much." It had been years since she'd really enjoyed the holiday season, not since her mother and sister had died. Without them, Christmastime held so many sad memories she and her father had mostly ignored it. After Papa had died and her uncle and his daughter had moved into Milford Park, Dunstan's lavish Christmas entertaining had only enhanced her feelings of loneliness and despair.

"It isn't all that far," the marquess was saying, "but we shall have to leave early if we intend to get there before the children are put to bed."

"All right. I'll make certain Aunt Winnie knows what time you wish to depart."

He smiled again. "I'll see you a little before six, then."

Kathryn nodded. She watched his graceful strides as

he walked down the hall and felt a soft, sweet stirring in the area around her heart. He seemed different today, less hostile, more the man he was before they married. The moment he disappeared into his study, Kathryn turned and dashed upstairs to find Winnie and decide what she should wear.

Both of them were excited. Kathryn had never been to the extravagant mansion that was the palatial home of the Duke and Duchess of Carlyle. And it was Christmas, after all. Her life was different now. She meant to enjoy herself.

Wearing a deep red velvet gown over wide panniers, the top cut stylishly low, the sleeves fitted to the elbow then flaring out with layers of velvet-trimmed lace down past her wrists, Kathryn checked the mirror one last time. She smoothed the chestnut curls Fanny had fashioned at the side of her neck, adjusted the heart-shaped patch at the corner of her mouth, and headed down the stairs.

The marquess was waiting at the bottom. He glanced up when he saw her and something dark and hot flickered in his eyes. It was a look she had noticed of late, on more than one occasion, but she had told herself she was mistaken.

If he wanted her, he would have come back to her room. He would have made love to her again. And he wouldn't have agreed to the annulment. Still, as she descended the last few stairs and took the arm he offered, there was no mistaking the hunger in his eyes as he assessed her from top to bottom, or the warmth of his kiss as he lifted her white-gloved hand and pressed his mouth against the back.

"You look lovely, my lady."

She moistened her lips, unnerved by that silver spark in his eyes that seemed to burn right through her clothes. "Thank you, my lord." He continued to watch her, wearing a lazy half-smile, and Kathryn didn't realize she was holding her breath until he turned away, fixing his attention once more on the stairs.

In a gown of pale blue fur-trimmed silk, her blond hair

piled in ringlets atop her head, Winifred Montaine DeWitt looked only a few years older than Kathryn. Lucien smiled at her with obvious pride and genuine affection. "I am the luckiest of men this night, escorting two of England's most beautiful women."

A slight flush rose into Winnie's cheeks. She glanced from her nephew to Kathryn and back, and seemed pleased with whatever it was she saw. "I think we are the lucky ones, my lord. Don't you agree, my dear?"

Kathryn smiled, suddenly lighthearted. She stared up at Lucien, felt the pull of those intense black eyes. "Indeed I do, Lady Beckford. To be in company with such a handsome man . . . fortune has smiled sweetly upon us this night."

Lucien seemed pleased. She wondered again at his change of mood, but decided to simply enjoy it. Accepting his arm while Winnie took the other, she let him guide her out the door and help them both climb into the carriage. They arrived by the light of an early rising moon, bowling down a long, tree-lined, oyster-shell drive up to the front of the house.

An elegant mansion surrounded by a seemingly endless landscape of open fields and forests, Carlyle Hall was even more magnificent than she had imagined. Palladian in design and built of Portland stone, its lovely balustrades and stylish pedimented windows glittered with dozens of beeswax candles.

A pair of red-liveried footmen stood at the doors leading into the house, men equal in height and build and wearing identical silver bagwigs. Walking next to Lucien into the entry, she paused beneath the painted ceilings to greet their host and hostess.

"We're so glad you could come," Velvet said, leaning over to buss Kathryn's cheek. "You look beautiful."

Kathryn swept into a curtsy. "Thank you, Your Grace."

Velvet waved away the formal greeting with a smile. "None of that. Not tonight. Tonight we are family and we are here to celebrate the season."

Oddly touched, Kathryn felt the unexpected sting of tears. She hadn't had a family for so long. She hadn't realized how desperately lonely she had been until that very moment. A memory arose of the Christmas she had faced last year, locked away in the madhouse, eating a supper of boiled potatoes, a piece of coarse rye bread, and a paper-thin slice of mutton—a special holiday treat instead of the gruel that was her usual fare. She thought of sitting in the dirty straw on the floor of her cell, missing her father and mother, weeping for the family she would never see again.

"Kathryn . . . ?" Lucien said softly. "Are you all right?"

She blinked, realized she had tears in her eyes, and saw that Velvet and Lucien were both looking at her with worried expressions. "I'm sorry. For a moment my mind wandered back to . . ." She tried to smile, faltered. "It wasn't a pleasant memory."

Lucien slid an arm around her waist, drawing her back against him. He kissed the top of her head. "You're free of those memories now. Tonight we'll make new memories. Happy memories."

"Lucien is right," Velvet firmly agreed. "Tonight will be the start of happy Christmas memories from now on." She looked lovely with her fiery hair just lightly powdered, her small, trim figure displayed perfectly in a gown of amber silk, the shiny gold trim matching the golden flecks in her deep brown eyes.

Kathryn discreetly brushed away a tear. "You're a wonderful friend, Velvet Sinclair."

Velvet squeezed her hand. "We are lucky to have each other. Go on now and join the rest of the guests. The children have been wanting to meet their uncle Lucien's new wife."

As she had been looking forward to meeting them.

With a last brief smile, Velvet returned to her duties as hostess, joining her husband to greet the new arrivals while Lucien led Kathryn into the Oak Room, a dark, richly paneled salon at the rear of the house. Beneath her feet, floors warmed by thick Persian carpets gleamed in the light of the candles. The ceiling was fashioned in a crisscross pattern of carved oak timbers, the walls covered with exquisite red-flocked paper.

Obviously chosen for its warm, cheery ambiance, the room had been decorated floor to ceiling with red-berried holly and mistletoe. Evergreen boughs draped over an oak-manteled hearth, where the huge Yule log waited to be lit.

The moment they entered the room, a small boy dressed in a miniature version of the fashionable *habit à la française* that included royal-blue velvet knee breeches and a matching blue velvet coat, raced up to greet them. Alexander Jason Sinclair, a diminutive version of his tall, handsome father with thick, dark coffee-brown hair and bright blue eyes, made a perfectly correct formal bow.

Then he grinned. "Uncle Lucien! I was hoping you would come." Lucien went down on one knee and the little boy raced into his arms.

"It's Christmastide, isn't it? Of course I would come."

Little Mary Jane, gowned in pale pink silk over tiny panniers, toddled up just then, her hair a vivid red, much brighter than her mother's auburn locks. She pulled her finger out of her mouth, looked at Lucien and giggled, curling her rosebud lips into an irresistible smile. Lucien kissed her cheek and began the introductions.

"Alex and Mary—this is your new aunt Kathryn."

Kathryn's head whipped toward him, her eyes wide in stunned disbelief. It was one thing for him, a longtime family friend, to use the affectionate pretend title of a relative, and another thing altogether for her. In less than a year, she would be leaving Castle Running. It was hardly fair to the children to let them form attachments.

The marquess simply smiled. "Say something, love. You'll frighten them if you merely stand there gaping."

The endearment washed over her and she nearly faltered again. Instead, she bent down and took each of the children's small hands. "It's a pleasure to meet you both.

Your uncle Lucien has told me all about you. I know we shall become great friends."

Alexander giggled and looked up at her with adorable blue eyes, and Kathryn fell instantly in love.

"Just like his father," Lucien teased, accurately assessing the besotted look on her face. "Only four years old and already he has every woman he meets falling hopelessly in love with him."

Just like you, Kathryn thought, noticing several of the female guests who eyed the marquess as if he were a tasty hunk of meat. From beneath her lashes, Kathryn studied his handsome dark profile, admiring the perfectly carved planes and valleys. Yes . . . something was definitely different tonight, had been different since the moment she had seen him standing at the bottom of the stairs.

Perhaps it was simply the holiday season and had nothing at all to do with her. Still, his eyes returned to her again and again, and she couldn't stop the frantic little flutter that leapt in her stomach.

Kathryn felt a tug on her skirt and shifted her gaze back toward the floor. "I'm almost three," Mary said, holding up two of her pudgy little fingers.

Kathryn laughed and hugged her. "Yes, you are, sweetheart, but don't be too anxious to grow up. Time goes by all too quickly as it is."

Mary just grinned and dashed off to join her brother. Kathryn followed the child's movements as she darted in and out between the guests, the image turning backward, to another child, this one a little older, blond and blue-eyed, sharing a lonely Christmas with the inmates at St. Bart's.

She bit down on her bottom lip, wishing she could speak to Lucien about the child and ask for his help, fearful of what would happen should he refuse.

"You're doing it again, love. You look so much prettier when you're not frowning." He tipped her chin with his hand. "Let it go, Kathryn. Tonight belongs to the future, not the past."

She swallowed hard and nodded, knowing he was right. Tomorrow, she would deal with her problems, tonight was the eve before Christmas and she meant to enjoy herself.

Lucien watched his new wife as he introduced her to the small group of friends Jason had invited: Lord and Lady Balfour, the Earl and Countess of Briarwood, Winston Parminter, the famous London barrister, half a dozen others.

Kathryn had met his solicitor, Nathaniel Whitley, at Castle Running and seemed to like him very much. The Earl of Haversham, the duchess's grandfather, had her laughing at tales of Velvet's misadventures and immediately put her at ease. After that, she seemed to relax and enjoy herself, slipping once more into the role of lady that she had been born to.

Standing next to Jason, Lucien watched her conversing with Aunt Winnie and the aging earl as she sampled an assortment of food from the vast array perched on a carved oak table that virtually groaned beneath the weight of its heavy burden: a perfectly browned roast goose, sweetbreads of veal, chicken fricassee, salmon with shrimp sauce, Florentine rabbits. There were kidney pies and meat pasties, buttered carrots, turnips and parsnips, mince pies, gingerbread, candied fruits, and custards.

Kathryn had been eating as if she couldn't get enough ever since he had left her at the table. It bothered him to think of the days she had spent eating less than nothing in that hellish hole of St. Bart's. Unconsciously a muscle tightened in his jaw.

"She's a beautiful woman," Jason said, following the path of his gaze.

"Yes, she is." Particularly tonight. With her hair swept up and soft dark curls at the side of her neck, she looked more beautiful than he had ever seen her. The deep red velvet gown brought out the highlights in her hair, and her small breasts formed delicate mounds that begged to be touched.

His body tightened painfully, reminding him how much he wanted her, and he forced his gaze away. "Since she has been living at the castle, she has regained a little of the weight she lost. And there is a glow in her cheeks that wasn't there before." He found himself smiling to think he'd had a hand in her transformation and turned to see his friend eyeing him strangely.

"All right, what's going on? I've been watching you all evening. Something's happened in that unfathomable brain of yours. Tell me what it is."

A corner of his mouth curved faintly. "I suppose you could say something has happened. I have finally come to grips with my situation. What happened at the lodge is over and done. The fact is, I am married. It is time to move on with my life, and that is exactly what I intend to do."

"Which means?"

"Put simply—I've decided to keep her. Kathryn thinks we are getting an annulment, but I have decided we are not."

Jason grinned. "So at last you have come to your senses."

"Perhaps I have. While I was recovering from that little scuffle I had at the tavern, I had time to do some thinking. It's a fact I'm in need of a wife, and no secret I'm attracted to Kathryn. I've come to the conclusion that the woman I'm married to will do as well as any, perhaps better than most. As you said, she is intelligent and strong. She comes from a noble family. In short, she is good breeding stock, and I believe she will make a fine mother for my children. Watching her tonight with Alex and Mary has made me even more certain."

"What about the fact she has interests in subjects of which you don't approve?"

Lucien shrugged. "She will have to give them up, of course. At any rate, once she is with child, she'll forget all that nonsense, settle down and behave as a proper wife should. It's time I had an heir and I mean to see it done as quickly as I can."

Jason looked as if he had his doubts, but didn't say so. "If Kathryn still wants an annulment, how do you plan to convince her?"

Lucien's gaze returned to his wife, who was laughing at something Lord Haversham said. "I don't. I intend to seduce her."

Jason laughed aloud, nearly spilling the mug of hot mulled wine he held in one big hand. "My friend, you never fail to amaze me. Wouldn't it be easier just to tell her you don't want to end the marriage?"

"It might be . . . if I were completely certain she would agree. However, since I am not, I shall have to go about it another way."

Jason's gaze swung to Kathryn, now joined by his wife and children. "Perhaps you are right. No use taking any chances."

No, indeed, Lucien thought. Kathryn was going to be his and soon. He wanted her in his bed, wanted to begin where he had left off the first time they had made love. Every time he looked at her, he remembered the way she had felt moving beneath him, the way her tight little passage had gloved him so sweetly.

And now that his decision was made, he wanted her heavy with his child. It was amazing how much he looked forward to the day that happened.

Winnie Montaine DeWitt sipped syllabub from the crystal cup she held and tried to look nonchalant, but beneath her long pale lashes, her eyes were fixed on the mirror above the hearth. Within the ornate gilt frame, a handsome man with thick, silver-tipped brown hair and clear blue eyes she recognized as Nathaniel Whitley was staring at her from across the room, studying her with an intensity that was nearly frightening.

It was an odd sensation, watching Nat watch her.

Standing at the angle she was, he didn't realize she could
see him, that the way he looked at her made hot, intimate
images appear in her mind. Memories she thought she had
forgotten, the first time she had kissed him, or the day
down by the stream when they had met in secret and he
had asked her to marry him. Memories of how one look
from the shy, gangly boy he was then could make her
heart trip with longing.

Other impressions rose up, not of Nat as a boy, but
Nat as a man, visions of how that kiss might have
changed, how those beautiful sculpted lips would move
over hers, kissing her in a way he hadn't before, how it
might feel to have him touch her breasts, to taste them
with his tongue, how it might feel to lie naked beside him.

Jerking her eyes from the mirror, she felt the heat in
her cheeks and forced the images away, but she couldn't
deny they had been there, and Winnie was ashamed.

"Well . . . Lady Beckford. I wondered if you might not
be here this evening." Her mind had strayed. She hadn't
seen him approach. He looked different now, harder, more
unreachable than he had in the looking glass.

She raised her chin, tried to look at him down her nose,
which wasn't easy since he was so much taller. "Mr. Whitley." It was all the greeting she could force past her lips.
Every time she looked at him, she felt guilty for her
wicked thoughts.

His gaze drifted down past her shoulders to the swell
of bosom that rose above the bodice of her gown. It lingered there a moment, then returned to her face. "I trust
you are enjoying yourself."

Winnie's hand fluttered nervously up to her throat. She
hadn't missed the mockery in his voice, nor the hard look
that turned his eyes the color of cold blue steel. "Yes . . .
yes, of course I am. Why shouldn't I be?" But she wasn't,
not really. Hadn't been since the moment she had spotted
Nat Whitley in the small salon next door to the Oak Room
in conversation with her nephew.

"I assure you, I wouldn't know," he said dryly. "When

you were speaking to Lord Cullinworth a little while ago, it certainly appeared as if you were well entertained. He's in the marriage mart, I hear. An earl, no less, and wealthy in the extreme—qualities a woman of your discerning standards is bound to find attractive." His mouth curved up, but it wasn't really a smile. "The earl is a client of mine. Perhaps I can put in a good word for you if that is your wish."

Winnie bristled even more. "What are you talking about? I have no interest in Cullinworth or anyone else. And I resent the implication that I would pursue his lordship for his title and fortune."

A fine dark brow arched up, but his eyes remained hard. "My apologies, then. But somehow I didn't get the impression you would be nearly so offended should his lordship wish to pursue a relationship with you as you were when I posed that suggestion."

Of all the gall! "It isn't at all the same and you know it!"

His attractive mouth went thin. "No, of course it isn't. My apologies, Lady Beckford." With a stiff bow, he turned away, walking across the room without a single look back.

Obviously he was still angry from their last encounter and now Winnie was angry, too. The nerve of the man! Had he actually expected her to engage in some sort of illicit affair? The more she thought about it, the madder it made her.

As usual, he hadn't brought his wife, not even at Christmastide. She wondered how the poor woman put up with such ill treatment.

She watched Nat join a small group of people clustered at a table near the rear of the salon, talking and laughing with Lord Briarwood's pretty auburn-haired daughter. It was impossible to imagine the cold, dispassionate man she had just spoken to as the same young man she had once thought she loved.

Still, there was something about him that stirred her.

Something that made her heart beat crazily whenever he came near. She hated herself for it, but it seemed there was nothing she could do.

For the balance of the evening, she tried to ignore him, but time and again, her eyes would stray in his direction, or she would hear his rich baritone as he laughed with one of the women. Each time it happened, an unreasonable tug of jealousy reared up. When the Yule log was finally lit and the Sinclair children put to bed, she watched him take his leave, saying a brief good-night to the duke and duchess before making his way out the door.

Restless, Winnie crossed the room that seemed empty without him and wandered out onto the terrace, desperate to feel the sobering bite of the cold December air. She rubbed her arms against the chill and yet she was grateful for it. Her body still felt hot and edgy from their earlier encounter. He was nothing but a rogue, an unscrupulous, unprincipled rake who cared about nothing but his own selfish interests.

But dear Lord she wanted him. She had never thought of herself as a woman of strong desires. Richard had been a kind, considerate sort of husband who came to her in the dark, left as soon as his needs were met, and ceased coming to her bed altogether once it was learned that she could not bear him a child.

She had never thought of Richard in the way she had once thought of Nat—the way she thought of him now— with a hot sweet yearning that burned through her blood. She was just as wicked, just as sinful as he was.

Winnie shivered. She might be angry at Nathaniel Whitley, but in truth, she was far more angry at herself.

# SIXTEEN

The days of Christmas slipped past. Happy days, warm, bright, cheerful days like those Kathryn had known as a child. Kathryn gifted Aunt Winnie with a lovely cashmere shawl and Lucien a finely engraved, beautiful silver snuff-box with his initials in gold lettering on the top. Lucien surprised her with an exquisite emerald and diamond necklace so lovely it took her breath away.

"Oh, my lord, I couldn't possibly accept this—it is far too valuable. In less than a year I'll be leaving and—"

"That is then. This is now. I'm giving you the necklace as a friend, and I want you to keep it." But he wasn't looking at her as a friend. His eyes were dark and hot and they made her stomach quiver.

She found herself wetting her lips, her fingers curling into her palms to keep them from reaching out to touch him. When he smiled, his mouth looked full and sensuous, and if she closed her eyes, she could feel those lips moving over hers, nibbling at the corners, kissing the side of her neck as he had done the night that they had made love. Heat rolled through her, pulled low in her belly.

The following day he took her for a sleigh ride over the freshly fallen snow. Beneath the thick fur lap robe she was warm and content, and Lucien was smiling. And everywhere they went, he watched her with those burning silver-black eyes.

He was being so wonderful, so solicitous, she began to feel guilty for the deception she waged. It had been going on for several weeks, since the day he had denied her permission to use the little stone cottage in the forest down by the stream. Though her husband had strictly forbidden it, Kathryn had ignored his dictates and begun working in the cottage. After all, she had reasoned, she was married to the man—at least for the present. That gave her a certain amount of leave to use what belonged to him.

Besides, she knew the only reason he had denied her use of the place was because he disapproved of her interest as a woman in what he termed "the vulgar practice of healing." Dabbling with herbs and potions and attempting to heal the sick was bad enough, but an interest in anatomy—it was still unacceptable even among the heartiest of men. Full-fledged riots had occurred when people simply discovered classes being taught that included dissection of a human corpse. Physicians were tolerated. Surgeons, on the other hand, men who engaged in the actual process of cutting into human flesh, were considered among the lowest elements of society.

Such interests were hardly appropriate for the Marchioness of Litchfield, Lucien had firmly told her.

Still, it was her life's work, the only thing that Kathryn was really interested in. Certainly she wasn't the type to sit around and fiddle with knitting or embroidery, or fuss with water colors in a futile effort to paint. She could play the harpsichord more than passably well and often found it soothing, but her love, her passion, was studying the ancient doctrines of herbal healing and using them to help sick people get well.

She loved to learn about the human body, to try to understand how it worked. She wanted to know how bones mended, how blood moved beneath the skin, how best to heal wounds, how to treat or perhaps even prevent disease.

But the marquess couldn't understand that. Perhaps no one could. It wasn't the sort of thing a lady was supposed to be involved in.

Kathryn didn't care. She had found her calling and she was committed. Even before she had set up her small, secret laboratory in the cottage, she had been dispensing herbs and potions to some of the people in the village. Now that she had a place of her own, word had traveled quickly that she might be able to help, and already several of the local peasants had come to her for treatment.

She usually worked in the cottage in the afternoons when the marquess was off surveying the fields, working with his tenants, or poring over his ledgers.

Aunt Winnie knew where she was, of course, and surprisingly, she seemed to approve.

"My nephew can be ridiculously stuffy at times. He has always envisioned a wife who was docile and obedient, but such a woman would bore him to tears. You must follow your conscience, Kathryn. You must do what is best for you. In time, my nephew will learn to accept you as you are."

But Kathryn didn't think so. Which was why she was convinced the best course still remained annulment, even though her heart ached every time she thought of leaving Castle Running. Every time she imagined being married to any other man but the Marquess of Litchfield, which she would have to do to stay free of her grasping uncle. She would be old enough to marry without his consent, but until she reached four and twenty, if she remained unwed, he would continue to be her guardian.

She thought about the earl and wondered what he would do once the management of her fortune was transferred to the marquess and his solicitor, Nathaniel Whitley. The papers were already being prepared, and secretly she hoped her uncle was squirming, that he was frantic with worry and rage. If his limited funds left him destitute, so be it. If she had any concern whatever, it was for her young cousin, Muriel, a pawn in her overbearing father's hands.

Perhaps she would speak to Lucien about it, see that the girl received a monthly stipend of some sort and enough for a proper dowry.

Aside from that, she had no pity for the Earl of Dunstan. She was certain one day the man would burn in hell.

Douglas Roth, Earl of Dunstan, sat at his desk in the exquisitely furnished study at Milford Park. Over the years, he had come to think of the masculine, oak-paneled room that had belonged to the late Earl of Milford as his. In fact, he considered all of Milford Park as belonging to him. For years he had imagined living out his life in the comfort and luxury of the parklike setting that had given the place its name.

Instead, thanks to his willful, conniving niece, he would soon be tossed out of the house like so much rubbish. He would be left to fend for himself and his daughter and, having spent most of the money he had earlier siphoned from her trust simply to maintain his extravagant lifestyle, he wouldn't be able to do so for long.

Douglas ground down on his jaw and his fingers tightened around the document he had been reading, crumpling the edges of the pages. It wasn't going to happen, he vowed. He wasn't going to let that deceitful little slut ruin the plans he had made.

Hearing the knock he'd been expecting, Douglas rose from his chair and strode to the door. The man in the hall made a slight bow of greeting and walked past him into the room, taking a chair in front of the desk while Douglas returned to his seat behind it.

"Well, you know what I want to hear," Douglas said without preamble. "What have you done about it?"

His estate manager, Evan Sloan, a lean, hard man with a sharp nose and sandy-brown hair, sat back in his chair. "I've made a devil's bargain, you might say." Sloan had been in Dunstan's employ for years, an invaluable asset both in running his estates—Kathryn's estates, he mentally corrected—and in a number of more personal matters.

And he was loyal to a fault. For the money Douglas paid him, and the fact he lived in the comfort of a large, well-appointed manor house at the edge of the estate, it wasn't surprising.

"A bargain with the devil, eh? And just what sort of bargain is that?"

Sloan steepled his hands in front of him. "I've offered a reward of sorts, for the accidental demise of the Marquess of Litchfield."

Douglas shot out of his chair. "Good God, man, are you mad? You'll have half of England out to kill him. If they connect the matter to me—"

"They won't," Sloan said with quiet authority. "And there are only two men involved. One has already made an attempt. 'Brigands' set upon your quarry outside the Quill and Sword Tavern in the village near Castle Running. Unfortunately, that attempt failed. The second man is conveniently in the marquess's employ. He has assured me he can handle the job without causing any undue suspicion."

Douglas rubbed his chin, mulling the matter over. "The reward, I take it, goes to whichever of these men succeeds."

"Exactly."

Douglas sat back down in his chair, his fingers absently drumming on the document. "All right. Perhaps the idea is a good one. We shall see if this devil's bargain of yours actually works."

"It will work, I assure you. Both these men are competent in his own way. It's only a matter of time until one of them succeeds."

"Not too much time, I trust. I've been asked to leave the premises in the next thirty days." Douglas smiled thinly. "I have no intention of moving."

Sloan rose to his feet, correctly reading the words as a dismissal. "Nor do I, my lord."

Douglas watched him leave. As soon as the door was closed, he picked up the papers he had received from Nathaniel Whitley just that morning. Grinding his teeth, he tore them in half, then in half again. A thin smile curved his lips as he tossed them into the shiny brass waste bin.

Lucien was worried about his aunt. She had been oddly withdrawn all through the holidays. He had thought, now that the season was past, she would return to her usual good humor, and for the most part she had. But in some strange way she still seemed distant and a little bit forlorn. Kathryn had noticed it as well, and her concern on top of his own made him even more determined to discover the cause.

Seeking Winifred out was the reason he had come home early this afternoon from a meeting with one of his tenants. Still dressed in his riding clothes, he had summoned his aunt into the Red Writing Room, a cozy little parlor at the rear of the house that Aunt Winnie seemed to favor.

"Good afternoon, my lord," she said, appearing at the door in a gown of soft blue wool. "Reeves said you wished to see me."

Lucien beckoned her in, seating her on a sofa in front of the large glass window that looked out over the garden. He took a seat in a wing-back chair across from her and motioned toward the tea tray on the table.

"It's chilly out. I thought you might enjoy a cup with me. Perhaps you would pour for us."

"Of course." Smiling, she bent to the task, filling two porcelain cups, adding a bit of cream and a chunk of sugar, as both of them liked. She handed him a cup and took one for herself, settling back against the sofa.

"I'm afraid I don't exactly know where to begin," he said.

Winnie smiled. "It is usually best just to jump right in."

"All right. Let me start by saying both Kathryn and I have been worried about you."

She looked surprised, her pale brows arching up, the gold-rimmed cup poised halfway to her lips. "Good heavens, why ever would you be worried?"

Lucien stirred his tea. "Something is bothering you, Winnie. I can see it in your eyes, and Kathryn has noticed it, as well. I want you to tell me what it is."

The cup trembled faintly in her hand. "But that's . . . that is ridiculous. Nothing whatever is bothering me."

He reached over and took the cup, set it back down in its saucer. "Please don't lie to me, Winnie. As the head of this family, your nephew, and your friend, I only want what is best for you. Trust me enough to tell me what is wrong."

Tears welled in her pale blue eyes. "I would tell you if I could. It simply wouldn't be fair."

"Why not?"

"Because it involves someone in your employ. If I tell you what happened, you might think differently about him and I wouldn't want that to happen."

Lucien's senses went on alert. "Has this man done something to hurt you? If he has harmed you in any way—"

"No, no. It is nothing like that. It's silly really. Men make advances to women all the time. I should have been flattered. If it were any other man, I might have been, but . . . well, I suppose I thought this particular man was different. Perhaps the fact that he is not is what has bothered me so much."

"There are any number of men who would find you attractive, Aunt Winnie. You're a very beautiful woman."

A hint of rose appeared in her cheeks. "Thank you," she said.

He smiled slightly. "Perhaps this man . . . whoever he is . . . simply couldn't help himself."

Winnie glanced away, her fingers toying with the folds of her pretty blue gown. "He is married, my lord."

Lucien frowned. "Married? For a moment I thought you were speaking of Nathaniel Whitley, since it is obvious how strongly he feels about you, but since Whitley is not married—"

Winnie's spine went straight, her face suffused with angry color. "Of course he is married. Nat married Emma Hanson two years after he and I ... That is to say, Nathaniel has been married to his wife for nearly twenty years."

Lucien smiled at her softly, a ray of understanding beginning to dawn. "Emma died two years ago, Winnie. I thought you knew. I'm sure Nat thought so, too. I realize you have only lived at the castle for the past six months, but since you and Nat were formerly acquainted, I assumed word of Emma's death must have reached you."

"Emma is ... Emma is dead?" Winnie rose to her feet on shaky legs, her cup of tea forgotten.

"Yes. I'm sorry."

She turned and stared off toward the garden, but she wasn't really seeing it. Her hands bit into her skirt and he could see that they were trembling. "If Emma is dead, then Nathaniel is a widower."

"That's right. Losing Emma was quite painful for him, but over the past two years he has mended."

"Nathaniel said ..." She swallowed, still staring off toward the garden. "Nat expressed an interest in me ... in pursuing a relationship, that is. I thought he was making improper advances. I thought ..." She turned to face him, and Lucien saw tears in her eyes. "I refused him—quite rudely. Nat would think the reason was ... Oh, dear God, what have I done?"

Winnie started toward the door and had almost reached it before she realized Lucien was staring after her. "I'm sorry, my lord, I'm afraid I must take my leave. There is a matter of some importance I must see to in the city."

He set his teacup down and rose to his feet. "Yes . . .

I can see that there is. I'll make the necessary arrangements. You and your maid may leave first thing in the morning."

He joined her at the door and Winnie swiped at the tears on her cheeks. "I would prefer to leave today, if you don't mind. I can be packed and ready within the hour."

"That isn't a good idea, Aunt Winnie. It'll be dark in London when you arrive. I would rather you waited—"

She reached out and gripped his hand. "Please, Lucien. I must go. I beg you not to stop me."

He had never seen her quite so unraveled. There was obviously more to the story than he knew, but whatever it was, perhaps this trip to London would correct the matter and his aunt would be returned to her old self again. He made a slight nod of his head. "I'll send a couple of footmen with you. You may leave as soon as you wish."

Winnie squeezed his hand. "Thank you." Turning, she hurried out the door.

Lucien watched her leave, still a little concerned but glad to have had a hand in righting whatever misunderstanding had occurred between his aunt and Nat Whitley. He ordered the carriage brought round and didn't see her again until she was out the front door and halfway down the front porch steps.

Lucien walked out on the porch behind her. "Have a safe journey and I'll see you the end of the week." Winnie smiled and waved and continued down the stairs. "By the way," he called after her, stopping her at the bottom. "Where has my wife gone off to this afternoon? No one seems to know where she is. I've been looking all over, but I haven't been able to find her."

The color in Winnie's cheeks slipped away. For an instant, her gaze flicked off toward the stream that meandered through the woods. "I'm afraid I don't know," she said, still not looking him in the face. "Perhaps she's gone into the village."

A muscle tightened in his cheek. "I suppose that must be it," he said, but he didn't believe it. Not for a minute.

Winnie was lying, and she wasn't very good at it, especially when her mind was already halfway to London. She was covering for Kathryn—but why?

His aunt climbed the iron stairs of the carriage and settled herself inside next to her maid. As the vehicle rolled away, she waved at him through the window, but her glance strayed once more off toward the stream.

In that instant, Lucien knew exactly where his wife had gone, and a shot of angry disbelief made the back of his neck go hot. "Bloody hell!" Striding back into the house, he stopped for a moment in the entry. "Reeves!" he called out. "Fetch my cloak and be quick about it."

"Yes, my lord." The butler returned with the heavy woolen garment and Lucien swung it around his shoulders. Furious at Kathryn and cursing himself for a fool, he strode out of the house and off toward the stables to fetch his horse.

It didn't take long to reach the small stone cottage that had once served as the caretaker's house, and as soon as he crested the rise, he saw his suspicions were correct. Kathryn's pretty little mare was stabled in the lean-to at the rear and a plume of pale gray smoke drifted out of the chimney.

Lucien cursed roundly and started down the hill.

"I hope it helps, Mrs. Finch. Boils can be very dangerous, to say nothing of how painful they are."

"Right ye are, dearie." The bony little woman grinned, exposing dark gums and the stumps of rotting teeth. "Me backside's feelin' better already."

Kathryn imagined it was. She had applied an ointment fashioned mainly of goldthread and pork grease, a salve she had discovered in the journal of a physician who had served with the army in India. It had worked wonders on the men he had treated. Kathryn hoped it would work for Mrs. Finch.

The woman's bony arm rooted around in the woven basket she carried, finally locating a small stoppered crock she handed over. "Here ye are, dearie. Some of me best plum preserves. And thanks be to ye again."

"You're welcome, Mrs. Finch, and good day to you." Kathryn closed the door with a satisfied sigh and returned to the book she had been reading, a volume of medieval Sussex folk remedies the duchess had discovered at Carlyle Hall and sent over as a Christmas present.

She had just sat back down in the comfortable old wing-back chair in front of the hearth when she heard the sound of the door slamming open and the marquess strode in. Kathryn shot to her feet so quickly the book tumbled out of her lap and landed in a heap at her feet. For an instant, she stared down at the ancient manuscript's bent pages, but she didn't reach down to pick it up. Instead, she tipped her head back and stared into the snapping black eyes of her husband.

His jaw muscles worked and his mouth looked thin and grim. Then his gaze moved away from her face to the vials and beakers on the narrow table along the wall, past the small clay pots on the windowsill where tiny green shoots of various herbs pushed up through the loamy soil. She had found a rickety wooden table in the attic and asked the cooper to brace it and shorten the legs to make it lower. Now it served as an examination table.

Though the cottage was clean and warmed by hooked rugs she had purchased from a vendor in the village, stacks of books littered nearly every available surface, many carted down from the marquess's library in the castle. Kathryn winced as he recognized several familiar volumes, then his hard gaze fixed once more on her.

"Perhaps my memory has begun to fail, but as I recall, when you asked for permission to use this place, I said no."

Kathryn swallowed and forced herself not to look away. "I realize I've gone against your wishes, my lord, but—"

"Gone against my wishes? Is that a polite way of saying you disobeyed my orders completely and did exactly as you pleased?"

She bit down on her bottom lip to keep it from trembling. The marquess was a formidable man when he was angry and he was beyond angry now. "The cottage wasn't being used and I needed a place to work. I was hoping you would approve. Since you didn't, I was left with no other choice."

"That is the way you see it? That you had no other choice but to disobey my wishes?" He clamped his jaw so tight a muscle jerked in his cheek. It took all Kathryn's will not to turn and run.

Instead she lifted her chin. "I'm your wife—at least for the present—I felt that gave me a certain amount of latitude."

His eyes ran over her, smoldering eyes that seemed to sear into her skin. "At least in that, madam, you are correct. You are definitely my wife." He took an ominous step closer, bringing them toe to toe. "The mistake I made was in not making certain you understood that completely. I believe it is past time I remedied that situation."

Kathryn gasped as Lucien gripped her shoulders and dragged her hard against him. His mouth crushed down over hers, and for an instant she simply stood there, feeling the heat of his lips, the hot glide of his tongue as he thrust it between her teeth. His arms tightened around her, drawing her closer still, and she could feel his hardened arousal.

Surprise changed to awareness as something in his manner shifted. His hands came up to cradle her face and she heard him groan. The kiss began to gentle, to seduce as well as demand, and desire rose like a hot wind out of nowhere. He tasted the corners of her mouth and his tongue slid like silk along her bottom lip. Her skin prickled and heat melted through her, pooling low in her belly. The slow, languid kiss turned hot once more, and Kathryn returned it with burning impatience, her own desire swelling with every heartbeat.

Unconsciously her hands slid up his lapels to twine around his neck and her legs began to tremble. He must have felt it, for he eased her backward till her hips touched the wall, giving her a measure of support. Another wet, fiery kiss and Kathryn softly moaned. He tasted the side of her neck, nibbled an earlobe, then began to unbutton the back of her simple gray wool gown. Looking down at her with scorching dark eyes, he tugged the pins from her hair one by one, and she heard each soft ping as they hit the stone floor, felt the weight of the heavy mass tumbling down over her shoulders.

"God . . . Kathryn." Lucien tangled his fingers in the softly curling strands, pulled her head back, and kissed her, ravishing her mouth and taking her deeply with his tongue. Kathryn kissed him back with the same fierce passion. She was trembling all over, hot and dizzy and weak.

With skillful, determined movements, he slid the gown off her shoulders, unfastened the tabs on her petticoats, and shoved the garments past her hips to the floor. Clad in just her chemise, stockings, and garters, she clung to him as lowered his head to her breasts, kissing them through the fabric, soaking the thin cotton with his tongue, watching as her nipple throbbed into tingling awareness.

"You belong to me, Kathryn," he whispered, sliding the strap of her chemise off one shoulder. "You're my wife now and that is the way it will stay."

"But . . . but what about . . . ?" He silenced her with a hot, hungry kiss that tore little whimpering noises from her throat. Then he was caressing her naked breasts, circling the tip with his tongue, and Kathryn's knees gave way beneath her. Only his sure grip kept her from falling. He eased his knee between her legs, setting her astride his thigh, and a hot, fierce ache bloomed at her core.

Her body tingled and throbbed. Sweet God, she was hot all over, embarrassingly wet and ready, her mind so muzzy she couldn't think. He filled his hands with her breasts, cupped them, teased them, tasted them. Her trembling fingers slipped into the hair at the nape of his neck, dislodging the ribbon that held it in place, and silky black strands slid over her palms.

He kissed her as his hands worked the buttons at the front of his breeches and he freed himself, then his hardened arousal pressed against her. He sifted through the dark curly hair at the juncture of her thighs and began to stroke her, gently at first, then more deeply, knowing exactly how to touch her, how to please her. Hot little jolts of desire burned through her and she heard herself crying his name.

Lucien stroked her with expert care. "I'm your husband," he whispered, his clever hands heightening her need for him. "Say it."

Kathryn whimpered.

"Say it," he softly coaxed.

"You're my . . . husband."

Urging her legs apart, he filled her with a single deep thrust that lifted her clear off the floor. Kathryn clung to his broad shoulders, her nails digging in, her bottom lip clamped between her teeth.

Lucien eased himself out, drove deeply in, and intense pleasure rolled through her. Out and then in, slowly, purposely, his muscles flexing, tightening, her own muscles pulsing around him. Lucien lifted her, guided her legs around his waist, and thrust into her again.

"God, I've wanted you for so damned long." He took her deeply, drove into her slowly and with exquisite care. She tried to think, but she couldn't, could barely remember to breathe.

She heard his voice as if from far away, low and thick and gruff. "You feel so good . . . so perfectly right." The words made her dizzier than she was already. Kathryn clung to his neck, her body trembling with heat and need, her stomach muscles contracting. Two more pounding thrusts had her clawing his shoulders, sobbing his name. Her body tightened, then spun away, exploding with such intense pleasure she thought that she might faint.

Lucien drove into her a moment more, then his body

clenched and he followed her to release, his long fingers gripping her bottom as he spilled his seed. Beginning to spiral down, Kathryn clung to him, thinking how much she loved him, how good it felt to be with him this way. How much she had wanted exactly this to happen.

# SEVENTEEN

Long minutes passed. Lucien pressed a soft kiss to the side of Kathryn's neck and lowered her back to her feet. His body felt sated and content as it hadn't in weeks. He could smell her soft perfume, still taste her on his lips. He liked the way she felt, standing slim and straight in the circle of his arms.

He gave her a last, brief kiss, bent down and retrieved her chemise. Kathryn slipped it over her head while he refastened the buttons on his breeches.

He hadn't meant to take her—not yet. He had come to the cottage to confront her, but anger had prodded him and desire drove him to act. Remembering how incredible it had felt to be inside her, he wasn't sorry.

He stroked her cheek even as his mind strayed backward, to other times, other women. Though he wasn't a selfish lover, with the rest he had simply taken his pleasure, using them as they used him and leaving nothing of himself when he was through.

With Kathryn it was different. Every time he looked at her, he wanted her. When he made love to her, he lost himself inside her in a way he never had before. He wanted to give her pleasure, wanted to absorb her into his skin, wanted to merge with her until he couldn't tell where he left off and Kathryn began. Kathryn fostered a need in him he hadn't even known he had, and that need seemed to grow each time they made love.

It frightened him to think a woman could affect him so, yet already he wanted to make love to her again.

He fastened the last button on his breeches and saw her staring up at him with big searching green eyes, confusion replacing the lazy contentment of moments ago.

"What about the annulment, Lucien? I thought we had agreed it was the best thing for us to do. It's what we both wanted."

"Is it? Perhaps there was a time I thought it was best, but not anymore. There isn't going to be an annulment, Kathryn. We are married and that is the way it will stay."

"But I thought . . . If you wanted a marriage in truth, why did you never return to my bedchamber? I realize that night was somewhat . . . that I did not please you . . . but I hoped in time—"

"That is what you thought? That you did not please me? Forgodsake, Kathryn, I've done nothing but think of bedding you since the day you walked into my study." And even as he looked at her now, her dark hair mussed and her lips kiss-swollen, he wanted her again.

"If that is so, why did you not return to my room?"

He trailed a finger along her jaw, felt a slight tremor pass through her. "Did you want me to?"

Kathryn glanced away, soft color rising in her cheeks. "Yes. I liked the way you touched me, the way you made me feel. I know most people don't think a woman should feel desire for a man, but I am not most women."

He couldn't argue with that. She was different from any woman he had ever met. It was that difference that disturbed him.

He sighed. "Perhaps that is the reason I stayed away. I was trying to sort things out. Once I did, I realized the best course was for us to stay married."

"Why? You might want me but you don't love me.

Why would you wish to stay married to a woman you don't love?"

Uncomfortable with the subject, he reached down and plucked up her simple wool dress. "Lift your arms."

Kathryn silently obeyed and he raised the dress over her head, settled it around her waist, and began to fasten the buttons. "Love is for innocents and fools, Kathryn. I am neither of those things. Companionship, common goals, parenthood. Those are the important matters to consider in a marriage."

Kathryn didn't argue, but there was something in her eyes that said she didn't completely agree. He turned away from her, frowned at his surroundings, started to stroll about the cottage. The displeasure he felt before returned with unsettling force.

"I realize you believe this work you are doing is important, Kathryn, but you know I don't approve." He picked up a pewter dish filled with a sticky syrup. "What is this?"

"It's a remedy for coughs I am making."

He held it beneath his nose and took a sniff, inhaled the scent of licorice and something sweet. "What's in it?"

"White wine, sugar candy, licorice powder, allicampane and arnica powders, trickle, and half a dozen figs."

He frowned and set the dish back down on the table. "You're the Marchioness of Litchfield," he said, continuing his survey, picking up a half-filled bottle here, a beaker there, finally making his way back to where she stood. "Fashioning potions and brewing elixirs isn't the way a lady of your position should behave."

"I'm helping people. How can that be bad?"

"You're lucky they aren't calling you a witch, and it remains to be seen whether you are helping anyone or not. Roger Ferris said his wife took to her bed for three days after she drank one of your potions. God knows what sort of havoc you might wreak on some other unfortunate soul."

"Roger's wife took to her bed as an excuse to avoid

her wifely duties. Apparently her husband is quite inept when it comes to making love."

Amusement flickered for a moment. One glance at the beakers and vials littering the room and it quickly faded away. "I don't give a fiddler's damn about Roger Ferris and his wife or anyone else. I want you to stop all of this nonsense at once."

"This is my life's work. Asking me to stop is like asking me not to breathe."

"Then you may as well start holding your breath. You are my wife and I forbid it. And in case you don't remember, you are the one who instigated this marriage."

"And you are the one who is now determined we shall both remain miserably locked within it."

He glared at her, his expression hard. Then he caught her chin with his hand, bent his head, and kissed her—a slow, lingering, very thorough kiss that had her clinging to his shoulders again.

"I don't think you shall hate being married to me so very much," he said with a trace of arrogance that Kathryn couldn't possibly have missed.

The mulish expression he had witnessed more than once settled over her features. "All right, you want me to stop, I'll stop. But I want something from you in return."

"And just what is that?"

"There's a child, a small boy at St. Bart's. I mentioned him once. Perhaps you remember."

He searched his mind, recalled the night he had awakened her from a nightmare in his study. "Yes, I remember you once said something about him."

"His name is Michael Bartholomew and he isn't the least insane—quite the opposite. He is bright and giving and a joy to be with. He was simply unfortunate enough to have been born in that place, the son of a woman who suffered a brutality from which she never mentally recovered."

Kathryn told him about Michael, how his mother had died right after the boy was born, how Kathryn couldn't bear to think of the lad being raised in a terrible place like St. Bart's.

"He's an orphan, Lucien. With nowhere to go and no possible future. As terrible as it is, it's a miracle they kept him there instead of tossing him out in the streets. He'd be dead by now if they had."

He studied her face, saw the anxiety there—and a desperate hope that he would agree. It wasn't precisely his plan to assume the burden of raising an orphan, but he had always liked children, he could certainly afford it, and if it gained Kathryn's cooperation it wasn't such a bad exchange.

He made a curt nod of his head. "All right, so be it. I'll arrange for the child's release and you will stay away from this blasted cottage and all that goes with it."

Some of the tightness left her features, but the tension remained in her shoulders. "As you wish, my lord." It was obvious she hated to concede to his demand, yet equally obvious she cared a great deal for the boy. "How long will it take, do you think?"

"I don't know. Probably not too long. I'll send a note to Nathaniel Whitley to complete the matter in all haste." His eyes moved over her, taking in her shining unbound hair, her disheveled clothes, the blush that lingered in her cheeks. The desire he had just sated rose up with amazing force. "In the meanwhile, I'll have your things moved into the marchioness's chambers."

The color deepened in her cheeks. She might not be the sort of wife he had imagined, but he wanted her, and now that their marriage was fact, he intended to have her. Striding to the door, he pulled it open and stood waiting for Kathryn to join him. As she crossed the room, she took a last wistful glance around the cozy little cottage. For an instant something unreadable flashed in her eyes.

Good Christ—surely she wasn't already scheming a way to return to the place! Lucien clamped down on his jaw at the thought. She wouldn't, he vowed, and tomorrow he would make certain. He would order the cottage cleaned out and put back in order, have Kathryn's so-called laboratory dismantled and disposed of. In the meanwhile, he would keep her well occupied in his bed.

It was time he got an heir. Lucien meant to see it done and the sooner the better. He glanced at Kathryn, felt his body stir, and thought that perhaps this afternoon would not be too soon to try again.

Winifred tossed and turned in the big four poster bed, unable to sleep, wishing dawn would come and she could go to Nathaniel. The journey to London had been uneventful. She should have waited till morning as the marquess suggested, but she had wanted to be there when Nat arrived at his office. And though she'd reached the city late in the evening, Litchfield's town house was kept fully staffed and her room was ready and waiting.

Thank heavens she hadn't the slightest idea where Nat lived—she might have disgraced herself and gone to his home like some doxy off the streets. Instead, she had retired to her room, hoping to sleep, knowing she would not. Now, as the hours rolled past, she lay awake, staring at the ceiling, imagining what Nat must have thought when she had spurned him so completely.

Just as she had before.

Her mind slid back more than twenty years, to that morning at Castle Running when she was a girl of eighteen, the day Nathaniel had come to ask her father for her hand in marriage. Winnie had awaited word upstairs, praying her father would agree, knowing in her heart that he would not.

"You're the daughter of the Marquess of Litchfield," he had said when he had called her down to his study. "Nathaniel Whitley is a commoner. I realize his family is wealthy—his father and I are friends or you would never have met him. Personally, I like the lad. He's intelligent and strong-minded. I have no doubt he'll make some young woman a very fine husband. But the fact remains, the boy is not a peer and that isn't going to change. You

are a lady, the only daughter of the Marquess of Litchfield, and Nathaniel is not the man you will marry."

Winnie had cried for days, but her father had not re-
lented. Instead it was the Viscount Beckford he chose as
her husband, and though she loved Nathaniel, it was the
way of things among the aristocracy and eventually Winnie resigned herself. In time, she had even convinced herself her love for Nat was merely a girlish infatuation.

But she had never forgotten him.

Winnie closed her eyes against a fleeting memory of
Nat sitting in the drawing room at Castle Running just
weeks ago, looking so unbearably handsome. *I've been
thinking about you, Winnie. I would very much like to see
you.*

Sweet God, the way she had behaved! Undoubtedly,
he believed she still didn't think he was good enough. In
truth it was her father who had felt that way, never her,
but unless she explained, Nat would not believe it.

Dawn finally arrived and Winnie rose from the bed
more exhausted than when she had arrived in London last
night. Still, she completed her morning ablutions and
dressed with care, choosing a dark blue taffeta gown with
scalloped ruffles on the underskirt and ruffled pagoda
sleeves, the stomacher softened by rows of mauve velvet
ribbon. Wide panniers made her waist look as small as a
girl's.

Her lady's maid, Florence Tauber, worked over her
hair, fashioning soft blond curls atop her head.

"You look lovely, milady." A woman in her forties
with a thin face and kindly eyes, Flo had been with Winnie since she was sixteen.

"Thank you, Flo." She fidgeted in front of the cheval
glass, hoping Nat wouldn't notice the faint lavender
smudges beneath her eyes, the trace of puffiness left over
from her tears.

Flo draped a fur-trimmed mantle over her shoulders,
enveloping her in its warm, soft folds. "You're all set,
milady. Whatever lucky man it is what's got you so head

up will surely take notice this fine mornin'."

Winnie felt herself blushing. How Florence had guessed there was a man involved she couldn't say, but the truth was the truth and she didn't bother to deny it. She just hoped Flo was right and that Nat would indeed take notice. More than that, she hoped he would forgive her.

"Do you think the carriage is out front yet?"

" 'Tis there, I'm sure." Flo smiled kindly. "I got poor Harry up before dawn to be certain it was ready."

Winnie smiled faintly and nodded. "Tell him I'm grateful, will you?"

Though it was unfashionably early and she wasn't sure Nathaniel would yet be in, Winnie climbed aboard the carriage and it rolled over the cobbles, off toward Nat's office on Threadneedle Street. It didn't take long. There wasn't much traffic at this hour of the morning, mostly peddlers and merchants, freight wagons, and hackney carriages carting passengers off to work.

The narrow brick building looked sleepy and uninhabited. Instructing the coachy to wait, she made her way to the door and found it locked, but lifted the heavy brass knocker and pounded away just the same, hoping he might have come in early.

To her relief, he opened the door himself, then stepped back in surprise when he saw who his visitor was, and a careful mask slid over his face.

"Lady Beckford. You are certainly up and about at an early hour this morning."

Winnie's fingers tightened on the front of her cloak. "I need to speak to you, Nathaniel. May I please come in?"

He opened the door a little wider. "Of course." A look of concern replaced his cool indifference. "I hope nothing untoward has happened. Lord Litchfield is not unwell? There hasn't been some sort of accident?"

"No, no, it's nothing at all like that." She watched him from beneath her lashes as he guided her into his private office and closed the door. She thought he looked even more attractive than he had the last time she had seen him, with his thick silver-tipped brown hair and blue eyes. "This isn't a business call. It is entirely personal. I needed to see you, Nathaniel. I . . ."

She let the sentence trail away, groping to find the right words, wishing in the long hours of the night she had been able to find them. But she hadn't, and now they seemed even more elusive.

"Perhaps you would care to sit down, Lady Beckford," he said with great formality, and the stiffness in his bearing tore straight into her heart.

"I should rather say this from right here if you don't mind." She stiffened her spine, determined to set matters straight. "I've come to apologize, Nathaniel."

"Apologize?" His smile turned slightly mocking. "Why would you apologize? If you are referring to conversations we have had in the recent past, it is I who should apologize. I spoke out of turn and you gave me the set down I deserve. I am a commoner, after all, while you are the Viscountess Beckford." Though some might have thought him sincere, Winnie didn't miss the sarcasm in his words. There was nothing about Nathaniel Whitley that gave the slightest indication he was anything less than her equal, and that was exactly the way Winnie wanted it.

She swallowed past the lump that had formed in her throat. "I'm afraid you don't understand. You see . . . when I said those things to you . . . I didn't know about . . . I didn't realize that you were . . . I've made a terrible mistake, Nathaniel."

"A mistake? Does that mean you have suddenly discovered you are lonely? Is that why you came, Winnie? You decided you need a man in your bed and as long as no one knows who it is—"

"Stop it! This has nothing at all to do with the fact you are not a nobleman—nothing in the least. The truth is I didn't know Emma was dead. I only just found out last night when my nephew chanced to mention it. Until then, I believed you were married. I thought you were proposing some . . . some sordid affair and I was . . . I was incensed. I didn't . . ." She glanced down at her hands. "I didn't think you were that sort of man, and it hurt me terribly to think that you were."

Nathaniel stood staring as if he didn't quite believe her. "You thought I was married?"

She nodded, fighting to hold back tears. "I'm sorry about Emma. I was staying mostly in the country at the time. It must have happened just before Richard took ill. He might have heard, but if he did he never said. I think he was always a little bit jealous of you."

"You thought I wanted to have an affair."

"Yes."

Nat reached out and took both of her hands. "Winnie . . . God, I'm so sorry. The terrible things I said. The awful things I thought."

A tear trickled down her cheek. "It isn't your fault, Nathaniel. I am the one to blame. I shouldn't have jumped to conclusions. Perhaps it was simply that you made me feel like a woman. I hadn't really felt that way in years and it frightened me. I hated myself for wanting to be with you when I believed you belonged to someone else."

She didn't know how it happened. One minute she was standing there looking up at him with tears in her eyes, and the next she was in his arms.

"I've been half crazy since the first time I saw you at Castle Running," he said against her ear. "It was as if the intervening years had never happened, as if time had gone backward and you were the same girl I once fell in love with."

Winnie clung to him, absorbing his heat, his strength. "It was the same for me, Nat. I wanted to see you and I felt so terribly guilty."

He drew back to look at her. "Say you will allow me to call. I realize it could pose problems for both of us. Your nephew employs me and he may very well disapprove. Others of your class most assuredly will. Perhaps there are steps we could take, some way to make things easier."

"I'm a grown woman, Nat. I don't care what people think—I never did."

His hand came up to her cheek. She saw that he didn't believe her, but in time, she would convince him. Winnie gazed into those clear blue eyes as he bent his head and very tenderly kissed her. She could feel him all around her, invading her senses, the same as it was before and yet completely different.

Nat ended the kiss before she wanted him to and she could feel his restraint in the shudder that rippled through his body.

"I'll call for you tonight," he said. "There is a quiet little inn at the edge of the city where no one will see us—"

"No," Winnie said firmly, her heart filled with so much joy it was nearly painful. "As much as I should like to keep you all to myself, I believe tonight I would rather attend the theater—if that is all right with you."

He understood what she was saying, that she really didn't care who saw them. At the brilliance of his smile, she nearly came undone.

"The theater, then," he said, accepting at last that being a peer was unimportant. "And afterward we shall take supper somewhere quiet where we can catch up on the years."

"Yes," she said, her hand still warmly clasped in his. "I should like that, Nat. I should like it very much." More than he could guess, she thought. Much more.

At last they would have the chance that had been stolen from them so long ago. And this time no one was going to come between them.

"Ouch!" Kathryn sucked a drop of blood from the tip of her finger and glared down at the pillowcase she had been embroidering. The stitches were small and even, like the ones she had used to sew the cut in Lucien's arm. But working over a patient was far different from sewing colored flowers onto a piece of cloth. Stitchery held no appeal for her and never had. To Kathryn it was tedious and boring.

She sighed and set the pillowcase aside. Rising from her chair, she ambled over to the window, her gaze drifting down to the little stream winding its way into the woods. Since the day the marquess had confronted her in the cottage, they had been existing in a fragile truce. During the days, Lucien worked at managing his estates while Kathryn fidgeted and wandered about, bored and longing to return to her studies.

At night, he came to her bedchamber and she forgot her work, her driving need to learn. One long, searing kiss, one touch of those clever, skillful hands, and Kathryn thought only of Lucien, of the pleasure he gave her, of how much she desired him. It wasn't until he left her in the early hours of the morning that she thought of the love for him that he did not return and a painful ache throbbed inside her.

During the day, he never sought her out. There were no soft looks of affection, no tender endearments. It was as she had feared—he wanted her but beyond that she barely existed.

Her heart squeezed hard to think of it. She wanted him to love her, wanted to share his life and for him to share hers. It made her sad to think of the loveless years ahead, yet the bargain of her marriage was now fact—a bargain of her own making—and she couldn't deny she had gained the protection she had so desperately needed. She was free of her uncle, free of the madhouse—she could endure if only she had her work.

With her little maid Fanny's help, Kathryn had managed to discover the marquess's plans to dismantle her laboratory and thwart his efforts in that regard. Since she had helped a few of his staff with her remedies, they were willing to risk Litchfield's wrath by packing and carefully storing the items away instead of discarding them.

Each day she thought of the herbs she had so carefully potted withering into dust and blowing away, the potions she had so painstakingly concocted that did no one the least amount of good. She had given up the work of her heart to save little Michael, but knowing he would soon be safe made the sacrifice worthwhile.

And it wouldn't be forever, she vowed. Thanks to the marquess's efforts, sometime on the morrow, the child would be arriving from London. Once Michael was there at the castle and safe, she would find a way to return to her studies.

Standing at the window, Kathryn stared down at the little brook, her gaze following a stick of wood that meandered along in the current and finally disappeared from view as the stream ran into the woods. She missed the serenity she found in the books she read in the little cottage, missed the thrill of helping someone who came to her in need. She couldn't live an entire lifetime stabbing at a piece of embroidery or pounding out tunes on the harpsichord.

And as much as she adored little Michael, even the child's presence in the house would not be enough to sustain her. She needed her work, just as the marquess needed his. Kathryn vowed, as she had done since her parents had died, she would do whatever it took to accomplish that end.

# EIGHTEEN

Lucien leaned against the railing at the top of the sweeping stone staircase that led down to the foyer. Below him, Kathryn stood beside the small blond boy, Michael Bartholomew. The child was clutching her hand, gripping it as if he would be lost in the bowels of the castle and never be seen again should he let go.

Michael had arrived by carriage the night before, accompanied by a footman from Lucien's London town house, the arrangements having been made by Nathaniel Whitley. With only a modicum of effort—and a goodly sum of coin—the boy had been released from St. Bart's into his care.

Lucien watched him now, the child small and thin and nearly towheaded, with big blue eyes that widened in awe at the elegant crystal, gleaming marble, and glittering gilt that decorated the house. Kathryn had said the boy had rarely been out of St. Bart's, only an occasional outing when one of the matrons took him along to pick up supplies. It was obvious by looking at him now how little of the world he had seen.

He pointed up at the painted ceiling. "Pictures," he exclaimed. "I never seen pictures on a ceilin' afore. 'Ow do ye s'ppose the fella got up there to paint 'em?"

Kathryn laughed and Lucien felt the pull of a smile. While his wife explained that craftsman had been brought to the castle from Italy a hundred years ago, he descended the stairs to join them.

They turned at his approach. "Good morning, Michael." Though he had met the boy last night, the child had said little, just clung to Kathryn's hand and stared at his surroundings as if he had arrived on the moon.

"Good mornin', sir," he said now, gazing up at Lucien with nearly the same look of wonder the painted ceiling had garnered.

"You are to call the marquess his lordship," Kathryn explained to him. "You should say, 'Good day, your lordship.' Or 'Good day, my lord.' "

He straightened. "Good day, ye lordship."

Lucien smiled. "I trust you slept well, Michael."

Small teeth flashed in a grin that displayed a bit more self-confidence. "Nearly suffocated, me lord, in all them deep feathers. But it were real nice, once I got used to it."

Lucien stifled an urge to laugh. "Have you two already eaten? I believe Cook has outdone herself, knowing we have a new arrival in the house."

Kathryn squeezed Michael's hand, then looked up at Lucien and smiled with such gratitude an odd tightness rose in his chest. "Actually we were just heading into the breakfast parlor. Perhaps you would care to join us, my lord."

"Yes, I believe I would." He waited for Kathryn to lead the way, but before she could take a step, Michael let go of her hand and walked over to where he stood at the bottom of the stairs. Tentatively, the boy's small hand reached out to touch the burgundy velvet trim at the bottom of his morning coat.

"Whot's it made of? I never felt nothin' so soft."

Lucien looked down at the child, at the coarse brown breeches and white homespun shirt Nat Whitley had provided, simple but undoubtedly an improvement over the dirty rags he must have worn at St. Bart's.

"The trim is velvet. The breeches are fashioned of a material called satin."

Michael touched the cloth encasing his thigh, testing the feel of the smooth, slick fabric. "They's the prettiest clothes I ever seed."

Lucien's mouth curved up. "There are times I would trade them for homespun, but you are right, I suppose— they are rather pretty."

"When I grow up, I'm gonna wear some just like 'em."

Kathryn bent down and hugged him. "I'm sure you will, Michael."

Mentally, Lucien made a note to call on his tailor. The child would be clothed appropriately, and soon—he would see to the matter himself.

"All right, now, why don't we get something to eat?" Kathryn extended a hand and the boy latched onto it.

"I 'ope it ain't gruel," he muttered, making Lucien's lips twitch again.

"No gruel today," he said. "Let's see how you like roast pheasant."

Michael Bartholomew adored it. As well as the sausage and coddled eggs, the Wilton cheese and apple pastries, and especially the steaming hot chocolate. Lucien had never seen anyone so small eat so much. He thought that perhaps he should stop the boy before he gorged himself to the point of being sick, but thought better of it.

In time the child would learn there would be plenty of food at every meal. For today, a bit of an upset stomach was probably a small price to pay for indulging in such a treat.

"I thought I'd show Michael the rest of the house," Kathryn said from her chair beside him, wiping her mouth with a white linen napkin then returning it to her lap.

The child watched her carefully and did exactly the same.

Lucien took a sip of his coffee. "Good idea. I've some

work to finish today, but perhaps on the morrow, we'll go out to the stable. I imagine Michael would enjoy seeing the horses."

Big blue eyes swung to his face. "You have 'orses?"

He nodded. "An entire stable full of them."

"I like 'orses. I seen some pretty ones pullin' them fancy carriages when people come to see the mad folk. Could I ride one, do ye think?" There was such yearning in the small boy's face, Lucien felt an unexpected tug at his heart.

"I imagine that could be arranged."

He grinned, his cheeks going bright with excitement. "Such a grand 'ouse, and 'orses, too! God's eyes, Kathryn, I never knew ye was so bloody rich!"

Lucien nearly choked on the coffee he was drinking while Kathryn struggled to stifle a laugh. God's eyes, indeed, he thought—how in heaven's name had he managed to saddle himself with such an outrageous pair?

Still, as he watched the boy climb down from the table, reach back when no one was looking, grab a length of sausage and hide it beneath his shirt, he couldn't help being glad the boy was there and no longer at St. Bart's.

As the marquess had promised, the following morning Kathryn walked with her husband and Michael out to the stable. The three of them had spent the evening otogether, Michael talking endlessly of the beautiful things he had seen in the castle, waving his arms and pointing, describing each incredible sight. He had enjoyed the portrait gallery and its lengthy row of paintings of Litchfield nobility, but he liked the Great Hall best of all, with its medieval suits of armor, ancient swords, fierce-looking axes and shields.

They had shared a quiet supper together, which they wouldn't often do once he was settled and a proper governess found. After such an exciting day, his eyelids drooping through the meal, Michael had fallen asleep as soon as he had stuffed in the last possible bite of food.

Lucien had carried him up to his bed on the third floor in a room next to the nursery.

In the morning, when Kathryn arrived downstairs, she found the child with Lucien in his study, standing next to the marquess's desk. She watched them from the doorway.

"I was wonderin', me lord . . . do ye think when I grow up I could learn to be a proper gent like ye?"

Lucien smiled. "You can be anything you want to be, Michael. All it takes is determination."

"Would ye teach me?"

"Teach you?"

"Aye, me lord. Would ye teach me to speak the way ye do? Like a proper gent should."

Lucien turned away from his work to scrutinize the child more closely. "I imagine we could work on it."

Michael grinned up at him and Lucien smiled back. Then his glance strayed to where she stood in the doorway, and the air seemed to heat between them. A soft buttery sensation slid into Kathryn's stomach.

The marquess shoved back his chair and came to his feet. "Good morning, my lady." His glance was long and penetrating, as if he were remembering the way he had left her that morning, in a pile of rumpled covers, naked and sleepy from his early bout of lovemaking.

Michael tugged at the hem of Lucien's coat. "Can we go out to the stables now, me lord? Ye said we could go as soon as Kathryn come down."

"It isn't *ye,* Michael. It's *you.* That can be your first lesson in how to speak. You should practice it until it comes naturally."

Michael grinned. "*You. You* said that we could go out to the stables as soon as Kathryn come down."

"And after we have had a bite to eat."

Food never failed to sway him. "It ain't gruel, is it?"

Laughter sparkled in the marquess's eyes. "I doubt you will ever be forced to eat the stuff again."

"Yeowee!" Michael lifted his arms in the air and

twirled around, then raced happily toward Kathryn, stopping at the door where she stood. At first she had been worried he might have been harmed by the guards in the weeks since she had left St. Bart's, but his happy disposition assured her he was not. "No gruel, Kathryn! Did ye—*you* 'ear what 'is lordship said? We never 'ave to eat the bleedin' stuff again!"

Kathryn bit down on her lip to keep from laughing, glanced sideways to see Lucien scowl, but she could have sworn it was amusement that faintly curved his lips.

"Your second lesson for the day will be that a child your age must not address his elders by their first names. From now on you will refer to Kathryn as my lady or her ladyship."

Kathryn inwardly winced. She hadn't had the heart to correct the boy, though she knew sooner or later she would have to. In the madhouse it didn't matter, but here . . . here life was altogether different. He would have to learn to follow the rules if he were to make his way in the world of the nobility.

Michael frowned as he looked up at Kathryn, then his buoyant spirit returned. "The guards always said ye—you was a lady. That shouldn't be too 'ard."

Kathryn bent down and hugged him. He was such an adorable boy.

They breakfasted together, then afterward headed out to the stable.

"Look, Kathryn! 'Orses!" Michael tore free of her hand and dashed to the pen at the side of the big two-story stone building where the horses were kept. At the end of a lead line, one of the stallions was being exercised by a groom. "Do ye—you think I could ride 'im?"

Lucien chuckled softly. "Not that one—at least not yet. He's young and full of himself. To begin with, you'll need an animal that's a bit easier to handle."

They walked into the darkened interior of the stable and the smell of hay and horses rose up. Dust motes swirled in the sunlight slanting in through the windows.

Above them, men were working with a big metal hoist, lifting heavy bags of grain into the loft.

"I think Robin might be a good horse to start with."

" 'Is name is Robin?"

"Gray's Robin is his full name."

As they approached the stall, Michael looked at the little dappled gelding with reverence. "Gray's Robin. 'E's a beauty, me lord."

The little horse whickered softly and Lucien smiled. "He's only fourteen hands and tame as a dog. He'll be a good horse for you to ride while you're learning." He turned to one of the stable hands and Kathryn saw it was Bennie Taylor.

"Michael, this is Bennie. He's very good with horses. He's the one who will teach you to ride."

Bennie bent down and shook Michael's hand. "Mornin,' lad." He glanced over to the dappled gelding. "His lordship's picked ye a good one."

Michael opened his mouth to correct his speech, but Lucien subtly shook his head. "When can we start?" Michael asked instead.

Bennie looked to Lucien, who simply nodded. "I'd say now's as good a time as any."

"Right enough!" Michael said, jumping up and down.

Kathryn watched the boy race off with Bennie as if they were long-lost friends. The child had never been shy. Michael had been born among strangers and, for the last seven years, they had been his life, his family.

She shifted her attention to Lucien. "You've been wonderful to Michael. I wanted him out of that place and safe. In truth, I never really expected you to welcome him so completely."

His dark gaze followed the boy. "He's an easy child to like. Tomorrow I'll arrange for a tutor so that he can begin his studies."

Kathryn smiled. "Believe it or not, he'll be pleased. Michael craves learning. He's fascinated by everything new he sees."

"So I've noticed." They turned and started walking, Lucien's hand at her waist as they stepped out from below the loft. The instant they reached the edge of the over-hang, Kathryn heard Michael's high-pitched scream.

"Me lord! Look out!" The child was running madly, trying to reach them, when Lucien looked up. Coming straight at him, the heavy iron hoist had snapped free of its rope and crashed down toward his head. Lucien slammed into Kathryn, knocking her out of the way, and both of them were hurled to the ground.

"Me lord! Me lord!" Michael reached them, Bennie Taylor at his heels, skidding to a halt just a few feet in front of them. "It nearly hit ye! God's eyes, it nearly kilt ye!" The child was shaking and so was Kathryn.

Lucien climbed to his feet, brushing dirt and straw from his coat and breeches. "Are you all right?" he asked Kathryn as he helped her to stand.

"I—I'm fine. Just a bit shaken up, is all." But she continued to tremble and so did Michael. Lucien reached down and picked the child up, holding him gently against his chest. "We're all right. Thanks to you, Michael, both of us are fine."

The boy's small arms slid around Lucien's neck. He buried his head against the marquess's shoulder. Michael had never had a father and it was obvious he had already adopted Lucien. Kathryn felt a painful tightening in her chest.

"It's all right, lad," the marquess soothed. "It was an accident. Sometimes those things happen." He set the boy down and Kathryn drew the child against her skirts while the marquess turned to inspect the fallen hoist. It was big and heavy, and if it had hit him, there was little doubt he would have been killed.

Another shudder rippled through her.

"What happened?" Lucien turned a hard look on the men who had been working up in the loft, all now clustered down below around the hoist. One of them stepped forward, his face as pale as Kathryn's.

"Can't say for certain, milord. We been workin' here all mornin' without a problem. Guess the rope musta been worn. If it was, none of us noticed." He straightened, squaring his shoulders, but his face was lined with tension. "I guess you'll be wantin' the lot of us to leave."

Lucien studied the men's stricken faces. Most of them had families to feed. "It was an accident. As I said, those things happen. Just be certain it doesn't happen again."

Relief and a smile broke over the man's craggy features. "Thank you, milord. We'll take better care from now on. You won't be sorry you let us stay."

Lucien nodded. "See that I'm not." Returning to Kathryn, he slid an arm around her waist in a more intimate manner than he usually did, and smiled down at the boy. "Go on with Bennie, Michael. Robin is waiting."

In the way of children, the incident was already forgotten. Michael smiled and nodded and raced off with Bennie while Lucien led Kathryn back up the path to the house.

"Michael was right," she said. "You could have been killed."

Lucien tossed a last glance at the fallen hoist. "I could have been, but I wasn't." A corner of his mouth inched up. "But I do feel an overwhelming urge to procreate. Perhaps we should retire upstairs for a nap."

"What? In the middle of the day?"

The marquess just smiled. "Come, love. I have plans for you that don't include a seven-year-old boy."

Kathryn flushed a bit and her heart kicked up as images of hard male muscle and clever, skillful hands began to flash through her head. But as he led her away, she glanced back at the fallen hoist and the group of men gathered around it. Twice in the past few weeks, the marquess had almost been killed. Surely it was simple coincidence.

Still, a thread of unease trickled through her. It niggled at her all the way back to the house.

•   •   •

Dr. Silas Cunningham tugged at the reins of his small black phaeton, pulling the horse to a halt in front of the massive stone castle. He had posted a letter, advising Kathryn Grayson Montaine, newly titled Marchioness of Litchfield, of his pending arrival, but he wasn't certain the sort of greeting he would receive.

In light of the fact he had failed her, a woman he considered a valued friend and in a strange way even a colleague, he wasn't sure what sort he deserved.

Silas set the brake, dragged in a fortifying breath, and jumped down from the phaeton, handing the reins to one of the stable lads who rushed up at his arrival. Even before he had reached the top of the front porch steps, the heavy wooden door flew open and Kathryn appeared in the opening.

"Dr. Cunningham!" She smiled in that warm, unaffected manner that had endeared her to him from the moment of their first meeting. "I was so excited when I received your letter—I can hardly believe you are actually here. Please do come in."

Some of his tension eased. He pulled his tricorn from his head, straightened his gray bagwig, and followed her up the stairs and into the house. The butler took his hat and greatcoat, and Kathryn led him into a sumptuous drawing room done in ivory and gold.

"I'm sorry my husband isn't here," she told him as she rang for tea. "I should very much have liked for you to meet him. Unfortunately, some sort of business came up in the city and he had to leave for a couple of days."

She looked as fresh and lovely as he remembered, none the worse for her terrible ordeal in the madhouse. Her smile was bright and welcoming, her hair a gleaming dark brown, and the color in her cheeks matched the hue of her rose silk skirts.

"You must be wondering how I found you after all this time. Actually, I learned of your whereabouts some weeks back through your husband's solicitor, Nathaniel Whitley. At the time, Mr. Whitley was working with the marquess in an effort to obtain your release from St. Bart's. He came to me asking about the events that took place at the time your uncle had you committed. I told him the truth, that it was all a pack of lies—but I had only the faintest hope it would be of help in obtaining your release. I did, however, ask him to keep me informed of his progress. When I heard from Mr. Whitley again, he told me of your marriage to Lord Litchfield and that I could find you here."

Silas surveyed the expensive furnishings, the gold brocade sofas and heavy velvet draperies, a far cry from the barren cell she must have occupied at St. Bart's.

Kathryn took his arm and led him over to a comfortable chair. "It's rather a miracle I am here and a very long story." She sat down across from him and a servant appeared with a silver tea tray, which was set on the table in front of them. Kathryn poured him a cup, adding sugar and cream. "Suffice it to say, thanks to the efforts of my husband, I am out from under my uncle's dictates and free of St. Bart's for good."

Silas shook his head. "Such a terrible thing to happen. I know I failed you miserably. That is one of the reasons I came here today. I hope you can find it in your heart to forgive me."

Kathryn stirred her tea with great precision, then very carefully set the silver spoon in the saucer. "I realize my uncle threatened to ruin you, Silas. I know you had a family to consider. You had no choice but to keep your silence."

"It was far worse than that. Lord Dunstan threatened Margaret and the children. He demanded I leave Wilford Village. He insinuated quite strongly that if I interfered in your defense in any manner, I might never see my family again."

Kathryn's slim hands trembled against the lace trim on her skirt. "My uncle is utterly ruthless. I am glad you didn't try to thwart him." She smiled, but it looked forced, as if the subject still pained her. "At any rate, all of that is over and done. Tell me about yourself. How are your studies progressing?"

"That, my dear, is the second reason I have come. I have recently accepted a teaching position at a small physician's college in Guildford."

"That's wonderful, Silas. Guildford isn't all that far away. Perhaps you'll be able to stop by on occasion for a visit."

"I should like that very much." He took a sip of tea. "You know how difficult it is to do research on human anatomy, public opinion being what it is. That is one of the reasons I accepted the position. The school is small and very discreet. So far the townspeople have only made mild rumblings of protest at the subjects we teach, and it is one of the few institutes that condones the use of human dissection as a tool of learning."

In medieval times, dissecting a human corpse had been banned by the church. Even now, hundreds of years later, the study of the human body was still highly opposed. Physicians received only the most cursory information. Most surgeons got their training in the military rather than the schoolroom, and their social status wasn't much higher than that of a barber—which many of them actually were. But a few men of medicine, men like Silas, believed the answers to healing lay in a greater knowledge of how the human body worked.

"I'm glad you've finally found a place to go forward with your studies," Kathryn said.

"It's been extremely productive thus far. I thought . . . if you are still interested in such things . . . that perhaps you might wish to come down to Guildford and take a look at some of the work that is being done there."

Kathryn's head snapped up so quickly she nearly spilled her tea. "Oh, Dr. Cunningham—I would love to! You can't begin to know how much I've missed our sessions."

"It would have to be done after hours, of course. It would be highly unseemly for a woman—especially one of your social rank—to be discovered in such circumstances. But I imagined you might wish to come, and it is the least I can do to make up for all you have suffered."

"Oh, Silas—yes! There are a number of things I've been working on as well, herbal remedies mostly, but some have distinct possibilities. I've been reading as much as I can, but modern texts are difficult to find and there are few on human anatomy." The change in her bearing made him inwardly smile. She was no longer the dignified lady of the manor, but the vibrant young woman he had known before, bubbling with enthusiasm, ready and eager to learn.

Silas described some of the projects they were involved in. Research, for example, to develop safe inoculations against smallpox. At present, though the patient himself might be saved, the inoculated person was so contagious, those around him often fell ill and died. Mostly they were working on more intricate delvings into the way the human body worked; the search for a way to stop pain when surgery was required; and the ongoing study of how they might learn to prevent putrefaction.

"It is really quite exciting," he said, "though progress is undeniably slow."

"I can hardly wait to get there," Kathryn said.

"And your husband? Will the marquess be coming as well?"

For the first time, she looked uneasy. "I'm afraid my husband disapproves of my interests in medicine nearly as much as my uncle." She smiled, somewhat sadly, he thought. "However, there is little fear he will have me committed should he discover I have gone to visit an old friend who happens to be a physician."

Silas returned the smile. "I am glad to hear it." He set his teacup down on the marble-topped table beside his chair. "And since it is certain that you are now in safe hands, it is time I took my leave." Kathryn rose and so did Silas. "Send a note when it is convenient for you to come. We've taken a nice, roomy house at the edge of the village. There is plenty of space and I know Margaret would enjoy your visit."

Kathryn took his arm and walked him to the door. He could almost see the wheels turning in her head. He had never seen a pupil more intrigued—or more determined to learn—than this one. It was a shame she was a woman. Still, he had wanted to give her something for the pain he had inadvertently caused, and he knew education was the thing she wanted most.

"Adieu, then," he said. "I look forward to seeing you."

"As I do, Doctor. It make take a while, but I'll arrange things at the first opportunity."

He left her in the entry and returned to his phaeton, climbed aboard and headed toward the road back to Guildford. He would see her, he knew, and soon. Kathryn Grayson Montaine was passionate about all aspects of life and her studies were certainly among them.

He thought of her husband and hoped he understood what a jewel he had in her. Rarely had he seen a woman of such strength and courage. Not even the cruelties imposed by her uncle could break her spirit.

He smiled to think of the studies going on at the college and found himself eager to share with his former pupil some of the knowledge he had garnered in the months that had passed.

# NINETEEN

Time ticked away. Though Kathryn had hoped an opportunity would arise to visit Dr. Cunningham, it did not. She consoled herself by spending time with little Michael, who had settled into the routine of life at the castle as if he had been born there. He had a tutor now and a governess, and at Lucien's insistence dressed as if he were the son of a lord instead of a homeless orphan the marquess had rescued from St. Bart's.

It was amazing the bond the pair had formed. Seeing them together, Kathryn realized how much her husband loved children and what a wonderful father he would make. Lucien wanted that above all else, she knew, perhaps more so now that Michael had shown him what it might be like to have a child of his own. He wanted a son and heir, and he set out to accomplish the task with driving purpose. There were times, late at night, when Lucien arrived at her bedchamber door and Kathryn resented him for it.

Then he would touch her, kiss her, whisper soft erotic words, and she would be lost. In those moments, she forgot his only use of her was to give him a son, that aside from the passion they shared, she held no special place in his life, in his heart. In truth, most of the time, he seemed to go out of his way to avoid her, to guard himself in some way whenever she was near.

Distressed at being unable to bridge the distance between them, Kathryn sought out Aunt Winnie when she returned from London. She found her in the conservatory, sitting on a wrought-iron bench in front of a mossy-bottomed pond. Winnie smiled when she looked up and saw Kathryn, and there was a softness, a serenity, in her face that hadn't been there the last time Kathryn had seen her.

"Good morning, my dear." Winnie patted a place on the iron bench beside her. "We've hardly had a moment to speak. Why don't you join me?"

"Actually, I've been looking for you, Aunt Winnie. Reeves thought I might find you here."

The blond woman sighed. "I should rather be out in the garden, but there is still a nip in the air. Besides, I do enjoy watching the fish."

Kathryn sat down on the bench, her apricot skirts spreading out around her. "You seem different since your return, Aunt Winnie. Brighter somehow than when you left. Are you so much happier living in the city than you were out here in the country?"

Winnie waved away the notion. "Don't be silly, my dear, it has nothing to do with that."

"Then what is it?"

For a moment, Winnie hesitated. She plucked at the lace on the sleeve of her blue silk gown. "I have something to tell you. I'm not certain what my nephew will have to say about it, but I don't believe that you will condemn me."

"Condemn you? Good heavens, Winnie, whatever for?"

That soft look reappeared and she smiled. "I've fallen in love, my dear. Totally and completely and without the slightest reservation. I'm in love with Nathaniel Whitley and he is in love with me."

Surprise, happiness, and a soft throb of pain moved through her. She was delighted for Winnie, yet seeing the joy on her face made the loveless void Kathryn lived in seem all the worse.

She leaned over and hugged the woman who had become such a dear and loving friend. "I think it's wonderful, Winnie. I couldn't be happier for you."

"Some people will think I'm a fool. They'll say Nat's a fortune hunter, even though he has money of his own. And they'll think I'm marrying beneath myself."

Kathryn squeezed Winnie's hand. "Well, I say you are lucky to have found a man like Nat and he is even luckier to have found you."

"He's wonderful, Kathryn. Nat is kind and caring. He is generous and good to a fault. He has asked me to marry him and I have agreed. He wished to speak to Lucien about it, but I asked him to let me talk to him first."

"Surely you don't think the marquess will oppose the marriage?"

Winnie glanced down at the water, watched one of the fish duck out of sight beneath a miniature ceramic bridge. "I'm not certain. It won't make any difference—I shall marry Nathaniel no matter what anyone says—but Lucien is family and I do so want his approval."

"I know he thinks a great deal of Nat. I can't imagine he'll be anything but pleased."

"I wish I could be sure. I've quite a sizable fortune. Lucien might think, as my father did, that I should marry a man of my own class."

Kathryn glanced away, her own situation rising up with painful force. "Lucien doesn't know what love is—you told me that yourself. He doesn't understand that there is nothing more important in this world than loving someone and being loved in return." She blinked against the sudden burn of tears. "I love him so much, Aunt Winnie. I would give anything if he were in love with me."

She felt Winnie's arms go around her. "There now, you mustn't despair, my dear. My nephew is a good man and

I believe he cares for you greatly. I have never seen him look at a woman the way he looks at you." She shook her head, searching for words to describe it. "There is such a terrible yearning in his face."

Kathryn scoffed. "What could he possibly be yearning for? I'm his wife. He comes to my bed whenever he wishes. Aside from an heir, there is nothing else he wants from me."

"Perhaps he wants your love, my dear. You see, my nephew may not know what love is, but that doesn't mean he doesn't need it, just like everyone else. I don't know how much you know about our family, but Lucien lost his mother when he was twelve and his father died not long after."

Kathryn looked down at the hands she rested in her lap. "The servants talk. I've heard some of the gossip. His mother ran off with another man, and his father was heart-broken. Apparently he loved her very much."

"William loved her—or at least thought he did. In truth, it was more of an obsession. Charlotte was beautiful and headstrong, and my brother was determined to have her. But Charlotte was never the sort of woman to be happy with just one man. After she left, William became so depressed he began to dabble with opium. He died one day when he took too much."

Kathryn felt a wave of pity. She had lost her own parents. She knew what it was like to feel so completely alone. "It must have been terrible for Lucien. He had already lost his mother. Losing his father must have taken a tremendous toll."

"I'm sure it did, though he never really showed it. My father—Lucien's grandfather—raised him after my brother died. My father saw William's obsession with Charlotte as a weakness, and he was determined his grandson wouldn't turn into the spineless man his son had become because of his love for a woman. Lucien was raised to guard his emotions, never to reveal his true feelings, to be completely self-reliant."

"Well, he certainly succeeded."

"Yes, he did. Too well for his own good. Charlotte was a strong-minded woman, outspoken, and determined. I think my nephew sees some of those traits in you and it scares him to death. The difference is, except for your strength, you are nothing at all like Charlotte. Perhaps in time, he will come to realize that." Winnie reached over and took her hand. "My nephew might have learned to hide it, but I know there are times he is lonely—and he has always been desperately in need of love."

"He loves little Michael. Already he is fiercely protective of the child."

"The boy is a pure delight and Lucien has always loved children. My nephew has a heart full of love to give. He simply doesn't know how to give it to a woman."

"Then you think that perhaps in time . . . ?"

"You must believe that. There is always room for hope."

*Hope.* It was a word she had clung to for years. Where her husband was concerned, she wasn't sure how much longer she could believe in the possibility. Forcing away the painful thought, Kathryn returned her attention to Winnie and her upcoming marriage.

"My husband may not know what it means to fall in love, but he respects Nat Whitley and I know he would want you to be happy."

Footsteps sounded behind them just then. "Happy?" Lucien strode toward them with a smile. "How could I possibly be happy when my favorite aunt is abandoning me for life in the city?" He'd been partridge-hunting with the duke. He still wore his shooting jacket and high black riding boots. With his dark hair slightly wind-tossed, he looked unbearably handsome.

Winnie nervously toyed with a wisp of blond hair, fallen loose from the soft curls atop her head. "I'm your favorite aunt because I'm your only aunt, and I am hoping you'll be happy for me because . . . because I am soon to be married."

"Married!" His eyes swung to Kathryn and for an instant there was something intimate and disturbing in his gaze. "Who is the lucky man—and it had better be Nat Whitley."

Winnie sputtered in surprise, then leapt to her feet, her solemn expression disappearing in a brilliant smile. "Then you don't disapprove?"

"Of course not. I can't think of a man who would make a finer husband than Nat, and I know how much he cares for you."

Her arms went around him and Winnie hugged him hard. "Thank you, Lucien. I love him so much and I was so worried." Winnie's eyes misted with tears. "Nat wanted to speak to you, but I couldn't bear the thought that you might not approve. My father turned him away from my door when he was a boy. I couldn't bear to think of him being hurt again."

"I'm happy to welcome Nat into the family. I hope you will tell him I said so."

"Yes. Oh, yes, I shall." She drew a pretty lace handkerchief from the pocket of her skirt and wiped at the wetness on her cheeks. "I can't remember when I've ever been so happy."

Kathryn smiled. "You deserve to be happy, Aunt Winnie." For an instant, her gaze strayed to the dark eyes of her husband. Something unreadable moved in their depths, then it was gone. She wondered what he was thinking, wondered if there was the slightest chance that one day he would come to love her as Nat Whitley loved Winnie DeWitt.

Knowing him as she now did, Kathryn didn't believe there was. She continued to smile, but her heart ached unbearably.

Lucien dug his heels into the sides of his spirited black stallion, urging the horse to a faster gallop across the fields. He was restless today, oddly disturbed in some manner. He wasn't certain what it was. He only knew that Kathryn was the cause.

In the past few days since his aunt had left to return to London, something had shifted between them. Kathryn had been listless and strangely remote, keeping to herself and rarely spending time even with little Michael. Sensing her withdrawal but unsure of the cause, he had left her alone, staying away even from her bedchamber at night.

Though his body craved the release he was accustomed to seeking, he had forced himself not to go to her, hoping in time her usual high spirits would return. So far that hadn't occurred. At night, lying alone in his big four-poster bed, his body ached with frustrated desire for her, but it was more than that. He wanted simply to be with her, to lie beside her and hold her while she slept.

It terrified him to think he wanted more from his wife than occasional companionship and the use of her body, but he was beginning to think that he did. He found himself straining to hear her voice, the warm sound of her laughter, as she passed down the hall. During the day, he stood at the window overlooking the garden just to get a glimpse of her, to watch the way the sunlight glinted off the auburn in her hair.

Two days ago, he bought her a small, leather-bound volume of Shakespeare's sonnets, hoping to distract her from the melancholy she had sunk into.

"You bought this for me?" She seemed incredulous he would do even such a small, simple thing, and he found the thought more than a little disturbing.

He cleared his throat. "I thought . . . hoped you might like it. You have seemed a bit out of sorts of late."

For an instant he could have sworn her eyes had misted with tears. "Thank you, my lord. I shall treasure it always." She had accepted the book and held it against her breast as if it were fashioned of gold instead of merely paper, smiling up at him with such sweetness something clenched hard in his chest.

Lucien reined the black toward the open fields and increased his speed, set the stallion into a steady pace toward the stone wall that loomed ahead. The stallion was an excellent jumper. He sailed over the wall with ease and Lucien turned him toward a tall hedge bordering the stream. The animal took the jump like the champion he was, and Lucien patted his neck in praise, then reined him back toward the house.

Two more jumps along the way. It felt good to be out in the warm spring air, to be free of his disturbing thoughts of Kathryn. The stallion approached the jump, a stone fence higher than the rest, a challenge another horse might have refused. Lucien knew Blade would not. As they approached the fence, the animal collected himself, Lucien lifted over the horse's neck at exactly the right instant, and together they flew over the fence. They had almost made it to the opposite side when he heard an ominous snap. The saddle shifted beneath him then dropped away and his weight lifted into the air.

The horse landed hard and slightly out of rhythm, nearly going down himself. Lucien's shoulder clipped the side of the high stone fence and he felt a jolt of pain, then his head hit the ground. He fought against the darkness closing in on him, then his vision grew dim, and the world spun into blackness.

He wasn't sure how long he lay unconscious, only a minute or two, no more. He staggered to his feet, shaking his head to clear it, leaning against the gray rock for support. His head pounded viciously. A bruise was forming on his shoulder, and his knuckles ached where they had been scraped, but otherwise he was unhurt. His white shirt hung open nearly to the waist, his jacket and breeches were covered with dirt and leaves. A soft nicker pulled his attention to Blade, who stood shaking a few feet away, his reins hanging down, his sides and nostrils flaring. The saddle lay in a heap near the animal's feet.

Ignoring the dizziness that assaulted him, Lucien made his way to the horse. Speaking to him softly, he smoothed the stallion's sides and patted his neck as he checked him for injuries. Gratefully finding none, he reached down to examine the saddle and saw at a glance the reason for his spill—the cinch had simply broken. He went down on one knee to survey the equipment more closely.

At first it appeared there was merely a break in the leather, but the saddle wasn't old and it had always been well cared for. He checked the severed edges of the leather again and this time he noticed there were faint circular marks where the leather had been weakened. A good hard ride, a moment of strain as he took a series of jumps as he had done today, and the cinch would give way.

Lucien cursed beneath his breath. His fall was no accident. And it was the third time in a few short months that he had nearly been killed. *Bloody hell!* Fighting the anger shooting through him, he gathered the horse's reins and started walking back to the house.

The servants were gossiping. Walking down the hall toward the kitchen, Kathryn could hear a group of them gathered behind the door. Then the door burst open and Fanny rushed out, running so fast she neared collided with Kathryn.

"Milady! Beg pardon! I didn't see you standin' there."

"What is it, Fanny? What's going on?"

She glanced around a bit furtively, then pulled Kathryn down the hall and around the corner where no one could hear. " 'Tis his lordship, milady. The cinch broke on his saddle and he took a pretty bad spill. He told the lads in the stable not to worry you, but we all thought you should know."

Kathryn's pulse began to race. "Where is he? How badly is he injured?"

"Joey says he's fine, just shook up a bit. As to where he is, I couldn't say for sure. He might still be out in the stables."

Kathryn didn't wait to hear more, just hoisted her skirts and took off like a shot out the back door. When she reached the stable, she found Bennie working over Blade, rubbing the sweat from his lathered black coat, but Lucien was nowhere near.

"Do you know where his lordship went, Bennie? I heard he had a riding accident."

"He went up to the house, milady. He were all right, though, just a bump on the head, nothin' serious."

*Nothing serious.* Those words, she had learned, were the standard reply all men made, no matter how severe the injury. She turned and started back to the house, but just inside the stable door, she spotted Lucien's saddle, and an unpleasant suspicion began to form. Changing course, she bent to survey the equipment, saw that the cinch had broken.

At first it looked as though the break was simply that. The edges were ragged, not smooth as they would have been if the leather had been cut. She started to breathe a sigh of relief when she noticed an odd pattern in the way the edges were frayed. The cinch had not been cut, but it was possible small holes had been made in the leather to weaken it. When it broke, if no one examined it closely, the edge would look frayed, as if the break were truly accidental.

Fear sent a chill down Kathryn's spine. Her throat tightened against the feeling of panic that lodged there. Lifting her skirts up out of the way, she raced back to the house and up the rear stairs, ran down the hall, and jerked open the door to Lucien's suite without bothering to knock.

He was still dressed in his boots and breeches, standing in front of the small oval mirror on his dresser, his shirt missing and his chest bare. He splashed a handful of water onto his face and gleaming droplets ran down his throat and into the curly black hair on his chest. Muscles stretched and tightened with each of his movements, rippled down his flat belly.

For a moment, Kathryn just stood there, admiring all that hard male flesh and wishing she could reach out and touch him. He hadn't come to her room in nearly two weeks and she had missed him.

Until she saw him standing there half-naked, she hadn't realized quite how much.

He blotted his face with a towel and his eyes swung to hers. "Obviously you heard I took a fall. I assure you I am quite all right. I've survived any number of similar spills and this one is no more serious than the others. If you have come to badger me with your potions and remedies, I'm afraid I shall have to disappoint you."

"Are you . . . are you certain that you are all right? Perhaps I should have a quick look."

His hard look softened at the worry on her face. "I'm fine. I bruised my shoulder and hit my head but I'm feeling much better now."

Unconsciously, she moved toward him, thinking of the saddle she had examined and uncertain exactly what to say. "I gather the cinch broke on your saddle."

He stiffened a bit, laid the towel beside the pitcher and basin on the dresser. "News travels fast."

"You could have been badly injured."

His face closed up. "I suppose I could have. Things like that happen."

"I saw the saddle, Lucien. I don't believe it was an accident. I don't believe you think so, either."

"Kathryn . . ."

She dug her nails into her palms to keep the tears from welling in her eyes. Lucien was in danger and it was her fault—again. "I'm sorry. I didn't know this would happen. I never thought for a moment he would go this far." As hard as she fought them back, tears surfaced and her vision blurred, his tall image swimming in front of her eyes. "I wouldn't have married you. No matter what he did—I wouldn't have put you in this kind of danger."

He moved then, with swift sureness, crossing the room to where she stood and wrapping her up in his arms. "Easy, love. It's all right. We don't know for sure who is behind this and, in any case, it certainly isn't any fault of yours."

"It *is* my fault," she argued against his chest, wishing with every heartbeat it wasn't the truth.

Lucien eased her back and looked into her face. "You want to tell me why?"

Misery washed over her in a sickening wave. "Because of my father's will. There's a clause in the will I never paid much attention to. It says that if my husband should die before I reach my majority, I am returned to the custody of my uncle. Even should I remain here at the castle, he would be in control of my money until such time as I remarried or turned four and twenty." She looked up at him through her tears. "He's trying to kill you, Lucien. Sweet God, what are we going to do?"

He eased her back into his arms and they tightened protectively around her. "I imagined it was Dunstan, though I hadn't quite figured out what he had to gain. As to what I intend to do, I'm not yet sure." He smiled down at her softly. "But I promise you, I don't intend to let him kill me."

Kathryn dragged in a shaky breath and nodded, her fear beginning to recede. For the present, Lucien was safe. They had discovered her uncle's scheme and the motive behind it. They would find a way to stop him.

"All right?" he asked, lifting her chin with his finger.

Kathryn nodded and tried to smile, but in truth she wasn't all right. She felt sick at what had almost happened and guilty that she was the cause.

"We'll talk more about this later," he said, letting her go and taking a step away as if he wanted to put some distance between them. "In the meantime, why don't you rest a while before it is time for supper?"

But suddenly she didn't want to rest. She wanted to be with Lucien. She wanted to touch him, kiss him, assure herself that he was safe.

She moved closer, reached out and rested a hand on his chest, felt those hard muscles tighten. "I would rather stay here," she said softly. "I know you aren't the sort of man who would ever need a woman, but there are times when I need you. I need you now, Lucien." Going up on tiptoe, she slid a hand behind his neck and dragged his mouth down to hers for a kiss. When his lips parted in surprise, she slid her tongue inside and heard him groan.

His arms tightened almost painfully around her. "Kathryn . . ."

"I want you, Lucien. I need you." She kissed him again and a shudder rippled the length of his long, lean frame. His answering kiss was fierce. Deep, wet, hot, hungry. His hands moved frantically over her clothes, unfastening the buttons and tabs, disposing of her garments, tearing a slight rip in her chemise in his haste to be rid of it.

His need of her made her own need swell. She was warm all over, her skin tingling and her breathing too fast. She wanted him. God, she wanted him so much. She cupped the front of his breeches, felt his hardness, the stiff pulsing length of him, and began to work the buttons that held imprisoned him inside.

His shaft sprang free, thick and hot and pulsing. With hands that trembled, Kathryn gently stroked him, and a rough sound came from his throat. He kissed her deeply, thoroughly, but Kathryn wanted more. She pressed soft kisses along his throat, pressed her mouth against the warm skin beneath his collarbone, trailed soft, moist kisses over his bare chest and down to the flat stomach below. He tasted salty from his morning ride and his skin was smooth and hot. She circled his navel with her tongue and a tremor passed through him, matching the one that tingled through her.

He whispered her name as his hands slid into her hair, dislodging the pins and freeing it to tumble down her back.

Kathryn circled his hard length with her hand, slid down to her knees and trailed kisses lower, heard him drag in a sharp, hissing breath. She wanted to taste the maleness of him, to know the intimate part of him he used with such skill. She kissed the smooth flesh over an arousal as rigid as steel and took him into her mouth.

Lucien's whole body tightened. His voice sounded thick and rough. "Kathryn . . . forgodsakes . . ."

But Kathryn refused to relent. For the first time, she was the one who wielded the power, a power she had only just discovered. Sensing how desperately he strained for control, she tasted him, stroked him, toyed with him until a fierce, low growl erupted from his throat.

Then he was lifting her up, carrying her over to his big feather bed and resting her in the middle. He paused only long enough to strip away the balance of his clothes, then he came down beside her on the bed. Kathryn's eyes widened as he lifted her up and settled her astride his hardened length. A hand fisted in her hair and he dragged her mouth down to his for a ravishing kiss that left her weak and breathless.

"Tell me what you need," he softly demanded, caressing her breasts and gently plucking the ends.

Kathryn tried to show him with her body, moving restlessly on top of him, feeling the heat as she settled herself more fully onto his arousal.

"Tell me," he commanded, determined to hear the words, watching her with fierce dark eyes that seemed to devour her. "Tell me what you need."

Kathryn touched his beautiful mouth with trembling fingers. "I need . . . you, Lucien."

With a low growl in his throat, he surged into her, impaling her completely, and heat roared like fire in her blood. "Then do as you wish, my love. Take whatever you need."

His words spilled through her, arousing her more than she was already. The feeling of power returned, stronger than it was before. Naked, she began to ride him.

Hard muscle tightened beneath her. Kathryn felt the tension in his lean, powerful body, the control he exerted in an effort to please her. Hot sensation rolled over her skin and dampness slid into her core. Kathryn gave in to the building pleasure, absorbing it, feeling it in every muscle and fiber. She rode him mercilessly, taking, taking, letting her head fall back as the pleasure grew more intense and her body tightened around him.

His hands caressed her breasts, captured her hips, and he began to move with her, driving himself deeper still. She cried out his name as a towering climax ripped through her, pleasure, heat, and need all merging into one. Holding her in place, Lucien thrust into her again and again, taking her deeply and stirring her to a second wrenching climax. Another hard thrust, and he followed her to release, both of them shaking with the force of it.

As she began to spiral down, Lucien gently eased her off him, drawing her down beside him on the bed, his arms curling protectively around her. Kathryn closed her eyes, grateful for the comfort of his body, feeling closer to him than she had in weeks. In this there were no barriers between them, only an eagerness to bring each other pleasure. Combined with love, such a powerful physical attraction could make a strong and enduring marriage.

Without it, eventually the passion would dwindle and fade. Kathryn couldn't help wondering how long this, the only real bond they shared, would last in the months ahead. Would it be severed once she carried his child? It hurt to think of it, to know that once she was round and heavy with his babe, Lucien would undoubtedly take a mistress, as other men of his station did.

Though the haze of pleasure still tingled in her body, a soft ache throbbed in her heart.

# TWENTY

Standing in front of the desk in Nathaniel Whitley's office on Threadneedle Street, Lucien signed the document lying in front of him and returned it to Nat, who carefully sanded it, folded it, and sealed it with a drop of wax.

"It is signed, witnessed by me, and dated," Nat said. "I shall place it in my safe along with the cinch and the other documents you've provided. Should anything untoward happen to you, I shall see the whole of it delivered to the magistrates' office." Nat looked up from the stack of papers, jerked the small wire-rimmed spectacles from his nose. "Forgodsake, Lucien—the man tried to murder you. He should be hanged from the nearest tree for what he has done."

Lucien ran a hand over his face, wishing it were that simple. "I should like nothing better, I assure you. At this point, however, we have little proof it was Dunstan who actually paid men to kill me. The men behind the attack at the Quill and Sword are long gone. The testimony of a groom will hardly stand up against that of an earl—especially not one as powerful as Dunstan."

The sworn testimony was the second sealed document Lucien had provided, wrung from a man named Oliver

Weed, a groom newly in his employ. Bennie Taylor had helped him uncover the man's identity. Weed had been among the group working in the loft when the heavy iron hoist had fallen and nearly killed him. Bennie recalled seeing the same man working over Lucien's saddle. At the time, he'd thought the groom was simply seeing to its care.

Captured and forced to admit the truth, Weed had confessed to the attempts on Lucien's life and named his employer—Evan Sloan, Dunstan's estate manager. But there wasn't nearly enough evidence to go after the earl himself—or even Sloan, for that matter.

"These documents will only prove useful should I die in some suspicious manner," Lucien said. "If that should occur, Douglas Roth will find himself charged with murder."

"But you will still be dead."

"Unfortunately that is true." His mouth curved faintly. "However, that is not going to happen. Not once Dunstan learns the threat these documents pose."

"And how do you intend to go about informing him?"

"I'm leaving for Milford Park on the morrow. Dunstan is supposed to be gone from the property by the end of the month—that is only a few more days. With my marriage to Kathryn, I'm now the owner of that estate and I fully intend to see that he leaves."

"You had better be careful, Lucien. The man has no conscience. Killing you wouldn't bother him in the least. Look what he did to his niece—his own flesh and blood."

"I'll be careful. And I'm taking along a friend just in case."

Nat paused in the act of stacking the papers on his desk. "A friend?"

Lucien smiled. "That's right. The Duke of Carlyle. With Jason along, there is no doubt that I'll be safe."

Nat relaxed at that. "You're right. Carlyle is a good man to have at your back." He rounded the desk to where

Lucien stood. "But still it could be dangerous. Be careful, my lord."

"Believe me, I shall." Lucien crossed the room and opened the door. "By the way—congratulations. I hope you know how glad I am that you and my aunt are getting together."

Nat smiled softly. "I've been in love with Winifred Montaine since I was a boy."

Lucien nodded, but the phrase, so unselfconsciously spoken, bothered him. Why was it men like Nat and Jason seemed to accept falling in love without the slightest qualm? It was ridiculous for grown men to believe in such fantasy . . . and yet. When he thought of Jason and Velvet, he had to admit there was something about their relationship that was different.

And Nat and Winnie shared something special, as well.

Lucien found himself thinking of Kathryn. Of how good it felt to make love to her, how protective he felt of her, how much he enjoyed just being with her.

Was it love?

Surely not. He wasn't the sort to fall in love.

But the notion stayed with him all the way back to Castle Running.

The day was blustery and cool, a crisp wind whipping the tiny budded leaves on the branches of the tree. Outside the front doors, the Litchfield carriage stood waiting, its four black horses snorting a frosty mist into the air as they stamped their feet and shook their heads, jangling their silver-studded harness.

Beneath the chandelier in the entry, Kathryn swung her fox-trimmed cloak around her shoulders, a matching fur muff in one hand, a small traveling valise sitting on the floor at her feet. Down the hall, Lucien and Jason approached from Lucien's study, and Kathryn steeled herself for the battle to come.

Her husband's dark eyes widened the moment he saw her. "Kathryn! What the devil are you doing up at this hour?" It was definitely early. She had known they would need an early start to make the two-day journey to Milford Park.

She forced herself to smile. "I am waiting for you, my lord."

Lucien stopped in front of her. Spotting her satchel on the floor, his thick black brows drew together. "You're dressed to go out. I hope you don't think you're going with me."

She smiled sweetly. "That, my lord, is exactly what I think."

A few feet away, Jason hid a grin.

"That is impossible," Lucien said darkly. "You know the reason we're traveling to Milford. Your uncle will be furious when he finds out his plans have been thwarted. I don't want you anywhere near him."

"I wish to see my cousin Muriel. I need to know that she is safe."

"No," Lucien said flatly, turning so that Reeves could drape his greatcoat over his shoulders. "Not this time."

"There may not be a next time," Kathryn argued, steadfastly holding her ground. "My uncle is leaving Milford. I need to be certain that Muriel is all right. Knowing him as I do, I should have done so long before this."

"There's no need for you to worry. I'll check on your cousin in your stead." His heavy coat swirled as he turned to leave. "I'll see you four days hence," he called over one broad shoulder, the duke falling in behind him.

Kathryn's next words stopped them at the top of the front porch steps. "I know the way to Milford, my lord. If you don't take me with you, I shall get there on my own. I am going to see my cousin—one way or another—and you are not going to stop me."

Fury settled over his features. He pinned her with a glare. "Threaten me and I shall lock you in your room. Unless you wish to remain there for the next four days, you will do as I tell you."

Ignoring the angry tic in his cheek, Kathryn smiled up

at him sweetly. "How can you be certain what I will do if I am not with you? Remember, 'He who trusteth not is not deceived.' " His mouth quirked at the Thomas Fuller quote, but his scowl did not lessen. Kathryn walked over and caught his arm. "I won't go near Dunstan, I promise. I shall simply check on my cousin. As long as you are with me, I will be safe."

What she had said was the truth—she should have checked on the girl before. But seeing that Muriel was well was only part of the reason she was determined to go along. She didn't trust her uncle, and even in company with the powerful duke, she was afraid for Lucien. "Please, my lord. I beg you to take me with you."

Lucien grumbled something beneath his breath. "In this Mr. Fuller is correct. If I could be certain that you would stay here, I wouldn't consider for a moment taking you along. Unfortunately, knowing how stubborn and willful you are, I have no choice but to take you with me."

Relief washed over her. "Thank you, my lord," she said demurely, as if she hadn't just blackmailed him into it.

The duke was still grinning.

"Cut that out," Lucien warned. "You have one at home just like her."

Jason laughed at that. "Touché."

Kathryn wasn't certain exactly what that exchange meant, but she was going to Milford and that was all that mattered.

Lucien assisted her up into the carriage, helping to arrange her heavy quilted petticoats, then he settled himself on the seat beside her. Draping a heavy lap robe over her knees, he leaned back against the tufted leather squabs. As soon as the duke was settled on the opposite side of the carriage, he signaled for the coachman to make way.

After spending the night at a small inn named the Dove, they reached Milford Park the following day. Though the marquess had hoped to find the earl making preparations to leave, there seemed to be no such activity.

In fact, Milford Park looked as lovely and serene as it had when she had left it over a year ago.

Kathryn had always loved the beautiful old brick mansion with its lush, parklike setting. As a girl, she had spent hours roaming the woods and picnicking with her family by the stream.

But her parents' deaths and Dunstan's arrival had destroyed the peaceful tranquility. During the years of his guardianship, she had only wanted to escape the place and all the ugly memories that went with it.

Now she had returned as the Marchioness of Litchfield and once again the house seemed the picture of her storybook dreams.

The carriage rolled to a stop out in front and a footman opened the door. Lucien helped her alight and they made their way up the stairs. They were ushered into the Blue Drawing Room, its high molded ceilings painted to look like a cloud-covered sky. Dunstan greeted them stiffly, his cheeks red with angry color. His nose was also red and slightly veined, but Kathryn recalled it had always been that way.

"So . . . you have come to see if I am yet removed from your property."

"Among other things," Lucien told him. "You know the Duke of Carlyle, I presume."

Dunstan made a stiff bow. "Your Grace."

"My wife has traveled here to see her cousin. I assume that she is in."

"I'll have the butler announce your arrival, Kathryn. You may await her in the Rose Room."

"Very well." She was hoping she wouldn't be forced to leave the men until Lucien had spoken to her uncle, detailing the evidence being held against him, but at least she was there should anything untoward occur. She made her way out of the drawing room down the hall to wait for Muriel, and to her surprise, the girl appeared only a few minutes later.

Kathryn smiled. "Cousin Muriel. I'm glad to see you

are looking so well." In the year since Kathryn had been away, the girl had begun to grow into her gangly frame. She was taller even than Kathryn, bigger boned, with long red hair that curled a bit too tightly. But her eyes were a pretty dark brown, she no longer slumped, and her figure was filling out nicely. Kathryn could see definite possibilities. She hoped Muriel could see them, as well.

"Father said you wished to see me. What is it you want?" The greeting was even less cordial than Kathryn expected. Muriel's looks might have changed but her disposition apparently had not.

"I was worried about you. You will be moving from Milford soon. I wanted to be certain that you had whatever you might need to make things easier for you."

"Father said we wouldn't have to move," she said, staring at Kathryn down her nose.

"Your father is wrong. My husband and I are the owners of Milford now. You will have to return to Dunstan Manor, or live somewhere else."

Her mouth drew down in an unpleasant line. "I hate that place. It is drafty and old. It is hardly fit for a pauper to live in, let alone the family of an earl."

"That is your father's problem. He inherited plenty of money when the old earl died. He managed to spend it on gaming and high living. Now you will both pay the price."

"This is all your fault."

"Is it? And whose fault was it that I was sent to the madhouse, Muriel? Both you and your father had a hand in that. No one cared a whit about what happened to me. In truth, I shouldn't care in the least what happens to you."

Muriel's freckled hands fisted. "I don't have to listen to this. My father will take care of you—just like he did before." She whirled away, wisps of her frizzy red hair flying out from the sides of her face.

Kathryn's voice stopped her at the door. "Listen to me, Muriel. I came here because I was worried about you. I realize you don't like me. Still, you are my cousin—one of the few relations I have left—and I don't want to see you hurt. If you ever need anything, you know where to find me. Just send word."

Staring straight ahead, Muriel pulled open the door as if Kathryn hadn't spoken, stepped out into the hall, and closed the door.

Kathryn released the breath she had been holding. The scene with Muriel had been more disturbing than she had imagined. The girl harbored a terrible anger Kathryn had never quite understood. She seemed jealous simply for the fact that Kathryn had come from a loving family while Muriel had been raised by her father, who showed her not the least amount of love.

With a sigh of regret that things could not be different between them, Kathryn walked over to the window. She wished she could join the men, discover exactly what was going on in the Blue Room, but Lucien would be furious if she interrupted, and she had pushed him as far as she dared. Clenching her hands together, she began to pace the floor.

"This is an outrage! You came here to accuse me of trying to have you murdered? That is utter and total nonsense. How dare you insinuate—"

"I'm doing far more than that, Dunstan." Lucien eyed the man across from him with a loathing that went beyond hatred. "I am warning you. I'm telling you that should you carry these efforts of yours any further, you and your estate manager—a Mr. Evan Sloan—will be prosecuted to the full extent of the law. And should either of you, by some quirk of fate, chance to succeed in bringing about my demise, the authorities will come straight to you. With the proof I have placed in safekeeping, should anything happen to me, there is no doubt you will hang for murder."

Dunstan sputtered and his face turned beet-red. "You are insane." He stood a good six inches shorter than Lucien, who took satisfaction in forcing the man to look up at him.

"You know very well I am perfectly sane—just as you knew that about your niece. Only Kathryn had no one to protect her as she does now. She fell prey to your ruthless schemes—I have no intention of doing the same."

Standing at Lucien's side, Jason cast Dunstan a hard look of warning. "You had better pray Lord Litchfield lives a long and prosperous life." The edge of Jason's mouth curled with distaste. "As he has said, should anything happen to him, you, my friend, are headed straight for the gallows."

Dunstan fell silent but his eyes darted back and forth between the two men.

"Heed my words," Lucien said. "You had better call off your hounds and quickly. Any other attempts made against me and I shall take the evidence I have and go straight to the magistrates. Even if you don't go to prison, in the eyes of society, you'll be a ruined man."

Dunstan took up a belligerent stance, his jaw set and his feet slightly splayed, but he said nothing more and Lucien made ready to leave.

"I expect you out of this house by the end of next week," he warned. "If you are not, the constable will be here to remove you." A thin smile edged his lips. "I imagine that might cause you a goodly bit of embarrassment." Turning the silver doorknob, he strode out into the hall, leaving Dunstan staring after him.

Jason followed in his wake, closing the door behind him. "I believe you have seen the last of Lord Dunstan."

Lucien worked a muscle in his jaw. "I meant what I said and he knows it. I believe he will leave us in peace." His boots rang down the corridor as he headed for the entry, Jason's long stride matching his.

He paused in front of the carved front door and spoke to the butler, a short, rotund man with very little hair. "You may inform my wife that we are ready to depart."

"I'm afraid I'm not certain where she is. She was

speaking to Lady Muriel in the Rose Room, but I believe I saw her leave."

"Find her and do so quickly."

He made a formal bow. "Yes, my lord."

But he didn't return quickly, in fact not for quite some time. Lucien began to frown as the minutes ticked past and Kathryn still had not appeared. Finally, he heard feminine footsteps and looked up to see her approach, a wide smile brightening her pretty face.

"I'm sorry, my lord. I was enjoying a stroll around the house. I had forgotten what a lovely place it is." Looking down at her, he felt his own mouth curving up. "Come, love," he said, taking her hand and resting it on his arm. "We'll return for a visit once the place is yours again."

Kathryn took a last glance at the only home she had ever really known, nodded, and let him guide her out the door, down to the waiting carriage.

"How did you fare with your cousin?" he asked once they were inside and headed down the road toward home.

Kathryn's dark brows pulled slightly together. "Not as well as I had hoped." She sighed. "Muriel resents me for some reason. Perhaps because I once had a family who loved me. My cousin never has."

"She is cursed with a father who cares for nothing but his own ruthless self-interests," Jason said. "I can't help feeling sorry for the girl."

"For the most part her father simply ignores her," Kathryn said. "Muriel craves his attention, but when he does seek her out, it is usually to berate her. He is cruel and domineering. The odd thing is, I think, deep down inside, she knows the sort of man he really is."

"We'll keep an eye on the girl," Lucien promised. "She is family now, whether she likes it or not. Perhaps in time, we can find some way to help her."

Kathryn flashed him a grateful smile. "Thank you, my lord."

Lucien leaned back against the seat of the carriage, settling himself in for the long ride home. Kathryn gazed

out the window at the passing landscape, and as the
wheels churned over the rutted road, he found his glance
straying toward her again and again.

In truth, he was glad he had brought her with him. He
enjoyed her company, enjoyed just having her around.
And last night at the inn, instead of sleeping in a cold
room by himself, Kathryn had been there to share her
warmth and her body, and he liked the feeling of waking
up beside her.

Looking at her now, the sunlight shining on her pretty
features and the pale mounds of her breasts, his body began to harden. He wanted her as he always did, but he
was content just to sit there beside her.

The thought occurred, if that was love, perhaps it
wasn't so terrifying as he had believed. Perhaps he might
even get used to the notion.

Lucien found himself looking at Kathryn and smiling.

From the corner of his eye, he saw that Jason was
grinning.

# TWENTY-ONE

After weeks of waiting, her chance had finally arrived. Kathryn folded another night rail and packed it into her small leather trunk. Anxious to be on her way, she paused at the window to check on the weather. It was early in the day, yet already a layer of clouds had begun drifting in. Wind flattened the new green grass springing up through the soil, and the air felt heavy and charged, as if the storm in the offing were impatient to get there.

Still, her husband had left for London and she was for Guildford at last. She glanced down into the courtyard, saw Michael running toward the stable, and smiled. The threat of rain hadn't affected the little boy, who was hurrying for his riding lesson with Bennie, Michael more eager than ever since his latest gift from Lucien. Her husband spoiled the child unmercifully, but Kathryn couldn't fault him. Michael was always so delighted, so grateful, so filled with utter joy.

Yesterday had been no different.

"Kathryn! Kathryn!" he'd cried, forgetting in his excitement that he was supposed to call her "my lady." "Come quick! Come see the new saddle me lord has bought. It come all the way from London just for me!

Please, Kath—me lady!" He tugged on her hand, pulling her relentlessly out of the drawing room and off toward the stable. " 'Urry—hurry, ye must come see!"

She laughed as he led her along the path, then, spotting her husband, smiled softly at the look of pleasure on his face. He flushed when he saw her, embarrassed to be caught indulging the child yet again, the skin beneath his high cheekbones turning a dusky rose.

"It's difficult for a boy of his size to master a proper seat," he gruffly explained. "It's important he have the right equipment."

"I'm sure it is," Kathryn agreed, stifling an urge to grin. Michael had won the marquess over completely. Lucien adored the child and he would do anything for him.

And so Blade had been saddled for Lucien, Michael's new saddle placed on the little dappled gelding he had already grown to love, and the two of them set off for an afternoon ride. As Kathryn stood at the window, she remembered their smiling faces, one so dark, the other so fair, and felt a swell of love that made a lump form in her throat. Lucien seemed so different of late, less distant, more open. Perhaps it was Michael, touching him somehow, breaching the wall of her husband's emotions that he had so carefully constructed around him.

If she weren't so restless, so eager to return to her studies—to continue the very course of action that would once more set them at odds—Kathryn might have allowed herself to believe things could actually work out between them.

But there was no way for her to remain on her present course. Not when she felt so caged, so useless. So completely bottled up. The life of a pampered nobleman's wife left her stifled and bored. She needed her studies, her interest in medicine and healing that had been her reason for living for so many years. She needed the work she'd been doing in the cottage, and though she had no desire to actually be a physician, she wanted to put her hard-won knowledge to some sort of use.

In that vein, Kathryn turned away from the window and returned to the bed to finish packing the last of the items she intended to take on her journey. She had already written to Silas Cunningham, relaying Lucien's plans to travel to London, and everything was set. Every year at this time, the marquess had told her, he spent the week with his solicitor, going over the past year's receipts, successes and failures, and projections for the coming term.

"You're welcome to come with me," he'd said. "In fact, I should be glad of your company. Unfortunately, I'll be busy most of the time. We'll have little chance to enjoy ourselves. Perhaps it would be better if we returned in a couple of weeks and stayed for part of the Season. The gossips might give us some trouble at first, but now that you are the Marchioness of Litchfield, it won't take them long to accept you into the fold."

Her husband would be leaving. Kathryn recognized the chance she had been seeking and latched onto it with greedy glee. "I should rather return for the Season, if you don't mind. It's time I came out of hiding and put an end to the scandal once and for all. Sooner or later there will be children. We have to consider what's best for them."

The thought of children made him smile, as she had known it would. "Then I'll make the arrangements for our return while I am there." He took her hand, pressed a kiss into her palm. For an instant, when she looked into those hot, dark eyes, she found herself wishing she were going along.

Kathryn thought of her husband now as she packed the last of her clothes, snapped the latches on her trunk, and rang for a footman to carry it downstairs. She was leaving with mixed emotions, half of her elated at the prospect of studying again with the doctor, the other half aching with the knowledge of how badly her husband would disapprove should he discover what she was about.

If only there was some way to make him understand.

Kathryn knew that there was not.

A distant rumble of thunder echoed in the entry, jiggling the crystal chandelier above her head. A faint flash of lightning brightened the sky, but it remained miles away and no rain fell. The journey to Guildford would take most of the day, but the roads were still clear and they would be traveling in front of the storm.

"The carriage awaits, my lady, as you have requested." Reeves eyed her with a hint of disapproval. It was obvious she hadn't discussed the trip with her husband, since he had made no mention of it, and though the butler held Kathryn in a certain high regard, he was ever loyal to his employer. "Should his lordship arrive, when shall I tell him to expect your return?"

"I shall be back before he gets here."

"And should he need to reach you?"

Kathryn chewed her lip. She considered lying, but her conscience instantly balked. She wasn't doing anything wrong, merely visiting an old friend and his wife for a couple of days. "I'll be in Guildford. I've an acquaintance there, a physician named Silas Cunningham. I'll be staying with him and his wife."

Reeves nodded curtly, but he seemed a bit less tense. "Have a safe journey, my lady."

"Thank you, Reeves." She stood as he draped a warm woolen cloak around her shoulders, then she made her way down to the carriage that waited out in front. It was a comfortable conveyance, not as extravagant as the marquess's traveling coach, but it was enclosed and snug and would certainly do to get her to Guildford.

It took most of the day to reach the busy but unpretentious village on the road leading north to London. At the doctor's instruction, they passed through the town to the far northern edge where Silas and Margaret lived in a pleasant-looking, two-story stone manor house.

As the carriage rolled to a halt in front, both of her friends came out on the porch to greet her, Silas in his usual silver bagwig, buttoning his waistcoat over his portly frame, Margaret shorter, but equally stout of build, her brown hair pulled back in a tidy bun. The children,

Kathryn learned, were away at boarding school, where they were both, as she could have guessed, excelling in their studies.

With a grand show of enthusiasm, Kathryn was ushered into the house and led upstairs to her bedchamber, a simple but spotlessly clean affair with a pale blue coverlet over the bed and ruffled blue curtains at the dormer window.

After a supper of jugged hare and venison pasties, she got her first real chance to talk to Silas about his work. Margaret smiled kindly as they rattled on about subjects that meant little to her but enthralled her guest and her husband.

"You won't be able to come to the college tomorrow until classes are ended," Silas said. "In the meanwhile, I've some texts that should keep you occupied. You can join me after the students are gone and I'll be able to show you some of our ongoing work."

Kathryn excitedly agreed. "I've been so looking forward to this. You cannot imagine what it's like being forced to ignore the single thing that one is most passionate about."

He nodded gravely. "I think I can imagine. With you, learning is a flame burning inside you that cannot be doused."

She smiled at his description, grateful to have at least one person who seemed to understand her. "I've brought a list of questions. I'm hoping over the next few days we might delve into some of them." Silas nodded, pleased by her eagerness, it seemed. Their discussion went on well into the evening, while Margaret politely listened without really hearing, her chubby fingers skillfully working the knitting she held in her lap.

The following day, Silas left for his duties at the Guildford Physician's College while Kathryn remained at the house with his books. She joined him late in the day and together they headed for his laboratory in the basement under one of the classrooms.

"Well, don't just stand there gaping," he said when she faltered for a moment in the doorway, staring at the cloth-draped table in the center of the room. "You have seen a cadaver before. If you wish to learn anatomy, there is no better way than to do so firsthand."

She took a deep breath, her mind racing back to the last time she had been involved with the sort of learning that was considered less than respectable. Then she squared her shoulders and walked in, determined to learn as much as she was able in the short time she was there.

Lucien had the oddest niggling feeling that something was wrong. For two days he had tried to shake it, but the sensation had only strengthened. Since his sixth sense for trouble had rarely failed him, he decided to cut short his meetings with Nathaniel Whitley and return to Castle Running.

After a tense journey from London, he arrived home late in the evening, and was only half surprised—and extremely annoyed—to discover his wife was not there.

"Where is she?" he demanded of his butler, who, reliable as always, had had the good sense to learn where she'd gone.

"Her ladyship is off to Guildford, my lord. She is visiting an acquaintance, a physician and his wife, a man by the name of Silas Cunningham."

*Cunningham.* The name registered immediately and Lucien knew exactly who it was. He also knew precisely why his wife had gone to see him and that she was dabbling once more in her blasted medical studies.

Defying his expressly forbidden command.

If the roads hadn't been so damnably muddy and he wasn't already tired from his journey, he would have gone after her right then. Instead, in a fury, he went into his study and poured himself a stiff drink of brandy, hoping it would help him to sleep, then left the room and climbed the stairs to his bedchamber. On the morrow he would leave for Guildford to fetch his errant wife home. She would face the full measure of his wrath and once and for all end her ridiculous obsession with a subject that was totally unsuitable for a lady of her station.

Lucien clamped his jaw. Whether Kathryn liked it or not, he vowed, the matter would finally be put to rest.

Dawn grayed the sky outside her window. Unable to sleep any longer, Kathryn lit the branch of candles beside the bed, pulled on her quilted wrapper against the faint morning chill, and went to work, poring over another heavy volume on anatomy that Silas had loaned her. She wished the books were more complete, that the workings of the human body were better understood. Perhaps they would be if so many people weren't still living in the Dark Ages, seeing any sort of tampering with the dead as sacrilegious and tantamount to making a pact with the devil.

She sighed, thinking that her husband wasn't much better; his notions of propriety were so strict he would never have allowed her to come had he known why she was there. Kathryn shuddered to think what he would say if he saw her working over Phineas, the name they had given the cadaver in the basement at the college.

She glanced at the clock on the mantel over the hearth, where a servant had arrived to lay a fresh layer of coals on the fire. Time to make ready. It was Sunday. They would attend morning service at the small parish church, then quietly slip away to their work at the school.

Tomorrow she would return to Castle Running.

Kathryn frowned, knowing she would do so with mixed emotions. She had missed her husband every day since she had been gone, but once she returned, she would miss her studies. She would be relegated once more to a life of stitchery, watercolors, and gardening, a life of boredom and uselessness to Kathryn.

Blowing out the candles now that the sun was well up, she dressed in a yellow wool gown and headed downstairs, determined not to dwell on problems that could not be solved. As they had planned, they attended the service at the Guildford parish church, but Kathryn found it hard to concentrate. Instead, her mind kept spinning ahead, forming questions about things she hoped Silas could explain as they worked in his laboratory.

After making the necessary farewells to the vicar and his family, they finally escaped, and Margaret returned to the house while Kathryn and Silas went immediately to his basement laboratory.

With an apron tied over her woolen gown, she studied the lifeless body on the table. The man had expired from a close-range accidental gunshot, Silas had told her, showing her the portion of the side that had been blown away. The shot had fractured the victim's ribs, and openings were made into the cavities of the chest and abdomen. The diaphragm was lacerated, and a perforation made directly into the cavity of the stomach.

"It was an utterly hopeless case from the moment the accident occurred," Silas said, "though the man miraculously lived for several days."

She didn't ask how the college had managed to obtain the man's body—she didn't want to know. As Lucien had said, there were unscrupulous men who engaged in the practice of providing cadavers to the scientific community. Resurrection men were little better than grave diggers. But she respected Silas Cunningham and she trusted that he had gone through legitimate channels. And she truly believed such studies were crucial to making advancements in medicine.

Dr. Cunningham adjusted the spectacles he wore on the end of his nose. "Take a look at the way the food in the stomach had begun to enter the bowel," he instructed, leaning over the table. Kathryn swallowed against the strong odor of pickling fluid used to preserve the body and focused her attention on the path he indicated with his scalpel.

"Take a look at—" The doctor broke off just then and Kathryn followed his gaze to the door. Her face went the same pasty shade as the man on the table when she saw her husband standing at the bottom of the basement stairs.

"Get your things," he said in a voice so tight and soft it was more chilling than if he had shouted. His eyes were flat and cold and even the anger that turned his lean frame to steel could not warm them. "You are leaving Guildford—now."

Kathryn wet her lips. "This is my friend, Dr. Cunningham. I was hoping you would have the chance to meet him. He has given me the rare opportunity to—"

"I see exactly what the two of you have been doing. I told you to get your things. I have already stopped by the doctor's house and collected the rest. Unless you wish me to drag you out of here by force, I suggest you do as you are told."

Humiliation warred with anger. She started to argue, to tell him she refused to be ordered about, but Silas caught her arm. "Go with your husband," he said gently.

"But I'm not going to—"

"Perhaps in time he will see things differently. For now, it is better that you do as he requests."

Lucien said nothing, just stared at her with an expression of tight control. Kathryn turned away from the accusation in those cold dark eyes, picked up her cloak and swung it around her shoulders.

"I appreciate your hospitality, Silas. Please convey my gratitude to your wife." She reached the door and Lucien jerked it open. He followed her up the steep stone stairs and into the sunlight. His carriage was waiting on the street in front of the college. He stopped her before they reached it.

"I thought you had more sense. Is your memory so short you don't recall the consequences you paid the last time you involved yourself in this sort of behavior?"

"Of course not, but I wanted to—"

"I know what you want—or at least what you think you want. I've warned you, Kathryn—time and again. Aside from that, you gave me your word."

Her chin angled up. "I told you I wouldn't go back to the cottage and I did not."

"You know my feelings on this matter. You waited until I left because you knew I would not approve."

"It's part of my life, Lucien. You can't ask me to simply give it up."

"I'm not asking you, Kathryn. I'm telling you." His glance strayed back toward the small basement room, his eyes dark and hard. "You're my wife, the future mother of my children. You will never again engage in that sort of abomination. Do I make myself clear?"

Kathryn didn't answer.

He gripped her shoulders, angry black eyes boring into her. "Do I make myself clear?"

Kathryn simply nodded. Her throat had closed up and it was difficult to speak. "Yes, my lord," she whispered. "You have made yourself perfectly clear."

They were the last words either of them spoke all the way back to Castle Running.

Even after their return, tension remained high between them. Though Kathryn often felt her husband's eyes on her, the marquess said little, and he had yet to return to her bed. She knew that he would, sooner or later. He wanted an heir above all things and as long as she played the role of marchioness exactly as he thought she should, eventually he would forgive her.

But Kathryn found it difficult to forgive him. Her life was in turmoil and she ached with loneliness and despair. She was desperately in love with a man who didn't love her, a man who disapproved of the woman she was and wanted only the use of her body. Tonight he had gone out for the evening. He hadn't said where. As she lay in her empty bed, staring up at the ceiling, Kathryn wondered how the future that she had imagined could be so different from the life she actually lived.

Lucien sat across from Jason in the smoky taproom of the Quill and Sword Tavern, where they'd come for a quiet evening of escape.

"In a way I feel like the veriest villain," Lucien said, running a hand over his face. "Watching her, you would think I have stolen her very reason for living."

"Perhaps as she sees it, you have."

"Kathryn is so damned bright and determined. I've seen few men with such a driving need to learn."

"But still you refuse to indulge her interest in medicine."

"She's a woman. She has no business engaging in that sort of pastime."

"And that, I suspect, is what you told her when you arrived in Guildford."

Lucien made no reply, which was answer enough.

"I gather you have yet to forgive her."

Lucien released a weary breath. "Kathryn believes I am still angry. Perhaps I am, but only a little. It is difficult to stay angry at the little witch for long." A corner of his mouth lifted faintly. "I may not approve of her studies, but I have to admit in some ways I admire her. And I want her as I never have another woman."

"Why don't you tell her that?"

Lucien glanced away. He couldn't imagine saying those words to Kathryn, yet deep down he wanted to.

Jason grinned. "Admit it. You're damned glad you married her."

Lucien sat back in his chair. "I always wanted a manageable little wife. In Allison Hartman, I would have had one. But I have to admit Kathryn intrigues me far more than Allison ever could have. I can't say I'm sorry things turned out the way they did."

Jason motioned for the tavern maid to bring them another ale. "It appears your wife isn't the sort for sewing and music lessons. She won't be happy unless she finds another subject that interests her, something that will challenge her."

Lucien mulled over Jason's words; it was a thought he'd had himself on more than one occasion. His glance strayed off toward the patrons in the taproom: the sailors gaming in the corner, Squire Thomas's son, Robert, laughing at a friend's bawdy joke, one of the young bucks from the village making eyes at Sadie Jensen. "I had hoped she would be with child by now," he said, "but as far as I know she is not. Perhaps Velvet could be of some help."

"I'll ask her if you like."

Lucien nodded. "I'd appreciate that. Perhaps Kathryn has mentioned something that she would find interesting."

"Kathryn loves children. As you said, a babe would surely help." Jason took a sip of his ale, eyeing Lucien over the rim. "I imagine you'll keep trying."

Lucien thought of Kathryn's soft mouth and willowy curves, of what it felt like just to hold her. "You may be certain I will."

But he returned too late that night and Kathryn was already asleep. Tomorrow, he vowed. Unfortunately, tomorrow had a way of being too late.

# TWENTY-TWO

Kathryn slept fitfully. When she finally drifted off, she awakened far later than she meant to. By the time she arrived downstairs, Lucien had gone off riding, leaving her to wander the house feeling listless and out of sorts. She went over the weekly menu with Cook, but was finished all too quickly. Running the household was second nature to a woman whose mother had died when she was a girl of ten, and the task provided little satisfaction.

Kathryn looked longingly out the window toward the stream that led off to the woods and the little stone cottage that had been her refuge. Just thinking about the place made her heart thud dully. Then she realized the hammering wasn't merely in her chest; a visitor was knocking at the tall carved front door. She made her way in that direction, waiting in the entry for Reeves to pull the heavy portal open.

At the sight of the stout build and white powdered hair of Constable Perkins, Kathryn's stomach instantly knotted.

"Lady Litchfield." He pulled off his tricorn hat and heavy coat and handed them to the butler. "Constable

Nivens and myself would like a word in private with you and your husband."

Kathryn moistened her lips, which suddenly felt dry and stuck together. She focused her attention on the butler. "Reeves, see if his lordship has returned from his ride. Tell him Constables Perkins and Nivens are here and that we are awaiting him in the Gold Drawing Room."

Reeves eyed the men with disdain, looking at the pair down his long, stately nose. "Very well, my lady." He disappeared around the corner, his steps long and urgent, while Kathryn led the men down the hall. Once inside the Gold Room, she rang for tea—anything to delay the conversation till Lucien arrived. He might still be angry, but he had always stood by her, and she trusted him to help her in this.

Kathryn instructed the footman on where to place the tea cart, then busied herself with the cups and saucers. She hoped she looked calm—on the inside she was shaking.

Sweet God, what on earth could the men possibly want? Were they here for her? Had word of her transgressions at the physician's college somehow reached them? Would it really matter all that much if it had? Or perhaps they had come for little Michael. Either way, from the grim expressions on their faces, it didn't look good.

Hoping her hands remained steady, Kathryn poured tea for each of the men. "My husband should be here any minute," she said, praying that it was true. If she ever needed Lucien's strength, she needed it today.

"Perhaps we should start without him," Constable Perkins suggested, ignoring the steaming cup she set in front of him and instead coming to his feet. Kathryn hated the fact she was forced to look up at him.

"I would rather wait," she said, "if you don't mind." As badly as she wanted to know why the men had come, she wasn't sure how long she could control her fear. It was growing stronger by the moment, making her hands shake and her pulse pound. Dear God, where was Lucien? Surely she had no reason to be afraid.

But she wasn't all that certain, and her growing fear made her insides tightened another notch. Kathryn moistened her dry lips and started to speak just as the double doors slid open. To her great relief, Lucien walked in.

"Gentlemen." Still dressed in his riding clothes, he instantly saw the terror she was trying so hard to hide and walked straight toward her. Kathryn knew a feeling of gratitude so strong it made her dizzy. She and Constable Perkins rose to greet him. On legs that trembled beneath her skirt, she closed the distance to his side and he settled a hand at her waist. His strong, reassuring hold gave her courage, and Kathryn thought, in that moment, she had never loved him more.

"All right," he said. "Now that I've arrived, why don't you tell us what this is about?"

Perkins arched a bushy eyebrow. "Put that way, I shan't mince words. Eight days ago, Douglas Roth was poisoned at his home in Milford Park."

"Poisoned . . . ?" The word squeaked out of Kathryn's throat, sounding strangled and choked. Eight days ago they had been visitors at Milford Park. "That . . . that is impossible."

"Completely impossible," Lucien agreed. "Eight days ago, Lord Dunstan was the picture of perfect health."

"That is quite correct, my lord." Constable Nivens plucked lint from the sleeve of his burgundy tailcoat. He was a gaunt man, sallow complected, with shrewd, accusing eyes. "At the time of your visit, his lordship was sound in both body and spirit. The night of your departure, however, he fell gravely ill. His physician, Dr. Harris, eventually put the cause of that illness to a deadly dose of poison."

Lucien's expression remained bland, but a muscle tightened along his jaw. "Are you telling us the Earl of Dunstan is dead?"

"Not yet," Perkins said. "Though Dr. Harris believes

it is only a matter of days at most. A decanter of brandy in his study is believed to be the culprit. The doctor says it was heavily laced with an extract of nightshade." Icy blue eyes swung to Kathryn. "It is a well-known fact that your wife has an extensive knowledge of the herbs and plants useful in medicine. She had motive and opportunity, since her uncle was the man who had committed her to St. Bart's, and according to the butler she disappeared for some time during her visit."

Dark spots danced for a moment in front of Kathryn's eyes. She felt as if the floor had dropped out from beneath her. She gripped Lucien's arm to keep from swaying on her feet.

"My wife did not poison her uncle. You have no way of knowing how long that brandy had been contaminated, and while you are looking for a motive, you might question some of the dozens of people Lord Dunstan has taken advantage of over the years."

"Advantage? In what manner?"

"In any manner he might find beneficial. Put simply, the man is ruthless in the extreme. There is no possible way to know what enemies he might have made over the course of his lifetime."

"If that is so, perhaps you can provide us with some of those names."

"With a little digging, I'm certain I can. I'm sure my wife will be able to contribute to the list herself."

Perkins stared at Kathryn. "Is there anyone at Milford Park who can vouch for your whereabouts during the time you were there?"

"I—I was with my cousin Muriel."

"We're aware of that. What about after Lady Muriel departed?"

"I wandered about the house. I hadn't been home for a while. It felt good to be there, to reacquaint myself with some of my family's possessions: portraits, embroidery my mother had done, a collection of thimbles I had admired as a child. I had missed seeing those things while I was away."

"And did you not go into your uncle's study?"

Kathryn faltered. Sweet God, she had only just gone in for a moment. The room was her father's favorite and she had liked to go there as a child, simply to feel his presence. She'd felt little of it there that day, now that Dunstan had taken over use of the room, and she had not tarried. "I—I don't remember. I walked about for quite a while before my husband summoned me to leave."

Perkins glanced at Nivens, who made a faint nod of his head. She wasn't sure but she thought that perhaps even Lucien had picked up on the lie.

"All right," Perkins said. "For the present that will be all. In the meanwhile, however, I suggest you both remain close to home. There will undoubtedly be more questions for Lady Litchfield. Should the earl expire, there is a distinct possibility that her ladyship will be charged with murder."

At the edges of her vision, Kathryn saw darkness and for an instant the room seemed to fade. She felt Lucien's arm go around her as he eased her down into a chair. "Stay here. I'll see the *gentlemen* out."

She simply nodded. Her mind was spinning, so full of fear she couldn't think. Her uncle had been poisoned. She couldn't deny she had every reason to wish him dead. In truth, she loathed the very sight of him. And she could easily have done it. She had often worked with poisonous herbs, even deadly nightshade, which in tiny doses could help ease pain and was good for indigestion.

And she had been alone in the house—in truth, even briefly gone into his study. Dear Lord, the constable must surely believe that she was the one who had poisoned him! Nausea rolled in her stomach. Even her husband must surely believe her guilty.

Kathryn thought of the troubled look she had seen in his eyes, and though at St. Bart's she had often wished her uncle dead, she found herself praying he would live.

Minutes dragged past. Kathryn crept to the drawing room door and stood listening to the low hum of the men's conversation. What were Perkins and Nivens saying to her husband? Were they convincing him she was guilty? She wished she could be there to defend herself, but she was afraid her presence might somehow make matters worse.

Instead, she strained to hear, waited tensely for the men to leave and her husband to return. At last the hall fell silent, the heavy oaken door opened and closed, and Kathryn breathed a sigh of relief. Then she heard Lucien's footsteps striding down the hall and steeled herself to face him.

He had almost reached the Gold Room when the sound of running feet and shouting servants halted him just outside the door. Kathryn's heart leapt as she imagined what new crisis must have occurred and stepped into the corridor beside him.

"What is it?" she asked. "What's happened?"

"I don't know." Turning, he started walking toward the rear of the house, Kathryn running to keep up with his long-legged strides. It was Bennie Taylor, she saw, racing toward them like a madman.

"It's Mikey!" he shouted. "Ye gotta come quick!"

Kathryn's heart lurched. Lucien started running and so did Kathryn, a new kind of fear rushing through her. Lucien reached the child first, pushing between the two grooms kneeling beside him on the grass. One held Michael upright while the other pounded frantically on his back. It was obvious the child had swallowed something and that it was lodged in his throat. Lucien didn't wait, just jerked the boy up by the ankle, holding him upside down in the air as he slapped and pounded, trying futilely to dislodge whatever it was.

Michael's face was slowly turning purple, and a sickening little wheezing noise rasped in and out of his throat. All the while, his big terrified blue eyes clung to Lucien, pleading for his help.

"Forgodsake, what did he swallow?" the marquess demanded, still trying to loosen whatever was wedged in the small boy's breathing passage.

"T'weren't nothin' but a piece of candy." Bennie's eyes filled with tears as Lucien rested the child once more on the ground and opened his mouth, his long fingers delving inside in an effort to extract whatever he had swallowed.

" 'E were hungry. Cook give us a piece of hard candy. That's all it was . . . just a piece of candy."

Kathryn bit back a sob. Her heart was slamming against her ribs, and her own breathing grew labored. Sweet God, the marquess was doing everything Kathryn knew to do, everything she had read should be done, but nothing seemed to be working. The little boy's face was completely purple now, his small hands clawing frantically at his throat.

Kathryn's pulse roared in her ears and she was shaking all over. For the first time in her life, as she looked at little Michael, heard the thin wheeze of air that was all he could gasp into his lungs, she thought she might actually faint.

Then Michael's eyes slowly closed and his small body went limp.

"He's unconscious!" Lucien shouted. His eyes swung to Kathryn and they were so full of pain Kathryn felt it like a blow to the stomach. "He's going to die, Kathryn! We've got to do something to help him!"

"We was suckin' on the candy." Bennie started rambling. "Then Mikey started laughin' at somethin' Joey said—"

"Kathryn!" Lucien shouted. "Tell me what to do!"

Hot tears rolled down her cheeks. "Turn him upside down again. Maybe this time—"

"That's not enough and you know it! Michael is dying! You've spent years reading those damnable books! Do something to save him!"

Kathryn swallowed, her chest aching with fear and

frustration. Dear God, not Michael! She loved the boy as
if he were her own and seeing him like this made it nearly
impossible to think. She dragged in a breath, clamped
down hard on her terror, shoved back the helplessness and
pain. Frantically, her mind began searching, going over
the knowledge she had gained. Lucien was right. There
had to be something she could do—some way to save
him!

"He has to breathe," she said, speaking her thoughts
aloud, her voice faint and shaky, barely under control.
"Nothing else matters but that. There is a sort of tube in
the body that goes down the throat. That's how the air
gets into his lungs. If I could open it . . . I don't know if
it would work, but maybe—"

"Do it!" Lucien commanded. Reaching inside his riding boot, he drew out the thin silver blade he had been
carrying since the attack he had suffered at the inn. "Do
it, Kathryn! If there is the slightest chance it will save
him, we have to take the risk!"

Kathryn wet her lips and took the knife he held out to
her. Though inside she was shaking, her hands looked
amazingly steady. "Get my medical supplies," she quietly
instructed Bennie, who dashed off toward the empty tack
room where the supplies from the cottage had been se-
creted away. Ignoring Lucien's sharp glance, she said a
quick prayer for guidance and began to run her fingers
along Michael's throat, searching for the breathing tube,
trying to recall from her recent studies exactly where it
was in relation to the big, blood-carrying tubes along the
sides.

Kathryn steeled herself, found the spot she thought
would be best, and inserted the blade, making the smallest
incision she could manage that would let in a sufficient
amount of air. Instantly, the boy's narrow chest began to
lift and fall in a more regular rhythm and Kathryn said a
silent prayer that at least so far she hadn't killed him.

"I need something to soak up the blood."

Another of the boys dashed away while Lucien jerked

off his coat and pulled his full-sleeved shirt off over his head. He shredded the thin lawn fabric, folded it into thick pads, and handed them over with shaking hands.

"He's breathing," Lucien said, "but the candy is still stuck inside."

"We need something round and hollow that the air can flow through until we can pull out whatever is in there. A reed or a quill of some sort."

"I'll get it!" Joey dashed off this time, all of the boys returning at nearly the same instant with their assorted supplies. While Kathryn kept the blood at bay, Lucien stripped away the feathers then broke off both ends of the quill pen Joey had brought and inserted it into the cut Kathryn had made.

"His breathing sounds better," Lucien said. "If we could just get the obstruction out of his throat—"

"Let me do it." Kathryn dragged a small pair of tongs from the satchel Bennie had brought. "These come in handy for a lot of things." Wiping the blood on her hands on her skirt, she carefully slid the tongs down Michael's throat and groped for the chunk of candy he had swallowed. Twice it slipped away and sweat poured into her eyes. She wiped it away with the back of her hand, leaving a smudge of red near the corner.

"I've got it." She drew out the obstacle victoriously and tossed it away, then returned to work on the incision she had made. Threading the needle she carried in her satchel, she carefully stitched the gash in the breathing tube together.

Through it all, Michael remained unconscious and for the moment Kathryn was grateful. Once he awakened— dear God, she prayed he would—the pain would be substantial.

"We need to get him into the house," Kathryn said. Lucien nodded and swept the boy gently up in his arms. They carried him into the room next to Kathryn's, and the marquess carefully rested him on the bed.

"As soon as he's awake, I'll give him something to ease the pain."

Lucien's gaze locked with hers. "Will he wake up, Kathryn?"

There was such despair in his eyes, Kathryn had to glance away. "I don't know."

"What about putrefaction?" he asked.

Kathryn swallowed. It was her worst fear and a very likely occurrence. "Once he's awake, that will be our biggest concern. I'll do everything I can to prevent it, but there is no guarantee."

Lucien said nothing. For long moments he just stood there, looking at her with an expression she could not read. Then he turned and walked out of the room. As she watched his tall figure retreat, Kathryn caught a glimpse of herself in the mirror above the dresser. At the sight, her face went even paler than it was already.

"Oh, dear God." Her lemon-yellow gown was soaked in blood. Her hands were blood-covered, specks of scarlet spattered her forehead and cheeks. In the eye of her mind, she could see Lucien's expression, so tight and carefully controlled, determined not to reveal his distaste.

"Oh, dear God," she whispered again and felt her stomach lurch. On trembling legs, she approached the dresser, poured water from the pitcher into the basin, washed and dried her hands.

"Kath . . . ryn . . ." The soft croak rolled up from the deep feather mattress.

"Michael!" She dashed toward him, sat down in the chair beside the bed, reached out and caught his hand. "It's all right, sweetheart. You had an accident, but you're going to be fine." Grabbing her satchel from the bedstand, she jerked it open and drew out several vials and a handful of ointments.

"My throat . . . hurts . . . so bad." Michael reached toward the place she had cut, but Kathryn gently caught his hand.

"I know it hurts, sweetheart. It was the only way we

could help you to breathe." She drew out a small bottle of liquid that held a tincture of opium. Remembering how the drug had once affected her, she worried for an instant about what effect it might have on Michael, but she knew it would help him handle the pain and for now that was the most important. She took a rag, soaked it in the liquid and dribbled it down his injured throat. She knew how badly it must hurt to swallow, but he didn't complain.

"I'm going to put some medicine on your throat and then bandage you up," she told him, placing a clean square of cotton she had doused with a mixture of barberry and milkweed over the wound and using a long strip of fabric to tie it around his neck. "You'll feel better in the morning."

At least she hoped he would. But if putrefaction set in—Kathryn's stomach clenched, but she shook her head, refusing to imagine the worst. By the time she had finished, Michael had fallen asleep. She glanced up to see Lucien standing in the doorway, the same unreadable mask on his face as before.

"He's sleeping now," she said. "He awakened for a moment, so we don't have to worry about that."

"Thank God." He crossed the room, his eyes on Michael. "I'll sit with him a while."

Kathryn simply nodded. Looking down at her bloody clothes, she gripped the folds of her skirt. She remembered the way he had looked at her that day in the basement and thought how repulsed he must be now. No gentleman—and especially not Lucien—wanted to see his wife looking as if she had just come from butchering a sheep. And to think she was covered in the blood of a child! She hurried away from him and down the hall to change.

For the next two days, she and Lucien took turns sitting by the little boy's bedside. Michael awakened with a fever at the end of the second day, and Kathryn prepared herself for the worst. Staying up round the clock, they alternated shifts, but otherwise rarely saw each other.

No word had come of Dunstan, but for now that didn't matter. Their concern, their prayers, were for Michael.

At the end of the third day, Michael's fever broke. Whatever small amount of putrefaction there had been seemed under control. Oddly, as soon as it was certain the child would live, Lucien had left the house and Kathryn hadn't seen him since.

That was two days ago. Two long, heartbreaking days for Kathryn. Every time she closed her eyes, she could see the tight, guarded expression on her husband's face. She could see the blood on her hands, and she knew what he was thinking. Disgust made his eyes go dark. Repulsion for a woman who could slice open a child as if he were no more than a bloody piece of meat.

She had heard it all before, during the days when she had been sent to St. Bart's. And Lucien felt the same—he had made that perfectly clear. Dear God, how could she ever face him?

Late in the afternoon of the second day, a messenger arrived from Constables Perkins and Nivens. The men would be arriving on the morrow for an audience with Lady Litchfield.

Kathryn's heart beat like a battering ram. Dunstan must surely be dead. The men were coming to arrest her. They would return her to the madhouse—or hang her. Her mouth tasted like ashes and her hands began to tremble. The men were coming and even Lucien believed her guilty. Terror rolled over her in harsh, unrelenting waves. Staring into a future too bleak even to imagine, Kathryn sank down on a chair in her bedchamber and started to weep.

# TWENTY-THREE

She had to leave. She couldn't face the possibility—no, *probability*—that she would be arrested for murder. Kathryn was the most likely suspect and everyone knew it. Even Lucien believed her guilty.

*Lucien.* In truth, he was the real reason she was running. She would never forget the look on his face as he had watched her with Michael. Or the mask he had assumed once she had finished her grisly task.

As bad as it had been when he had seen her working in the basement, this was far worse. He would never look at her again without seeing her blood-soaked gown, without wondering what sort of woman she really was. Certainly Allison Hartman wasn't that sort. Lady Allison was the epitome of feminine womanhood. Lady Allison was the woman Lucien had wanted.

Kathryn's hands shook as she stuffed a third simple gown into her satchel, tossed in the silver-backed hairbrush on the dresser, two clean white night rails, and another pair of shoes, the second a bit more comfortable than the sturdy leather pair she wore for her upcoming journey.

She glanced toward the window. The hour was late,

the servants sleeping. Darkness enveloped the castle but a sliver of moon emerged from between the clouds. Kathryn dragged in a shaky breath and took a last glance around the room she had become so fond of and knew how badly she would miss it: the lovely velvet draperies, so elegant yet they kept the room cozy and warm, the bed she had so often shared with Lucien, the hours of pleasure they had found in each other's arms.

Kathryn rubbed her shoulders and hugged herself, fighting back a shiver of despair. She wouldn't think of Lucien—she wouldn't let herself. If she did, she would never leave. Her gaze strayed for a moment to the note she had left him on the small French writing desk in the corner. She was giving him his freedom, urging him to make the sort of life for himself that he had always wanted. He deserved at least that much after all the trouble she had caused.

Kathryn brushed at a stray tear that had somehow managed to escape from beneath her lashes, closed the lock on her satchel, and left the bedchamber.

It took sheer force of will not to stop by Michael's room to check on him one more time, but she knew his nursemaid would be sleeping at the foot of the bed and she didn't dare wake her. Michael was healing rapidly. He was going to be just fine, and once Lucien returned, the boy would be in very good hands.

Kathryn no longer worried about Michael. Once again, it was she who was in danger. Leaving Castle Running one step ahead of the constables' men was the only choice she had. More than that, she was running from Lucien. She was in love with a man who didn't love her, a man who cared only for the woman he wanted her to be, not the woman she was inside. She had to leave before he returned, before he looked at her with disgust in his beautiful dark eyes.

She had seen that look in her uncle's eyes, in the eyes of Bishop Tallman, and the doctors at the madhouse. She had to leave and it had to be tonight. As before, she would do whatever she had to in order to survive.

Escaping the house proved easier than Kathryn had imagined. She thought of taking a horse, but decided against it. Once she reached an inn, she could travel by mail coach, which would be faster, her route less easy to follow. Things would be different this time, since she had money to pay her expenses. Lucien had been extremely generous in her allowance and she had spent very little. She wouldn't be cold and dirty. She had warm clothing and she had a plan.

By morning, after walking throughout the night, Kathryn had reached an inn called the Peregrine's Roost. The mail coach arrived before noon. She paid the fare and climbed aboard. Over the next few days, she changed coaches four times, heading one way and then another, fearful her movements might be traced. By the time she reached St. Ives, on the distant, remote Cornwall coast, she was certain no one would be able to find her.

She had been to the tiny fishing village years ago, with her parents when she was a child. She had loved the place then, and as she peered out the window of the mail coach, listening to the crash of the surf on the cliffs below, she saw that the stark beauty of the region hadn't changed.

Perhaps she could make a life here, Kathryn thought, the notion easing the dull pang of loss that throbbed beneath her breastbone. Then she thought of Lucien, thought of his silver-black eyes, the soft way he smiled at her, the way he had always tried to protect her, and deep in her heart where no one could see, Kathryn silently cried.

It was so hard to admit he was wrong.

So impossibly hard that it had taken him three days to work up the courage to do so. He wasn't sure what to say, how to broach a matter of such importance, her interests, her beliefs, the heart of his problems with Kathryn.

And so he had left the castle and gone off by himself, gone to ponder all that had happened, events that had drastically changed his way of thinking, changed his whole life. He had needed to see things clearly, to think things through. He'd wanted to be certain.

By the time he returned, it was too late.

Sitting behind the rosewood desk in his study, Lucien smoothed the crumpled edges of the note Kathryn had left him. After six days and a thousand readings, the paper was tattered and frayed. He didn't need to look at the words; he knew the message by heart. But this small scrap of paper was the last word he had of her and he would keep it until her return.

Lucien flattened the paper on his desk, the letters taunting him, reminding him what a fool he had been.

> *My dearest Lucien,*
>
> *By now my uncle is surely dead. I beg you to believe I am innocent of the crime of his murder, though under the circumstances, that must be difficult for you to do. I leave in the hope that the trouble I've caused will end, and because I am afraid.*
>
> *In leaving, I also wish to set you free.*
>
> *Obtain the annulment we spoke of and marry a woman of your choosing. Though I wish things could be different, I could never be the kind of wife you want. After what happened with Michael, I am certain your disgust of me makes the truth of that more than clear.*
>
> *Take care of yourself, my love, and please take care of Michael, as I am sure you will. I leave with but one regret—that I never had the courage to tell you that I love you and that I always will.*
>
> > *Your friend forever,*
> > *Kathryn*

The letters blurred and ran together. Lucien rubbed his eyes, folded the sheet of foolscap, and stuffed it in the pocket of his waistcoat, letting the letter fall back into place over his heart. For six days he had searched for her. Six of the longest days of his life. He was exhausted to the bone, worried and heartsick and filled with regret. But he wouldn't give up until he found her.

When he did, he would tell her what he had discovered as he had watched her saving the life of the little boy who had become so dear to him. He would tell her that he had been wrong about her studies, that what she was doing *was* important. That it did not matter that she was a woman. In saving one small child, all her years of learning, all that she had suffered, had been worth it.

And he would tell her that he loved her. Though he hadn't truly believed in such a thing, watching her in those fearful moments with Michael, he had never felt such pride in another person, such an intense feeling of connection with another human being.

He was in love with her. Totally and without the slightest doubt. In the back of his mind, buried so deeply he hadn't realized it was there, he had imagined she was a woman like his mother and that had made him afraid. But the truth was Kathryn Grayson wasn't the least bit like Charlotte Montaine. She was good and decent and worthy of his trust. He loved her beyond measure, and he ached with the need to tell her. In her letter she had said that she also loved him, and for the first time he understood just how lucky he was.

And just how desperate he was to have her safely returned to him.

Lucien raked a hand through his hair, shoving it back from his forehead. His clothes were mud spattered, his face in need of a shave. He didn't care. As soon as Jason arrived, he would set off on his search again. Somewhere there was someone who had seen her, someone who remembered her, who knew which way she had gone.

She wasn't in immediate danger from the law, although her departure had made her appear even more guilty. Her uncle had not died as everyone had been certain he would. Instead, he was slowly recovering. It looked as though he would live, and since there was no hard evidence that Kathryn was responsible for the attempt on his life—and

Dunstan wanted to silence the gossips and put the matter to rest as quickly as he could—the constables were no longer breathing down their necks.

As for him, he had to admit there was a single moment when he had doubted her, knowing the terrible treatment she had suffered at Dunstan's ruthless hands—but one look at her face and he had known she wasn't guilty. Kathryn was a healer, not a killer. Should the law threaten her again, whatever it took, he would find a way to protect her. She would never have to be afraid again.

The door swung open just then and Jason's tall frame ducked through the opening. "The horses are waiting. Are you ready?"

Lucien nodded. "Let me get my coat and gloves and I'll meet you in the entry." Catching the duke's quick nod, Lucien felt a tug of gratitude for his friend's unwavering support.

"We'll find her," Jason had said the moment he'd heard the news. "We won't stop until we do." The hard edge of determination rang in Jason's voice and Lucien had believed him. Grabbing his jacket off the back of a chair, ignoring the pounding in his head and the tiredness in his limbs, he followed his friend out the door.

Kathryn left her small slate-roofed cottage on the cliffs at the outskirts of St. Ives and hurried down the path toward the village. She had been living in the seaside town for nearly two months, working as a midwife, among myriad other tasks.

Today she'd been summoned by Agnus Pots, an ancient woman so stooped and withered she looked like a gnome, to help a fisherman's young wife deliver her first babe. Agnus had been the town's midwife until Kathryn's arrival, but she was getting too feeble for the job and was grateful to take on an assistant.

In the first few weeks, it was apparent Kathryn was capable of more than just birthing babies, and her duties expanded. People of every age, description, and ailment began coming to her cottage on the outskirts of the village, and Kathryn did her best to help them.

It was the sort of life she had always imagined. Her work was important. She felt useful. Needed.

And desperately, achingly, alone.

She missed Lucien more than she ever could have guessed. She missed his smile, the sound of his voice, missed just seeing him walk into a room. She missed little Michael and she worried about him. She missed her home in Sussex, missed her husband and family with a piercing ache that never left her. She prayed that Lucien would forgive her for upsetting his life once more, and in the days ahead that he would find a measure of peace.

The fisherman's cottage loomed ahead. Kathryn forced her sad thoughts away, shoved open the rough-planked door, and stepped into the room where young Lisette Gibbons lay whimpering on the bed.

"How is she?" Kathryn asked Agnus, her eyes on the girl's swollen belly beneath the clean but well-worn sheet.

"She's hurtin' somethin' fierce, but I don't see as anythin's wrong. The child oughta be comin' soon."

Kathryn moved to the side of the bed, wrung out the wet cloth lying in a basin of water on the table beside it, and sponged the perspiration from Lisette's glistening forehead. She was a big girl, blond and blue-eyed, with wide hips that would help to ease the child's way.

"Just take it easy," Kathryn soothed. "The babe will be coming soon and all of this will be over."

"I'm gonna die," Lisette moaned. "I'm gonna die just like my sister." Panting and sweating, she muttered curses at the pain, curses at her big, unwieldy body, then cursed her husband for putting her in this situation.

Kathryn gently squeezed her shoulder. "It's all right, Lisette. You aren't going to die. Just try to stay calm. When the next contraction comes, I want you to push as hard as you can."

The girl whimpered and bit down on her bottom lip so hard a drop of blood appeared on the surface. She was drenched in perspiration, her night rail damp and clinging to her cumbersome body. Her wrists had been tied to the headboard of her cornhusk bed.

"Do as she tells ye, child," Agnus Pots instructed, "and be grateful the girl is here. I'm too old and feeble to do the job meself, like I done for so many years."

Kathryn smiled at the ancient midwife and mopped her own sweaty brow with the back of a hand. The next series of contractions came swift and hard, but a screaming Lisette did exactly as Kathryn told her and a tiny boy child slid into the world.

Kathryn handed the babe to Agnus, who cooed over it as she wiped it clean and wrapped it up in a woolen blanket, then settled it in the crook of its sleepy mother's arms. Kathryn watched the woman's tired, gentle smile, saw the pride and love on her face, and knew the same sense of awe she always did at the sight of a newborn child. Life was so precious. And so uncertain.

Unconsciously, her hand slid down to her slightly rounded stomach. For the past three weeks, she'd been sick nearly every morning, unable to hold down even a bite of bread. She knew well enough what that meant. She had tried so hard to forget the man she had fallen so desperately in love with, to put his tall, dark image out of her mind and accept the life she was making for herself in St. Ives. She wanted to forget, to leave the pain of losing him behind.

Now that she would be bringing his child into the world, Kathryn knew she never could.

She sighed as she washed her hands in the basin on the rickety table. At least she would have some part of him with her through the years. Kathryn thought of the beautiful girl child she prayed she carried, imagined the silky black hair and silver-flecked eyes the babe was certain to inherit, and a pang of longing knifed through her.

She ached for the father her child would never know.

She ached for Lucien, and for herself.

•    •    •

*Six months. Six long, agonizing months and still no sign of her.* Lucien descended the sweeping staircase on the way to his study. He had just returned from a journey to the village of Maidstone, having received a tip from the town smithy that a woman of Kathryn's description was living in a cottage there. It wasn't the first such futile journey.

After the first two weeks of fruitless searching, he had posted a reward. Any number of people wished to claim it. Nat Whitley hired men to check out as many leads as they could manage and most of them were discarded. But those that looked promising Lucien followed up on himself.

"Me lord! Me lord! You're home!" Michael raced toward him and Lucien scooped him up in his arms, balancing him up on one shoulder.

"I got in about an hour ago. I didn't want to interfere with your lessons."

"Old Parny's teaching me French. God's eyes, why's a man got to learn to speak like them pansy Frogs?"

Lucien bit back a smile. The child was the most precious gift Kathryn had ever given him. There were times, like today, after running into another dead end, if it weren't for little Michael he would surely be the one being carted off to the madhouse.

"Mr. Parnell is concerned that you should fit into society," Lucien explained. "You told me you wanted to be a proper gentleman. Well, learning to speak French is part of what you need to learn."

"I bet you can't speak like them Frogs."

"*Those* Frogs. And you are wrong if that is what you think. *Je parle français assez bien. Comprenez-vous?* It is expected among members of the upper classes."

Michael frowned. "It sounds pretty when you say it. Old Parny sounds like a toad in a rusty bucket."

His mouth edged up. "Well, then, you learn the words and I'll help you to say them properly. All right?"

Michael grinned. "Right enough!"

Lucien set him back on his feet and the boy raced away, heading back up the stairs to join his tutor.

"My lord?" Lucien turned at the sound of Reeves's voice. "I'm sorry to interrupt, my lord, but it seems you have a visitor."

"A visitor? Who is it?"

"Lady Allison Hartman. I told her you were not receiving, as you had only just returned from a tiring journey to Maidstone, but she insisted on seeing you. I told her to wait in the Green Room. Shall I send her away, my lord?"

*Allison Hartman.* Lucien inwardly sighed, suddenly more tired than he was before. Good God, of all the people he hadn't expected to see.

"My lord?"

"What? Oh, no . . . it's all right, Reeves." He dragged his mind back to the present, away from memories of Allison that couldn't begin to compare with those he held of Kathryn. "I'll speak to her."

When he opened the door to the Green Room, he found her sitting on a dark green brocade sofa, as blond and fair and lovely as she was the first time he had seen her. He thought of the constant fatigue and worry for Kathryn that had etched deep lines in his face and imagined that to her he must look ten years older.

"My lord?" She came to her feet as he walked in, looked up at him and smiled. "It's good to see you."

He glanced past her, his gaze searching for her mother, the baroness, the stalwart chaperone, but the woman was nowhere to be seen.

"Lady Allison . . ." He made a formal bow over her hand. "You're looking as lovely as ever."

She flushed prettily. "Thank you, my lord."

"I hope your mother and father are well."

"They are fine, my lord. I, on the other hand, have been ever so worried of late."

Lucien arched a brow. "Worried?"

"Yes, my lord. I've heard the terrible stories . . .'tis no

secret your wife has left you. I've heard the awful accusations about her."

Lucien bristled, his jaw going tight. "My wife is innocent of any wrongdoing. She has never harmed anyone in her life."

Allison glanced down at the hands she clasped in front of her. "I would have to doubt that, my lord," she said softly. "You see, she has very greatly wounded me."

Whatever anger he felt left on a harsh breath of air. Kathryn wasn't the only one responsible for hurting Allison Hartman. He had handled things poorly, made a muck of the whole affair. "Kathryn has always regretted what happened, my lady. As I do myself. At the time, she was desperately in need of my protection. I believe it was her feeling that our marriage would last only a short duration and that you and I might still one day wed."

Bright blue eyes came to rest on his face. "She thought that, in truth?"

"Yes."

Allison moved toward him, rested a small, white-gloved hand on his arm. "Perhaps that is the reason she left, my lord. So that you and I could be finally be together."

Lucien looked down at the delicate hand perched on his sleeve, perfectly graceful, utterly feminine. He couldn't begin to imagine that small, delicate hand doing what was necessary to save a small boy's life.

"Perhaps that was part of the reason," he said, gently disengaging himself and purposely stepping away. "At the time she left, she didn't know how much I had come to love her. She didn't know that I was glad we had married and that I felt privileged to call her my wife."

Allison's body went rigid, her gloved hands fisting against the lace of her cream silk skirt. "I thought you didn't believe in love. That is what you always told me."

"I was a fool," he said simply.

Allison's blond brows narrowed. She tossed him a disapproving glare. "I had hoped that we might mend things

between us. I can see now that I was wrong. I shall accept
Reginald Dickerson, Lord Mortimer's proposal, as my
mother has insisted I should." Lifting her chin, she picked
up her skirts and started past him. Lucien caught her arm.

"You may not believe it, Allison, but we are lucky we
did not wed. You deserve a man who loves you, whether
that man is Mortimer or someone else. Be certain that he
is also someone you can love in return. It is the key to
finding true happiness."

Allison said nothing but something flickered for a moment in her eyes. He watched the sway of her panniers
as she walked down the hall and out to her waiting carriage. Allison was sweet and innocent, the kind of woman
he had always believed he wanted.

Now he knew he needed a woman of intelligence, of
passion, and commitment. A woman who wasn't afraid to
challenge him, one he found challenging in return. He
needed Kathryn Grayson and he was determined to find
her. He wouldn't stop until he did.

# TWENTY-FOUR

Days turned to weeks. Weeks became months. A lonely Christmastide came and went. Outside the cottage, a frosty January wind beat against the shutters. An icy sea pounded against the shore, and a blanket of snow lay like a cold hand over the frozen earth.

Inside the thick stone walls of Kathryn's cottage, a small fire blazed in the hearth, sending heat into the dark oak timbers above her head, and the soft yellow glow of candles flickered over the cradle in the corner.

Kathryn looked down at the tiny black-haired child curled up in peaceful slumber and felt a swell of love so strong her hand shook as she tucked the blanket under the sleeping baby's chin. That the child was a boy and not the girl she had prayed for no longer mattered. She had carried him in her womb for nine long months, suffered the agony of childbirth, nursed him through fits of colic and croup, and loved him since the moment he had gasped in his first breath of air.

He was hers, she vowed, hers and hers alone.

That he was Lucien William Montaine, heir to the fifth Marquess of Litchfield, was unimportant. Even for the sake of the child she had named after its father, she could never go back to Castle Running. With her uncle most likely dead, God only knew what fate awaited her outside the remote, protective confines of Cornwall. Death by hanging, or a return to the madhouse. Neither of them were possibilities she wished to face.

And there was Lucien to consider. She couldn't intrude in his life again, no matter that she wanted to return with every heartbeat, thought of him every day, missed him and little Michael, and loved them both more than ever.

She would hardly be welcome even if she tried. Not after all that had happened between them. If she closed her eyes, she could still see Lucien's face as she had worked over little Michael. Surgeons were no better than barbers.

And a woman—heaven forbid! No female of breeding would ever undertake such a deplorable task. No, Lucien could never accept the woman she really was, and as much as she longed to see him, ached to be with him, she knew she could never return.

The baby started crying. Kathryn gently picked him up and cradled him against her breast.

"Hush, little Luke, don't cry. Mama's here." But the child refused to be silenced. He was, after all, the son of a marquess, a high-ranking member of the nobility, and perhaps he was demanding his rights.

The thought haunted Kathryn day and night. *If only you'd been a girl,* she thought, though she loved little Luke with all her heart. She could justify in some way keeping a little girl with its mother. But Luke was a boy and a boy needed his father. He deserved the title and holdings that were his birthright. Guilt that she would deny him these things ate at her like a cankerous sore. Knowing how much Lucien wanted a son only made the feeling worse.

Kathryn quieted the child, crooning to him softly until he hiccuped and slowly drifted back to sleep. Tired after a day of setting broken bones and dispensing ointments for everything from boils to blisters, she gently settled the baby back in his rough-hewn cradle and lay down on her bed in the small alcove behind the curtain at the end of the parlor.

She tried to fall asleep, but as tired as she was, sleep eluded her. She closed her eyes and for an instant drifted off, but a sound near the bed snapped her eyelids open again. A tall man stood in the shadows. She could see the high curve of his cheekbones in the flickering light of the candle, the hard line of his jaw, the straight nose and well-formed lips. Raven-black hair, queued back from his face with a spreading black bow, gleamed like onyx in the thin blade of flickering light.

"Kathryn . . ." he whispered, reaching out to her. "I've looked everywhere. God, I've missed you so much."

She went into his arms, her eyes filling with tears, the wetness slowly sliding down her cheeks. "Lucien . . . I love you. I love you so much." He cradled her face in his hands and kissed her as if he couldn't get enough. His hands came up to her breasts and he cupped them through her thin white night rail, his long fingers gently caressing the ends. Kathryn kissed him fiercely, clinging to his shoulders, whispering how much she loved him. When his hands slid along her hips, she whimpered, eager to feel him inside her.

He found her feminine softness, skillfully stroked her, and Kathryn cried out his name, begging him to take her. "I need you," she whispered. "I've missed you so much."

He filled her then, and Kathryn moaned at the pleasure, at the feeling of oneness that she had been missing for so long.

"I've come to take you home," he whispered and her heart leapt with joy. She thought that he said that he loved her, but another sound intruded, muffling the words. The noise grew louder, the crying of a baby, and Kathryn's mind drifted off in another direction. As the son's crying grew, the father's image wavered.

"No . . ." she pleaded, reaching out to him. "Please don't go." But his handsome face dimmed even more and his tall frame drifted backward toward the door. The baby's sharp cries increased, erasing the last traces of slumber, and Kathryn opened her eyes. Her heart clenched to discover that she was alone.

Only a dream. Another in a series of nightly encounters that left her aching with need, mired in despair, and filled with unbearable grief. Shuddering against the cold that had settled in the room, Kathryn brushed away the wetness still clinging to her cheeks, dragged herself out of bed, and went to soothe her crying babe.

Following the butler down the hall, Jason Sinclair ushered his petite wife into the study at Castle Running. A smiling Lucien beckoned them in. "It's good to see you," he said, rounding the desk and coming forward to kiss Velvet's cheek. "It seems as though it's been forever."

Velvet smiled up at him. "That's because it has," she gently chided. "We decided since you continue to ignore our invitations to come for a visit, we would simply come here."

Lucien motioned them toward a comfortable leather sofa in front of the fire, his fingers dark against the white lace on his cuff. "I'm glad you did. I suppose I've been a bit of a recluse of late."

That was the understatement of the year, Jason thought. Since Kathryn's disappearance, Lucien rarely left the house, unless it was in pursuit of some vague clue that might lead him to his wife. Sad though it was, Jason had come to believe the girl wasn't going to return, and not even the Herculean effort his friend had undertaken to find her was going to change that. It was as if she had simply disappeared.

"I realize you have any number of pressing affairs," Velvet said lightly, taking the seat he offered. "But even a recluse has to come out of hiding on occasion."

"I suppose that is so," Lucien agreed. "Why don't I start right now? It's past time for luncheon. I'll have Cook prepare something for us to eat."

"Good idea." Jason forced himself to smile as he watched his friend cross to the bell pull, but he was thinking how clearly he could read the worry still etched in Lucien's face. In the months that had passed, the marquess had begun to fear that Kathryn's uncle—now completely recovered from his near demise—might somehow be involved in her disappearance. In that vein, he had searched the sanitariums and hospitals all across England, again to no avail.

In truth, Jason believed, it was Kathryn herself who had somehow outsmarted them. She had left Castle Running determined not to be found and, as she had in most things she set out to do, cleverly succeeded.

He wondered if she had even the slightest notion what her disappearance had done to his friend.

"Reeves will let us know when the meal is ready," Lucien said, taking a seat across from them. "So how is it I am fortunate today to be honored by your esteemed presence?"

"Actually, we came to put an end to your seclusion," Jason said. "We're planning a short trip into London. We were hoping you and Michael might come along."

The edge of a smile curved his lips, but Lucien shook his head, as Jason had been certain he would. "I appreciate the invitation, but I'm afraid I'll have to pass this time. I'm terribly busy right now. I'm working with some of my tenants, making plans for the coming year. I couldn't possibly leave."

No, he couldn't leave, Jason inwardly grumbled. He didn't want to do anything but sit in his bloody castle and grieve. Too late, his friend had discovered he was desperately in love with his wife. He had lost her because of his damnable pride and arrogance, and the pain of that loss was eating him up alive.

"I realize you are busy," Jason said. "You've always been busy. You always will be. But that isn't the only reason you won't go and you know it. The truth is you don't want to leave because of Kathryn. You're torturing yourself over your wife. You feel guilty for driving her away. You love her and you want her back. Well, it doesn't look as if it's going to happen, my friend. I'm sorry, but it's time you faced the truth."

Lucien stiffened, but he didn't argue, just rose to his feet and crossed to the window.

"When Kathryn left," Jason continued a little less harshly, "she intended for you to go on with your life. Whether you like it or not, that is exactly what you've got to do."

Lucien stared out the window. He was thinner than Jason had ever seen him, his eyes lackluster, with none of the silver fire that usually blazed out of the inky darkness. "I know you're right. I'm just not ready. In time, I suppose I'll have no choice, but for now . . ." He shook his head. "I don't know, Jason. I can't get her out of my head. Every day I worry about her. I wonder if she has enough to eat, if she is warm enough, if there is anyone she can turn to if she should need help."

He glanced toward them and there was such misery in his eyes, a heavy weight seemed to settle on Jason's chest.

"I know she isn't coming back," Lucien went on. "I've resigned myself. But the truth is I miss her more than I ever imagined. I'm not ready to face life without her . . . at least not for a while."

Jason said nothing. When he glanced down at Velvet he saw her discreetly wipe away a tear. "If only she knew," Velvet said softly. "She loves you, Lucien. She would never want to see you hurting. If there was only some way for her to know what she has done to you."

Lucien cast a hard look at Velvet. "What she has done to me?" he repeated harshly. "What about what I have done to her? This is my fault—all of it. None of this would have happened if I hadn't been such a stubborn fool."

Velvet came up off the sofa and crossed to where he stood. She rested a small hand on his sleeve. "You mustn't be so hard on yourself. Kathryn is partly to blame, as well.

She should have come to you. She should have talked to you, trusted you. You never failed her, Lucien—not once."

For a moment, he glanced away. "No," he said softly. "I wouldn't have failed to protect her, but I never once tried to understand her. That is the real reason she left."

Jason cleared his throat, hurting for his friend as he had each time he had seen him. "Are you sure you won't change your mind and come with us? The children would love to have you both along."

Lucien smiled sadly and shook his head. "Perhaps next time."

Velvet went up on tiptoe and kissed his cheek. "I wish there was something I could say . . . something I could do . . ."

"Coming here is enough. Thank you both for being my friends."

Jason just nodded. His throat felt uncomfortably tight. The butler appeared just then, announcing that luncheon was ready.

"Shall we?" Lucien smiled and motioned toward the door.

Settling at hand at his wife's tiny waist, Jason ushered Velvet out of the room, thinking he was perhaps one of the few men who knew exactly how his friend must be feeling. Recalling the dark days of his past, he could too easily imagine how his heart would shatter if he ever lost Velvet as Lucien had lost Kathryn.

# TWENTY-FIVE

Why she timed her journey to end on March 15, Kathryn could not say. It was exactly a year ago that she had left Castle Running. Perhaps, considering what she had come to do, it was fitting she return on that same terrible day.

Kathryn pulled her cloak more closely around her and leaned back against the seat of the carriage she had let for the journey. Grady Bosworth, the plump young widow she had hired in St. Ives to help care for the baby, sat on the seat across from her. Grady had lost both husband and child to diphtheria when the child was two weeks old. She had milk and she had been nursing little Luke so Kathryn could continue to work. She was a friend Kathryn would miss when she returned to Cornwall.

"Are you sure his lordship will be wantin' me to stay?" Grady had asked that same question at least a dozen times since they had left on their journey.

"*I* want you to stay, Grady. Luke needs you. He'll be frightened at first. As long as you're there with him, he'll know that he is safe."

"It doesn't seem right," Grady muttered. "Just doesn't seem right a'tall."

Kathryn didn't answer. Whether or not Grady approved

didn't matter. After months of agonizing, of torturing herself with reasons to keep the child with her, she had made the decision she had known was right from the start. Luke Montaine was heir to the Marquess of Litchfield. He deserved his birthright and even though it tore out the last of her heart, Kathryn meant to see that he got it.

She dragged in a shaky breath. She was tired from the long days of travel but the end of her journey was near. She longed to reach her destination, to accomplish the painful task she had set for herself.

And she never wanted to get there.

The carriage rattled over the muddy roads. During the year since she had left the castle, she had managed her money well, earned a modest living for herself, and still had a goodly sum left, enough to afford this conveyance and travel in at least a passably comfortable style. It didn't lessen the agony she would face once she arrived at Castle Running.

They passed through the village of Gorsham. Kathryn kept herself carefully hidden behind the curtains, fearful someone might recognize her and turn her in to the authorities. They surely must still be looking for her in regard to Dunstan's murder. The village was quiet; the drizzle kept most people inside. A stray cat sat on the front porch of a cottage and the glow of candles flickered through the windows of the Sword and Quill Tavern.

In a few short minutes, the town disappeared behind them and Kathryn opened the draperies enough to see out, her heart thudding painfully as the castle grew near. The carriage rounded a bend in the rutted, muddy lane and pressed on. Through the trees up ahead, she could see the crenellated towers of Castle Running reaching into an iron-gray sky, and a shiver of dread slid into her stomach.

The coachman turned the conveyance up the gravel drive. The wheel hit a bump, tossing her against the squabs, but the baby didn't awaken. The gray stone walls loomed ahead, high and forbidding, more ominous than she remembered. Kathryn steeled herself, hardening her heart to complete the dreaded task she had come for.

Cradled in her arms, Luke began to squirm inside his soft wool blanket. He fussed for a moment, yawning and thrusting his tiny fist into the air as if he had something to say. Kathryn kissed the downy black hair on his head, crooned to him softly, and he quieted. Closing his silver-flecked eyes, he drifted back to sleep.

The carriage rolled to a stop and Kathryn's heart seemed to stop with it. For twelve tortuous months, she had yearned to climb those front porch steps and return to her home. Now that she was here, she dreaded each of the coming moments.

A footman came forward, opened the carriage door. She remembered his name was Dickey. Kathryn drew her hood up over her head against the drizzling mist that continued to fall and gave him a tentative smile as he helped her down, his eyes widening as he realized who she was and caught sight of the tiny babe she carried.

Racing ahead of her, he pounded furiously on the heavy oaken doors, and a grumbling Reeves pulled it open, allowing Kathryn into the entry. The astonishment on his long, stately face turned to a rare, teary smile when he caught sight of her and the babe.

"May I say, my lady, we are all of us so pleased to see you. We hoped you were well and safe but there was no way to know for sure."

It was the longest speech Reeves had ever made and it brought an ache to her heart and a faint mist of tears she quickly blinked away. "Thank you, Reeves." He took her dripping cloak but didn't take time to hang it up.

"I'll get his lordship. He wasn't feeling quite himself this morning . . . today being what it is. Why don't you wait for him in the Great Hall? You always liked it there."

She felt oddly pleased that he remembered. "The Great Hall . . . yes, that would be nice. Thank you, Reeves." While the butler scurried off, Kathryn made her way to the most ancient room in the castle. A huge fire blazed in the massive hearth and she moved to warm herself in front of it. Her chest felt leaden. Her heart ached unbearably.

The room reminded her so much of Lucien. What would he say when he saw her? What would he think when he first saw his child? What had happened in the year they'd been apart? She wondered if they were still married and the thought sent a jagged edge of pain slicing through her.

She prayed for the strength to do what she must and glanced up just as the marquess walked in. He paused a few feet in front of her, his spine ramrod straight, and she thought that he looked even taller than she remembered. He was thinner, she saw. Perhaps that was the reason.

Aside from that, his handsome image was so familiar, so achingly dear, that for a moment she thought she must be dreaming again. Staring into those silver-black eyes, at the strong jaw, and beautiful, sensuous lips, she ached to go to him, to touch him, to rest her head against his shoulder.

Kathryn knew that she could not.

Lucien stared at the woman in front of him and for a moment his legs refused to move. In the past few months, he had finally resigned himself to the fact that he would never see her again. Now she was here, standing in front of the massive hearth as if she had never been gone, as slender and lovely as he remembered. Her hair seemed darker, her eyes a deeper shade of green.

His gaze left her face, moved down to the small blanket-wrapped bundle she carried in her arms. A child, he saw, and confusion stabbed into him, warring with uncertainty.

"It's good to see you, Kathryn . . ."

She wet her lips. She was nervous, he saw, her body faintly trembling. Was the child hers or someone else's? Was it the reason she had left him? Had something happened he didn't know about? Did the child belong to him—or another man? At the last thought, a stab of bitterness rose inside him. Lucien forced it down.

"You must be cold," he said. "Let me get you some brandy."

"No . . . please, I'm fine." Kathryn reached out as if to call him back, stopping him before he reached the sideboard. "I'm sorry I didn't send word," she said on a shaky breath. "I know you didn't expect me . . . why should you? I've been gone this past year. I didn't mean to come back at all, but . . ." The words trailed away. She glanced down at the child and Lucien's stomach knotted.

"The child . . . is yours?" he said softly, groping for words, afraid he would say the wrong thing, afraid of what Kathryn might tell him.

"Ours," she said softly, and his eyes slid closed on a wave of pain. "Luke is the reason I returned."

"Luke?" he repeated, his head spinning oddly, the word coming out tight and strained.

"Lucien William Montaine. I didn't know I was with child when I left, but I suppose it wouldn't have mattered. With my uncle dead—"

Lucien shook his head, fighting to remain in control. "Dunstan didn't die. You're safe from the authorities. They're no longer looking for you." All least not at the present.

Her shoulders sagged with relief. She looked so pale, so terribly unhappy. It was all he could do not to go to her, to crush her against him. He forced himself to stay where he was, afraid that she would once again flee.

"I didn't poison him."

He swallowed past the tightness in his throat. "I know you didn't. It is not yet known exactly who did, but I don't believe you are capable of such a thing."

She studied him a moment, deciding whether she should believe him. She glanced back down at the child, who briefly awakened. His child, it was clear, with the same black hair and dark Montaine eyes. For a moment his throat ached so badly he couldn't speak.

She looked up at him and her eyes filled with tears. "I had to come," she said. "I couldn't keep him from you. I wanted to. God knows I wanted to. But Luke deserves his birthright and I knew that you would be good to him, that you would love him just as much as I do."

There was something beneath the words, something he was missing. He found his voice but only with an effort. "He's beautiful, Kathryn."

"He's a very good baby. He rarely cries at night and he has the sweetest laughter. When he looks at me I always think of you and I—" She didn't finish. Tears spilled onto her cheeks. "Do you want to hold him?"

His hands were shaking. Very carefully he reached out and accepted the small blanket-wrapped bundle that had once again returned to slumber.

"He'll need a wet nurse," Kathryn was saying. "I brought a lady from the village, Mrs. Bosworth. She's been with us almost from the start. She's waiting outside in the carriage. I'll send her in when I leave."

There it was—the truth she hadn't said or he had refused to hear. His eyes burned. Surely she didn't mean to give up her child? Surely he hadn't heard her correctly.

She brushed at the tears on her cheeks. "He likes to feel the sun on his cradle in the mornings. That always makes him smile." Reaching out a trembling hand, she fussed with the baby's blanket, pulling it up around the child's tiny shoulders. "Sometimes he gets the colic, but Mrs. Bosworth will know what to do. I wrote a list of the things you'll need. I'll leave it on the table."

Lucien stared into the beautiful, pain-filled face of the woman he loved and he thought that surely his heart must be crumbling inside his chest. "I cannot begin to imagine the sort of man you must believe me to be."

Her eyes met his through the glitter of tears and her brow furrowed slightly. "I think you are the very best of men. I wouldn't have brought Luke to you if I did not."

"But you believe that I will let you give up this child you so obviously love. That I will let you walk out of this house without your son."

Fat droplets rolled down her cheeks. "Don't . . . please.

There is nothing in this world that I want less than to leave him, but he is your son, too. And I owe you. For everything that's happened, I owe you your son."

His chest hurt. He couldn't seem to drag in quite enough air. "I beg you, Kathryn, with each of your words I am burning in the hell I have made."

She seemed not to have heard his words. "Are we still . . . is Luke of legitimate birth?"

His throat hurt. "There has been no annulment. I'll have no wife but you."

She stared at him a moment more, as if she memorized his features, then she glanced away. "I have to go," she said. "I have to leave."

Lucien stepped into her path, carefully cradling the child against his shoulder. "You can't leave, Kathryn. I won't let you." Something blurred his vision. His heart seemed a broken, useless thing as he struggled to find the right words.

"The day of the accident . . . everything went wrong. The constables came, then there was the terror of losing Michael. Everything was so confused, but that was the day I knew. For the very first time I knew. I saw you working over that child and I knew without doubt that I loved you. I saw how much of yourself you risked to save him, and in that moment I understood all that you are, all that you have taught yourself to be—and I loved you even more. I left because I didn't know how to tell you. How to say that I was wrong." He looked down, saw that his hands were shaking. "I nearly lost my mind without you, Kathryn. You thought that I didn't need you, but you were wrong. I love you, Kathryn, and I need you so damned much."

Her eyes looked huge and her face was bathed in tears. "Lucien . . ." She stepped toward him and he reached out to her, pulled her into his arms, holding her and his child hard against him and fighting the tears that burned to escape.

"I've missed you every day, every hour," he whispered

against her hair. "I love you, Kathryn. I love you more than life itself and I don't want you to leave."

Kathryn wept then, deep, wracking sobs that tore into his heart and threatened to undo him completely. He stroked her hair and whispered how much he loved her over and over again. For long minutes they just stood there, two people who had suffered too long and too much, holding the beautiful child who had brought them back together.

"I'll never let you go again," he said.

"I don't want to go," she whispered. "I never did. I love you, Lucien. I love you so much." She cupped his cheek in her hand and looked up at him with a soft, sad smile. "This is where I always wake up. Night after night I dreamed of you saying those words and then I wake up and discover it is only an illusion."

He bent his head and very softly kissed her. "I promise you I am very real. From now on, I shall make certain that all your dreams come true." His eyes ran over her face, drinking in the elegant lines, the curve of her soft full lips. "As soon as you are ready, my love, I intend to show you how very real I am."

Kathryn's cheeks flushed a bit, but just then the baby stirred and awakened, interrupting the sensual moment. Kathryn stepped back to accept the squirming bundle and Lucien handed the child into its mother's care.

"Are you certain?" she asked, gazing up at him with only a flicker of doubt. "If you meant those things you said, this is the last chance you'll ever have to get rid of me."

His heart felt suddenly weightless, seemed to take flight inside his chest. "Then I suppose we shall be stuck with each other forever."

Kathryn broke into the most beautiful smile he had ever seen and he thought that no memory he held of her had ever done her justice. And no person or thing would ever come between them again.

There would be problems, he knew. Once the constable's office discovered Kathryn was in residence once more at the castle, they would arrive with questions about her untimely departure. The attempt on Dunstan's life had never been resolved and, though no other attempts had been made, the case remained open and Kathryn was still a suspect.

But none of that mattered. Not anymore. Kathryn was home and safe, and he meant to see that she stayed that way. No matter what it took, Lucien vowed he would protect her.

He never wanted to lose her again.

The storm heightened. Bright slashing shards of lightning ripped across the landscape and thunder shook the windows in the towering stone walls of the castle. A fierce March wind howled into the quaking branches of the trees.

In the drawing room of the master's suite, gowned in deep green silk, Kathryn sat across from Lucien at a small round table draped in white linen, her hair unbound as he had requested, sipping the last remaining drops of wine from a crystal goblet that shook faintly in her hand.

She had yet to see little Michael, who was visiting the Sinclair children at Carlyle Hall, but the baby had been put to sleep hours ago, and the intimate supper she had shared with Lucien in the marquess's suite was now ended. Over an elegant meal of roast partridge and creamed whiting that Cook had prepared in honor of her return, Kathryn had told her husband of the year she had spent in St. Ives, while he had recounted the months of his futile search for her.

Though Lucien had glossed over his own personal pain, the depth of his suffering was obvious from the lengths he had gone to in order to find her. Kathryn had cried to think she had caused him so much anguish. It had simply never occurred to her that he might care enough to be so badly hurt.

As supper progressed, topics turned to her uncle and

the crime that had been committed. Lucien gently explained that the authorities would most likely approach her again with questions, but no matter what happened, he promised to keep her safe. This time, Kathryn believed him.

They spoke of Aunt Winnie, who had provided the single note of happiness Lucien had known during the terrible year of their separation.

"My aunt is happily married to Nat Whitley and living at his town house in London. I think she understood better than anyone why you had to leave, but she never gave up hope that you would return."

Kathryn caught a tiny tear with the end of her finger. "I hurt so many people. I never meant to, Lucien. I thought by leaving I was doing the best thing for everyone."

He reached for her hand, brought it to his lips. "All of those sorrows are past. We have two glorious children and a bright future ahead of us. That is all that matters."

Kathryn smiled at him through a mist of tears. Lucien was right. The present was all that mattered, and a future that would begin tonight, she fervently hoped—in her husband's massive bed.

His white linen napkin looked stark against his dark hand as he tossed it on the table beside his plate, moved behind her chair, and helped her to her feet.

"I imagine you are tired," he said, but his eyes said something different, as they had all through the meal . . . or at least so Kathryn had believed. He was dressed impeccably, in a silver-trimmed black velvet coat, matching waistcoat, and breeches. Silver threads edged the fine lace at his cuff and draped over the backs of his hands.

Kathryn studied him from beneath her lashes. "Perhaps I should be tired, my lord, after such an eventful day, but in truth . . . I am not tired in the least."

Something moved over his features, tightening the finely carved lines, the beautifully sculpted planes and valleys. "I realize a great deal has happened in the year we've been apart. You've birthed a child. I know very little about that sort of thing, but—"

"Do you want me, Lucien?" Her gaze met his, seeking the truth. Perhaps she had been wrong. She was a mother now, with changes to her body. Perhaps he felt differently about her.

Lightning cracked outside the window, outlining the subtle curve of his lips. "Do I want you? I've wanted you every day since you left the castle. Today has been the happiest day of my life—and a total living hell. From the instant you walked through that door, I've wanted to kiss you senseless. It's all I can do not to tear away your clothes, drag you down on the floor, and make wild, insatiable love to you. I want to be inside you so badly I ache with it."

Kathryn's stomach contracted at the hot sensations flooding in. Reaching out a shaky hand, she rested it against his cheek. "Would you kiss me, Lucien?"

His eyes, black as pitch, seemed to burn with a silver light. He tipped her head back with his fingers, the delicate lace on his cuff brushing softly against her cheek. Just a feather-light brush of lips, the most innocent of touches, but the moment his mouth came down on hers, desire flared between them like a jagged bolt of lightning and both of them were lost. Lucien kissed her chin, her eyes, her nose, then took her lips in a hot, devouring kiss that had Kathryn clinging to his shoulders. He kissed his way down her throat, trailed hot, damp kisses across the bare skin above her breasts.

Need overwhelmed her. She wanted to touch him, hold him, wanted to see him naked as he had so often been in her dreams. Sliding her trembling hands beneath his black velvet coat, she urged it off his shoulders, worked the silver buttons on his waistcoat, and helped him slide it off, as well. She drew off his snowy stock and tossed it away, then trembled at the powerful muscles expanding beneath his shirt.

All the while he kissed her, deeply, thoroughly, almost

savagely, while his long dark fingers fumbled with the buttons at the back of her gown. With a muffled curse, he tore the last two recalcitrant offenders away. Sliding the gown and her chemise off her shoulders, he bared her breasts, then paused and lifted his head to look at her, his eyes glinting in the ragged patch of moonlight spilling in through the mullioned windows.

Kathryn couldn't breathe.

"You are even more beautiful than I remembered," he said softly, reverently, reaching out to gently cup a breast.

Kathryn moaned as he bent his dark head to lave first one and then the other. Heat boiled through her and Kathryn arched toward him, her head falling back as he took the plumpness into his mouth. Faint little panting sounds slipped from her throat and her fingers curled into the front of his full-sleeved white shirt. He suckled her nipple and fire seemed to lick downward, into the very core of her.

"Lucien. Dear God . . ." When he kissed her again, her fingers slid into his hair, dislodging the ribbon that held it in place and letting the heavy black strands fall free.

Lucien unfastened the tabs on her panniers, shoved her gown and chemise past her hips to her feet, deftly knelt and removed her slippers, then swung her up in his arms. Kathryn leaned her head against his shoulder as he strode out of his private drawing room through the door leading into his massive bedchamber.

Wearing only her pink satin garters and white silk stockings, she found herself perched on the edge of the bed, her legs slightly parted and Lucien kneeling between them.

"Open yourself to me, Kathryn," he softly commanded, finding her feminine core and beginning to stroke her. "Let me love you as I have imagined a thousand times since you have been gone."

"Lucien . . . please . . . surely you don't mean to . . ." She gasped as he urged her back on the bed and lifted her stocking-clad legs onto his shoulders. Kathryn quiv-

ered at the feel of his mouth and tongue on her most
sensitive parts, at the heat and overwhelming sensations.
Her hands fisted in his hair and she cried out his name,
writhing upward, wavering on the edge of control, but
Lucien was relentless. With skillful care, he brought her
to climax, forcing the cry of his name from her lips.

He silenced her with a ravaging kiss, coming up over
her as he buried himself deeply inside. He filled her completely, and the snug, heavy feeling of rightness was so
profound, so exquisite, Kathryn felt tears burn the backs
of her eyes. Out and then in, deep, forceful strokes that
reached her very core and set off hot waves of pleasure
that rippled and grew. Kathryn bit down on her bottom
lip and clung to his neck as she surged nearer and nearer
to climax.

Dear God, Lucien! She had missed him so much, loved
him so long, and she had been so desperately lonely.

Release broke over her like a warm summer storm,
drenching her in sweet silvery rain. Kathryn's fingers dug
into the muscles across his shoulders as he reached his
own release, his body going rigid, straining forward, then
relaxing, his forehead coming to rest against her own.

She could feel his smile like a gentle ray of sun. "I
love you, Kathryn. Don't ever leave me again."

Kathryn slowly shook her head. "No, my love. I promise I never will."


The Earl of Dunstan sat in the drafty rear salon of Dunstan
Manor reading an article in the *London Chronicle*. It was
a small item he almost skimmed over, one that mentioned
the return of a certain lord's wife who had gone missing
for nearly a year. A lengthy stay "on the Continent," the
Marquess of Litchfield had claimed, was all that had kept
his wife away. It had nothing in the least to do with the
fact the woman had left under a cloud of suspicion that
she might be guilty of the attempted murder of her uncle.

Douglas ground his jaw, anger boiling through him in
great torrential waves. *Might* be guilty? Of course the chit

was guilty! She loathed the very sight of him. She had discovered his plans for her overprotective husband and she meant to insure they failed.

Douglas scoffed. Well, the chit hadn't managed to kill him, but she had succeeded in wrecking his life. Thanks to Kathryn's defiance and cunning, he now lived in near solitude on his crumbling Bedfordshire estate. His plans for a brilliant political career lay in ashes at his feet and the scheme to marry his daughter to a man of power had disintegrated even before it had had time to mature.

Douglas crumpled the newsprint in his hand and hurled it into the fire. Damn her! Damn her to bloody perdition!

Shoving to his feet, he strode out of the room and down the hall, feeling the chill of the grim old house the moment he left the fire. With coal at a premium, they couldn't afford to heat the whole bloody place, and even if they tried, the house was in such ill repair the warmth would simply escape through the cracks in the walls.

"Ludlow! Ludlow, where are you?"

The butler scurried from around the corner, wearing mittens and bundled in a blanket that wrapped around his coat and breeches.

"Yes, milord?" The end of his nose was red and a slight shiver ran through his bony frame.

"Where is my daughter? I haven't seen her all morning."

"I believe she is still abed, milord. Shall I fetch her downstairs, sir?"

Douglas's irritation swelled. "Do so at once. And tell her she had better not keep me waiting." Another useless chit just like the rest, whining and complaining every minute since they'd left Milford Park. This one gave him nearly the grief Kathryn had done. If she didn't mend her ways and soon, he would marry her off just to get her out of his hair. He might not be able to snare a powerful young aristocrat, as he had once planned, but in her own odd way, Muriel was a tasty enough little morsel. He could surely barter her off for a goodly bit of coin to some wealthy old lecher who itched to get between a young girl's legs.

The object of his irritation descended the stairs in a pink quilted wrapper that appeared even more ghastly against the frizzled red of her unkempt hair.

"You are beginning to look like a slattern," Douglas told her. "Why are you still abed?"

"It's too cold to get up. This house is as drafty as a dungeon. The only time I'm warm is when I'm beneath the covers."

"If you are so fond of lying abed, perhaps I should find you a husband. I am certain Lord Tilbert would keep you warm enough beneath the blankets."

Muriel's face went pale, washing out some of her freckles. "Lord Tilbert? Lord Tilbert is a doddering old man. Surely you wouldn't consider marrying me off to a man like that?"

"I'll do whatever I have to, my girl, and you had better not forget it. In the meanwhile, I wanted to tell you I shall be leaving for a couple of days."

"Leaving? Where are you going?"

"That is none of your concern. Suffice it to say, I am seeking a bit of justice." He turned and called to his butler, who also served as his valet. "Ludlow!" The bone-thin man creaked toward him from around the corner. "Pack my traveling valise. I shall need clothes for at least a week."

"Yes, milord." The scrawny man scurried away.

"As for you, Muriel. I would suggest that you find a better means of keeping warm than lying in your bed complaining. If you don't, I warn you—Lord Tilbert will be the better choice of the suitors I shall find for you to marry."

With that he strode off, leaving the girl to stare after him, pale and shaken. Good, he thought. At least one of the women in his care had learned her place.

The other was about to learn what happened to those who opposed him.

# TWENTY-SIX

At last Kathryn was home! Every dream of Lucien she had ever dreamed had come true twice over. He loved her, he needed her, and he accepted her the way she was. At last she had found a place of true refuge and it felt so right, so incredibly good.

She stood next to him in the master's suite, where she slept now each night.

"I want you to move in here," he had said the evening of her return. "You may still keep the room next door as your own but at night I would have you sleep in here." He looked at her with a bit of uncertainty. "Would you mind terribly?"

Kathryn had smiled, her heart overflowing. "I should love that above all things, my lord."

She remembered those words now as he smiled, still the handsomest man she had ever seen. She had an embarrassing urge to slide her arms around his neck and press her mouth against those sensuous lips. Though they had made love just hours ago, when she looked up at him, his eyes were dark and smoky. Lucien framed her face with his hands and bent his head to kiss her, but the shout of a little boy running pall mall up the stairs had both of them pulling guiltily away and turning toward the door.

Michael was due back from his visit to Carlye Hall today, where he had been staying, giving them a chance to be alone for a while, after such a lengthy separation.

"Papa! Papa!"

At the word, Kathryn's eyes swung to Lucien's in surprise, and a faint flush rose beneath the skin across his cheeks.

"The process has been started for the boy's legal adoption," he said gruffly. "In a few weeks' time, he'll be Michael Bartholomew Montaine. Since that will be the case, it seemed only fitting that he should address me as his father."

"Of course." Kathryn fought a smile and felt a fierce swell of love for him. For the first time it occurred to her that she might have been wrong in leaving. If ever there was a man to trust with her life, her heart, it was the man she had married.

Michael rushed in just then, sliding to a halt right in front of them, the thick Oriental carpet bunching at his feet and nearly knocking him over. " 'Tis truth! God's eyes, Kathryn, you've finally come 'ome!"

There were tears in his big blue eyes and neither Lucien nor Kathryn bothered to correct the poor grammar he had used in his excitement at seeing her. Kathryn knelt and opened her arms, and the small blond child rushed into them. Kathryn hugged him hard, swallowing past a tight ache in her throat.

"I missed you, Michael. I missed you so much."

"I missed you, too . . . me lady." He hugged her neck, his small head tucked into her shoulder. "We all missed you, 'specially me lord."

Kathryn smoothed back his shiny blond hair, hugged him again, then drew back to look at him. "From now on . . . if it's all right with you . . . I should like it very much if you would call me Mama."

Michael looked up at her with teary blue eyes, then his thin face split into a grin. "Are you gonna be my mother?"

"If you want me to."

"Oh, yes—ever so much. Now I'll 'ave . . . have a mama and a papa just like everyone else."

She straightened the lapels of his velvet-trimmed jacket just to have a reason to touch him. "That's right, Michael. And you have a new little brother. His name is Luke. Would you like to see him?"

Michael looked up at her with wonder. "I have a brother?"

"Yes."

"Then I should like very much to see him," he said quite properly.

Above his head, Kathryn looked at Lucien and both of them smiled. Kathryn had to blink to assure herself she wasn't dreaming again.

It was that same day that she returned for the very first time to her little stone cottage, amazed to discover it ready and waiting for her. In the weeks after she had left the castle, Lucien had restored the cottage and supplied it once more with the items from her laboratory she had hidden in the stable.

Now that she was home, with the children to consider, she didn't intend to devote herself so completely to her work, but it was there whenever she had time for it, challenging her, making her life complete.

Smiling to herself, Kathryn set off for the cottage now, on this the first warm day of spring. Though the sun shone brightly outside, inside the thick stone walls, a fire had been laid in the hearth to dispel the chill, and smoke curled invitingly from the gray stone chimney. In the cheery little parlor, Lucien had returned the medical texts she had borrowed from his library and added to them tenfold. It appeared he had been scouring the countryside for reference volumes and they sat now stacked in piles all over the floor.

Kathryn grinned to think of it, of her husband actually encouraging her eccentric, once-forbidden interests. Humming to herself, she set to work straightening the cottage, watering the pots of herbs that sat on narrow wooden tiers in front of the sunny window. She barely caught the faint grating of iron as the latch was lifted on the door. Certain it was her husband, she smiled and turned, but the man who had just stepped into the cottage wasn't Lucien.

It was Douglas Roth.

A chill swept down through Kathryn's bones. "Uncle Douglas," she said, barely able to force out the words. "I am surprised to see you here."

His thin lips barely curved. "I don't know why you should be. In the years you spent under my care, you must have learned I believe in retribution. As I recall, you suffered a caning or two before you learned you could not thwart me without receiving some punishment in return."

Kathryn stiffened. How could she ever forget her uncle's harsh treatment of her? The early years had merely paled in comparison to the suffering she had endured at St. Bart's. "How did you know I was here?"

He moved farther into the room, closing the door behind him, careful to keep his immaculate bottle-green tailcoat from coming in contact with the myriad beakers and vials on the tables. Unconsciously he checked to be certain his silver bagwig remained perfectly in place, which, of course, it did.

"Finding you was hardly a difficult task. I've been watching the house for several days. In the course of my surveillance, I chanced upon the cottage. It was obvious that such a haven for herbs and potions could only belong to you, so I waited for your arrival. I knew I wouldn't have to wait long."

Kathryn wet her lips, more nervous by the moment. "Why have you come here? What do you want?"

His brow arched up. "What do I want? Surely you can guess." His lips curled into the cold, ruthless smile that had haunted her nights at St. Bart's. "I want you to pay for destroying my world." He moved toward her, his nose wrinkling in distaste at the unusual smells in the cottage. "You took my livelihood, Kathryn. You ordered me removed from Milford Park. You destroyed my reputation among my peers, to say nothing of the fact that you attempted to kill me—an effort, I daresay, I couldn't help but admire. Still, your attempt grimly failed. I assure you mine will not."

A wave of fear swept over her. Douglas Roth had come here for revenge and he clearly meant to kill her. Her glance strayed frantically toward the door, but Dunstan stood firmly in the path of escape.

Kathryn stiffened her spine. "I didn't try to kill you. I've wanted to—on any number of occasions—but I am not the one who tried. If I had, I wouldn't have failed."

A muscle throbbed in his cheek. "You were always an arrogant chit. I almost believe you. Almost. But even if you were telling me the truth, it wouldn't change things. You've ruined my life and destroyed my plans for the future. I intend to see that you pay."

Kathryn didn't wait for more, just bolted for the door, dodging right and then left around her uncle's larger frame in a futile effort to get round him.

"Oh, no you don't!" He was quicker than he appeared—and stronger—and he caught her in a savage grip and whirled her in the opposite direction, dragging her away from the door.

"Help! Somebody help me!" But no one could hear through the thick stone walls and all she received for her trouble was a vicious slap across the cheek. He shook her so hard her teeth rattled against each other.

"No more of your screeching—do you hear? It won't do you the slightest bit of good and we both know it."

It was the truth and the knowledge made her heart race even faster than it did already. Struggling against his implacable hold, she kicked him hard in the shins, and bolted once more for the door, but her skirts blocked the blow and slowed her escape. Dunstan was on her in an instant. Jerking her around, he drew back and slammed a fist into her jaw, and Kathryn went down in a heap. The last thing she remembered was the pain shooting into her head and her uncle's ungodly peals of laughter.

Then there was only darkness.

Lucien nudged his black gelding into a canter as he headed home from the fields. It was early yet, but he had been restless. He'd been determined to leave Kathryn alone this day, allow her to work in her cottage in peace, but the sun was simply too brilliant, the sky too bright a blue, and in truth, after missing her for so long, he needed to feel the warmth of her smile, hear the reassuring sound of her laughter.

At the top of the hill, he changed course, reining the stallion toward Kathryn's small cottage, and that was when he saw the smoke. It was coming from that direction, more than the single plume rising up through the chimney.

His heart leapt hard against the wall of his chest. Lucien leaned over Blade's neck and set the horse into a ground-eating gallop. By the time he reached the bottom of the hill, he could see the first flames burning through the eaves of the roof and Kathryn's little mare tugging frantically at the rope that bound her to the lean-to at the side of the cottage.

Lucien set the stallion into a flat-out run.

Charging down the hill and splashing across the stream, the animal nickered wildly as Lucien reined him to a sliding halt in front of the cottage. He was out of the saddle and running before the gelding had come to a stop, slamming through the heavy oak door and racing inside, forced to a halt by a blistering wall of flame.

"Kathryn! Kathryn—forgodsake, are you in here?" His eyes searched the smoky darkness; the cottage was burning so badly he could barely see. "Kathryn! Kathryn!" He moved along the walls, stumbling over stacks of books, knocking over beakers and vials, glass splintering on the tables, slicing into his hands. "Kathryn—it's Lucien. Forgodsake, answer me!"

A muffled groan rose up from a smoky corner. Eyes stinging, coughing and fighting to breathe, Lucien staggered in that direction. A length of sturdy brown wool shone through the wreckage on the floor, the upturned pots and broken glass, the pages of books that had been ripped out and scattered across the floor to kindle the flames.

Fighting against the fear that gripped his chest, he knelt beside his wife's body, saw that she was breathing, saw that her hands were bound and a gag stuffed into her mouth. Swearing savagely, he scooped her into his arms and started toward the door.

"Easy, love. Everything's going to be all right, just as soon as I get you out of here." Kathryn groaned in response and he held her more tightly against his chest. Lurching toward the burning door, he stumbled across the room and out into the cleansing spring air. He didn't stop until he reached the safety of the trees, where he rested Kathryn gently on the ground and dragged the gag from her mouth. Pulling the knife from his boot, he cut the bonds on her wrists, carefully checked her for bleeding or broken bones.

Kathryn's eyes fluttered open and she dragged in a shaky breath. She tried to speak, but the smoke had roughened her voice and it came out as an undecipherable croak.

"Don't try to talk. I'll be right back. I've got to get your horse before the fire can reach her." He left her a moment, freed the little mare that Kathryn had been riding, then returned to where his wife was trying to right herself against the trunk of the tree.

"Take it easy," he coaxed, coming down on one knee beside her.

"Dun . . . stan," she croaked in her smoky voice. "He tried to . . . kill me. Be . . . careful, Lucien. He might still be . . . here."

The cocking of a pistol followed the belated warning. "Why is it you always turn up where you are not wanted?"

Lucien's jaw clamped hard on a wave of fury; he had an urge to slam a fist into the preening bastard's face. If he tried, he'd be dead before he'd taken two steps. "I might say the same of you."

"In this instance, your timing is most unfortunate. You see, as much as I wanted you dead, it was strictly a matter of business. With Kathryn, it's an endeavor of personal satisfaction. Once she's gone, however, there is no real benefit to doing away with you. Now you have left me no choice." He glanced at the burning cottage, saw the flames beginning to reach up into the sky. Soon someone would spot them and the alarm would spread. "There isn't much time if I am to dispose of your bodies." He raised the pistol, pointed it directly at Lucien's heart. "I wish I could say I was sorry, but . . ."

His finger tightened on the trigger and Kathryn screamed as Lucien dived toward him, knowing there wasn't the slightest chance the shot would miss. The sound of the blast echoed in his ears the same instant he slammed into Dunstan's chest, hurling them both to the ground. Lucien waited for the searing agony that would signal a mortal wound but none came, and beneath him, Dunstan's body lay limp and unmoving.

Dragging himself to his feet, he stared into the open, sightless eyes of the earl, then past him to the girl who still held the smoking pistol pointed at her father's back.

"He was evil," Muriel said just above a whisper. "He killed my mother. I found a letter she wrote in one of her old trunks. She knew he was trying to kill her. He only married her for her money. Once it was gone, he grew tired of her. He said she was too much trouble. He cared about nothing . . . no one but himself. Now he's dead."

Lucien approached her slowly, took the gun from her trembling hands. "It's all right, Muriel. You saved my life. Both of our lives. No one is going to fault you for that."

"I guessed he was coming here. I should have come sooner, but I was afraid." She glanced over at Kathryn, whose face was deathly pale where it wasn't covered with soot. "I'm the one who poisoned him. I knew they would blame it on you. You were always kind to me, but I was just so jealous. I'm sorry, Kathryn. Sorry for everything."

Kathryn pushed herself to her feet. Stumbling slightly, she walked toward Muriel, her eyes glazed with tears. She wrapped her arms around the girl, who turned and began to weep on Kathryn's shoulder. "It's all right, Muriel, it's over. It's over for all of us."

A bevy of servants appeared over the rise just then, armed with buckets and hoes. Reeves was among them. As they set to work, forming a bucket brigand that led up from the stream, dashing bucket after bucket of water onto the roaring flames, the butler broke away from the rest and hurried toward them.

"Are you and her ladyship all right, my lord?" His worried glance traveled from their dirty, soot-covered faces to the dead man lying on the ground.

"We're fine. Take Lady Muriel back to the house and see that she's made comfortable. Have Bennie get a wagon and take care of the body."

Reeves cast him a questioning glance, but merely agreed. "As you wish, my lord." Shedding his coat, he tossed it over Dunstan's still form, then led a pale-faced Muriel away.

Lucien strode over to Kathryn and pulled her into his arms. Holding her against him, he ran a finger along her blackened cheek. "Are you all right?"

She nodded, leaning into his embrace. "I'm fine, thanks to you."

"And Muriel."

"Yes." She looked over at her uncle's still form, then turned away. "I can hardly believe it's finally come to an end."

"It's the end for Dunstan. It is only the beginning for the rest of us."

Kathryn smiled up at him, her face glowing with the same deep love he was feeling. He brushed her mouth with a kiss, loving her more than ever and silently vowing he would keep the promise he had made. In the years ahead, he would see that all of her dreams came true.

"I love you, Kathryn," he said, meaning it more than she would ever know. Once he hadn't believed in love. Now the notion felt so right, so perfectly true, it was amazingly easy to say the words.

Lucien looked down at the woman in his arms, felt alive as he never had before, knew there wasn't a luckier man on this earth, and he smiled.